INTERNATIONAL BESTSELLING AUTHOR
KAYDENCE SNOW

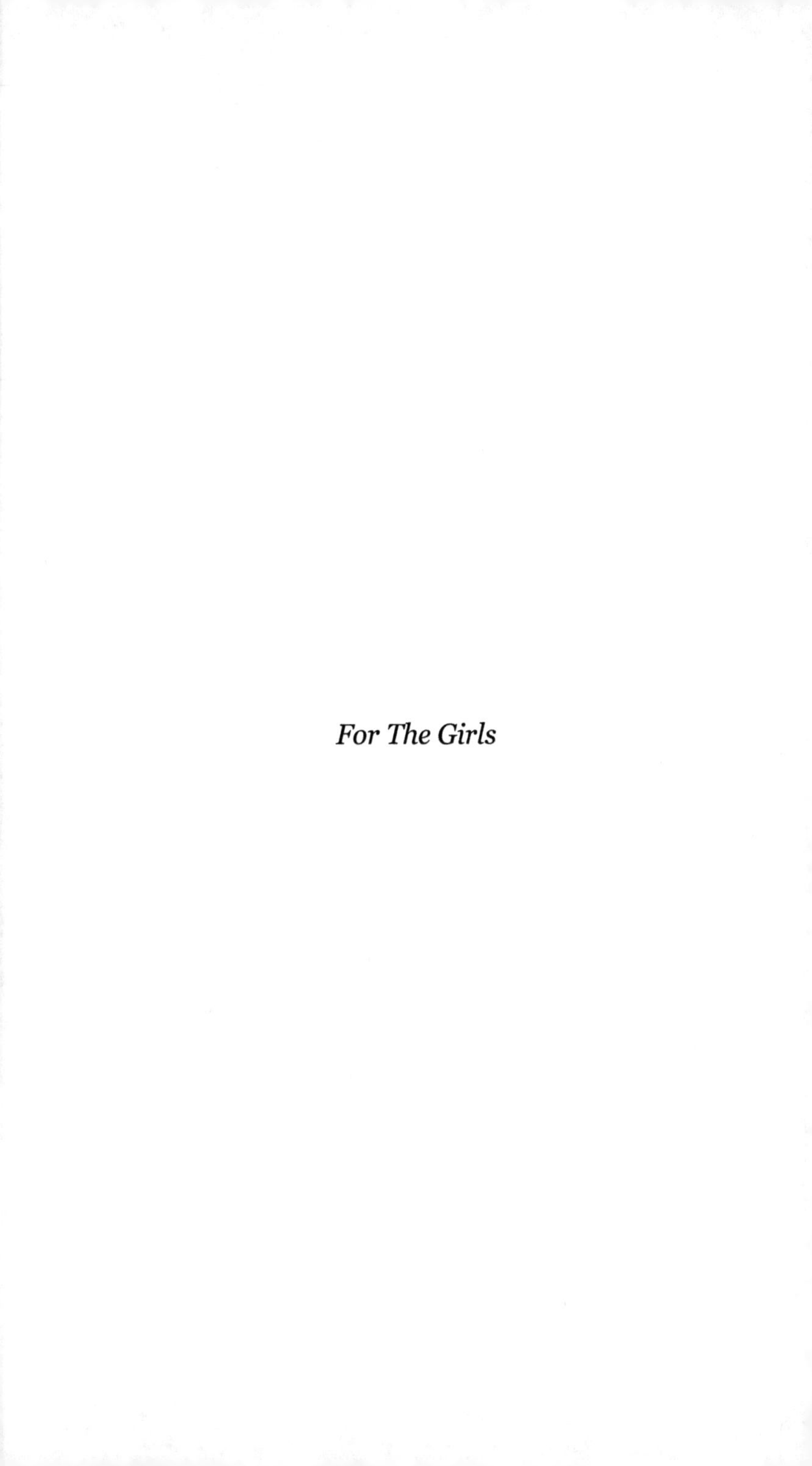

For The Girls

CHAPTER 1

Donna

MOM WAS SITTING AT THE BREAKFAST NOOK alone, the delectable spread in front of her way more than four people could realistically eat. Dad must've been away for work again, and if Harlow wasn't up yet, she wouldn't be eating breakfast. Looked as if it was just us two.

Magda marched in from the kitchen, a fresh pot of coffee in hand. "Good morning, beautiful, smart girl. How you want your eggs this morning?" The woman had worked for my family since before I was born, but her heavy Eastern European accent persisted.

I smiled. "Poached, please."

She set the coffee on the table and patted my arm as she passed.

"Morning, sweetheart." Mom flashed me her perfect teeth before returning her attention to the iPad next to her bowl of granola. She was impeccable in a linen shirt dress and a full face of makeup, not a hair out of place—all before 8:00 a.m.

"Morning, Mom. You look nice. Big client?" I smoothed the front of my skirt as I sat down, running my fingers down the gray-and-teal tartan pleats. Emily Mead Interiors was in high demand, and if Mom was going to meet with someone herself instead of sending one of the designers she employed, it was probably someone high-profile.

"Thank you." She gave me another bright smile. "Yes, a potential new client, demanding to meet with me personally."

"Celebrity," we said at the same time, rolling our eyes.

I grabbed a piece of toast and started spreading mashed avocado onto it as Mom scrolled through her tablet again. A bird chirped outside, the California sun shining brightly through the open French doors.

Everything, down to the weather, was pristine and neat.

I couldn't wait to put on a pair of scuffed boots and feel them stick to the filthy floors . . .

I shook my head. I had to focus. Get through the day. It was only one day.

Magda returned with my poached eggs as I was crumbling some feta onto the avocado.

"I have my dinner with my friends tonight. Will you and your sister be OK alone?" Mom took a sip of her coffee.

I smiled around a bite of gourmet breakfast, wiping

the corner of my mouth with the starched napkin. "Yes. I have some extra-credit homework to finish, and Harlow will be fine."

My sister, younger by exactly eleven months, would be glued to her computer. Friday nights were her gaming nights—nothing but her bladder could drag her away from the keyboard.

"Good. I won't be late."

She never was. Not that it mattered. I was eighteen and Harlow was seventeen. We were more than capable of taking care of ourselves—despite being raised with a permanent staff, managed by Magda, making sure we never wanted for anything. We may have been obscenely rich, but my parents had made sure we weren't spoiled. They'd instilled the value of hard work in us from an early age. We were Meads—nothing short of excellence was acceptable.

But everyone had to let loose once in a while. Dad had the frequent extensions to his business trips so he could play golf. Mom had her fortnightly boozy dinners with her friends, ensuring she was fast asleep by midnight. Harlow had her computer games.

I had my thing too. I'd be going there tonight. Just thinking about it made a rush of adrenaline shoot down my spine, like rough hands on bare skin.

Shifting in my seat, I pushed the thought away once again. No one could know about that. They wouldn't understand.

I just had to get through one more day at school, one more afternoon of homework, *one more day* of being driven, determined, perfect Donna Mead.

And then I could spend all night being whoever the fuck I wanted.

I took another bite of toast to hide my smile.

Harlow appeared downstairs just as I finished eating. Her Fulton Academy uniform was as perfectly neat and ironed as mine, but her knee-high socks were still pooled around her ankles, and it looked as if she hadn't bothered to brush her hair before tying it up. Her long blonde ponytail hung just past her shoulder blades.

My hair was a little lighter than hers, ashier, and I kept it maintained in a short, sharp style with monthly visits to the salon. It was closer to Mom's color, although she put lowlights in hers.

"There's my baby girl." Mom beamed at her youngest child, and Harlow gave her a sleepy smile back as she poured coffee into her travel mug. "Sit down and eat some breakfast."

Harlow grunted, and I answered for her. "We have to get going to pick up Mena."

Mom frowned. She liked that we were picking up our cousin, but it was warring with her typical-mom need to shove food down our throats. But I knew Harlow couldn't stomach anything solid until lunchtime—especially when she stayed up half the night doing god knew what on her computer.

Screwing the lid onto her travel mug, Harlow leaned down and gave our mother a kiss on the cheek. The big white headphones hanging around her neck were blaring some EDM shit that became audible as she got close. "Love you," she croaked.

I cringed internally. Had she been to bed at all?

Hoping to distract our mom from how tired my sister looked, I leaned over and gave her a kiss too. "Love you, Mom. Good luck with the delusion of grandeur."

She laughed as we headed for the garage. "Is it delusion if the majority of the country knows their name? Have a good day, girls."

Magda wordlessly pressed a granola bar into my hand as I passed the kitchen, shooting a meaningful look in Harlow's direction. I gave her a withering smile. I'd try, but no promises.

With a yawn, Harlow dropped into the back seat of my pearlescent white BMW 8, while I smoothed my skirt down and stepped in more carefully to avoid creases.

The garage door silently slid open in front of us, revealing a pair of long legs clad in the same knee-high socks my sister and I were both wearing—white with a teal stripe at the top. Next came a flash of creamy brown-skinned thigh, the skirt length flirting with inappropriate, followed by the top half of the most fabulous bitch I knew.

Our friend Amaya Ellis-Lahari lived one street over and rode to school with us almost every day, even though she had her own car. Us girls liked to stick together. She and Harlow had offered to take turns driving, but I shot that down. I liked to be in control of where I was going and how fast.

Amaya was scrolling through her phone in the

middle of the driveway, arms crossed and hip cocked, her designer backpack slung over one shoulder. I started the car and revved the engine, but she completely ignored me, running a hand through her long black hair.

With a smirk, I disengaged the handbrake and revved the engine again, then lurched forward and slammed on the brakes just inches away from Amaya's ridiculously long legs.

She didn't even flinch.

I laughed, and she looked at me over the top of her sunglasses and gave me the finger.

After taking her time to shoot off a text, she leisurely slid into the passenger seat. "Meads."

"Hey, girl." I gave her a kiss on the cheek as Harlow grunted from the back. As I took off, my sister jammed the headphones over her ears and closed her eyes. Amaya buried her nose in her phone, and I put on some Billie Eilish.

This part of the journey was spent in relative silence, all of us trying to wake up and get ready for the day—especially Harlow.

We drove out of the estates area and took the main road through downtown Devilbend. The homes got smaller, the yards more cramped and untidy. Eventually we pulled up outside of a big, run-down apartment building.

Mena walked up the cracked concrete path and jumped into the back seat.

"Morning!"

Her bright greeting made me smile. That girl had

been through some horrific shit at her last school—which is why my parents were paying for her to go to Fulton with us now—but it hadn't made her bitter or angry. Mena was the kind of person whose inner beauty oozed out of her pores, her energy infectious.

We chatted and sang along to "You Should See Me in a Crown" as I drove us to school. Even Harlow perked up and took her headphones off, the massive coffee she'd finished finally doing its job.

I retraced our path through downtown, passed the turnoff to our neighborhood, and drove up the winding tree-lined road toward Fulton Academy.

Every other day, we got up half an hour early and drove in the exact opposite direction of school to pick up Mena, because she needed someone to show her she was worth it—that she belonged with us. The other days, she took the bus to our house, and we still drove in together.

I parked in a spot near the front. Even with the student parking lot almost full, everyone knew not to park in my spot.

Glancing in the mirror, I checked my makeup and smoothed an errant strand of hair back into place. Surreptitiously, I checked on Harlow at the same time. She'd retied her hair while we drove, and as we got out of the car, I was pleased to see her socks were pulled up and her shirt tucked in.

We all knew the strict uniform rules, and my sister wasn't an idiot, but I couldn't help but make sure everything was in place. I didn't want any of my girls getting in trouble needlessly.

Walking in through the grand front doors of one of the most prestigious high schools in California—if not the country—I kept my gaze trained forward. Amaya was at my side, Harlow and Mena joking and carrying on behind us. I envied how oblivious they were to all the people watching us, some wishing they had the guts to talk to us, others hoping I'd fall on my ass.

Perfection was fucking exhausting, but it was all I knew.

There was only one thing that could completely take my mind off it. The buzz of conversation around us reminded me faintly of another kind of buzz—*the kind I'd be feeling reverberate through my body tonight.*

Shit, I really needed this. It was the third time that morning I'd had to push the thought away. I had three AP classes on Fridays, and I needed to focus.

I got through my busy morning without incident and repressed a yawn as I shoved books into my locker at lunch.

"Cafeteria? Or you wanna head out to eat?" Amaya leaned on the locker next to mine.

Harlow appeared next to her. "Can we just do caf? I'm starving."

"That's because you didn't eat breakfast after staying up all night." I was kicking myself for not shoving the granola bar under her nose earlier.

"I second the caf." Mena nudged my shoulder and smiled before unloading her own books in her locker.

Mena had ulterior motives. She couldn't afford to eat out all the time and didn't like us constantly paying for her, so she always preferred the cafeteria—the option already paid for as part of tuition.

I rolled my eyes, and they landed on an unfamiliar face.

The guy walking toward us in the busy hallway was tall, his brown hair kind of wavy and messy on top but with a precise fade-cut underneath. The gray pants and white shirt of the uniform fit his frame perfectly— probably tailored, just like all the other uniforms on all the other spoiled rich kids in this place. His teal tie hung perfectly in place, but his blazer was draped over the books he had tucked against his hip.

I leaned back on the locker and watched him as he passed, his free hand tucked into his pocket, his face blank.

He didn't look at anyone. He didn't have that uncertain, worried demeanor that almost always marked a new kid obsessing over where they would fit in at a new school. Which told me he didn't give a shit about his place here, or maybe he was just putting up a brave front, a hard exterior to mask his nervousness.

His gray eyes flicked to the side and connected with mine for the briefest of moments. I didn't smile like half the basic bitches in the hall with hearts in their eyes. I didn't frown or show my confusion either. I didn't react at all, watching him with as steady and cool a gaze as he was me.

He stopped at a locker near the end of the corridor. Only seniors had their locker in this hall, so that was at least one piece of the puzzle.

"Who is that?" I asked, keeping my gaze locked on him. I may have been bad with names—something I was working on—but I never forgot a face. I certainly wouldn't have forgotten those piercing eyes, the strong jaw.

How had I gone all morning without knowing there was a new senior at Fulton? I hated not knowing things.

I wasn't delusional. Of course I couldn't control everything, but knowing as much as possible allowed me to be prepared for all scenarios. I had a spreadsheet with the names of each student at Fulton Academy, the names of their parents and what they did for work, any dirt we had on them, and any other pertinent information that was useful—or could be in the future. The girls were the only ones who had access to it, or even knew about it.

Information made the world go round. So did networking.

"That must be the new guy." Harlow shrugged. "Not in any of my classes, but I heard whispers."

"And you're only mentioning this now?" I glared at her, but she flipped me off with a sweet smile, and I couldn't resist smiling back. She entertained my need to know everything, and I distracted our parents from her weird online activities and less than impressive grades.

"He wasn't in any of my morning classes either." Mena looked at him over her shoulder. "I think I would've noticed that level of hotness."

"You have a boyfriend." Harlow laughed and smacked her.

"So? I'm only human. I can look."

"Amaya." I cut across their banter. Amaya would've already texted me if she'd known about this.

"Already on it." She was typing furiously on her phone.

New guy closed his locker and walked out of the hallway, heading in the opposite direction of the cafeteria. I didn't like having him out of my sight, but I chased after no man, and I certainly didn't change my plans for any.

Looping my arm through Amaya's so she could continue to text, I led the way into the bright, bustling cafeteria.

Tall windows lined one wall, letting in natural light, with several French doors providing access to a courtyard for alfresco dining. Along with the various seating scattered throughout the space, a lounge area in the back corner housed an assortment of comfy couches and low tables. The full-service food counter was closer to a buffet than a school lunch line and included an espresso station—complete with a full-time barista.

We waited until we were seated at our usual table, trays of sushi and berry parfaits in front of us, before Amaya leaned in to deliver her information.

"His name is Hendrix Hawthorn. He started at Fulton today but spent most of the morning in the office—something about paperwork—which is why no one's seen him much yet. He moved here from the East Coast, but I can't seem to get any info on where exactly he transferred from."

Her fingers tightened around her chopsticks. Amaya liked the lack of information about as much as I did.

"I wonder if he has any friends here," Mena mused. I left the comment alone for now. I needed to know more about him before I decided how close we would become.

"Hey, girls." Nicola joined us at our table, her bleach-blonde hair bouncing at her shoulders. She was nice enough, and her mom was a household name due to her film career—as well as a client of Emily Mead Interiors—so she hung around us at school. But she wasn't a part of my core group. Harlow, Amaya, and Mena were my soul-deep friends.

We greeted her warmly anyway. Within a few minutes, a bunch of other people joined us too, and the new guy was the topic on everyone's lips. I kept quiet, listening to what everyone else had to say. The girls at the table kept glancing in my direction, waiting to hear what I thought. One negative word from me, and Hendrix Hawthorn would not be getting into the La Perla panties of a single Fulton student.

Unfortunately, I had a feeling I'd have to tackle this one head-on and speak to him directly. There just wasn't enough information to decide if he was going to be trouble—or if he was *worth* the trouble.

Before long, the conversation moved on. William complained about Mrs. Watson's surprise quiz in Calculus, Harlow threw in a completely random fact about the Fibonacci sequence that I had no idea where she'd learned but was positive was correct, Drew loudly and half-jokingly hit on Mena, and half the table reminded him she had a boyfriend.

Business as usual.

Lunch ended, and we dispersed to our next classes. Mulling over the new guy proved to be a good distraction through the afternoon, and I pulled at the waist of my skirt only once, thinking about how I couldn't wait to change into something very different and go to my dirty little secret. *Only a few hours to go.*

I was the first one of us girls out at the end of the day, so I threw my bag into the car, put my sunglasses on, and leaned back against the hood to turn my face up to the sky. There was a chill in the breeze, but the sun was driving it away.

Hendrix Hawthorn came striding down the steps as if he owned the place. He looked casual enough, but that neutral mask was still in place, and his Ray-Bans were already over his eyes. Nicola and a few other senior girls were trailing a safe distance behind him, whispering to each other, trying to get up the courage to talk to him. Tess even adjusted her boobs to put her cleavage on better display.

I rolled my eyes behind my shades and gritted my teeth. I didn't know why his presence bothered me so much. Maybe it was the blasé attitude. Maybe it was the fact that I had no idea what his deal was, and I really hated not knowing things.

But I was never one to let things fester.

As he passed my car, I pushed up into a standing position and called out, only slightly raising my voice. "Hendrix, right?"

I glanced at the girls behind him, pleased to see they were dispersing, even if their focus hadn't left us. Most people nearby had slowed down and were throwing us surreptitious glances. They knew just as well as I did that this interaction would determine where the new guy would fit in the complex social hierarchy of Fulton Academy.

Hendrix pressed his lips together and looked as if he might just keep walking, but then he seemed to notice all the attention too. He slowed his steps and half turned his body to face me.

Well, at least he was smart enough to realize that ignoring me would be a bad move.

"Yeah." His deep voice was as disinterested as his facial expression. He stuffed a hand into his pocket and chewed on something, adding an edge of frustration to his impassive posture.

"Welcome to Fulton Academy." I folded my hands in front of myself, giving him my polite but professional smile—a smile I'd perfected at twelve years old. "I'm Donna Mead."

"Uh-huh." He smacked the gum. "I've already had the welcome speech from the people in the office."

"This isn't official business." Maybe he wasn't as smart as I thought.

He looked me up and down. "No thanks."

"Excuse me?" I raised my eyebrows.

He flashed me a grin, mashing the pink gum between his perfectly straight teeth. "If this isn't an official welcome, then it's clearly ... personal." He leaned in as if he were sharing a secret, but I kept my back ramrod straight. *Was that cinnamon?* "And I'm not interested in getting personal with you."

My right hand twitched with the urge to slap him. Luckily, my left was wrapped around it. I shoved down the rage, removed my sunglasses, and cocked my head, giving him an amused smile. "That's really presumptuous of you. I just wanted to introduce myself. Starting at a new school after the year has already begun can't be easy. I can help ease the transition. I could make your time here very pleasant."

I left the implications hanging in the cold breeze between us. I could make his time at Fulton incredibly fucking *unpleasant* too if I wanted to.

He watched me for a moment, his sharp jaw working that gum a little faster. Then he turned to face me fully and took his own sunglasses off. "I know girls like you. You think you rule this school and that you're going to grow up to rule the world. I know exactly what you think you can control. But I don't give a shit, princess. I don't want to be in your court. I don't give a flying fuck about making friends or *getting personal* with you or your hangers-on, so just pretend like I'm not here and continue to live your perfect little life. I'm just here until I can graduate and join the real world."

He blew an obnoxiously loud bubble, jammed his sunglasses back on, and walked away from me.

He fucking walked away from me. It was doubtful anyone had heard our exchange, but plenty of people were looking, watching for a hint of what my decree would be on Hendrix fucking Hawthorn.

I resisted the urge to chase him down, scream at him, smack that smug look off his face. Instead I smiled and replaced my sunglasses, keeping everyone in suspense for a little longer.

The smile was even a little genuine. He'd pissed me off, disrespected me, and was downright antagonizing. But I had a feeling I was going to have fun breaking him.

CHAPTER 2

Donna

GRAVEL CRUNCHED UNDER MY FAVORITE PAIR of thigh-high boots. The red miniskirt was tight around my thighs, the sheer top showed off my lacy bra underneath, and I was wearing more makeup than I ever did in public.

But I wasn't perfect, polished Donna Mead with starched uniforms and manicured nails tonight.

I was . . . someone else tonight.

Dark Donna.

The gaudy green neon above the metal door read *Davey's.*

A smile pulled at my ruby-red lips as every step I took toward the shiftiest establishment I knew took me away from myself.

Mom had come home from her boozy dinner, and I'd heard her snoring through the door as I passed her bedroom. Harlow was on her computer and had been oblivious to anything going on around her for hours. She'd be going to bed soon, and she'd leave early in the morning for tennis while Mom slept in. Meaning no one would notice *me* sleeping in.

My Legal Studies extra-credit assignment was done.

I'd mentioned a headache to the girls, ensuring they wouldn't try to get me out.

My to-do list for next week was written up in order of importance.

Hendrix ... *ugh*! Hendrix was tomorrow's problem.

The girls had witnessed the tail end of our conversation, and I'd told them every detail in the car. Amaya swore profusely, calling him some very colorful names. Harlow mostly laughed, amused that someone was getting a rise out of me. Mena didn't like that he'd said mean things to me, but in the same breath she hoped he was adjusting to a new school OK.

I still hadn't decided what to do about him, but as I pushed through the rusty metal door, thoughts of the infuriating guy melted away. Instead, the pumping bass sent chills of anticipation down my spine.

I paused in the entrance area only long enough to slip a fifty to Anton—the burly bouncer whom I had a standing arrangement with. Not that Davey's was that strict with checking IDs anyway. Anton was paid for his discretion as much as for my entry. He gave me a nod, tucked the bill away, and readjusted himself on his stool. I didn't think I'd ever seen him crack a smile.

The Davey's clientele was as questionable as the stale trail mix they served up at the bar, but I didn't come here for stimulating conversation or to meet my future husband. I came here to have fun—to let the loud music and edge of danger drive all other thoughts from my mind.

I swayed my hips to the music as I made my way through the middle of the room, checking out who was on the dance floor. A lot of bikers hung out here, drug dealers, hookers—basically unpredictable people with questionable morals. People who made a thrilling jolt of fear race down my spine.

When I reached the bar, I wedged myself between a couple of bikers and a prostitute named Gina (she'd spilled her whole life story to me on one of my previous visits but had no memory of it or me—so I didn't bother saying hello). I stuck my ass out, crossing my booted feet at the ankles and arching my back. My gaze stayed forward, but I could practically *feel* hungry male eyes caressing my curves.

Three busy bartenders were working the bar, but luckily Bea spotted me first.

"Hey, girl." She greeted me with a fist bump. Bea was in her thirties, had dreadlocks and a penchant for leather vests, and took shit from no one. "Usual?"

"Yes, please." I gave her a genuine grin. We'd never spoken much beyond that exact exchange, but just like Anton, I had an understanding with Bea.

She dropped a glass of what looked like vodka and soda in front of me, but it was actually just soda. Even when I ordered an alcoholic drink in front of other people, Bea knew not to serve me alcohol, and she knew to keep her mouth shut about our agreement. I slipped her a fifty as I paid for the drink, and she gave me a wink before moving on to take the next order.

I was here because it made me feel alive. I didn't actually have a death wish. There was no way I was going to risk getting intoxicated in *this* crowd.

I turned to lean back against the bar, sipping my drink as I scanned the room. There were a few guys with potential. I liked the ones who were taller than me in my heels. I didn't really care what color his hair was, what his voice sounded like. I hardly even bothered with his name half the time. But he had to be strong, confident, with some intensity simmering around the edges. *He* had to be the one to approach *me*.

The boys at my school couldn't handle me. But these lowlifes—these criminals with dark pasts and nothing to lose—they could handle me in the best, most depraved ways.

That's why they had to be older. How could they handle me if they couldn't handle themselves? Even so, I still never went for anyone who looked older than late twenties. I had control issues, not daddy issues.

In the bathrooms, in their cars, against the rough brick at the back of the building. One guy had even taken me to the back of the parking lot and bent me over his vintage Mustang. That was a fun night . . .

I never hooked up with the same guy twice, and I never let them think they could get more than one night of fun—not that any of them were interested in anything serious.

As my gaze wandered the crowd, I spotted the only man I'd ever slept with more than once.

I knew him only as Shady—yes, I was sleeping with someone who went by Shady, which pretty much told you all you needed to know about him. Not that he ever told me what his "business" was, but he was at Davey's a lot, all the staff knew him, and he was always talking to some new face.

Like right now. Shady was standing with his shoulders slouched, one hand holding a drink and the other in the pocket of his tracksuit pants, talking to someone in a very expensive suit who looked as if he didn't want to be there.

When the suit walked away, I sauntered over.

"Donna." He smirked at me from under his baseball hat. He only knew me as Donna.

I pressed myself against his side and brought my lips to his ear. "Hey. You busy tonight?" I made my intentions perfectly clear by giving his ear a little bite.

He groaned and gripped my hip.

Shady wasn't my usual type. He was only a little taller than me, and while he was lean and fit underneath those ridiculous tracksuits, he wasn't the size of a fridge. But he had the dominant confidence—bordering on cockiness—in spades. And his cock was huge.

"I wish I could, Donnie baby," he answered, and my face fell. "But I got some important business I gotta take care of tonight. If you're still around after close . . ."

But I was already shaking my head. I was never there that long. I couldn't risk getting home too late.

"Next time." I winked at him and walked away, making sure to sway my hips a little extra as I moved to the center of the dance floor.

He'd send me a bunch of texts later, telling me what he wanted to do to me. I was already looking forward to the thrill of reading them—a little slice of danger in my normal, clean life.

I didn't always pick up when I came to Davey's. Sometimes I just wanted to dance, to thrash out my frustration with the world on the sticky floors. Sometimes I liked to sit in a corner and people-watch, wondering what these people's lives were like. Were they easier than mine? Harder? What secrets did they have?

As I walked away from Shady, I had a feeling no one would approach me tonight. Sometimes, when he was in a shit-stirring mood, I thought maybe Shady *made sure* no one approached me. I didn't know if he was actually possessive or if he just liked to fuck with me, but I didn't care either way. If anything, it amused me. And I refused to give him the satisfaction of my reaction.

***

I rolled out of bed sometime after ten the next day—a good three hours later than my usual wake-up time. Harlow was still at tennis, and Mom liked to sleep in and have breakfast brought to her in bed when Dad was away. He was more active, like Harlow, and usually dragged Mom out to the pool or for a walk in the mornings.

The house was silent as I made my way downstairs, yawning and enjoying the fact that no one was around to make me feel as if I had to cover my mouth.

The hour alone before Harlow got back from tennis was the only peace I had all weekend. Mom got up not long after, just as Dad returned from his work trip and insisted on a family lunch.

I spent Saturday night at Amaya's with the girls. We stayed up late, watched movies, gossiped—and discussed the Hendrix topic ad nauseam.

"God." Amaya groaned, letting her phone drop to the couch next to her. "That is the sixth text I've gotten from a basic bitch fishing for info on the new guy. Do your own damn research!"

I chuckled and ran my hands through the ridiculously soft faux fur of the cushion in my lap. Mena and Harlow were throwing bits of popcorn at each other, trying to catch them with their mouths between fits of giggles, and only half paying attention.

"No boy talk!" Harlow yelled, then launched herself to the side to try to catch a kernel.

Mena laughed so hard she had to wipe tears away before she could speak. "I don't get why everyone's obsessed with him. He's just a guy."

"Because we go to school with a bunch of thirsty bitches," Amaya deadpanned.

I laughed. She wasn't wrong. People were

fascinated because he was a shiny new toy, but he'd made it perfectly clear he didn't want to be played with. *We may as well give him what he wants . . .*

"Reply to them." I gestured at Amaya's phone, and she picked it up.

"What should I say?"

"Just write . . . Hendrix who?" I grinned. "And nothing else."

Amaya nodded, already typing. "Brutal."

I spent most of Sunday doing homework, and on Monday, while most people were dragging their feet into school, I marched in with a faint smile. Every time something annoyed or frustrated me, I'd remember the loud music thrumming in my chest, the smell of beer and sweat and cheap perfume, the feeling of eyes on me as I danced like a stripper. Shady must've been in one of his moods, because I ended up not finding a guy to have dirty sex with, but it was still a fun night—exactly the break and distraction I'd needed.

With the help of a few depraved texts from Shady, my Davey's high lasted well past the weekend, and I was still feeling loose as I pulled into the school parking lot on Tuesday morning.

"What the fuck?" Amaya growled. She'd spotted the Tesla in my spot the same time I did. I came to a stop and gripped the steering wheel, taking a deep breath.

"Whose car is that?" Harlow leaned between the front seats.

Everyone at Fulton knew not to park in that spot— everyone except one infuriating new asshole.

"I'll give you three guesses." My buzz was wearing off, and I hadn't even stepped foot into the school yet.

"We'll just have to park somewhere else today." Mena squeezed my shoulder. "It's no biggie."

She didn't get it. It may have been just a parking spot to everyone else, but I knew how these things worked. If I gave them a parking spot crumb, those vultures would devour my whole carcass—scrape my dignity, influence, and power from me strip by bloody strip. I had to remain in control.

"You guys go ahead. I'll drive to the back of the lot and look for a spot."

"No way, girl. We stick together," Amaya protested immediately, but Harlow was already undoing her belt.

"I can't get another late mark. Sorry, sis!" She sounded genuinely sorry but also a little satisfied at my ire—*little sisters*.

"I'll walk with you," Mena said to me.

I checked the time and shook my head. "Thanks, girls, but there's no sense in us all being late. Get your fine asses out of my car."

I flashed them a smile to show I really didn't mind, and they got out, rushing for the front doors. There were hardly any students still outside. I had five minutes to find a spot and get to my first class.

Just as I was about to take off, the door to the Tesla opened, and Hendrix fucking Hawthorn stepped out, completely unhurried and unfazed.

I quickly put my car in neutral and pulled the

parking brake, then got out too. If I had to be late, so would he.

"Hendrix." I raised my voice, letting the edge cut into the single word.

He looked over his shoulder and rolled his eyes. "What now? I'm gonna be late."

"You're in my spot." I folded my arms and glared, showing him exactly how pissed I was.

"Excuse me?"

"You." I pointed at him, speaking as though I were explaining a complex idea to a child. "Are in." I pointed to his car. "My spot."

He stared at me for a beat, then made a show of checking the ground around his car before raising his brows and holding his arms out at his sides. "Don't see your name on it."

I took a deep breath and pinched the bridge of my nose. "I've tried to be nice, but you threw that in my face. You said you wanted to be left alone, but here you are antagonizing me. Everyone knows I park here. I'm now going to be late because of you. Move your car, and don't let this happen again."

He threw his head back and laughed, his broad shoulders shaking under his blazer. When he looked at me again, the mirth fell from his features, replaced by an intense stare.

"The spots are not allocated. Much as you like to think so, you don't own this school, princess, you don't own this spot, and you will never own *me*. I don't respond well to being ordered around." He locked his car and stalked toward the school as the bell sounded, leaving my profanity-filled response on the tip of my tongue.

I resisted the urge to stomp my foot like the brat he thought I was. Instead, I got back into my car, drove to the back of the lot, found one of the last remaining spots, and took the walk to the entrance to calm myself.

I was already late, so I didn't bother to rush; no sense in ruining my appearance too. His blatant disrespect in front of the entire school—everyone would walk past and see his car in my spot—made it impossible to do nothing. And my seething rage and determination to remain in control allowed me to formulate a rough plan by the time I entered the main building.

I sent a message to the girls in our group chat. "I've changed my mind. He needs to be taught to heel."

If he was going to act like a disobedient puppy, pissing on things he thought he had a right to, then I would treat him like a dog.

CHAPTER 3

Hendrix

I FROWNED AT THE BULLETIN BOARD. I KNEW for a fact I'd put my name down on the sign-up form on my second day at Fulton Academy, yet there was the spot, covered in white-out with some other dickhead's name scrawled over the top.

I gritted my teeth and fought the urge to hunt down this Thomas Booth and make sure he could never walk again, let alone kick a football.

It was for the best—I'd come here to remove my own name anyway. Playing football was too close to my old life. Apparently the school was holding tryouts this late in the year because four of the players had been injured in some car accident—one was off the team permanently for breaking the coach's strict no-alcohol-during-the-week rule. The dumbasses were getting wasted and driving around Devilbend on a Wednesday night. It was something I would've done—before.

Only nostalgia had made me put my name down in the first place—misplaced longing for a life I now knew was a fucking joke. I flexed my fingers and bunched them into a fist, remembering the feel of the ball as it slapped into my waiting arms. I hadn't played in over a year, and it was all my fault. All my stupidity and carelessness and . . .

I dug my nails into my palm and forced myself to focus on my surroundings, the chatting of students as they passed, the opening and closing of lockers in the distance.

The teal tie felt stiff and tight, and I tugged at it before adjusting the bag on my shoulder. I wasn't used to the uniform yet.

A short woman with glasses and a pencil skirt hugging her generous curves stepped out of the office and reached for the form I'd just been staring daggers at. She spotted me and paused, giving me a warm smile.

"Did you want to sign up? It's not too late." She wiggled the form in front of my face.

"No thanks." I kept my voice even. There was no need to take my frustration out on the nice reception lady.

I did my best to ignore the other students as I walked to my locker.

She may not have whited my name out herself, but I had no doubt Donna Mead was the person behind its removal. It didn't matter though. I didn't belong on their stupid football team, especially if I wasn't welcome. You couldn't build a team if the team didn't get along.

I'd been at Fulton just over two weeks, and other than a few early verbal sparring matches with Donna, I'd hardly had a conversation with another person. The first few days had been a nightmare. It was a new school, all new people, the other fucking side of the country. I knew I was good-looking and tall, and now the giant chip on my shoulder gave me the edge of bad-boy danger private school girls creamed their panties for. A few guys had been friendly initially too, probably hoping I'd join the football team and help save them from a disaster season.

I'd either brushed off or ignored them all, wondering how long I'd have to endure this torture before they got the hint. I just wanted to be left alone, finish my senior year, and never see any of these stuck-up, rich assholes again.

By the end of the first day, it was clear who the "queen bee" was. Donna Mead strutted the halls with her predictable gaggle of girls and the confidence of a spoiled brat who'd never been told *no*. The guys all checked her out as she passed; the girls all glanced in her direction, as if waiting for permission to exist.

Donna was exactly the type the old me would've gone for. If this were a year ago, before I went and ruined everything, she would've been riding my dick within a week, and I would've been throwing punches at any guy who dared look in her direction as we both got off on the power of being the most popular couple in school.

A lot had changed. I had nothing but contempt for

girls like Donna and guys like me now.

I hated her for what she represented, but I hated myself more for what I used to be.

I'd hoped to just sail under the radar, but it became apparent very quickly that wasn't going to happen. Antagonizing Donna was the best and most efficient way of making sure everyone left me alone.

So, I was rude to her, really embracing the cocky attitude, the side of myself I tried to push down.

I could tell she was pissed, but the stares from chicks wanting to get in my pants didn't stop. So I parked in her spot deliberately. Of course I knew it was her spot. I'd seen her park there, seen other students leave the prime space free. I got up extra early and sat in my damn car for nearly twenty minutes, waiting for her to show.

It was almost cute, the way her nose scrunched up in derision. It took a lot not to chuckle while she was berating me. That was the first time I noticed she had one green eye and one hazel. So unusual. It was distracting, watching both the mesmerizing colors blaze in fury at me. I'd planned to hang around longer, really rile her, maybe even get her to raise her voice. But I'd started to forget all the hurtful things I'd planned to say to her and walked away much sooner than planned.

It worked anyway. I'd goaded the queen of Fulton Academy into declaring war on me. I got what I wanted . . . and then some.

The next day, a group of freshman girls were standing in the parking space, blocking my car with their gangly bodies. I laughed to myself as I passed. I had no intention of ever parking there again. I'd made my point. But the parking-minders remained for a solid week, faithful subjects trying to impress their queen. Most likely she hadn't even had to ask. They'd probably only needed a vague mention of how inconvenient it was for her and jumped to her defense.

I deposited my bag in my locker and gripped my biology books with one hand, slamming the locker shut with the other.

As I walked the halls, no one looked at me anymore. Donna had made her declaration, and her loyal subjects were doing her bidding—excommunicating me.

Just before I reached the end of the hallway, some junior with a wonky tie and acne around his nose deliberately bumped into me in an attempt to knock my books out of my hand. His intentions had been obvious in his jittery steps and nervous glances, so I'd had plenty of time to tense my core and grip my books tighter. The kid bounced off me like a tennis ball.

Eyes wide, he stared up at me. I gave him a disparaging look, and he nervously shot a glance to the side before hanging his head and rushing off.

I followed his gaze. *Of course.* Donna was walking up the corridor with her short friend—Mena? The guy had been trying to impress her and failed miserably.

I rolled my eyes and went on my merry way.

It had been two and a half weeks of this. At first, all the early attention for a hot new guy had abruptly stopped. Exactly what I wanted. Then people started throwing me openly hostile scowls wherever I went. Not unexpected, and definitely something I could handle. Then losers wanting to impress Donna started bumping into me, attempting to shove me into lockers, trying to intimidate me, while the chicks—also wanting to impress Donna, although mostly for different reasons—started saying bitchy things about me as I passed. Having the entire school against me was more than I expected, but I could still handle it. There were only seven months until the school year ended, and I'd never be seeing any of these people again. What did I care what they thought of me?

I never fought back, never reacted more than to tense up and stop my ass from hitting the ground. I just sealed that impassive look on my face, turned my nose up as if none of these bastards mattered more than dirt on my shoes, and kept walking.

Inside, I was *writhing*.

Old habits die hard, and every time someone showed me aggression, I itched to drive my fist into their face, spear tackle them to the ground, knee them in the gut, do something *violent*. I knew it would make me feel better . . . momentarily. It just wasn't worth it anymore. Not after what went down at my last school.

As I neared my classroom, a football came sailing at my head. I'd seen the quarterback throw it. I caught it, not even flinching at how close it got to my nose or how my hand stung from the impact. The guy had a good arm, had to give him that. I was pretty sure his name was Drew—I'd seen him hanging out with Donna and her group.

I fixed him with a deadpan stare. *Nice try, asshole.* A smile pulled at his lips as he stared at me in shock. He was as grudgingly impressed with my catch as I was with his throw. *Suck on it—that's exactly what you missed out on by scratching my name off the sign-up.*

I let the ball bounce to the ground and walked into my classroom to take my seat, like a good little boy. As I opened my textbook, I allowed myself a little smirk of satisfaction.

The bell sounded, everyone settled, and Mrs. Shepard—a middle-aged woman with a killer rack that I'm sure was in the spank bank for half the boys at the school—started the lesson.

And my fucking pen ran out of ink. I scratched it aggressively against the paper, hoping to get the blue stuff flowing by force, but it refused to budge. My grip on the pen tightened to the point that I could feel the plastic about to snap. Dropping it onto the desk, I took a deep breath and, without even thinking about it, turned to the chick in the seat next to me.

"Hey, you got a pen I can borrow?" I whispered.

The look she gave me was so full of derision and outrage you'd think I'd asked her to get on her knees and blow me in the middle of class. It was just a fucking pen.

She looked away without even a response.

I'd wanted to be left alone, but this was ridiculous. How hard was it to be polite every once in a while?

Someone tapped my shoulder with a pen, and I

turned in my seat. The chick one row back and to my right was holding out a black pen with a friendly smile.

I frowned and eyed the pen, wondering if it was laced with arsenic. She was one of Donna's girls—and I'd picked up enough from overheard conversations to know that Mena was Donna and Harlow's cousin and very close with them both.

So what the fuck was she doing acknowledging my existence?

"It's just a pen." She rolled her eyes, but with a hint of humor.

I took it and nodded. "Thank you."

"You're welcome." Her smile seemed sincere as she sat back and returned her attention to the front of the class.

"Mr. Hawthorn." Mrs. Shepard's voice had me doing the same. "Am I boring you?"

"No, ma'am." I held the pen up. "Just borrowing a pen."

She gave me a skeptical look and got back to the lesson.

I did my best to pay attention, but I couldn't stop thinking about the anomaly that was Mena. From what I'd seen, the girl was genuinely friendly and sweet. She had a purple birthmark on the right side of her nose that would've made her a target for bullies at my old school. Fulton was almost identical, but Mena was one of the most popular girls, protected by her close friendship with Donna.

It didn't fit my assessment of who Donna Mead was

and what she was about, and I didn't like that. I didn't like that I was suddenly wondering what made her tick. It had been a long time since a chick had made me curious, and I didn't have time for it.

I drove home in the brand-new Tesla Model S my parents hadn't even questioned the price tag on. I resented having to take anything from them in the first place, but public transport in this part of Devilbend was a joke, so I'd caved and let them buy me one. But I'd chosen a ridiculously expensive one just to spite them, and the most environmentally friendly one to put some semblance of good into the world in a vain attempt to make up for all the bad I'd done. They'd just paid the bill, not even an angry message to their disappointment of a son.

Being sent to the other side of the country to live with my aunt was almost as much a relief for me as it was for them.

Aunt Hannah lived on the edge of the nicest part of Devilbend. Her townhouse was spacious and nicely decorated, but she didn't have the sprawling land some of the ostentatious estates boasted—the kind of property I grew up on back in New York.

I parked on the street, not wanting to block the one-car garage when she got home.

As soon as I finished shoveling a sandwich into my mouth, I changed into sweats and spent the next couple hours zoning out with the help of video games. I got so engrossed in the explosions on the TV I didn't even notice the front door opening.

"Hendrix?" My aunt's voice made me startle. She stood next to the couch, her arms crossed over her silk blouse.

I immediately ended the game and dropped the controller on the coffee table. "Hey. Uh . . . how was work?"

She ignored my question. "Have you been playing video games all afternoon?"

"Yeah." I cringed. I was eighteen and she wasn't my parent, but I was here and not with my asshole parents because she allowed it. "I'm going to do homework after dinner."

She just sighed and gave me a disapproving look. She'd looked at me with disapproval a lot in the month I'd been staying with her. It grated on my nerves, but I kept my reaction tightly under wraps. Considering the reason I was here, what I'd done, I deserved the disapproving looks.

I got up and started clearing the plates, cups, and chip packets. I liked to eat while I played. "Um . . . how was your day?"

"Fine." She followed me into the kitchen and dropped her oversized purse on a barstool.

"Cool." I nodded and pressed my lips together.

Hannah was working her way up through the ranks at some marketing company. She worked hard, sometimes doing long hours and often bringing work home, her laptop and piles of paper spread over the dining table. She was in her early thirties, had no kids, and had no idea how to handle me. I wondered, almost daily, how my parents had gotten her to agree to let me move in while I finished high school. She and my dad weren't exactly on good terms. I'd only met her a handful of times at family events—where she generally kept to herself in a far corner, scowling and getting slowly but surely drunk. But she'd been kind to me as a kid, bringing me little gifts and dropping the scowl if I happened to come up to her.

"I'm staying at Robbie's tonight." She leaned on the counter. Robbie was her boyfriend, whom she rarely talked about and I had yet to meet. "Do you need me to leave you some money to order takeout for dinner?"

"No, that's OK. Bank of Dad has it covered." I gave her a wry smile. My credit card had a very generous limit. My father may have sent me away like the blight on his reputation that I was, but he wasn't about to cut me off.

"Right. Good." She stared at the counter, and I shuffled my feet. I was glad she was finally spending more time with her partner. My guess was she'd been spending every night at home because of me, and I felt bad.

"You're not to have anyone around." She finally straightened and fixed me with a firm look. So, this was what was making her pause. She needed to lay down the law.

"That won't be a problem." There wasn't a single soul in Devilbend I would consider a friend.

"I'm not messing around, Hendrix. I need a night to spend with my boyfriend, but leaving you alone makes me nervous. I won't tolerate . . . insubordination."

If I hadn't felt like shit to my very core, her attempts at a firm reprimand would've been amusing. She was a petite woman with strawberry-blonde hair and a tasteful manicure. I had a foot and a hundred pounds on her. There wasn't much she could do to make me do anything, which made the fact that she hadn't had her boyfriend over to intimidate me even more perplexing. I admired her, really. She was taking me on all on her own. But she had nothing to worry about.

I'd spent the month since I'd arrived doing nothing but what she'd told me. She had only two rules, which she'd made crystal clear within half an hour of my arrival: maintain a B average, and stay out of trouble. The slightest hint of my breaking either rule would result in immediate removal from her home. I had no intention of letting her down.

We'd hardly spoken since then, but I'd been respectful, cleaned up after myself, gone to school, stayed out of her way. I was doing all I could to show her I was serious, but she still felt the need to remind me I was on thin ice every few days. As if she was worried I was just waiting for her to let her guard down so I could go back to being the douchebag I'd been before.

I'd avoided talking to her about it because I really didn't want to discuss the reason I was here in the first place. But I needed to man up and say something. As frustrated as I was with the constant side-eye, I knew I deserved it, so I made sure my voice was calm, contrite even, as I leaned on the counter opposite her.

"Aunt Hannah, I know my being here isn't easy for you. I don't know what you discussed with Mom and Dad—they don't really tell me anything—but I want you to know I'm not here because my parents made me. I want to be here. I want to be anywhere but . . . there, where it all happened and everyone looks at me like I'm a monster." *Because I am . . .* fuck it. I swallowed and made myself own it. "I know it's because I am. But I'm trying not to be. I'm really, really fucking sorry for what I did, and I promise I'm not interested in causing any trouble at all. Sorry for cursing."

She straightened her shoulders, and her expression visibly softened as she scrutinized me for a few minutes. "I believe you. I don't know if I would've handled the situation like your parents did, but I'm not your parent. But then, I guess you're not your father either . . ." She looked to the side, lost in thoughts I suspected weren't directly related to our current situation. "Anyway, I'm sorry if I've been a hard-ass. I'm just still trying to figure out how to navigate this."

"It's OK. I don't want you to change your life on my account. Go out, spend time with Robbie. Have him over if that's what you used to do. Just know I won't cause any trouble. I can take care of myself, and as soon as school is over, I'll be out of your hair. I'll figure something out."

"Tell you what, I'll stop being such a bitch and be more relaxed if you promise to come to me if you need help with something or if you're struggling. I agreed to this for many reasons, but I do want to be here for you,

Hendrix. If I can."

I had to clear my throat around the lump that had suddenly formed there. If my parents had, even once, made me feel as supported as this virtual stranger had, maybe things would've turned out differently. "Deal."

"And I don't think you're a monster." My gaze flew up to hers, the emotions flying around in my chest too many to process. "I think you made a mistake—a very bad one that you have to live with for the rest of your life—but I don't believe you intended to . . . for things to go the way they did."

I held her gaze for a long moment, then nodded. It was all I could manage.

"Right!" She slapped the counter and literally shook the tension out of her shoulders. It was the most animated I'd ever seen her. "Good talk! Should we hug it out?" She tilted her head and gave me an awkward, questioning grin.

I chuckled. "That's not necessary."

"We'll work up to it." She waved her hand. "I'll get a stepping stool to prepare."

"A stepping stool?"

"Yeah. You're way too fucking tall. I need to assert my adult dominance by gaining a height advantage."

I let a genuine laugh bust out of my chest. "So, you're OK with cursing then?"

She tapped her chin and squinted, then shrugged. "Yeah, fuck it. You're an adult, and I have a potty mouth."

"Excellent." I grinned. This was feeling more like a

nephew-aunt relationship, and a little weight lifted off my shoulders.

She left a few minutes later, and I got on with exactly what I said I'd do—homework.

My phone went off just as I started packing my books up, yawning so wide my jaw felt as if it might dislocate. I checked the message and sighed.

> Heard you were in my neck of the woods. Hit me up if you need anything—even if it's just to shoot the shit over a drink.

The number was unknown, but I knew the name at the end of the text. This had the potential for trouble—trouble I didn't need, wasn't interested in, and just told my aunt I was avoiding. But even I knew not letting off some steam every once in a while could result in even worse trouble.

I decided to ignore the message for now and flopped into bed. It was well past midnight, but I still had trouble falling asleep, thoughts of a certain interesting blonde keeping me tossing and turning.

CHAPTER 4

Hendrix

MY LUNCH TRAY WAS YANKED OUT FROM UNDER my nose before I had a chance to pick up the silverware. It clattered to the ground, pasta puttanesca splattering everywhere as a green apple rolled away.

"Oops." A girl with curly black hair held a hand to her mouth in mock shock, her friends snickering behind her.

Half the kids in the cafeteria froze, their full focus on the scene, just as Donna and her friends walked past.

I took a deep breath and released it through my nose. Fixing the wannabe bitch with an unimpressed look, I bent sideways to grab the sauce-covered pudding cup and—without breaking eye contact—removed the lid and licked it in a slow, deliberate move. I almost smiled at how her face slackened, her lips parting a little in shock even as she frowned in frustration at my lack of response. She was no doubt wondering what my tongue would feel like between her thighs, questioning how her brilliant plan to humiliate me had backfired so badly.

I dropped the lid onto the mess at my feet and dug into the pudding as she walked away, her shoulders tight.

Shit was escalating. In the last few days, the girls had started getting physical too. None of them dared try to shove me—they weren't that stupid—but pushing my books off desks, throwing their trash in my direction, and other aggressive moves were getting more common.

If something didn't change soon, I'd have to make a stand. I wasn't interested in being anyone's friend, but I wasn't going to be anyone's punching bag either. Even though I deserved it, ultimately, they didn't know that, so was it really penance for past crimes if my tormentors' hearts weren't in it for the right reasons?

People buzzed around Donna's table, laughing and joking, not paying any attention whatsoever to the rest of the cafeteria. The wannabe bitch was neither getting rewarded for her stunt with the queen bee's attention nor being chastised for her stupidity by anyone else. This thing had taken on a life of its own. Donna wasn't behind the continuing escalation of shitty behavior toward me, but she wasn't doing anything to stop it either.

Only Mena and Donna's sister, Harlow, glanced in my direction every once in a while, sitting at the end of the table in their own private chat.

My knee bounced under the table, but I made myself eat the pudding at a leisurely pace. Then I got to my feet, cleaned up the mess as best I could with napkins, and returned my tray to the staff, letting them know there was an accident and apologizing for the mess. None of these brats would bother cleaning it up, expecting "the help" to do their bidding even at school. I was one of these brats until not too long ago.

I left halfway through lunch, needing to get away from all those idiots even if it meant not getting a proper meal. The bag of chips I had stashed in my locker wouldn't be enough, but it was better than nothing until school ended.

Footsteps echoed behind me in the mostly empty hall, and I slammed my locker shut, preparing for whatever bullshit was coming next.

Turned out it was a serving of hot fries and not bullshit. Mena came to a stop next to me and held out the steaming offering. My mouth watered. Who didn't love hot fries?

"I noticed you didn't really eat." She was wearing makeup today, her birthmark invisible.

I arched a brow at her. "How can I be sure no one pissed on them?"

She scrunched up her face. "Who would defile the sacredness of hot fries like that?"

My lips twitched. She almost drew an actual smile from me. "Wouldn't put it past your friend."

"Donna wouldn't do that." She sighed as I took the fries. "And she didn't tell that girl to throw your lunch on the ground."

I gave her a skeptical look and spoke around a

mouthful of hot potato. "She didn't tell her not to either."

"No, but Donna isn't the boss of everyone."

I snorted and gave her a withering look.

"OK, fine. She has a lot of influence around here, but . . ." Mena trailed off, searching for words to defend her cousin, just as the girl in question appeared with the other two at the end of the hallway. Lunch was coming to a close.

Donna stopped next to us and clasped her hands in front of her. I shoved another three fries into my mouth to distract myself from the exposed skin between the tops of her socks and that infuriating skirt. Who the fuck decided to put a bunch of hormonal teenagers into porn-fantasy outfits and make them spend every day of the week together? Idiots . . .

"You OK, Mena?" Donna asked as she stared at me. There was genuine concern in her voice.

Mena huffed. "I'm fine. He's harmless."

I shoved more fries into my mouth. If she only knew how decidedly *not* harmless I was . . . I should've just walked away, but instead I found myself leaning back against the locker.

Donna finally faced her friend. "Hendrix has made it perfectly clear he wants to be left alone."

I finished the last of the fries and cut in before anyone else could speak. "Thanks for the fries, Mena. You seem like a genuinely nice person. I really don't understand why you hang out with these vapid bitches."

Harlow fixed me with a scowl so deep she bared her

teeth. Amaya stopped texting for longer than a few seconds and narrowed her eyes. Donna surprised me once again by leaning back just a fraction, a tiny smile pulling at her lips.

But it was sweet Mena who surprised me most. She stepped right into my space and poked me in the chest. "No. I know you're new around here, so you don't know us, and I don't really understand this bizarre feud between you two, but I'm not going to stand here and let you talk about my friends like that. You're being a judgmental douche—and not the vagina kind. The butt kind." She jabbed my chest again, and my eyes widened. I'd inadvertently unleashed some kind of attack koala, and she was coming for my head. "I'm trying to be nice to you because I think that's the right thing to do, but make no mistake—I would do anything for those three. They're like more than sisters to me. No one fucks with Devilbend Dynasty."

Without waiting for a response, she spun on her heel and stalked away. Harlow and Amaya trailed after her, but Donna remained, a smug smile on her lips as she crossed her arms.

I crushed the empty, greasy bag in my fist and straightened to my full height. She didn't even waver, somehow still managing to look down her nose at me despite having to look up to meet my eyes.

"Don't fuck with my friends. Then you'll know what I'm really capable of."

"You're already making my life difficult enough. What more could you possibly do?" I gritted out, showing my frustration for the first time.

"You wanted nothing to do with me, any of the other students, or this school." She shrugged. "I simply let a few people know."

"Yeah, well, they're really running with your suggestion now, so consider this a fair warning. If shit keeps escalating, I'm not just gonna take it lying down. I'm not expecting to be anyone's bro, but I'll have to start swinging back if it comes to it."

I dumped the greasy bag in the trash and shoved my way through the crowd. It was the most aggression I'd shown since I started at Fulton, and surprised students started getting out of my way.

It was a lie, of course. If the violence increased, I wouldn't do shit to fight back. I'd never swing a fist again, as much as I wanted to. *I'd rather die.*

The pent-up frustration had to be released somehow though. By the time the day ended, I'd snapped three pens.

As soon as I got in my car, I slammed the door shut and resisted the urge to punch the steering wheel. I couldn't go home. Video games wouldn't cut it today. Plus, I'd been slacking off with my fitness.

Because I was a good, responsible boy now, I shot off a text to my aunt.

> Going to sign up to a gym. May be home after you.

Her response was immediate.

> No worries. Staying at Robbie's tonight. Be
> safe!

The words on my phone screen melted some of the frustration from my system. *Be safe.* Not *be good* or *don't disappoint me* or *don't embarrass me.* I was beginning to wish Aunt Hannah had raised me and not the two emotionless robots I had for parents.

I drove to downtown Devilbend and parked at Exert. There were several gyms in town, two closer to where I lived, but I chose this one because it was on a busy street in the center of everything. I wanted the anonymity of a crowd.

The young guy behind the counter looked up from the computer screen and gave me a polite smile.

"Hey. Welcome to Exert." He was in shorts and a workout top with the gym branding, and his messy blond hair gave him a little bit of a surfer vibe.

"Hi. I'd like to join up."

"Great!" His smile widened, and he tapped at the keyboard before pointing to a touch screen facing me. "Just fill this out."

I filled out the form and handed over Dad's credit card, and he gave me a membership card and key fob. "We're open twenty-four hours, but the desk is only manned during business hours and evening classes. I've sent you an email with the schedule if you're interested. Can I help organize a PT session? The first one is complimentary."

"Nah, man, I'm good. Just here to work out." I was

already swinging my bag over my shoulder.

"No worries. I'm Turner, by the way. Just let me know if you need anything."

"Thanks, Turner," I called over my shoulder as I headed toward the changing room.

I thrashed my body for nearly two hours, alternating cardio and high-intensity weights. I hadn't played football in a year, and with everything going on, my visits to the gym had been sporadic at best. No question I'd be feeling it the next day.

When I got home, starving, I made myself two microwave dinners and slumped into a stool at the kitchen island.

My phone vibrated when I was halfway through something resembling chicken and pasta. I checked the message and sighed. It was from that same number.

> Hey, man. Wanna come out? Maybe play some pool? I'll be here all evening. No pressure.

At the bottom was an address two towns over.

I'd ignored the fucker's first message, and I knew I should ignore this one too, but the thought of spending another night in this empty house, alone, made me want to claw my eyes out.

I'd hardly had a conversation with anyone besides my aunt in nearly two months. I hadn't heard from my parents since the day they put me in a town car headed for the airport. The kids at school were on a collective campaign to make my life hell. And I hadn't spoken to any of my old friends in a long time. Most of the large group that used to hang on my every word disappeared pretty quickly after they realized I would no longer be going to school, let alone playing football—not after what I did. The rest I cut off myself. I couldn't stand to look at them. It was like looking in a mirror.

My aunt was supportive, but she was still my aunt, not my friend. Not someone I could chill with.

Shady wasn't an ideal companion—especially with a nickname like that—but he was all I had at the moment. I shoveled the rest of my dinner into my mouth and headed for the shower. My aunt wouldn't even know I'd gone out, but it didn't matter. I had no intention of breaking my promises to her. I was staying out of trouble. This was simply an excuse to get out of the house before I went completely batshit and started collecting cats and putting on tea parties for them.

When I pulled into the parking lot of the address he'd given me, I sighed. The neon name above the door—*Davey's*—glowed in the dusk. It had taken me forty minutes to get there, and it was probably going to be a giant waste of time. Shady hadn't bothered to mention it was a bar, so I hadn't bothered to bring my fake ID. I wasn't even sure I still had it.

I sent him a text.

> Just got here but can't join you. Did you forget I'm underage?

I was hoping I could convince him to grab a burger or something. I really didn't want to go home yet.

After five minutes, he still hadn't replied. Then a lean guy in a black tracksuit came swaggering around the back of the building. I'd only met him once, when he came to visit his cousin in New York about six months before my life was turned upside down, but there was no forgetting that cocky swagger, the wide grin.

Everything about this guy screamed trouble. You could tell with one glance he was Shady by nature and not just by name.

I got out of the car and walked toward him.

"Hendrix, my man!" he called out, spreading his arms wide.

I gave him a half-hearted wave and a smile. We shook hands, and he pulled me in for a good thump on the back too.

"Hey, Shady. Nice to see you again."

"You too, man, you too. Come 'round back—no bouncer." He led the way, then leaned sideways as if telling me a secret. "Between you and me, this place isn't exactly too bothered with shit like that."

"Shit like . . . legal drinking age?" I raised my eyebrows with a smirk.

He laughed, throwing his head back. "Yeah, yeah, yeah. So, how you been, man?"

Without giving me a chance to answer, he started chattering away about nothing specific as we walked into one of the dirtiest bars I'd ever seen. It was dingy, smoky, and full of people who looked even more like trouble than Shady—and that was saying something. I followed him to a seating area in the back, and he introduced me to a handful of other guys, who gave me their best tough-guy head nods in greeting.

Before I could sit down, he led me away again, still talking shit. I'd never met someone who could talk so much without actually saying anything.

We settled into a couple of barstools, and he turned to me. "Had to intro you to the businessmen. It's a respect thing."

I just nodded. If those guys were legitimate businessmen, then I was a professional cupcake baker. "They own the club? You work for them?"

"Nah, nah. The owner doesn't come 'round much. That was the manager and a couple other guys. We all have an arrangement. What's your poison?"

That was all he was going to say on the matter of his "business," and I didn't want more details anyway. "Just a soda or something. I'm not drinking."

"I told you, bro. No one's gonna check your ID here." He thumped me on the back, waving a bar chick with dreads over.

Shady ordered vodka and OJ, and I got a Coke, then turned to him. "It's not that. I have to drive back to Devilbend, and I can't get in any more trouble, man."

He nodded and dropped the grin. "Hey, man, Wiley told me what went down. That's some heavy shit."

Wiley was Shady's cousin and a friend of mine from New York. He didn't go to my school, but I'd met him at some party, and we clicked. We used to egg each other on to do the stupidest shit. He didn't have a lot of money, so I always insisted on paying when we went out for food and shit, but he provided an outlet for me— dangerous access to getting into some dumb trouble. He was one of the only people who stood by me when "shit went down," as Shady said. But I'd stopped returning his calls too. I didn't deserve anyone's support, and I needed to cut ties to that life anyway.

Yet there I was, sitting in a dodgy bar with his cousin, who was already downplaying the single biggest mistake of my life. Maybe this wasn't a good idea . . .

"What went down?" I arched a brow at him.

The bar chick delivered our drinks, and he took a sip. "Yeah. You know, what happened . . . the incident."

"The incident . . ." I glared at him. "I don't need you to play it down, man. As much as my parents wish I wouldn't, I actually own my shit. You can just say it. I—"

"Hey, look," he said, cutting me off. "I'm not trying to piss you off or fish for info. We don't even have to talk about it. Wiley told me you were out this way and asked me to reach out. I'm happy to be a drinking buddy or intro you to some chicks if you wanna get laid, or you can just ignore my ass and come here whenever you like. I'll let the bouncers know you're a friend. They'll take care of you. That's it, bro. Take it or leave it."

He shrugged and took another sip. I watched him carefully for a few moments, then sighed and drank my Coke.

Maybe I'd let his words get to me too much. This

lowlife seemed to genuinely have a sliver of heart in his skinny chest. And it would be nice to hang with someone without pressure—someone I didn't have to pretend with, someone who knew what I'd done.

"Sorry, Shady. I'm a little touchy."

"Forget it." He waved a hand, then swiveled on his stool to look at the dance floor. "Now, tell me. Are you an ass man or a tits man?"

I chuckled. As long as I kept a wide berth from Shady's "business" here, this could be exactly what I needed to chill out from time to time.

CHAPTER 5

Donna

THE CAR WAS EERILY SILENT WHEN THE GIRLS piled into it at the end of the day. Amaya didn't launch into the day's gossip, Mena didn't crack jokes, Harlow didn't throw out any random facts. I sighed and turned the music up. I wasn't sure if they were pissed at me or worried about me, but I hated this.

We needed some girl time, so instead of turning off toward home, I continued on into town.

Amaya turned the music down. "Where we going, D?"

The use of my childhood nickname made something in my chest constrict, and I forced some levity into my voice. "We're ignoring all our responsibilities and getting something greasy to eat."

Harlow snorted. "It's Friday afternoon—you're the only one who has responsibilities."

They all laughed at my expense, and I couldn't

help joining in.

We parked our asses at a Portuguese joint and shared a massive plate of Peri Peri chicken and fries. When the plate was empty, Amaya crossed her arms on the table and fixed me with a look. "Is the new guy situation getting out of hand?"

I groaned. "Maybe. He's been a giant pain in my ass since he showed up."

"I think you need to tell people to back off him," Mena said.

"I never told anyone to lay into him in the first place." I hadn't been lying when I told Hendrix I wasn't telling people to make his life hell.

"I know that, but people listen to you. They'll stop if you tell them to."

I bristled. That would feel like admitting I was wrong. "Look, I know some people have started taking things too far, but that's not my fault. He was a complete jerk to me, and he turned his nose up at every single person in our school. He's been disrespectful and antagonizing every time I've spoken to him. I'm not gonna just stand there and take that. I'm going to defend myself and you guys, no matter what it takes. He started this."

Mena looked down into her lap and frowned. She clearly didn't agree with everything I'd said, but she knew firsthand how far I'd go to protect the three people sitting at that table with me.

When we'd found out she was being bullied at her last school, I pulled every thread I could think of to make her tormentors pay. I'd called in favors I was holding on to for after college to protect her.

"He started it." Harlow mimicked my voice, and I smacked her shoulder. She pinched my thigh in response.

"Ouch!" I yanked her ponytail, and then we both burst into giggles.

"Seriously though"—she straightened her hair—"I've never seen you this worked up. He's just an asshole with an ego. If I didn't know any better, I'd think you had the hots for him."

"Oh, *please*." I crossed my arms and rolled my eyes.

"Holy shit." Amaya sat up. "Is that why you don't want to call the dogs off? You're worried the other girls will think it's open season?"

"No." My answer was immediate and firm. But now that she mentioned it, I didn't like the idea of a sea of teal pleated skirts hanging off his every move. But that was only because I didn't want him to have anyone to hang out with—as he'd insisted he didn't want. That was all. It wasn't because I secretly liked him.

"You're bullying him." Mena finally raised her gaze, making Amaya and Harlow pause in their taunting and poking at my sides.

I reeled back as if she'd slapped me. "No, I'm not."

"Yes, you are. You all are. The entire school. He may be big enough to defend himself from most physical attacks, but what happens when people decide to gang up on him? What happens when they get a group together, drag him out to the football field, tie him to the goalpost . . ." She swallowed as I shared a wide-eyed look with the other two. "Because they decide they need to prove a point. Prove *your* point."

She was describing the horrific things that had been done to her.

I reached across the table and took her hand. "I'd never let that happen, Philomena."

"Not intentionally." She slowly pulled her hand out from under mine. "But can't you see that you're doing to him what they did to me?"

I sat back and really thought about it. Was I instigating the mean, petty shit Fulton students were doing to Hendrix? No. But did I start the campaign against him to prove a point? Yes, I absolutely did. And did I get satisfaction from how thoroughly he was being punished for treating me with disrespect? I'd be lying if I said no. It was why I'd let it go on.

But the thought of being as bad as her bullies in Mena's eyes broke my heart.

Tears stung the backs of my eyes, but I forced the emotion back. I refused to cry in front of other people.

"I think she's right." Harlow fiddled with her napkin. "We need to take Mena's view on the situation seriously, considering."

Amaya nodded. "D, we know you're not intending to bully him, but I do think we need to be wary of this escalating. Fulton is a whole other ballgame. You know that if any of those shits pulled the kind of stunt Mena went through, they wouldn't even see the inside of a police station before their parents' money took care of the problem."

"You're right." I nodded and licked my lips. "You're all right. I refuse to let him talk to me like shit, but I don't agree with how things have been escalating. I'll do something about it on Monday."

"*We* will." Harlow smiled, reminding me I wasn't alone in this . . . even though it sometimes felt like it.

"It'll be fine." Amaya flipped her long black hair over a delicate shoulder. "We just need to remind those idiots they have reputations to uphold. Nothing brings rich brats into line like the threat of embarrassing their parents."

Mena smiled, already looking lighter. "I love you girls."

"Love you," the three of us chorused.

"Ugh!" Amaya slapped the table. "Enough heavy shit. Let's go get Starbucks."

We walked two blocks to the nearest one and got giant cups of sugar and caffeine.

Out on the sidewalk, Mena sucked on her straw while typing out a text. When Harlow and Amaya joined us, she put the phone away.

"Turner is about to go on his break. Mind if we swing by his work?" she asked.

"Not at all!" I looped my arm through hers, and we took off down the street. Her boyfriend still went to her last school—Devilbend North High School—and the two of them were adorable together. But Mena worked at a diner closer to where she lived, and Turner had just recently gotten a job at a gym downtown, so they had less and less time to spend with each other. I couldn't blame them for seizing every opportunity.

As we rounded the corner and strolled toward the gym's front doors, our steps gradually slowed to a stop; each of us was staring through the window, transfixed.

My first response was a spike of annoyance—I couldn't seem to get away from this jerk!—but it was soon replaced with a grudging appreciation.

Only a small part of the gym was visible through the front window, the neat rows of machines disappearing around the corner. Hendrix was on a machine close to the glass, sitting on a bench with his knees spread wide, his arms pulling down on some weighted contraption. He was shirtless and so sweaty he was fucking *glistening*. It seemed as if half the muscles in his body danced under his skin at every movement.

"Wow," Harlow breathed, sucking the dregs of her drink with an obnoxiously loud slurp.

"I have a boyfriend, and even I can't look away." Mena tilted her head to the side, eyes glued to the show.

"You're only human." Amaya shrugged. "But fuck me. Why is it always the assholes that look like *that*?"

"Is that a tattoo?" If I'd been with anyone other than my three best friends, I would've been embarrassed at how breathy my voice sounded. There was definitely some ink on the left side of his back, just under his shoulder blade, but we were too far away to make it out.

That didn't stop us from leaning forward as one, our foreheads nearly touching the glass, as we tried to see what it was.

"You ladies wouldn't be objectifying our newest member, would you?" A deep, masculine voice made us all jump. Mena even made a little squeaking sound in the back of her throat that had us all cracking up in embarrassed laughter.

Turner leaned against the wall with his arms crossed, smiling in amusement. We'd been so entranced by the frustrating guy on the other side of the glass we hadn't even heard him walk up.

Mena was the first to recover. "You know I only have eyes for you," she cooed, rising up on her tippy-toes to give him a kiss.

He glared at us all with a thin-lipped smile and shook his head. "You four are worse than the creeps who only pretend to do weights while they stare at the women on cross trainers."

"We are not!" Harlow smacked him.

"We kinda are." Amaya shrugged, taking another sip of her drink.

I took one last surreptitious glance at the window—to make sure Hendrix hadn't spotted us, not to cop another eyeful, of course. Unfortunately . . . I mean, *fortunately*, he'd disappeared into the back of the gym.

Turner slung an arm around Mena's shoulders.

"Come on. I've only got another twenty minutes of my break, and I need to get something to eat."

We said our goodbyes and left the lovebirds alone.

***

I hadn't planned on going to Davey's that night, but I was so agitated after I got home I couldn't even focus on my homework. Harlow had changed into sweats, carried armfuls of junk food into her room, and parked herself in front of the computer, so she wouldn't be noticing jack shit for the remainder of the night. My parents were home, but I figured if I left after midnight, they wouldn't even notice. They'd both had long days at work, and their bedroom was on the opposite side of the house.

I just had to be extra cautious and make sure it was a short visit. Everyone would be home in the morning, so I'd have to skip sleeping in, but I could handle one day of sleep deprivation.

What I couldn't handle was another week—another *day*, another *hour*—of this clawing, pressured feeling inside me.

My to-do list was growing instead of diminishing, no matter how hard I worked, and now I had the added problem of trying to figure out the Hendrix situation. I couldn't let Mena down; I just had no idea how to fix it. Not to mention I was suddenly finding myself thinking about Hendrix's sweaty muscles instead of focusing on how annoying and rude he was.

Black stiletto boots in hand, I tiptoed down the

stairs and into the garage without making a sound. I didn't stop listening and looking out for someone to bust me until I was at the end of the driveway and putting my headlights on.

The leather seat was cool on my bare back. I'd kept the all-black outfit simple—halter top and short, loose skirt. Heavy eye makeup, messy hair, and no panties.

I didn't always fuck some random when I went to Davey's, but I was going to make sure I did tonight. I needed more than the illusion of freedom that came with dancing and anonymity. I needed the oblivion of a strong body looming over me, making me *feel* for a little while instead of *thinking* all the fucking time. I just needed a break . . .

The anticipation built as I drove, only speeding a little in my eagerness. I just knew I'd feel better in the morning, even if I was a little tired. I'd be more clearheaded and ready to tackle school, college applications, and Hendrix fucking Hawthorn.

I parked, tucked my keys into my little cross-body bag, and resisted the urge to sprint to the front door.

A grin spread over my face when I spotted Shady at the bar. I wouldn't even need to be here an hour. But as I got closer and saw who was on the stool next to him, my heart instantly jammed up into my throat.

Why was he ruining *every single* aspect of my damn life? Why was I being punished like this?

Hendrix was in jeans and a black T-shirt—an expensive one with the brand in bold white letters near the bottom hem. It was a loose style, but the fabric still stretched taut over his muscular shoulders and arms. Immediately, flashes of what he looked like shirtless and sweaty assaulted my mind.

I clenched my thighs against the pressure low in my belly. I *wasn't* turned on by him. My body was just already primed for sex, that was all.

But now that I was staring at the root of all my recent problems, my body was starting to make me think the solution could be to just . . . fuck him out of my system.

A group of chicks heading for the dance floor, drinks in hand, bumped me out of my stupor.

I clenched my teeth and retreated back into the crowd, then found a spot by the wall and leaned back, crossing my arms and keeping him in view.

"Hey." A deep male voice made me glance to the side. "Can I get you a drink?"

He was exactly what I'd come here looking for: tall, late twenties, in worn jeans and boots, his tattooed arms exposed. He had the confidence to approach me within five minutes of my arrival, and he'd already made physical contact, dragging the backs of his rough knuckles up the side of my arm.

"Fuck off." I shrugged him off and focused back on the problem at hand.

The big, bad man chuckled and muttered "feisty" under his breath as he headed for the bar. My body groaned in protest as I watched him walk away, but I had to figure Hendrix out first.

What the hell was he doing here? And how did he

know Shady? Having my fun for the night ruined was frustrating, but his presence here could have much heavier implications. If he told anyone … I couldn't even bear to think about it. I had to speak to Shady and get some info, then I had to either make sure Hendrix didn't see me or find some way to make him keep his mouth shut.

My mind churned, adding more weight to the already massive amount of pressure I was there to get a break from. This wasn't fair. This was supposed to be *my* place. *My* reprieve from my life.

What … how … ugh! *Why*?!

I couldn't even think straight anymore. All I could do was glare and grind my teeth as worst-case scenarios flashed through my mind.

Shady got to his feet, did that manly handshake/slap-on-the-back combo, and disappeared into the back area. I'd never been over there—even Shady had warned me off a time or two, so I was pretty sure it was where morals went to die.

Hendrix downed the rest of his drink and turned on his stool, ready to get up, but his eyes locked with mine and he froze. A frown wrinkled his brow, then his eyes widened a little.

Well, at least now I knew this was a coincidence. He definitely hadn't been expecting to see me.

Fuck it.

I glared back, then pushed off the wall and strutted toward the bar.

I needed to clear my head before attempting

damage control, and I figured half an hour wouldn't make a difference.

Hendrix settled back on the stool, watching me intently as I approached, but I changed direction just before I reached him.

I tapped tall, dark, and dangerous from earlier on the shoulder.

The man turned and grinned, leaning back against the bar. "Hey, feisty."

I smirked, he raked his eyes up and down my body, and I knew I had him.

CHAPTER 6

Hendrix

I FLOPPED MY ASS BACK ONTO THE STOOL AND gripped the edge of the bar about as hard as I was gripping the edge of my sanity.

It was really her. Donna Mead—spoiled rich bitch, queen bee of Fulton Academy—had a dark side. A dark, *sexy* side that had her looking as if she knew her way around a bar I was pretty sure was owned by gangsters.

Gone was the pleated skirt and pristine white shirt of the Fulton uniform—replaced by a black miniskirt and halter top. In place of the sensible Mary Janes she wore to school was a pair of thigh-high boots that had my cock stirring in my pants.

I surreptitiously adjusted myself and got more comfortable on my stool. No way in hell was I attempting to leave until my sudden stiffy went down.

It had taken me a few seconds to place the gorgeous blonde as she sauntered toward the bar. She was wearing dark makeup, and her short hair was in a messy rock-chick style. I wanted to run my hand through the soft strands, mess it up even more, maybe grab a fistful and pull until her mouth was turned up to mine. I'd make her tell me exactly how much of a bad girl she was.

I blinked, forcing the sudden and vivid fantasy from my mind. She was on her way over, and I had to remember who I was dealing with. Come Monday, she'd still be perfect princess Donna, and she'd still be responsible for making my life at Fulton hell.

But as it turned out, I didn't need to worry about what I'd say to her. She changed direction and went up to a guy ordering at the bar. I frowned, confused. Maybe it wasn't her after all.

But then I dismissed the thought. She'd seen me, recognized me. There was no mistaking the rage-filled glare she'd thrown my way. I'd been on the receiving end of it countless times now.

A pang of annoyance had me grinding my teeth. It was the bullshit from school all over again. She was determined to make me feel as if my very existence was of no consequence to her.

I wanted to just get up and walk out. If she didn't give a shit about why I was here, then I wouldn't give a shit about why she was.

Instead, I found myself waving the waitress over and ordering another soda.

A few feet over, the bastard who looked like an enforcer for a motorcycle club handed Donna a drink and wrapped a meaty hand around her delicate waist, leaning in to whisper something in her ear. She smirked, a devious glint in her eye, and ran her hand up his massive arm as she murmured a reply to whatever vulgar shit he'd surely just said to her.

My hand tightened around my drink as I sized him up. I wasn't sure if I could take him. We were about the same height, but I'd only just gotten back into the gym that afternoon, and he looked as if he bench-pressed his Harley every damn day.

His hand lowered to her hip, and Donna took a drink before lifting her gaze. Our eyes met, and she frowned slightly—at the fact that I was still there? Had she forgotten I even existed? *Bitch . . .*

I looked away first and mentally slapped myself. Why the fuck was I letting her get to me like this? And why the fuck was I thinking about the best way to put a guy—who I was positive was armed—on his ass? Especially considering I'd vowed never to throw another punch for the rest of my life.

Better to leave Donna to whatever fucked-up game she had going here. This was exactly the kind of drama I didn't want. That guy was *exactly* the kind of trouble I was trying to avoid.

Shady had left for the night. The vague excuse he'd given made me think he was up to shit I didn't want to know about. But I couldn't be mad. He'd spent nearly two hours with me at the bar, talking about three times as much as I did, pointing people out, giving me his opinions on movies and recent events, making vulgar commentary on the women. He'd even managed to make me laugh a few times. It had taken my mind off my problems and made the risky decision to come here worth it.

If only I'd left five minutes earlier. If only I hadn't seen her . . .

Now I couldn't leave, couldn't tear my gaze away as she finished her drink and let the biker dude lead her out to the edge of the dance floor.

Shady had pointed out a lot of people, and I wasn't really trying to remember names, but this guy's towering frame and mean mug had stood out. One of the very few times Shady had lowered his voice was when telling me to avoid this fucker—*Bronson.* He'd made it clear, in that way criminals had of speaking without coming right out and saying anything concrete, that Bronson was a murderer and basically untouchable because of the "people he rode with." Yep—definitely an enforcer for an MC.

"But don't sweat it!" He'd slapped me on the shoulder. "Davey's is a neutral place. Only a select few people are permitted to do business here, and no other bullshit is tolerated. We don't need the pigs sniffing around because some dickhead couldn't take his fun elsewhere."

He probably hadn't meant to conflate murdering people with fun, but that was Shady for you.

Donna didn't strike me as the kind of chick who did anything without knowing exactly what she was getting into, but behind all the annoyance and frustration, there was a sliver of worry deep in my chest too—*very deep,* buried behind all the other not-so-favorable emotions I had for this infuriating woman.

She may've been a bitch, but I still didn't want to see her end up dead.

I sat on the damn stool and sipped my drink, frozen in indecision.

It was none of my business. I didn't need this shit. Hell, maybe I could use it to get what I wanted from her down the road—I was pretty sure she wouldn't want her devoted followers, or college admissions boards, finding out she was hooking up with lowlifes and criminals. The scandal . . .

On the other hand . . .

I couldn't shake the feeling that something wasn't right. That guy was serious trouble. And I really didn't like how he was grinding his hips against her in time to the music.

It *really* didn't fucking help that she kept glancing in my direction.

At first, her gaze held nothing but contempt, but as the flirting between her and Bronson increased, her glances became more neutral—as if she was simply checking I was still there. By the time they were pawing at each other as though moments away from fucking in a bar full of people, her glances were . . . well, if I didn't know any better, I would've said she was looking at me with heat in her eyes. And if they were brief glances, I would've put it down to her being really into her hookup. But the way she looked at me—it lingered, our connection across the crowded room palpable. It was almost as if she wished it was *me* palming her ass, that it was *my* neck she was placing a sultry kiss to. Her eyes stayed glued to mine as she dragged those full lips up the column of his throat.

I was torn.

I didn't come here to watch my new nemesis get it on with some douche—the anal kind, as Mena had put it. But my dick was convinced I should go over there and pull her out of his arms and into mine.

I forced myself to turn away. Placing both clenched fists on the bar, I took three deep breaths of the sweaty, smoky air and focused hard on the peanut shells littering the chipped wood.

You're going to get up off this fucking stool, and you're going to march to the exit. You will not look in her direction, and you will not stop until you're in the goddamn car.

I gave myself a mental slap, then chugged what was left of my flat soda. Determined, I got to my feet . . . and my eyes immediately met her mismatched ones.

She smirked as she passed within a foot of me, her hand tucked into Bronson's as he led the way past the bar.

My whole body tensed, refusing to do as I'd just decided. Instead, I stared like a creep after them. For a second, I was worried he was about to drag her to the back—where even Shady told me to avoid. But they didn't turn down the dark corridor. He pushed open a back door, giving me a glimpse of the night sky and a dumpster as they made their way through it.

Just before the door swung closed, Donna turned her head and looked at me again.

I ground my teeth.

Leave, Hendrix. Just go. You don't need someone else's problems making your life any more difficult. Let the princess get herself out of her own mess.

Except I was pretty sure she was exactly where she wanted to be, and that made me want to throw something.

Fuck it. I gave up. I wouldn't be able to live with myself if I left and she turned up dead in a few weeks. I'd just check that she was—*ugh!*—enjoying herself. I'd make sure she left safely, and then I'd use this information to blackmail the shit out of her. There wasn't much I needed from her other than to get those bratty kids off my back, but I was going to milk it for all it was worth—payback for putting me through this mess of a night.

I made my way through the crowd, following their path past the dark corridor and to the back door. With my hand on the handle, I braced myself for what I might see—would sex or violence affect me more?

The music from the club faded as I stepped out into the night.

He had her up against the wall, right next to the dumpster, a string of condoms hanging from one thick-knuckled hand.

I clenched my teeth and let the heavy door slam shut.

Donna looked over his shoulder, but it was too dark

to make out her expression. Bronson paused what he was doing and half turned his head. "Find some other place to piss, man. I'm kind of busy here."

He lowered his mouth back to her neck.

He was going to fuck her in a disgusting alleyway, where people routinely pissed? Real class act, this guy.

A breathy moan escaped the darkness shrouding them, and I suddenly realized that was exactly what she wanted. The perfect princess liked to get down and dirty with dangerous men.

I didn't even know where to begin trying to guess what her damage was, but it looked as though Donna was just as fucked up as me—albeit in a different way.

But I'd inserted myself into this clusterfuck of a situation, and I wasn't about to walk away. If she wanted to be there, I'd have fun ruining her fun.

I rolled my shoulders—preparing, just in case this got violent—then relaxed and shoved a hand in my pocket, trying my best to look casual.

Bronson turned his head and shoulders, raising his voice. "What's your problem, dude? Fuck off."

"I don't have a problem." I shrugged. "Just making sure my schoolmate here is safe."

CHAPTER 7

Donna

"SCHOOLMATE?" THE BIKER DUDE SNEERED IN my direction. In the distance, thunder rumbled.

I rolled my eyes. "Oh, you suddenly want to know things about me?"

He smirked and gripped my waist. "I don't give a fuck how old she is. Get lost, pretty boy."

"Do you give a shit that her rich daddy will have half the police in the state on your ass if you so much as touch her?" Hendrix cocked his head to the side, his voice amused.

Biker dude growled, and not in the fun, sexy way.

I was losing my patience too. "Are you gonna man up and get rid of him, or do I need to get *myself* off?"

"Listen here, you little slut." He jabbed a finger in my face while his other hand tightened into a fist, the leather of the fingerless glove creaking. "You know what? On second thought, I don't need this high school drama bullshit."

Without waiting for a response, he turned around and stomped back toward the bar, boots pounding on the concrete. I narrowed my eyes and gritted my teeth.

"You know what, asshole?" I yelled after him, taking a few steps in his direction.

His back stiffened under the leather vest, but suddenly Hendrix was taking long strides in my direction, eyes wide and mouth firm. The suddenness of the movement and the intensity of his stare made me pause long enough for biker dude to disappear back inside.

With my evening entertainment and outlet for my rage gone, I turned my ire on the jerk who had been a thorn in my side for weeks now.

"What the fuck are you doing?" I got in his face. The killer heels helped put me closer to eye level, but I still had to tip my head up.

"Saving your ass." He huffed.

"My ass was just fine, thanks. My ass was about to *get* some ass, you arrogant, presumptuous, cock-blocking *dumb*ass."

"Your ass was about to get killed. Bronson has a reputation for leaving his girlfriends in dumpsters." He wasn't backing down. We were practically chest to chest.

"I'm not his girlfriend. He was just a hookup. What the fuck do you take me for?"

"Honestly, I have no idea what to make of this.

What . . ." He shook his head and sighed. "Donna, what the fuck are you doing here? What are you wearing? Do you have any idea how dangerous—"

I cut him off with a shove against his chest. It took him by surprise enough to make him stumble a step back, but I followed, getting in his face. "Screw you and your assumptions." I shoved him again, but this time he was prepared and hardly budged. "Screw you and your patronizing bullshit." I shoved hard, but his whole body was rigid, muscles tense under my palms. "I'm not a fucking idiot. I know exactly what I'm doing and who I'm doing it with. I can take care of myself."

Thunder grumbled again, making me wish I could growl like that—with the force of nature behind me.

Hendrix was breathing heavily even as he stood there, as still as a statue and as hard as one, but a muscle was ticking in his jaw, and his eyes narrowed. Something in me liked that. He'd been so dismissive of me at school, so blasé about everything I threw at him, that getting a rise out of him was like a drug. My favorite kind—unpredictable.

Like a junkie, I shoved his chest again.

This time his hands shot up to grip my wrists—not painfully, but tightly enough that I couldn't wrench out of his hold. I tried anyway, thrashing against him as my adrenaline spiked.

"Let go of me, asshole."

"I'm not going to hit you, Donna," he growled, the sound low and controlled but with menace simmering just below. "But I'm not just going to stand here and not defend myself. Get your shit together."

I leaned up and shouted right into his face, "Fuck you!"

The corner of his lip twitched, an almost smile. "I thought we established that wasn't going to happen?"

I was getting more and more worked up, basically throwing a tantrum, while he just stood there like a pillar, getting calmer and calmer. It was *maddening.*

Well, I was over letting him feel as though he had the advantage. He could deny it all he wanted, but he was attracted to me. I could see it in the way his eyes searched my face. His lips were smirking, but his eyes couldn't lie—those beautiful, intense gray eyes.

I used the leverage of his grip on my wrists, lifted up onto my toes, and kissed him.

For a second—a bare breath of a moment suspended in time—he froze.

Lightning flashed, illuminating the dirty alleyway and this thing between us. Then, as the thunder roared, he moved his lips against mine, his tongue darting out, his mouth claiming me.

He released one of my wrists to wrap an arm around my body and walk me backward.

I gripped his T-shirt, pulling the fabric as if the thin fibers could tether me to some semblance of control. I'd kissed him so I could prove something, but within seconds, he had the upper hand, and my head was spinning in the most delicious, most excruciating way.

My back hit the rough brick, and he lifted my other wrist above my head, keeping it trapped in his strong grip. His free hand went to my waist and made me arch—made my body mold to every hard, unyielding inch of his. He moaned into my mouth and kissed me harder until the back of my head ground into the wall.

His erection pressed against my front, and I wanted it inside me. I wanted *him* inside me—my body, my mind, my soul. I wanted him to consume every fiber of my being until all I could see, hear, smell was Hendrix Hawthorn. Until I forgot everything and everyone and there was only *him*.

It was exactly what I came here for—to forget, to lose myself in something for a little while . . . but part of me bristled at the fact that it was with *him*. Why was my body responding to his more than it had to any other man in the past? I'd been fighting to keep command of the Hendrix situation for weeks. Now here he was, smashing through my careful control with one mind-shattering kiss?

I took his bottom lip into my mouth and sucked. Then I took it between my teeth and bit.

He hissed and pulled away, another bolt of lightning throwing his confused expression into sharp relief.

Some of the heady weight of his body on mine lifted, and he released my wrist. But I didn't like that either. Fuck, I had no idea what I wanted with this infuriating son of a bitch. *And I hated it.*

Before he could completely back away, I wrapped my arms around his neck and kissed him again. The thunder rumbled, so close now that the ground under my boots vibrated.

Hendrix growled too, his own thunder rumbling through his chest. I could taste his blood on my lips, the metallic flavor as distinct as the need coursing through my body.

He broke the kiss again and shook his head, breathing hard.

I gripped his T-shirt, my body clinging to his even as my mind screamed. "If you want to go, go! See if I care!"

"Listen." He licked his lips. "I'm not into this rape fantasy bullshit. If you want me inside you, I'm gonna need to hear you say it."

I blinked. I was not expecting that. Not once had any man I'd had dirty sex with bothered to check if I was enjoying myself. They didn't give a shit, and I didn't even care enough to learn their names. That was the whole appeal of the situation—I was using them as much as they were using me, and the edge of danger that came with the unknown, the uncertainty, was intoxicating.

Why the fuck did Hendrix even care? "You are such a pussy. You're killing the mood."

He watched me for a beat, shadows falling over his face, then pushed himself off the wall.

I didn't doubt for a second he would leave. My hand shot to his belt to stop him. "What do you want, an engraved invitation into my cunt?"

Usually, men were surprised to hear such a filthy word coming out of my mouth, but Hendrix didn't even falter. "Any form of explicit consent will do."

I rolled my eyes. "Jesus, would you just fuck me already?"

"Is that what you'd like?" I could hear the smirk in his voice. The lightning that flashed a second later let me see it too. I wanted to sit on that smug face and ride it so he'd shut the fuck up already.

"Yes," I gritted out.

"That'll do." He'd barely said the words before he was on me again, reaching behind my neck to pull on the bow that held my halter top in place.

The two pieces of shimmery fabric fell away, and he palmed my breasts. He didn't take it slow or explore—just grabbed two firm handfuls of my flesh and kneaded, his thumbs teasing my nipples.

I threw my head back against the brick and moaned into the night as Hendrix started kissing and licking at the sensitive spot on my neck.

A drop of water hit my cheek, and my eyes opened in confusion just as another landed on my forehead. Another rumble of thunder reminded me a storm was rolling in, but then Hendrix took one of my nipples into his mouth, making me forget everything.

He teased me with his mouth before pulling away again.

"Do you have a condom?" His breath was hot on my cheek as his hips gyrated against mine.

"Huh?" It took a moment for his words to register. "Yes, in my . . . fuck. No. You chased biker dude off with them all." I groaned.

"Shit." Hendrix planted a hand on either side of my

head and pressed his forehead to mine, sighing deeply.

I ran my hands down his front. He felt so good under my touch, his muscles coiled, his T-shirt getting damp from the softly falling rain. I liked to flirt with danger, but I wasn't stupid. I never fucked anyone without a condom. But Hendrix wasn't one of the degenerates I usually hooked up with. He was . . . I didn't want to think about what he was to me in that moment. I just wanted to get off with him.

"It's raining anyway . . ." He let one hand drop to his side, inching his body away.

I wrapped my arms around his waist and licked the rain off the side of his neck. "I'm on birth control and I'm clean. Are you?"

I felt him swallow under my lips. "Honestly, I don't know. Haven't been tested. And I'm not willing to take the chance. No offence, but I don't know where that thing has been."

White hot rage coursed through me almost as intensely as desire. I bit his neck, and he yelped, pushing me away by the hips.

"Offence taken, asshole." I scowled at him.

It was too dark to really see, but I could've sworn he looked amused, and his hands were still on my hips.

"Did you just bite me?" He chuckled. "Under that perfect princess mask, you're just a feral animal, aren't you?"

"Yeah. Whatever. I wanna get off, and if you're not game, then get lost so I can get on with my night." His rejection was starting to sting, and if I couldn't have him, I wasn't really in the mood to pick someone else up. I really hoped he wouldn't walk away from me—because I couldn't seem to make myself walk away from him.

He licked his lips, collecting some of the rain that was dripping down his face. Droplets fell from the tip of his nose, trailed down his neck. I wanted to lick every single one.

Just as I was about to cover my boobs back up and try to gather enough pride to walk away, he spoke.

"If the guys you've been with think the only way to get a woman off is with their cocks, I feel really bad for you—you must've been having some mediocre sex."

Before I could throw a witty response back at him, his strong hands were shoving my hips around so I was facing the wall. He pushed forward, his front flush with my back, and I had to throw my hands up against the brick to keep my balance. A shot of adrenaline raced down my spine, amping up the lust. I had no idea what he was about to do to me, and I *loved* it. This was exactly what I needed, what I craved.

He kicked my feet a little farther apart, then gripped the back of my neck.

I practically melted at his touch, my very being diluted in the steady rain and his intoxicating presence.

He trailed his hand down the rain-slick skin of my back, and then both hands were at my hips, dipping lower, down my thighs. When he reached the hem of my skirt, the heat of his body disappeared as he stepped away slightly—as his hands moved under the fabric and up my legs. He traced his thumbs along the underside of my ass before dragging his palms over it to cop a good feel. His fingers went all the way to my lower back, then back down, and he laughed softly.

"No panties. You dirty whore."

I bristled at his use of the derogatory term, the logical part of me offended. But my logical part wasn't in charge—my dirty whore part was, and Dark Donna was only more turned on by his words.

His hand appeared at my neck again, and he pushed—his touch not rough but firm, demanding—until my cheek was against the wall. My nipples brushed the rough brick, and rain pelted my bare back. Every place his skin touched mine felt as if it were on fire. I was nothing but heady sensation—putty in his strong hands.

I arched my back, sticking my ass out even farther, and he flipped my skirt up to expose me to the dark alley.

Done wasting time, he reached between my legs and stroked me firmly, and my already heavy breathing kicked up another notch. His appreciative moan hummed at my back as his fingers glided through my wet folds effortlessly. He put one finger inside, making me gasp at the sudden intrusion, then twisted it as he removed it. Another finger joined the first, and he slid them in and out of me at a steady pace.

The hand at my neck disappeared, but my incoherent sound of protest morphed into one of ecstasy as Hendrix wrapped his arm around my front. His body crowded me once again, that cinnamon scent mingling with the fresh rain. With one hand still fucking me with his fingers from behind, the other went to my clit and started stroking in rhythm.

Another clap of thunder shook the ground, and the rain beat down even harder, plastering my hair to my face as I grunted. With every punishing thrust of Hendrix's fingers, his other hand rubbed me up and down, and my tits scraped against the brick.

It didn't take long before my orgasm was washing over me as intensely as the rain. I squeezed my eyes shut, seeing stars, as I clawed at the wall, desperately seeking something to hold on to as every muscle in my body tensed up in ecstasy.

"That's it. I want your cream all over my hand." Hendrix's voice was strained and gravelly in my ear, his words only intensifying my orgasm as I writhed under his touch.

He removed his fingers and stroked me gently as I came down, my knees shaking, my breathing ragged. His hands clasped either side of my head, his forehead rested against my temple, and his warm breath caressed my cheek as the rain washed away the slick evidence of my pleasure from his hand.

After a few moments, he placed a gentle kiss on my cheek, my neck, my shoulder—his soft, warm lips such a contrast to the sharp, cold rain. He cupped my breasts, making me gasp, then surprised me by lifting the two front bits of my halter top over my chest and backing away to tie them.

I frowned. Didn't he want me to return the favor,

get him off? But I didn't really have time to think about that.

My knees buckled, but before I ended up on my ass in a dirty alleyway, Hendrix's strong arms wrapped around me and held me against his chest. His steel-hard erection dug into my ass, but he didn't rub up against me. He just whispered against my wet skin, "I got you."

What the fuck is happening? Usually, the guy would make sure he got off, regardless of whether I did, and within about two minutes, he'd tuck himself back into his pants and disappear. I was fine with it—preferred it, actually. But I found myself leaning back against Hendrix, allowing myself to relax farther into his arms.

When he bent down and scooped me up, the voice in my head demanding that he "put me down this instant, you Neanderthal" hardly even sounded convincing. I rested my head on his shoulder, breathing him in, as he grabbed my purse off the top of the dumpster and dropped it in my lap.

"Where'd you park?" he asked as he set off toward the front of the building. The words reverberated through his chest, just loud enough for me to hear over the rain.

I lifted a lazy hand and pointed to the back corner of the lot. It was nice to have someone take care of me for a change. I'd worry about the terrifying implications later.

CHAPTER 8

Hendrix

EVEN SOAKED FROM HEAD TO TOE, SHE WAS light in my arms. I'd gone hard at the gym that afternoon, but I felt as if I could carry her all the way back to Devilbend if I had to.

My shoes squelched in the gravel as I trudged through the easing rain past rows of parked cars. Donna readjusted herself in my grip and turned her nose into the crook of my neck. She took a long inhale, then licked me.

My steps faltered.

My cock was straining against my jeans, demanding I bend her over the hood of one of these cars and do as she asked in the first place—fuck her raw. But I'd promised myself I was done doing risky, stupid shit, and having unprotected sex with a chick I barely knew was the definition of risky. Donna was probably on the pill and clean—she was wound way too tightly not to be on top of every little detail of her life. But her very presence here indicated a streak of recklessness too. I couldn't take the chance.

I chuckled and decided to ignore her hot little tongue on my throat and the steel rod in my pants. "What are you doing?"

"I just wanted to see if you taste as good as you smell," she murmured and scratched the back of my head, sending tingles down my spine that had nothing to do with the cold rain.

"What do I smell like?"

She sighed. "Like expensive cologne and cinnamon and . . . sex." She punctuated the sentence by licking my neck again.

I hid my groan beneath a clearing of my throat and looked around, desperate for something, anything, to distract me from this torture.

"Fuck." I stopped and turned. I'd walked right past my car.

Donna finally lifted her head from my shoulder, and just like that, she had my full, undivided attention again.

We stared at each other—only inches between us—and I forgot I even had a car, let alone where I'd parked it. Wait. Wasn't I supposed to be taking her to her car anyway?

"Hendrix," she whispered, leaning forward.

I mirrored her movement, pressing my forehead to hers. "Yeah?"

"What . . ." Her gaze bored into mine with

increasing intensity. The orgasm high was wearing off, and her mind was kicking back into overdrive, trying to make sense of it all. I held her just a little closer, fully aware of what was about to happen but hoping to prolong the moment anyway.

"Shit." She squeezed her eyes shut, as if trying to wash a nightmare from her mind's eye. Then she licked those delicious lips and leaned away, no longer looking at me.

She pushed against my chest and wriggled her legs. Resisting the urge to hold on tighter was a Herculean effort, but I managed it.

"Put me down," she growled, but I was already bending down, already releasing my hold, already missing her warmth . . .

I'd known it was coming, but it still made me want to throw something when she looked at me with a sneer.

"Ah, there it is." I stuffed my hands into my pockets and smirked. No choice now but to go back to our bickering default. I wasn't about to show her how badly I wanted to pull her back into my arms when she was looking at me like that. "The instant regret. Aren't you glad I only fucked you with my fingers now?"

"There isn't a single thing about this night I'm glad about." *Ouch* . . .

As the rain petered out to a pathetic drizzle, she turned and started to walk away.

I watched her hips sway, her spine straight and shoulders back. She'd just spent time in the seediest establishment for miles, had let me fingerfuck her in the dirty alley next to a dumpster, had a face covered in smeared makeup, yet she was still walking away with confidence. As if she *owned* this place.

I took one step back and wavered. My car was a few spots away; she was nearly safely to hers. I should just leave, end this torture.

But I couldn't tear my gaze off her. And not because I was still hard and her ass looked amazing in that skirt. Despite how much of a bitch she was being to me, I couldn't help worrying about Donna Mead.

I was seeing in her some of the same shit I'd seen in myself a year ago. It had taken something truly catastrophic to make me realize it, but with hindsight, I could see there had been signs. I'd been doing all kinds of reckless shit, just as Donna was now. I didn't want her to end up where I was.

If someone had asked me that morning who I thought Donna was, I would've told them she was a spoiled rich brat with delusions of grandeur. She had everything handed to her and always got what she wanted. She was perfect in every way she could control—her looks, her grades, her reputation—and would never let anything jeopardize that.

Never in a million years would I have expected her to have a bad-girl streak. I had no idea what Donna was running from, but after what went down between us, I was no longer confused about why she'd come to a place like this. She was escaping. She was using the thrill of danger as a distraction and the high of meaningless hookups to numb whatever pain was deep in her chest.

The way she'd come at me in the alley—that first kiss had been almost violent in its intensity. It was the first time I'd felt truly alive in a long time. Too bad it was delivered by someone spiraling toward death.

I may have used slightly different means when I was spiraling a year ago, but she was chasing the same thing I'd been chasing—oblivion. It was a fucking miracle she didn't have an addiction yet. Maybe she did. What did I know?

I sighed and looked up to the stormy sky. The rain had stopped completely, and I wiped the moisture from my face before glancing in her direction again, wanting to make sure she made it to her car before I left.

To my surprise, she was walking back toward me with a determined look on her face, those killer boots crunching in the gravel.

"I thought you were leaving." I crossed my arms. I wasn't sure I could handle more of this in one night.

"I never leave loose ends. No matter how badly I want to take a shower."

"Loose ends?" I scoffed, ignoring her dig. "What're you gonna shoot me in the head and stuff my body in the trunk of your Beamer? You lack the upper body strength."

"What are you doing here?"

"What are *you* doing here? Oh, wait!" I gave her a wicked smirk. If I couldn't fuck her, I'd taunt her. "I already know. Come here a lot? How many degenerates have you fucked?"

Her nostrils flared. I was getting to her, but she

managed to keep her voice even. "Hendrix, I don't have time for this bullshit. What are you doing here?"

"None of your business." I dropped any levity from my tone. If she wanted to get serious, I was ready to get serious. "I've made it perfectly clear you don't own me. I don't have to tell you jack shit."

"Fine. Whatever. I don't actually care. You don't have to tell me anything, just . . . don't tell anyone else either."

There it was—she'd hung around to make sure I wouldn't tarnish her perfect reputation.

She dropped her gaze, showing the first sign of vulnerability since she'd wriggled out of my arms, and pushed her sopping wet hair back with both hands. Taking a deep breath, she fixed me with an indecipherable look. "Listen, you have your reasons for coming here, whatever they are, and I have mine. All I'm saying is, let's just pretend we never saw each other here and be done with it. OK?"

I cocked my head to the side. "Yeah, but I don't actually give a shit if anyone finds out I was here."

Her shoulders drooped in defeat, but she kept her gaze on mine. Brave little princess. "Please understand the gravity of what I'm about to say—because I think I've only said this to about six people my entire life. Hendrix, *please*, don't tell anyone you saw me here."

I nearly cracked—nearly told her I'd do whatever she wanted before pulling her into a hug. But I was certain the affection wouldn't be welcomed, so I just squeezed my hands into fists and sighed. "I've got no one to tell. You made sure of that, remember? No one would believe me anyway."

She laughed, the sound low and devoid of humor. "You don't understand what it's like. Reputation is everything in my world. Even the breath of a rumor . . ."

"I understand better than you know." Spoiled rich brats in California couldn't be that different from spoiled rich brats in New York.

She eyed me up and down, the question clear in her gaze. *Who are you? What's your story?*

But I wasn't in a sharing mood.

She licked her lips. "So, what do you want then? What's it gonna cost me?"

"I don't need your money. My daddy has a platinum card too." She wasn't stupid. She'd seen my car; I went to the same exorbitantly expensive, pretentious school. But for some reason, I wanted to point out that we had some things in common, that I understood her better than she thought.

Now it was her remaining silent, watching me with a raised brow, waiting for me to fill in the blank.

There was only one thing I wanted from her—well, two, but there was about as much chance of me getting her to lift that skirt as getting Americans to use the metric system, so I went with the practical option.

"You already know what I want." I shrugged. "Call off your attack dogs. I don't need any friends here, but I'm not interested in making any enemies. And trust me, if I start swinging back, it's going to get ugly. So do us all a favor and get this shit under control."

"Done." Her answer was instant. Part of me bristled, wondering if I should've asked for more, but that was the old me talking. More would only get me into trouble. I got what I wanted. Nothing else mattered.

With a nod, I turned and walked away, forcing myself not to look back.

***

Monday started in much the same way it always did. I got to school, parked, walked to class. As usual, some students made a point of turning their backs to ignore me, while others openly sneered in my direction. But I made it to my first class without anyone trying to prove he was a big man by shoving me. No one smacked my books off my desk in my classes; a few people even got out of my way as I headed to lunch.

I'd been planning to go off campus for lunch but decided against it, turning right toward the cafeteria instead of left toward the doors at the end of the hall. I hadn't seen Donna all morning, and I wanted to remind her of our little chat, test if she was taking it seriously.

I walked in, head held high, and smacked my gum loudly. A few people turned in my direction at the sound, but I ignored them. My full focus was on the girl in the perfectly neat uniform, not a blonde hair out of place under her teal headband, the smeared black makeup gone.

Donna was sitting in her usual spot, Harlow on the table with her feet on the chair next to her. The other girls weren't there yet, but some of the other assholes they hung out with were.

I looked right at her as I passed but kept my expression neutral—doing the whole pointing-at-my-eyes-and-then-her bit felt like overkill. She glanced up, met my gaze, and looked away again as if I didn't matter. As if I hadn't brought her to orgasm sixty hours earlier. As if we hadn't struck a deal in the rain right after.

I had to hand it to her—she had impeccable self-control. If only that trait weren't driving her to do stupid-ass shit just to feel alive.

Not my problem. *Not my problem.*

I forced myself to look away, grabbed some gluten-free paleo salad thing and a drink from the food counter, and picked an empty table.

No one flipped my tray. No one even said anything to me.

By the end of the day, it was clear everyone was leaving me alone. Donna had done what she'd promised. As if there was ever any doubt she could accomplish whatever she set that pretty little head to.

I had exactly what I wanted.

Except I no longer had any excuse to speak to a certain infuriating blonde, and as I drove home, the victory felt hollow.

CHAPTER 9

Donna

MOM TURNED SIDEWAYS IN FRONT OF THE ornate mirror by the front door and smoothed her midnight-blue cocktail dress.

"How do I look?" she asked no one in particular.

"Gorgeous, as always." My auntie Eleanor smiled at her, then shoved her out of the way with her hip to take up the mirror. "How do *I* look?"

"Like me. So gorgeous, as always," Mom shot back.

Mom was older than her sister by two years, but they were as close as Harlow and me. I knew there was a period of time—when I was a young child—that they didn't speak. It had something to do with my aunt moving away to marry a man Grandmother didn't approve of and ending up without an inheritance, but every time I tried to dig more up about it, Mom shut me down with some version of "Leave the past in the past."

I just wanted to know everything. It was

interesting: shoot me.

But Mena's family had moved back to Devilbend just before we all started high school, and our moms reconnected. They looked really similar, and even though they were teasing each other in front of the mirror, they were smiling and laughing.

"You're both stunning." Dad came down the stairs, fiddling with a cuff link. "Brad, back me up here or we'll never leave."

"Yes. Absolutely ethereal. We're the luckiest men on earth," my uncle Brad deadpanned, but I could see his lips twitch as he fought a smile.

While my mom and aunt started smacking and berating him for his attitude, Dad came to a stop next to me.

"Help me out, sweetness. I can never get the right one." He held out his right wrist, and I fixed the cuff link in place. "Thank you." He kissed the top of my head. "You girls have fun. And call us if you need anything."

"I will."

My parents had both stopped bothering to warn me to be safe and make good choices. It was a given. I was their perfect little girl. I'd make sure everything was fine, and I'd take care of the others.

It was Mena's birthday, and we were throwing her a party. She'd originally insisted on a small gathering, maybe at the diner where she worked. But when we sat down to write a list of who to invite, she was the only one surprised to see over twenty-five people on the list. The girl just wasn't used to having that many friends, and I was pretty sure she'd never had a real party to celebrate her birthday.

It didn't take much to convince her after that, but the guest list had grown . . .

During the afternoon, we'd had a family lunch together and opened presents. Now our parents were graciously leaving for the night. They planned to go to dinner in San Francisco and stay at our apartment in the city. The staff were given the night off, although cleaners would be arriving at ten in the morning to make sure the house was pristine before my parents returned. Everything was nearly ready.

As soon as our parents disappeared outside, I rushed to the back of the house, where the others had been listening out for the sound of the front door closing.

"Freedom!" I yelled, sliding across the kitchen tiles with my hands in the air.

Everyone whooped, and Turner pushed the button on the blender, getting the first batch of margaritas going as Mena grabbed glasses from the cupboard. Harlow pushed a few buttons on her phone, and music started pounding through the speaker system installed in the ceiling.

"Thank fuck." Amaya headed straight for the back patio, lighting a cigarette before she was even fully out of the house.

Harlow handed me a margarita, and I took it absentmindedly, mentally running through the checklist.

The staff had put up balloons and streamers in the main areas and cleared away some of the expensive, breakable items.

It was too cold to go in the pool in October, so the party would be in the main living area and on the patio where Amaya was smoking. A fire pit with chairs and blankets was set up and just waiting for the strike of a match.

Magda had prepared mountains of food.

I had a cake with eighteen candles ready to go in the fridge.

Drew and Will were bringing enough beer and spirits to give us all alcohol poisoning.

"Harlow, is the playlist ready to go?"

She nodded and planted her ass on the island counter next to the blender. "Yep! All of Mena's faves mixed in with some bangers!"

"Amaya!" I called out to the patio as Turner poured the drinks.

She startled me by leaning over my shoulder and stealing my untouched margarita. "No need to shout. I'm right here." She took a sip, giving me a teasing look over the salted rim.

"Guest list update," I demanded.

"Should be just over a hundred. There's always a few last-minute additions though."

Mena choked on her drink. "A hundred?! We don't even have that many people in our senior year. I don't even *know* that many people!"

"You can't have a Devilbend Dynasty party and

expect under a hundred people." Amaya shrugged and took another sip.

I stole my drink back and glared at her before addressing my cousin. "It's just one of those things. If you invite certain people, certain others expect an invitation too. Then word spreads, and everyone wants to come so they can be seen at one of our parties, and it just kind of snowballs. Don't worry about it. All your friends will be here, and we'll have a great time."

"Yeah, baby. Just enjoy it. You deserve a fun night." Turner wrapped an arm around Mena's shoulders and kissed her temple.

Harlow, Amaya, and I made a loud, over-the-top *aww*. They were so cute it was making me sick. Will never made me smile the way Mena was smiling at Turner now.

I finally took a sip of the margarita, and my eyes widened. "Jesus, fuck!"

Harlow had been the one putting the ingredients in the blender when I'd gone to the foyer to see our parents off. I frowned reproachfully at her.

"What?" She smiled sweetly.

"This is really strong."

"So?"

"So let's not write ourselves off before the party even starts, OK?"

"Yes, mom." She rolled her eyes, and the others chuckled.

I glared at them but chose to let it go. This was Mena's day.

We hung out for a bit, chatting and laughing, then headed upstairs to get ready.

A few hours later, I felt as if I could declare this party a success. Music was pumping, and a dance floor had been established in the living room. The cake had been presented to the birthday girl as a hundred people sang her "Happy Birthday." People were drinking, laughing, and talking around the firepit, some of them smoking pot.

I'd hardly had time to have two drinks all night, but now I could finally take a bit of a break. My indigo dress rode up my thighs as I leaned over the island. Amaya had helped me pick it out the last time we went shopping. It clung to my curves and had long sheer sleeves and a completely sheer back. Careful not to knock anything over, I grabbed the vodka bottle.

Someone came up behind me, beer breath washing over my cheek as their hands landed on my hips. "You look smokin' tonight, princess."

I gritted my teeth but made sure my voice was even when I answered. "Thank you, William."

When he called me *princess* it was an endearment, an attempt to make me feel special. When Hendrix said it, it was delivered with derision. But why was I thinking about that asshole now?

I poured the vodka and searched the absolute mess in front of me for some kind of mixer, trying to sidestep out of Will's grasp. "Are you having a good night? Where's Drew and the others?"

He moved up next to me and slung an arm over my

shoulders. "Who cares? I was hoping I could steal you away. It's been a while since we . . . caught up."

There were a lot of people in the room. I had to be careful about my reaction.

I was probably going to marry Will. He was the son of a prominent businessman and planned to follow in his father's footsteps, and his mother was on the board of every charitable organization she could find. Our parents were friends and approved of us being together. Our life plans matched. He'd be the perfect husband, and I the perfect wife.

We'd dated exclusively for about six months in junior year, but I put a stop to that. I made it clear to Will I needed some time. It was around then that I started going to Davey's. As much as I'd made peace with my future with Mr. Carboard, I couldn't commit to it fully just yet.

We'd hooked up a few times since, but I'd made it very clear I wasn't interested in anything serious until maybe a few years into college. I needed to focus on my studies.

I *did* need to focus on my studies and my volunteering and all the other things that would help me achieve my goals. But the truth was, Will was about as interesting in bed as you'd expect. He had an average-sized penis, he liked to do it missionary, and he had no idea what a clitoris was.

Maybe I was being a bit harsh, but Will just couldn't give me what I needed.

"Hendrix?" Will sounded half-confused, half-angry.

Shit! Did I say something out loud? I wasn't even drunk. "What?"

"What the fuck is he doing here?" Will took another swig of his beer as I whipped my head around.

Sure enough, there he was, making his way through the crowd and craning his neck as though he was looking for someone. He was in tight ripped jeans and a plain white tee under a dark green zip-up jacket, his hair messy in that intentional way. As he reached the other side of the island, he spotted me and froze, his eyebrows slamming into a frown.

I stiffened, ready to shrug Will off, but then Hendrix noticed his arm around me. When his eyes narrowed just a fraction, I decided to lean into my future husband's side instead.

"What the fuck are you doing here?" He asked the question that was on the tip of my tongue.

"It's my house, asshole. What the fuck are *you* doing here?" I crossed my arms and cocked my head.

He looked even more confused "Clearly I had no idea. Otherwise I wouldn't have willingly put myself in your proximity."

"Clearly. So why are you *still* here?" I leaned on the counter, getting out from under Will's drunken slouch. He was starting to lean a little too much weight on me.

"Turner invited me. I had no idea the girlfriend he can't shut up about is Mena. Although I should've known. The two nicest people in Devilbend—of course they're together."

I snorted, failing to contain the smile. He was so right. "They're so cute together it's sickening."

"Right?" He laughed.

I wiped the smile off my face, remembering we were in a room full of people who thought we hated each other. Because we did. Will kept looking between us, trying to solve some puzzle, but he was probably too drunk to even remember why he'd come over to me in the first place.

"Go find Drew and the guys, Will. Your beer is nearly gone." I gestured with my head toward the back patio, and he gave me a smile.

"Good idea," he slurred and stumbled away.

"Good boy," Hendrix cooed after him once he was out of earshot. "Now fetch your balls."

I bit my tongue to stop myself from laughing. I didn't want to give him the satisfaction. I didn't even want him here. But this was Mena's birthday—it wasn't about me. "Fine. You can stay. But only because it's Mena's special day. Just don't steal anything."

He smirked. "Lighten up, Mead. It's a party—and you don't even have to find a way home. Have a drink or five. It might make your personality bearable."

"I was just about . . ." I looked for my half-made drink, but he was already walking away. "Asshole."

I downed the vodka in my cup straight, then spotted the bottle of OJ in the sink. *Naturally.* I poured myself another stronger one, then added the juice.

I would never admit it—not even to save the human race from extinction—but Hendrix was right. I wanted to lighten up and have a drink. I also *needed* one now that he was here.

I sipped my vodka and OJ as I mingled, trying to ignore the fact that he was in my house. Will had passed out in a chair by the fire, Drew and the others keeping an eye on him.

"Don't let him puke in my house." I pointed to him and raised my brows at Drew.

"On it." He took another puff of what was clearly not a regular cigarette and passed it to Amaya. Harlow was in a fit of giggles next to her, she and Nicola losing their shit over something on her phone. Laughter bubbled up in my chest too. I had no idea what was so funny, but their mirth was infectious.

I was about to find a spot and join them, but then I noticed Hendrix just a few feet over, talking with Mena and Turner. They looked as if they were really getting along. And the mirth in my chest died. He was in my house, with my friends, in my life. And I wanted him gone . . . but I also kept trying to remember if my room was messy or not and what he'd think of it if he made his way up there. And that was just . . . ugh! Insane!

Shoving some skanky chick in platform heels out of the way, I headed back inside and downed the rest of my drink, dropped the empty cup into the mess on the counter, and located the vodka.

With the smooth glass of the bottle clutched firmly in my hand, I made my way back outside. Keeping my gaze ahead, I avoided everyone and took the stone steps down to the path leading to the pool.

As soon as I was away from everyone's judgmental gazes, I could finally take a deep breath. The cool night air filled my lungs as I walked the manicured path, leaving the raucous sounds of the party farther behind me with every step.

It was chilly but still, and the water in the pool looked black—smooth glass reflecting the stars above. I sat at the edge and crossed my legs. The cap came off the bottle, and I took a swig, the alcohol burning my throat on the way down as much as the cool air had soothed it. The thumping bass and cacophony of laughing, talking voices in the background grew fainter with every sip.

I'd been looking forward to hanging out with my friends, having some fun now that the party was pretty much taking care of itself. But then *he* showed up and ruined everything. I couldn't think about anything else with him so close.

The way he'd worked my body at the back of Davey's just one week ago . . . if I closed my eyes and allowed my mind to go there, I could still feel his fingers on my rain-slick skin, still feel the ecstatic oblivion he'd provided without wanting anything in return.

He'd given me one of the best orgasms of my life, but it was what happened after that I couldn't seem to work out. Hendrix had taken care of me. He'd met my physical needs, then taken me into his arms and made me feel . . . safe? I couldn't quite put my finger on the warm, fuzzy emotion it had brought up.

Then, naturally, we'd argued. He'd gone right back

to the asshole he'd been from the start, and I knew there'd be no repeat performance, even if I wanted one.

So, when I wasn't fighting memories of how good he'd made me feel, I was obsessing over how he could ruin me with one carefully worded sentence delivered to anyone in my orbit.

How had I allowed myself to get into a situation where a man like Hendrix fucking Hawthorn had that much power over me?

I sighed and took another swig. At least the alcohol was making it easier to not give a shit for a little while.

Setting the bottle on the ground, I pulled a cigarette and lighter out of my cleavage. I'd stolen it from Amaya's pack earlier in the night when no one was looking. I didn't really smoke, especially not where anyone might see me—not that I judged my friend for doing it, but I couldn't afford to have anyone think I had any bad habits. When people thought you had one bad habit, they tended to start wondering what others you might have. If they only knew . . .

I lit the cigarette and inhaled, then pulled my knees to my chest and stared at the still, dark water as I blew the smoke out.

The sound of someone approaching made me turn my head and lower the cigarette out of view. I was fully prepared to dump it in the pool, but when I saw who it was, I just faced forward again and took another resigned drag.

Why couldn't I get away from him? Even in my own house?

Hendrix came to a stop right next to me, his boots touching the edge of the pool, and whistled low. "Nice view."

I glanced up at him. He was looking out past the pool, taking in the twinkling lights of Devilbend and the Californian landscape beyond.

"Best in Devilbend," I deadpanned.

He folded his tall frame down next to me and draped one arm over his bent knee. Gripping the neck of the bottle with the tips of his fingers, he twirled the vodka on its base; the glass crunched against the travertine pavers. "There really is no happy medium for you, is there? It's either one extreme or the other."

I raised a questioning brow and took another drag.

"You're either the perfect princess, headed for the ivy league, or you're drunk on vodka, smoking, and going to Davey's dressed like sin."

"You think you know me?" I shook my head. He wasn't wrong, but I'd die before admitting it to his face.

"Can I have a drag?" He held his long fingers out for the half-smoked cigarette.

I sighed and handed it over. He was taking everything else anyway.

He pulled on it, squinting at me, then blew the smoke in my direction before handing it back. "You try to be what everyone expects you to be, but deep down, even you must know you can't control everything. And that thought terrifies you. But you don't know how to deal with it, so you go out and do stupid shit as a *fuck you* to the universe. Or just to prove to yourself that you can. Or just to let off steam. I haven't figured that part out yet."

Yet. As if he was actively trying to figure me out. As if he was convinced he would eventually. The arrogance . . . I wanted to punch him in the throat for his assumptions, but part of me also liked that he wanted to know more.

"You have no idea what you mean . . . what you're talking about." Shit. I was wasted. I hated how slurred my words came out, that I stumbled on them. I didn't want to show him any weakness.

"Yes, I do." He stopped swirling the bottle and put it behind him, out of sight and reach. "I didn't have your control issues, and I definitely didn't give a shit about my reputation like you do, but I used to do reckless shit in order to feel alive too. I know the high you're chasing, and trust me, it can only end in disaster."

"Is that what happened?" I let my knees drop to the side, brushing up against his leg, and leaned on one hand for balance. After one last drag, I put out the cigarette and left the butt on the ground. "Is that why you moved here? You did something disastrous? Did you crash daddy's Porsche?" I stuck my bottom lip out and mock-pouted.

He scoffed. "I wish. I . . . I'll never forgive myself for what I did."

He stared at the pool, and the mocking expression fell from my face. He was serious. And I was too drunk to deal with this conversation. My head spun, and I involuntarily tilted into him, grabbing his shoulder for balance.

Immediately, he gripped my elbow. He smelled like cinnamon, like that night in the rain, but there was a hint of cigarette smoke too. It was heady, alluring, and in my inebriated state, I couldn't stop myself from leaning in to get more of it.

My lips were inches from his, my body remembering how infuriatingly good it felt to have his body pressed up against me. I wanted him—badly, the pressure between my legs building. But in that moment, in the cold night, with the still pool water reflecting all our flaws, I realized what I craved more was how he'd made me feel *after*. When he picked me up and told me he had me, and I believed it with every fiber of my being.

"Shit." I dropped my head to his shoulder, squeezing my eyes shut, my breaths coming in pants.

He sighed and ran a hand down my spine, the touch gentle, hesitant. "You're wasted. Come on."

He pulled away, but he didn't disappear as I expected him to. He helped me to my feet, steadied me, and wrapped an arm around my waist as he slowly walked me back toward the house.

The sounds of the party got louder, the weight of my life heavier, with every step.

I pushed down the confusing emotions in my chest, blinked back the perplexing tears.

Just before the last bend in the path, I made him stop and took a step away from him, breathing deeply, willing myself to sober up. It was fine to have a few drinks, have fun with my friends—I didn't want people thinking I was a robot—but I couldn't have anyone seeing me completely wasted either.

Hendrix held on to my elbow until it was clear I wasn't going to faceplant, then let go, the last connection between us severed.

I pulled my shoulders back and ran my hands over my dress to check for dirt. Hendrix stepped in front of me, and I froze as his gentle fingers smoothed down a few errant strands of my hair.

"You're perfect," he whispered, brushing the very tips of his fingers across my cheek. I gritted my teeth to resist leaning into the feather-soft touch.

"I'll go around the side of the house. So people don't get the wrong idea." He smirked, then turned and walked away.

I watched his broad back until he disappeared into the darkness, then I walked back into the chaos.

CHAPTER 10

Donna

I WOKE UP THE NEXT MORNING HUNGOVER AS fuck. But I still woke up. Harlow and Amaya were both out cold in Harlow's bed. Turner and Mena may have been up, but the door to the spare bedroom they'd slept in was firmly closed, and the faint noises coming through were a pretty good indication they didn't want to be bothered.

Did I want to sleep off the previous night's poor choices, stay in bed, and ignore the world until sometime in the afternoon? Of course. But someone had to let the cleaners in and check in with the parents so they wouldn't rush home early. So I dragged my ass out of bed at nine thirty and was dressed and showered when the professional cleaning crew rang the bell at precisely ten.

Sundays were Magda's days off, so I pressed the button to open the gate and put on a pot of coffee myself.

I stood in the silent kitchen, the cold from the tiles seeping into my feet as the water percolated, and tried not to think about Hendrix.

Even though I should've stayed down there to supervise the cleaners, I took my steaming black coffee upstairs, grabbed a throw off the end of my bed to wrap around my shoulders, and went out to my balcony. It looked out over the yard and had a stunning view of the town and landscape beyond. The sunshine made my head hurt even with my sunglasses on, but I embraced the pain, letting it work with the caffeine to wake me.

The pool was visible from my vantage point, and the bright morning sun glistened off the water, making me wonder if I'd imagined how dark and still it had been the night before. Maybe it hadn't ominously reflected all my darkness back at me. Maybe my bizarre drunken talk with the boy I was supposed to hate never happened. Maybe his touch and his declaration that I was perfect—which had given me the strength I needed to go back to the party for another hour, pretend I was having a grand time before I managed to slink away to bed—had all been imagined.

I took a big sip of the bitter coffee and sighed, pulling the throw tighter around my shoulders. It was wishful thinking. I hadn't been *that* drunk, and there was no way in hell I'd imagined how amazing he smelled, how good and strong his shoulder felt under my hand.

I couldn't let Hendrix Hawthorn get under my skin. He was not part of the plan. College was my plan. A law career and a perfect reputation that would allow me to one day run for office were my plan. William was my plan.

My stomach roiled; saliva gathered in my mouth. I threw out a shaky hand and steadied myself on the railing. I must've been more drunk than I thought.

I forced several deep, cleansing breaths into my lungs and pushed thoughts of boys out of my mind. Then I sat down and finished my coffee before heading back downstairs to tackle the day.

The others shuffled into the kitchen one by one after the cleaners left, looking worse than me—rubbing their eyes, grunting in greeting, dragging their feet.

"Whoa! It doesn't look like there was even a party here last night." Turner looked around in awe, then rushed to the window to check the patio area.

Harlow put some chill music on, and we ordered in for breakfast. By the time our parents got home, everyone was showered and feeling more like themselves.

Thankfully, the evening was quiet, and I was able to get some homework done before going to bed early.

I spent Monday and Tuesday avoiding Hendrix as much as I'd warned everyone else to. Tuesday evening provided another good distraction, with the added bonus that I could accomplish something for my future and for the greater good.

After school, I changed into plain black clothes and headed straight into Devilbend's downtown for my volunteer shift with Devilbend Community Legal

Center. I worked there for four hours every second Tuesday.

I mostly just made coffee, did filing, and took a few phone calls, but my two-year commitment would look fantastic on my college application, and I was gaining invaluable insight into family law. While the clinic covered various areas of practice, Tuesday night was devoted to family law appointments. Lawyers from some of the best firms in the area volunteered their time to provide advice to members of the community who couldn't afford legal help otherwise. I'd met partners and associates from the law firm I was hoping to intern at over the summer, plus I was building relationships and doing good in my community.

It was the right thing to do, but it secretly felt more like an obligation than anything else. I'd never admit it to anyone, not even to myself out loud, but these Tuesday nights had turned into a boring chore.

"Here's your coffee, Jasmin." I gave the manager of the center a smile.

"Thanks, Donna." She shoved several dirty cups out of the way so I could place the new one next to the pile of files on her desk.

I frowned but chuckled. "How many have you had today?"

"Uh ... four? No. Six. I don't know. An even number. Are the volunteer lawyers here yet?" She was the cliché of the overcaffeinated community lawyer, with cheap suits, tired eyes, and her chestnut hair in a messy bun. But clichés existed for a reason. She was overworked. She was underpaid. She really needed the caffeine to get through her day.

"Yes, ma'am. Mr. Horowitz just got here, and the first clients should arrive any moment now. The interview rooms are set up, and I've got everyone coffee or tea. Also, here's a phone message from James. His son has strep throat again, and he won't be able to come in tomorrow."

Her shoulders sagged. "Great. Perfect. First they cut my damn funding, then three people call in sick. I'm going to have to reschedule a dozen appointments tomorrow."

"I'll do as many as I can tonight."

"That would be really great. Thank you, Donna."

"It's no problem. How bad is the funding cut?"

She winced. "Bad. I'm probably going to have to lay someone off—when I actually need to hire two more to keep up with demand for services. And donations are down. It's one of those days where the coffee is the only thing keeping me going." She saluted me with her mug and took a long drink, then frowned. "I'm sorry. You don't need me unloading all this on you. Thank you for volunteering your time. It makes a difference."

"It's no problem. On both fronts."

The little bell above the rickety glass door chimed, and I had to go welcome the first clients.

The rest of my shift passed as usual as I assisted the lawyers and made those calls, but the mundane admin tasks didn't do much to quell my frustration at how much this woman had to deal with on top of all the obstacles constantly being thrown in her way. I helped Jasmin tidy up and close for the night, and we left together just after eight.

"Thanks for your help tonight, Donna. I'll see you in two weeks." Jasmin deadlocked the front door, waved at me, and headed for the bus station around the corner.

I was parked a few blocks away in the opposite direction, so I pulled my coat in tight and started walking.

Even this late at night, the lobby beyond the glass windows of the BestLyf building was bright and lit up as I passed. DCLC's offices were in a dingy two-story building right next door, which also happened to be owned by BestLyf. I probably wasn't supposed to know that, but I'd glimpsed a rental statement once when I was doing some filing. The rent was astronomical. I understood that real estate in the heart of Devilbend was in high demand, but DCLC was a nonprofit, for fuck's sake, and BestLyf owned the biggest building in Devilbend and half the other properties on the block. It wasn't as though they couldn't afford to give a charitable organization a discount on rent for the shittiest building on the street. I guess they wanted to help everyone live their best life, but only if you weren't poor.

Glaring at the pavement as I powerwalked, I didn't notice the other people approaching on the sidewalk until a deep throaty laugh slammed me right back to Saturday night. My steps faltered, and my head shot up.

Sure enough, there was Hendrix, walking toward me with a man and a woman next to him. He had his hands stuffed into the pockets of a dark blue coat, the collar popped against the harsh wind, and his hair was even more disheveled than usual.

Our eyes locked, and we both slowed until we were standing in front of each other. His companions stopped too, throwing curious glances between us.

I recovered first, clearing my throat and shifting my feet. "Hey."

Ugh. I'd figured just walking away without saying anything at all would be worse, but . . . *Hey?* I mentally slapped myself.

The side of his lip quirked. "Hey," he said, his jaw slowly working a piece of gum as he stared at me.

The woman cleared her throat. "Hendrix? Are you going to introduce us to your friend?"

"We're not friends," we both rushed to say. Laughter bubbled up in my chest, but I kept it contained and smiled at her instead.

"Oh." She raised her eyebrows. "Girlfriend?"

I snorted, and Hendrix laughed. "Definitely not. This is my aunt Hannah and her partner, Robbie." He gestured to the couple. His aunt gave me a friendly smile, and her boyfriend waved, stomping his feet against the cold. "Guys, this is Donna. She . . . goes to my school."

For some reason, I enjoyed how hard he was finding it to define who I was to him. Remembering my manners, I turned to face them and reached out my hand. "It's a pleasure to meet you."

They both shook my hand, and then Robbie asked,

"Are you all right out here on your own? It's getting late."

"Yes, I don't like you walking around downtown on your own," his aunt added. "Would you like to join us for dinner? We can drive you home after." She was genuinely friendly. How the hell was that surly asshole related to her?

Hendrix stiffened next to me, his jaw clenching on the gum. I decided to put us both out of our misery.

"That's very kind of you, but I'd like to get home. I just finished a volunteering shift at Devilbend Community Legal Center, and I'm tired. I'm parked just up ahead. I'll be totally fine." Without waiting for them to insist or ask more questions, I started sidestepping away. "Enjoy your dinner."

"It was lovely to meet you," his aunt called after me.

"You too!" I waved and tore my gaze away before I was too tempted to march back over there and demand to know why Hendrix was frowning at me so hard.

When I got home, I headed straight for my father's study at the back of the house. The door was ajar, and warm light was spilling onto the marble tile in front of it. I could hear soft voices and the clinking of ice.

My mother's soft laugh made me smile. They had evening drinks in here from time to time. Mom used to take a drink in to Dad to distract him from work until he gave up, and eventually it had turned into a nonregular ritual.

I knocked on the door as I pushed it open. "Daddy?"

"Oh, shit." Mom laughed, leaning her elbow on the

arm of the leather couch in the corner.

Dad squeezed her knee and swirled his scotch with his other hand. "You must want something big if you're calling me Daddy."

I placed my hand on my chest and plastered an outraged look on my face. "Can't a girl show affection to her father without being accused of manipulation?"

"When it comes to most teenage girls, no." Mom took a sip of her own scotch.

"When it comes to you, sweetness, definitely not. You don't do anything unless it's with intention. You get that from me." There was pride in my father's eyes as he leaned back against the couch.

My parents knew me so well, and yet . . . no one knew that part of me that came alive by throwing myself at dangerous men in seedy bars. Other than Hendrix. And he'd still called me perfect.

I pushed him out of my mind and sat on the soft rug, helping myself to the cheese board. "So rude," I said around a mouthful of brie and cracker. Other than with the girls, this was pretty much the only place I'd allow myself to speak with food in my mouth.

My parents each raised a brow, waiting.

I rolled my eyes. "OK, fine." They burst into laughter, and I had to raise my voice. "But it's not for me."

"What's going on?" Dad set his glass on the table and leaned his elbows on his knees.

"DCLC is having its funding cut. Jasmin says she's going to have to let someone go, and they're stretched so thin already. It's just not fair."

Dad nodded and gestured for me to continue. I sat up straighter and met his gaze head-on. I'd never asked my parents for this much money before.

"I'd like you to make a donation. An anonymous one."

"How much?"

I laid out several levels of monetary assistance and what that would do for the center.

"That's a lot of money." Dad popped an olive into his mouth.

"They help a lot of people."

"Our charity fund has already allocated the donations for this year."

"Yeah, but we have the money, and you're in charge of the fund. You can expand the capacity if you want. Or we can make it a personal donation."

He eyed me for a few minutes, chewing on the olive. "Tell you what, prepare a proposal for me, outlining in detail the funds needed and where they'll go, and I'll consider it."

I grinned and jumped to my feet. "Thank you, Daddy!"

His answer was as good as a yes. He was just using the opportunity to get me to work on my report-writing skills, and I knew I'd crush that report.

I finished drafting it well after midnight and fell asleep instantly afterward, exhausted after a long day—but a certain infuriating guy invaded my dreams anyway.

With the donation all but locked in, I thought my frustrating week was finally turning around, but the next day made me want to throw a tantrum in the middle of Fulton Academy—let everyone see how done I was with their shit.

I was sitting between Amaya and Mena at lunch, slowly eating a roast veg salad while checking emails on my phone, when I saw it.

"Motherfucker." I smacked my fork down and gripped my phone so tightly I was surprised the screen didn't crack.

"D? You OK?" Amaya leaned in, her dark hair falling over her face and screening her concerned expression. The cafeteria was as raucous as usual—no one had noticed my quiet outburst of rage.

Grinding my teeth, I showed her my phone. She skimmed the email that had just come in, the one informing me I would not be awarded the internship I'd been working toward for the past year.

"What the fuck?" Amaya's frown deepened. "I was positive you had that in the bag."

"Me too." I got to my feet and stuffed my phone into my pocket. "Keep this in the Dynasty for now, OK?"

"You got it. Where are you going?" She waved Mena's curious glances down.

"To get to the bottom of it."

I marched out of the cafeteria, through the school, and up to the third floor, where all the faculty and admin staff had their offices.

Mr. Kirke was the Legal Studies teacher and in

charge of facilitating students applying for scholarships, volunteering, and other opportunities in the legal field. I'd have bet my hefty inheritance he knew exactly what was going on here. I wiped all emotion off my face as I approached his open office door.

He was hunched over some papers on his desk, making a mess of the sandwich clutched in his hand. When I knocked on the doorjamb, he looked up over his rimless glasses and swallowed his bite of food.

"Miss Mead." He pressed his lips together. "What can I do for you?"

Taking that as an invitation, I walked into his office and perched myself on one of the two chairs facing his desk. "Mr. Kirke, I'm sorry to interrupt your lunch. I just wanted to clarify something before my next class."

"What's that?" He leaned back in his seat, crossing his fingers over his beer belly.

"I just received an email from Horowitz, Ross, and Shore informing me I would not be interning at their offices this summer. It was brief and uninformative. Seeing as you help organize the internship, I'm hoping you can enlighten me."

He was not at all surprised I hadn't gotten it. I pushed the rage down. I was the only Fulton student who'd applied. He should've had my back. "Hundreds of people apply every year, Miss Mead. There is only one position."

"I am aware of how competitive the position is. I am also aware of what they look for. My grades are unblemished, I'm taking several AP classes, I'm volunteering with a nonprofit with ties to the firm, and my planned career path is exactly what they nurture in potential interns. I am the perfect candidate. I'd simply like some insight into why I was not chosen."

I wasn't being arrogant—I was confident I'd done all the right things. I'd worked my ass off. And if there was something else that would've given me the edge, he should've told me. It was *literally* his job.

Mr. Kirke gave me a small, patronizing smile. "There were three dozen perfect candidates. Sometimes, life's just not fair. Take this as a life lesson and move on, Miss Mead."

That condescending mother—

"May I ask who the successful student was?" The information would be public within a week anyway.

"A bright young man by the name of Jacobs." He didn't even hesitate, didn't have to look up the name. How long had he known?

This whole situation was infuriating. I crossed my legs but kept my posture perfectly straight. "Mr. Kirke, I did my research, like I always do, but tell me if I'm wrong here."

He frowned slightly but nodded for me to continue.

"Horowitz, Ross, and Shore has been practicing law in the state of California and the West Coast since 1938. The internship has been running since 1963."

The bell rang, and he sighed, but I rushed to keep speaking.

"In that time, only two women have been awarded the position: Jemima Holt and Miriam Randle." I'd been determined to be the third—but I'd severely underestimated entropy, nepotism, and the fucking patriarchy.

"What's your point, Miss Mead?" His nostrils flared. I was pissing him off. Good, because I was livid.

"As you yourself said, there are hundreds of applicants each year, dozens of ideal candidates. How is it that year after year, a male student is chosen?"

He scoffed and waved his hand dismissively. "Female students don't generally have the same level of interest in studying law as male students. It's probably just a numbers thing."

"Females make up just over 50 percent of all students enrolled in law schools nationally. This number has been steadily growing over the decades, yet the percentage of women in leadership positions, *higher paying positions*, remains woefully low. Judges—27.1 percent. Deans—32.4 percent. Private law firm partners—22.7 percent. I would've thought you'd know these basic, easily accessible statistics as the Legal Studies teacher in one of the best schools in the country." He sat up, his belly digging into the desk and his face turning red, but I refused to let him get a word in. "And if this were a post-graduate position in the legal field, your argument of 'it's a numbers thing' may check out, but as it stands, it seems blatantly obvious Horowitz, Ross, and Shore is extremely biased toward male applicants when choosing their interns. I would expect an educational institution such as Fulton Academy—which prides itself on its progressive and exceptional approach to education—to take issue with such egregiously sexist practices.”

“Miss Mead, that's quite enough.”

“No. What's enough is your apathy, the ingrained sexism in the legal field, and no one doing anything about it.”

He shot to his feet. I refused to have him looking down on me, so I stood too.

“You are not privy to the selection process at Horowitz, Ross, and Shore,” he growled, “and you are not aware of how the real world works. But you will be very soon, so let me give you one quick lesson now. Women who throw around those kinds of baseless accusations against institutions such as Fulton Academy and Horowitz, Ross, and Shore very quickly find themselves unemployable. I would've thought that as a student of law, you'd know not to make accusations without proof. I'm sure you could cause a media storm in a teacup what with all this social media and the Twitter and such, but I'd be very careful who you make enemies of, Miss Mead, if you wish to have any chance of being employed after you finish college.”

I immediately wanted to post, tweet, fucking TikTok about this and show him just how fast I could cause some trouble. And his suggestion that I'd be ruining all my carefully laid plans by doing so was . . . weirdly freeing? I guess I was just in a “fuck everything” kind of mood.

He gathered some papers off his desk, walked to his door, and held the handle. “The bell rang ten minutes ago. I'm late for a meeting, and you should be in class."

I was clearly dismissed, but it was probably for the best. The urge to grab his too-short tie and twist until he couldn't speak nonsense anymore was growing by the second.

"This is bullshit," I muttered as I stormed past him and down the corridor.

He let the cursing slide, pulling the door shut and rushing off in the opposite direction.

CHAPTER 11

Hendrix

MY MEETING WITH THE GUIDANCE COUNSELOR was mandatory, but missing most of lunch to sit in an office with a woman who had no concept of my past turned out to be as big a waste of time as I thought it would be. When she asked why I hadn't graduated last year as I was supposed to, I told her that information should be in my file and I wasn't comfortable talking about it. I resented that it had even been brought up in such a casual way.

Then she spent a stupid amount of time rambling about college applications and areas of study while I tried to keep my bored mask in place. In reality, my skin was crawling, and I wanted to storm out of there the entire time. To her credit, she did try to ask me questions about what I wanted to do after high school, but I didn't give her much in the way of responses. Because I had no fucking clue. I just wanted to get through the school year and graduate. I couldn't bear to think about what would come after, what kind of future I might have.

I was so wrapped up in thoughts of a potential future I didn't deserve that I almost missed the blonde ball of anger barreling toward me from the other end of the hallway.

Seeing Donna made me pause and look around. Where the hell was I? Somehow I'd wandered into a quiet, locker-free corridor I wasn't familiar with. I was still getting the lay of the land—the school was massive.

"What the hell are you doing in the administrative wing, Hendrix?" Donna stopped directly in front of me and somehow managed to look down her perfect little nose—despite being a good foot shorter. She was seething.

I knew she couldn't stand the sight of me, but even I couldn't elicit *this* level of rage. What was up her ass?

I made sure not to let my amusement show as I frowned down at her. "None of your business."

Oh, she did not like that at all. She took another step closer, her chest just inches from mine, and gritted her teeth, but she didn't seem to have a witty comeback. I kept perfectly still, stifling the chuckle that was bursting to tumble out of me.

When it became apparent she wasn't going to say anything, I looked around the corridor, careful not to give away how affected I actually was by her proximity, by her sweet, girly smell in my nose. "Why's it so quiet here?"

She finally found her voice. "Because anyone who's not teaching a class is currently in a meeting."

She blew a big breath out through her nose, as if the meeting were being held specifically to make her life more difficult. Then she cocked her head, and a tiny smile twitched at the corner of her mouth before it disappeared. What a strange, frustrating woman.

As abruptly as she'd gotten in my face, she grabbed my wrist and turned on her heel. Stunned by the sudden movement and flowery scent of her shampoo wafting past me when she flicked her hair, I let myself be dragged like a naughty puppy. Shoulders back, head held high, she marched past two office doors and opened the third.

When she tried to pull me into the office, I came to my senses and pulled my wrist out of her grasp.

She rounded on me immediately. "Get inside."

"No." I folded my arms. "You're acting even more batshit than usual, and I really don't have time for whatever this is. I need to get to class."

"The bell went fifteen minutes ago. Is there even any point?"

"Of course there is. I'm very interested in Mrs. Shepard's hot take on string theory."

"Please. Like you even know what string theory is. You'd pick science over a blow job?"

"What ... the fuck is happening?" My eyes widened, and I allowed myself a quiet laugh. Her erratic behavior was worrying, but fuck if it wasn't intriguing too. She was a bitch, but there was no denying she was hot, and I'd be lying if I said I hadn't been thinking about what I'd done to her that night in the rain. I knew what her pussy felt like clenching around my fingers as she came. And now that she'd put the suggestion into my brain, I wanted to know what her mouth felt like around my dick.

"I have a score to settle, and I need to burn off some steam. Meeting lets out in about twenty. You want your dick sucked or not?"

"How do I know you won't bite it off instead?" I narrowed my eyes.

She leaned in, lifting onto her toes to whisper into my ear. "You don't. But that's the risk you take any time you stick your dick into someone's mouth, isn't it? The danger, the teeth." She nipped me on the ear. "That's what makes it fun."

Her words made some things click into place in my mind—why she was at Davey's that night; the intense, controlling personality; why she was about to do something reckless on school property. Donna liked the rush of danger, the adrenaline of almost getting caught.

But I didn't have the time to fully consider the implications of all that. I was hard as a rock, and I was an eighteen-year-old guy. I was never going to say no to a blow job.

I wrapped an arm around her waist and shuffled us the rest of the way into the office.

As soon as I pulled the door shut, her hot little tongue invaded my mouth. She placed both palms flat against my chest and shoved me, and I let her, relaxing back against the wall as I grabbed her ass with both hands. She had a great ass under that scandalous tartan skirt.

But I lost my grip on it almost immediately as she slid down, rubbing her body down my front until she was on her knees in front of me.

I had to take a breath to steel myself. Part of me had figured she was talking shit and I was calling her bluff. But I should've known. Women like Donna Mead rarely said things they didn't mean, and even less often did things they didn't want to do.

Holy shit, this is really happening. She made quick work of the button and fly on my neat gray uniform pants as I tried not to pant as if I'd just run a marathon. I was acting as though I'd never had head before, for fuck's sake.

Although, to be fair, I'd never had head on school property. I'd gotten into plenty of trouble, did some fucked-up shit at my last school, but this was a first even for me.

As Donna pulled my pants and boxers down in one efficient maneuver, I could see what she saw in these moments of recklessness. It was a thrill; an exciting, tantalizing buzz of adrenaline made my suddenly free cock even harder.

I shouldn't have expected anything less, but Donna still surprised me a little when she leaned forward and immediately took me into her mouth. No teasing strokes of the tongue, no exploratory kisses. She just wrapped her full lips around the head of my cock and sucked.

"Fuck." I no longer cared how hard I was breathing. Her mouth, her lips, her tongue, *holy shit*—the back of her throat . . . I was lost, such a fucking goner for this complicated, infuriating, spoiled rich girl and her hot little mouth.

She sucked me off the same way she did everything else—with confidence and determination. As with everything else in her perfect life, Donna excelled at this too.

She used the perfect amount of suction, swirling her tongue around the head, working the base with her hand. The occasional scrape of her teeth made me shiver, the hint at pain and destruction.

She'd said we only had fifteen minutes, but I had a feeling this was going to be over in two. How fucking embarrassing. I tried to think of unsexy things to slow down the orgasm already building, stem the increasing pressure in my groin.

Puppies.

Algebra.

The intricacies of my Tesla engine.

The grating sound of nails on a chalkboard.

Austin's face as he—no, not that. I pushed that back into the lockbox deep in my mind.

For a moment, I worried I was about to go from one extreme to the other—go completely flaccid in Donna's mouth while she was giving me the best goddamn blow job of my life. But then I opened my eyes, looked down at her, and groaned, all other thoughts driven from my mind.

I could see down her perfectly ironed shirt, her perky cleavage and a hint of pink lace. Her lips were plumped up from the friction, her unique eyes watching me, unashamed and unabashed. She was perfect.

Her light, soft hair bounced as she bobbed her head up and down. Without thinking about it, I reached out to run my hand through it, then stopped myself just in time. Most chicks didn't like it when you grabbed their heads while they were sucking you off, in my experience.

But Donna frowned a little and grabbed both my hands, placing them on her head and digging her nails into my skin. As soon as I threaded my fingers into her hair, she let go, and her hands went to my hips.

I groaned again—too loudly, considering our location—but some noise is kind of unavoidable when the chick giving you a BJ actively encourages you to pull her hair and hold her head.

I was getting close, panting, the pressure building. My hips twitched, involuntarily driving my dick forward, and I fought to still them.

Again, Donna surprised me. She moaned around my cock, the vibrations feeling incredible. Both her hands moved to the wall on either side of my hips, and she gave me a challenging look, practically begging me to fuck her mouth.

I watched her carefully, just in case I'd read the signals wrong, but I started thrusting. She met me stroke for stroke, taking me deeper and moaning. The head of my cock started hitting the back of her throat repeatedly, but she just kept going, encouraging me with her eyes, sucking me down with her mouth.

For a few glorious moments, Donna gave herself over to me completely. The sight of her on her knees before me as I thrust my cock in and out of her mouth, her eyes starting to water a little, was addictive. Better than any porn I'd ever seen.

The feel of her soft hair in my hands, and her even softer mouth . . .

My whole body tensed, and I banged my head against the wall, bending slightly at the knees as the most intense orgasm washed over me. I couldn't have warned her if I wanted to—the climax came over me so suddenly and with such force. For a second, my vision went black, stars sparking at the edges as I exploded down her throat.

She swallowed it all, sucking and licking as I gasped for air as though I were drowning.

I slumped against the wall. My legs and arms felt like noodles as I slowly caught my breath. Donna sat back on her heels and gave me one small, satisfied smile. She looked happy with herself—as she should, that was fucking phenomenal—but she also looked more relaxed, not as worked up as she'd been in the hallway just moments before.

Without another word, she reached into her pocket, popped a mint into her mouth, then smoothed her hair and uniform before getting to her feet and walking out of the office.

"What the f . . ." I scrambled to tuck myself back into my pants and rushed after her, leaving the door wide open.

I caught a glimpse of her turning the corner at the end of the hallway and took off jogging after her. When I was halfway up the hall, several people rounded the corner and started walking toward me. The meeting must've finished, and all the teachers and admin workers were heading back to their offices. I slowed down to a respectable speed and plastered a neutral look on my face until I passed them.

As soon as I was out of the hall, I booked it toward the stairs.

"Donna!" I called out, taking the stairs down two at a time. I caught up to her just as she reached the halfway point.

She turned to me, a little confused, but didn't stop walking. "What?"

"What do you mean *what*? Are you OK?" I leaned in, keeping my voice low. She'd left without a single word. Had I hurt her? Was I too rough? "Did you not want to . . . did you change your mind or something?"

She laughed under her breath. "No. You finished, didn't you?"

I blew out a big breath. "I mean, yeah. I finished spectacularly." There was that satisfied smirk again. "But did I do something to make you uncomfortable? You just left without saying anything."

"Oh, I'm sorry. Did you want to cuddle? You'll have to get yourself a girlfriend for that."

"I don't want a fucking girlfriend," I barked, a little too loudly. Voices were starting to reach us from below—people were making their way to their next classes. We were about to be swallowed up by the student body once more. "I just want to make sure you're OK."

She finally stopped and faced me, rolling her eyes before glancing down at my crotch. "Your vagina is showing."

"What?" I glanced down, then looked at her as if she was crazy—I was starting to think she was. "I'm just trying to be a decent human being and make sure I didn't choke you out with my dick. Why do you have to be such a bitch about it?"

"I'm fine. You're more than fine. That was a hookup and nothing more, and I didn't think we needed to compare notes. Also, I didn't want to get caught in Mr. Kirke's office. So I left. Nothing else to it. Now stop acting like a pussy and wait a few minutes before coming the rest of the way downstairs. I don't want to be seen with you."

She fixed my collar, gave me a sweet smile, and walked away.

I stood there for a moment, trying to figure out if I wanted to smile or punch something.

Donna Mead was a fucking force of nature, and if I wasn't careful, I had a feeling she would knock me to my knees like a goddamn landslide.

CHAPTER 12

Donna

THE HEAT FROM THE MASSIVE BONFIRE warmed my right cheek, but not as much as the heat from Hendrix's stare was warming my left.

It had been stupid to hook up with him again, get on my knees for that cocky son of a bitch. It had definitely been stupid to do it at school, where anyone could've caught us. But that was part of the thrill, wasn't it? It was a reckless thing to do, but I was enraged after my chat with Mr. Kirke, and I'd needed an outlet. He was just there, that was all. It could've just as easily been Will if he'd happened to walk down that corridor toward me.

I'd avoided him for the next few days, to make it clear it meant nothing, but there he was, invading my Saturday night. *Again.*

Even through his Jason mask, I could tell he was watching me. He'd worn plain black jeans and a black jacket, but the mask from *Friday the 13th* was iconic enough to make his lazy costume clear. I huffed and took a drink of my soda, careful not to ruin my lipstick. Mena had spent hours doing our makeup, insisting on getting it perfect.

I was dressed as Britney Spears in the flight attendant uniform from the "Toxic" video. My sister was the perfect "Baby One More Time" Britney, with the slutty uniform and her long hair in pigtails. Amaya had opted for the skimpiest Britney outfit, but the look from her performance of "Slave 4 You" at the VMAs looked perfect on my stunning friend. She was so committed to the look we'd had to talk her out of buying an actual snake to wear around her neck all night. Mena was in head-to-toe denim and had somehow talked Turner into dressing in all denim too so they could be Britney and Justin in their matching outfits.

Half the reason we'd decided on these costumes was so we could say hi to people when we arrived and declare, "We're Britney, bitch!" The first half hour at the party had been a lot of fun as we ran around greeting people we knew.

Last year we'd planned to go to some party at Nicola's parents' penthouse loft in San Francisco, but we'd ended up staying in to watch horror movies instead. Mena had worked all day and fallen asleep halfway through the first one.

This year, Harlow talked us all into going to a not-entirely-legal party. We'd driven nearly an hour out of town, into rural land, then down some dirt track to a party in a field. With every bump in the track, every ding on the outside of my car, I wondered how much damage I was doing. Should've taken the jeep Dad got for fishing trips he never went on.

There was a massive bonfire in the middle of the clearing, dark woods edged one side, and a wheat field stretched as far as the firelight could illuminate and beyond.

Easily several hundred people were there. Some of them were Harlow's gaming friends who'd invited her in the first place—a bunch of gangly nerds who hadn't even bothered to dress up. She'd introduced us all, and we'd made small talk, but it became apparent pretty quickly we had nothing in common. I was pretty sure every one of those computer geeks wanted to get into my crazy smart, adorably beautiful sister's pants.

There were college kids there, and some people from Devilbend North High—Mena's old school. At first I was surprised to see how many people there were Fulton students, but it made sense. Harlow had invited all our friends, and they would've told others, and Amaya couldn't keep her mouth shut about a party if she tried.

I ignored the tingly sensation of eyes watching me and turned to look at Amaya. She was in her element, several college guys hanging around her as she flirted and drank from the only champagne glass in sight. Literally everyone else was making do with shitty red cups. Where did she even get that?

"Donna." Harlow bumped into me, breathless. I

stumbled but righted us both. She hung off me, her hands on my shoulders and her face really close to mine. "Donna, I can hear the fire," she whispered, her eyes going really wide.

I gave her a confused look. "Yeah, Harlow. We can all hear the fire. The wood crackles as it burns."

Her eyebrows rose, and she blinked once. "Oh yeah." Then she burst into laughter.

"How did you get drunk this fast?" I asked, getting a little worried. We'd only been there an hour.

"Uhhhhhmmmmmm." The guilty look on her face was almost caricaturish.

I rolled my eyes. "What did you take?"

"Just a little." She held up her finger and thumb and squinted through the gap at me.

"A little what?" I led her a few steps away from the fire and the crowd.

"Ooh, you want some? I feel *great*!" She pulled a little baggie out of her skirt pocket and held it out to me.

I took it from her and inspected it. The baggie had several little white pills in it—E. She was going to have a fucking fantastic night . . . but she was going to come down hard. I guided her over to a bunch of coolers and opened a few until I found one filled with bottled water, then stuffed one into her hand and made her look at me. "Harlow. You drink this or I'm going to take you home, got it?"

She straightened and saluted me. "Yes, ma'am!" Then her eyes wandered to something over my shoulder, and her mouth fell open. "Donna, there are freakishly tall people walking in the big grass.”

"What?" I turned to follow her gaze and pinched the bridge of my nose. "You're not seeing shit. Those are performers. People on stilts." Someone—probably from Fulton, as I was pretty sure no one else could afford the extravagance—had hired a bunch of performers for the night. Several people on stilts were wandering the wheat field, coming into the crowd every once in a while, and contortionists in grotesque costumes twisted themselves into scenes reminiscent of the exorcist. I'd even seen a few very convincing "werewolves" leap out of the woods, scaring the absolute shit out of a group of girls, who sent high-pitched screams into the night. I had to hand it to whoever had done this—it had taken the mediocre rave in a field to the next level. Everyone was on edge, the adrenaline mingling with the alcohol (or drugs) as they waited for what might happen next.

"Oh. OK." With a grin, she snatched the baggie of fun out of my hand and ran off, pigtails bouncing as she barreled through the crowd of college dudes to Amaya's side. They chatted, the dudes laughed at some joke she cracked, and then she passed Amaya the little baggie.

Great. Now I'd have two off-their-faces idiots to haul home tonight. I was starting to wish I'd taken Will's offer to drive us so I could drink too. But he always got drunk at parties, and I couldn't rely on him to get us home. And it wasn't as if I'd be able to get an Uber to come out here, so . . . someone had to be responsible.

Mena appeared at my side and bumped my shoulder with hers. "Hey, you. Having a good night?"

"Yeah." I smiled at her. "You look really pretty."

"Thanks." She glanced down at the swathes of denim and gave a little twirl from side to side. Her eyes were a bit glassy, and her own lipstick was starting to get smudged. I could smell alcohol on her breath. She leaned down and fixed herself another drink from the coolers.

"You're glaring again." She chuckled.

I shook my head and pulled my gaze away from Hendrix. I hadn't even realized I'd gone back to staring at him.

"I didn't mean to. I just don't like him being here." I crossed my arms. He was standing with Turner, talking, laughing, chatting with some of Turner's friends. He looked as if he was having a good time, and for some reason, that pissed me off more than anything.

"Why?" Mena wrapped an arm around my waist and took another sip of her drink. "Things have been fine since you made everyone at school back off him. You guys haven't even yelled at each other in weeks. But he's kind of getting close with Turner, so I've been talking to him a bit, and he's really not that bad."

All my friends had seen was him being an arrogant smart-ass to me, me laying down the law, and us bickering those few times at school. They had no idea what he had over me, what I'd let him do to me, what I'd done to him. Hendrix and I were getting all twisted up in each other, and I didn't like it one bit.

I wrapped my arm around her waist too and turned us toward the fire. "OK. No more glaring. Let's talk about something else."

"OK. What do you want to talk about?"

"How about our trashed friends?" I pointed at Harlow and Amaya, who were dancing as if they could feel the music moving through their bones, heads rolling in ecstasy. They were sweaty and rubbing up on each other in the middle of the dance floor—and had the attention of half the guys at the party and a few of the girls too.

Mena laughed. "I wish I had Amaya's confidence. And Harlow's complete lack of care for what people think of her. And your . . . fuck, everything."

"You don't want to be me, trust me." It came out low, way more somber than the self-deprecating joke I'd intended it to sound like.

"Donna?" Mena frowned at me. I could see the question on the tip of her tongue—the "are you OK?" A twinge of panic squeezed my chest. I wasn't sure I could lie to her if she asked me so directly.

But Drew saved me from having to.

"Ladies!" He draped himself over us both, one arm around Mena and the other around me, his athletic body towering over us. He smelled like expensive cologne and bonfire smoke.

"Hey, Drew." I gave him a kiss on the cheek, grateful for the distraction.

"Come on, Mena—my other cheek feels left out." He leaned his head between ours and wiggled his eyebrows.

She whacked him in the stomach. "No. We've been over this. How drunk are you?"

"Not at all." He took a swig from his beer and immediately returned his arm to my shoulders, then lowered his voice. "Actually, I'm just trying to make a girl jealous."

Biting his lip, he gave Mena a look that would've had her dragging him off to find a secluded tree in the woods—if she was actually into him.

"So, your strategy for picking up is to make it look like you have two other chicks on the hook?" I gave him a skeptical look.

"Yeah, you know most girls are put off by that, right?" Mena backed me up.

"Not this girl." He grinned. "Trust me."

"What girl?" Turner appeared in front of us, blocking our view of the fire and cocking his head to the side. I bit my lip to keep from laughing. This was going to be good.

Drew grinned. "You must be Turner."

"And you must be Drew," Turner deadpanned.

"Aw. You talk about me. I knew I had a place in your heart," Drew cooed to Mena, pulling her closer as she rolled her eyes.

"Only to tell me what a pain in her ass you are," Turner shot back.

"But what an ass!" Drew dropped his arms and turned, sticking his butt out and wiggling it in Mena's direction.

Turner pulled Mena to his side and shook his head at Drew. I'd known him long enough to see the amusement in his eyes, but Drew hadn't. He dropped the clown act and cleared his throat, standing to his full height.

"Hey, man, I don't mean anything by it. I'm just messing around. I know she's taken—she talks about you all the time. You're a lucky man. Mena, am I making you uncomfortable?"

I coughed to cover up the giggle that was threatening to bubble over, but when Mena and Turner finally cracked, I gave up and joined them, all of us bursting into laughter at the wide-eyed look on Drew's face.

Mena, ever the sweetheart, put him out of his misery. She stepped forward and placed a hand on his shoulder. "I know we're just messing around. I would've said something if it was bothering me."

"And I would've made you pay." I wiped the tears from under my eyes.

"And I would've come down to that fancy-ass school to whoop your ass long ago," Turner added.

Drew chuckled and jumped right back into his default setting, covering Mena's hand on his shoulder with his. "Well, if we have the boyfriend's blessing—"

Abruptly, his face fell as his attention snagged on something in the distance.

"Shit," he muttered. "Nice to meet you, man. I gotta run."

Without any explanation, he took a swig of his beer and rushed toward the edge of the clearing where the cars were parked.

Mena watched him with a confused expression.

"What was that about?"

I shrugged. He'd joined a group of guys who had just shown up—all of whom I recognized as Fulton Academy students, most of them on the football team. Two were gesturing wildly and getting in each other's faces. Drew dropped his beer and got between them, keeping them apart. Others helped him stop the fight before it started, but then it looked as if they all broke into a heated discussion.

"What the hell is *that* about?" Turner voiced what we were all thinking as we stood there, watching the scene from afar.

"I don't know, but I'm gonna find out." I squared my shoulders.

"Want me to come with?" Turner asked. "That looked pretty heated."

"No, that's OK. Thanks." I patted him on the arm. "I know all those guys. You two go have fun."

I marched off before they could argue.

The closer I got, the more apparent it became that I knew each one of them. Some were in Halloween costumes, masks, and grotesque monster makeup, but others were just in jeans and their Fulton varsity jackets.

Will was leaning on the hood of his gray Bentley, watching the others argue with a passive, if not bored, look on his face.

"Boys!" I raised my voice a little to get their attention. "It's a party. What's with the hostility?"

"Donna, baby, I got this. It's just some guy stuff." Drew threw me an easy smile, but his shoulders were tense, and he was still shooting looks at Luke and Donnie—the two who had nearly started throwing fists earlier.

"What happened?" I demanded. An uneasy feeling crept up my spine, leaving a chill in its wake despite the heat of the bonfire. This was how they'd been acting after Luke crashed his car over the summer and injured himself and three other guys on the team. His left arm was still in a cast.

"Nothing, Donna. It's fine." Luke rubbed the back of his head and turned away from everyone.

"Is someone hurt?" I folded my arms. Then someone shifted, allowing a streak of bright light to fall over Donnie's face, and I gasped and rushed forward. "Holy shit. What the fuck happened?"

His left eye was black and blue, and there were scrapes on his chin. He glanced over my shoulder and swallowed audibly, then gave a hollow chuckle. "Football is a contact sport. Shit happens." He pulled me into a hug. "But thanks for the concern."

I narrowed my eyes at him, stepped back, and eyed them all. They were acting shifty as fuck. And they hadn't played a game last night, so that made no sense. Was I seeing shit, or were the others sporting bruises and scrapes too? Maybe it was just the masks and makeup, the uneven light of the fire deceiving me.

Before I could pull my phone out and turn on the flashlight to check either way, Will pushed off the front of his car and wrapped his arms around my waist. "Hey, D. Wanna go somewhere quiet?"

He smirked and pulled me in close. His eyes weren't glassy, and he wasn't swaying. Will was stone-cold sober at a party. Something was definitely up.

"Not tonight." I pushed at his shoulders, and he let go, but then he grabbed my hand and tried to turn me around.

"OK, cool. Then let's go get a drink and find the girls."

"No." I wrenched my hand out of his. "Will, what the fuck . . ."

"Everything OK here?" Suddenly Hendrix was there, his mask sitting on top of his head and his dark eyes taking everything in. Why was he *everywhere*? And why was no one telling me the truth?

A motherfucking werewolf jumped out from between the parked cars, growling and raising its paws in the air. Some of the guys jumped in surprise while the others laughed nervously at the performer.

"Not now, asshole!" I screamed, and the guy in the suit gave me a hairy middle finger and stalked back into the shadows.

I turned on Hendrix. "Everything is fine, Hendrix! Mind your own business." Then I turned on Will. "No, I don't want to get a drink or go find a quiet place with you, William." I looked around at the crowd of idiots from my school. "You're all about as subtle as a sledgehammer. I don't know what this shit is about, but I don't like it, and I'm going to get to the bottom of it."

With that, I turned on my heel and stomped back toward the crowd and the fire and the music . . . and yet another thing I had to manage.

I came to a stop at the edge of the dance floor and looked up to the pitch-black sky, begging whatever deity was listening for strength.

Amaya and Harlow were still dancing lasciviously, but now they were also making out. It was nothing new—they kissed from time to time at parties and shit. Amaya liked to tease the boys, and Harlow liked to subvert people's assumptions about her. It was just a bit of fun, but there were a lot of people here we didn't know, and they were both high, and the college guys were dancing a little too close. I didn't want them to do anything they'd regret . . . or worse.

I caught Turner as he came past with a couple of beers. "Hey, can you get Mena home? I need to take care of this . . ." I gestured to the dance floor. Amaya was now shirtless, nothing but a delicate, lacy bralette covering her perky B cups.

"Yeah, I'll take her home. We have a designated . . . whoa . . . okay . . ." His eyebrows rose as he stared.

"Hey!" I snapped my fingers in front of his face and shoved him. "Go find your girlfriend."

He cleared his throat. "Yes. Yup. Good idea."

"Shit," I muttered as he moved away. I had no idea how I was going to get two trashed people into the car.

Once again, Hendrix appeared uninvited at my side, popping an obnoxiously loud bubble with his gum. "I'll get the little one. You get the naked one."

I glared at him for a moment. He was sticking his nose in my business again. But Turner was busy with

Mena, and they were both kind of drunk, and the football guys were pissing me off . . . I really didn't have any other choice.

"Fine." I barreled through the crowd, which looked as if it was about to turn into an orgy any second now. More people had started taking clothes off, and several were making out and grinding on each other.

"Hey!" I clapped my hands next to Harlow's and Amaya's heads.

"Donna!" they both yelled, as if we hadn't seen each other in years.

"Time to go." I picked up their discarded clothing and Amaya's Louis Vuitton bag.

"Where are we—oop!" Harlow descended into a fit of giggles as Hendrix picked her up and swung her over his shoulder in one smooth move. I wrapped an arm around Amaya's waist and pulled her along.

Trying to get them into the car was like trying to wrangle several cats into a bath with one arm tied behind your back. There was screaming and uncontrollable laughter, and I got scratched on my arm. In the end, we managed to shove them into the back seat, and I turned the child lock on so they couldn't let themselves out.

I slammed the door and leaned heavily back against it, blowing my hair off my forehead. Hendrix leaned his hip next to me and laughed.

"Thanks for helping. You didn't have to do that," I said, unable to look at him for some reason.

"You're welcome."

There was a long pause. I stared out into the dark woods. Why was I always the one taking care of everyone else? Maybe I wanted to get trashed every once in a while and know someone would get me home safe.

My friends had said to me more than once I was the strongest person they knew. But that's the thing about being seen that way—you don't feel as if you have permission to be vulnerable. You don't feel as if you're ever allowed to fall apart.

I didn't know why I was letting this shit get to me in the middle of the night in a field in bumfuck nowhere, but suddenly my throat felt tight, and tears stung the backs of my eyes.

Hendrix sighed, reminding me he was still there.

Before I could gather myself, put my strong mask back on, he reached out and squeezed my shoulder. His thumb rubbed smooth circles at the base of my neck.

I grabbed his wrist, but instead of pushing him off me, I found myself leaning into him. "I'm just so fucking tired."

"I know." His deep voice had me feeling in my bones that he really did know. I wasn't talking about just tonight.

He pulled me into his chest and held me tightly, and even with my face buried in his shirt, I was suddenly able to breathe better. I took a long inhale, closing my eyes as the scent of his expensive aftershave mixed with cinnamon hit the back of my throat.

When he'd embraced me at Mena's birthday party, I was drunk. I could blame my momentary lapse in judgment on my impaired decision-making skills. But as he held me at the edge of fire and chaos, dancing and drama, I had no such excuse. Being in his arms felt so *right*.

But it *wasn't*. It *couldn't* be.

My heart hammered.

I straightened, pushed out of his hold.

Our eyes met in the dim light.

The urge to kiss him was palpable, but I forced myself to turn away, get into the car, drive off.

My hands shook the entire drive home, silent tears streaming down my face.

What the fuck was happening to me?

CHAPTER 13

Hendrix

AUNT HANNAH FLICKED THE SWITCH, AND THE multicolored twinkle lights came to life.

"Ahh. Now it feels like Christmas!" She beamed, backing away from the ugliest tree I'd ever seen. But it was also the first one I'd gotten to decorate myself, so my smile back was genuine. Growing up, we always had at least five trees spread throughout the house, and each one was professionally decorated. I'd been scolded anytime I reached for a shiny ornament.

"You forgot the main bit." Robbie waved the red-and-gold star at her. We'd met over dinner that night we bumped into Donna in Devilbend. He was actually a nice guy, and he and my aunt were good together. They were both sarcastic and liked to talk politics and had this weird kind of calm about them. It was nice being around an adult couple who liked each other. I was pretty sure they actually *loved* each other.

"Shit!" Hannah propped her hands on her hips, then pointed at me. "You. Tall, surly teenager in the armchair. You can reach."

"So can he!" I pointed at Robbie, who promptly pointed at my aunt. We both frowned at him.

"What?" He shrugged. "Everyone else was pointing. I just wanted to be cool."

It was such a lame joke, but I laughed anyway. Was this what it was like to be part of an actual family?

Without having to be asked again—another first for me—I got to my feet and secured the star on top of the gaudy tree.

It was only a week until Christmas, but everything felt different. Back in New York, the temperature would be hovering around zero, while here in California, it was just chilly enough for a coat. Back home, I'd probably be going to my hundredth charity event of the season, playing the perfect son for my perfect parents. Here, all I'd done was go to school, hang out with my aunt and Robbie, and train with Turner at the gym.

He'd managed to drag me to that Halloween party only after assuring me it wasn't being thrown by one of the kids from my school. He said Mena would be there with her friends, and realistically I knew that meant Donna would be there too, but I'd hoped the party would be big enough to avoid her. I'd obviously forgotten how fucking hard it was for me to stay away from that chick.

The air hostess outfit and ample cleavage had made her look like temptation incarnate. My eyes kept wandering over to her without meaning to, but what surprised me more was that I caught her looking my way too.

She'd made it clear after the incident in that teacher's office that I meant nothing to her, but we'd hooked up twice now—and it was *good*. Our chemistry was off the charts. Even she couldn't deny that.

We'd had a moment at her car. Another moment where unspoken things passed between us. And then that bitch ran from me again.

Why the fuck was I doing this to myself? I'd been so frustrated after she drove off that I made Turner and Mena leave as soon as I found them, basically telling them they were either coming with me now or finding their own way home.

They were silent and tense on the drive back to their apartment building, while I gripped the steering wheel way too hard and breathed through my stupid fucking emotions.

By the time I dropped them off, I'd calmed down enough to apologize. They both forgave me immediately and even asked if I was OK. Because that was the kind of people they were.

Why couldn't I be more like Turner? Calm, happy, steady.

Why couldn't I be interested in a girl like Mena? Nice, sweet, low drama.

No, I had to find the biggest bitch in town with the biggest fucking secret and make it my mission to get all up in her life.

I was seeing something in Donna I knew was inside me too. That twisting, writhing darkness had ruined my life, along with several others. I didn't want a single other person to go through what I went through. To go through what I put those people through. Even if that person was treating me like dirt on her shoe.

Still, there was only so much I could take. If Donna wanted to ruin her life, who was I to stop her?

After that party I took a long hard look in the mirror, realized I didn't need her rich brat problems, and redoubled my efforts to steer clear. For the next few weeks until Christmas break, I went to school, kept my head down, avoided her in the halls, and ate my lunch off campus or in my car. The only person my age I spoke to was Turner.

My phone buzzed on the coffee table, and I picked it up as I took a sip of eggnog. Who the hell invented this crap? And why was I still drinking it? I made a face and put the cup down, then froze as I read the message.

> We won't be able to make it to Devilbend for Christmas. Your father has had a work situation come up, and I really must oversee the Christmas Eve charity ball. Have a safe holiday with your aunt. Kisses, Mom.

I gripped my phone so fucking hard the screen actually cracked, the line through the glass cutting through my mother's indifferent words. I stared at the message until the screen went black. Then I shot to my feet and stormed out the door, slamming it behind me, ignoring the things my aunt and Robbie were calling after me.

I wanted to hit someone, feel bone crunch under my knuckles. I wanted to drink an entire bottle of something expensive and let the alcohol obliterate everything. I wanted to find a chick and bury myself in her so deep this feeling would just melt away.

A flash of short blonde hair and mismatched eyes mixed with that last image, and suddenly I was thinking about fucking Donna. I growled and sped up.

I wanted to do a lot of things I used to do—things I'd vowed never to do again. Instead I walked. Even in my T-shirt and jeans, I didn't feel the cold, hardly noticed when it started raining lightly.

I wasn't sure how much time passed, but I didn't go back until I was calm, my breathing even, the urge to do reckless, destructive shit gone.

As I walked back inside, I checked the front door for damage. Thankfully it was fine. When I popped my head in the kitchen, both Aunt Hannah and Robbie had already gotten to their feet and were on their way to the front of the house.

"Hendrix—"

"Hey, guys." I cut my aunt off. "I'm really sorry about before. I'm just gonna grab a shower."

I rushed up the stairs before they could answer.

After showering and getting dressed, I checked the time. It was after nine. I'd been out stalking the neighborhood for over three hours. I'd missed dinner.

They had to be mad at me. I'd have to apologize again—do it better. I couldn't handle it if Aunt Hannah kicked me out.

A knock sounded at the door, followed by my aunt's soft voice. "Hendrix?"

"Come in," I called, straightening my sheets and kicking some dirty clothes under the bed. I really needed to make more of an effort to keep my room clean.

"Hey." She plopped onto the bed. "I got a message from your father."

I sank down next to her, hanging my head. What was there to say?

"I'm sorry, honey." Her warm hand rubbed my shoulder.

I frowned at her. "You're not mad?"

She sat up a little straighter. "That your parents are dicks? Yeah, I'm pretty fucking mad about that. But how's that your fault? Not mad at you."

"I'm sorry about storming out." I still felt the need to apologize. "And I'll clean my room. And I'll do more around the house."

"Hendrix. Stop. You were upset. You went for a walk. I'm actually proud of you."

"Proud of me?" What the fuck was this feeling in my chest? It felt as if it were about to bust open, spilling blood and guts everywhere, but . . . in a good way?

"What would you have done a year ago? To deal with something that upset you?"

The booze and drugs, the horrific violence, the depraved sex. I cringed.

"Exactly!" She laughed. "You did good, kid. And I don't need a housekeeper." She waved her hand. "Just stick to what we already discussed—good grades, no trouble—and we're sweet. I'm not going to kick you out for not making your bed."

Fuck. There it went again—blood and guts everywhere. Why were my eyes stinging? Oh my fucking god! I was about to cry. I cleared my throat and pushed that shit down. Maybe I needed to go for another walk.

"So, your father said something about a work thing coming up?"

I dragged my hand down my face. "Yeah, that's what my mom said too. But it's bullshit. There's always a work thing, always a charity. It's just an excuse."

I hadn't seen my parents since they'd shipped me off to Devilbend, and we hadn't spoken in that entire time either. Most of my messages had gone completely ignored. It was OK—I knew I deserved it for what I'd done. But I'd been on my best fucking behavior. My grades were the best they'd ever been. I wasn't expecting miracles, but some part of me had been looking forward to seeing them for Christmas, away from the pressures of their lives in New York. I hadn't realized how big that part was until I got my mother's text message.

Her excuse was almost certainly a copy/paste from some other message she'd sent to get out of another commitment. I didn't even warrant a genuine explanation, let alone a phone call.

What had I expected? It wasn't as though my

parents had given a shit about me before—why would they start now?

I hated myself a little for still craving their approval, their attention.

If I was really honest, that's what had gotten me into this mess in the first place.

"All right, let's hug it out." Hannah got to her feet and waved her hands at me to get up. "I think we've worked up to it."

I stood and reached for her, but she sidestepped me and jumped onto my bed. I gave her a withering look but couldn't help the laughter bubbling up.

"Height advantage." She held her arms out, and I gave her a hug, fighting chuckles the whole time. Despite being so small, she had a strong grip, and after the first-hug weirdness wore off, it was actually pretty damn comforting.

Like a champ, she didn't hang around and make it awkward after.

"We'll have a great Christmas, I promise. Even if it's just the three of us," she said as she jumped off my bed and left me alone in my room.

My phone went off, reminding me I'd need to get the screen fixed. It was another text from a person I hadn't spoken to since leaving New York.

> I'm going away during the holidays and won't have service, so I wanted to get in touch and say merry Christmas early. And a happy New

Year. I hope you make the most of it—for all the reasons we discussed. I truly wish you well, Hendrix.

I typed out and deleted my response a dozen times before giving up. She was probably leaving her home over Christmas because she couldn't stand to be there—because of me. I'd taken so much from this woman, and here she was, wishing me well.

I didn't deserve it, and I didn't deserve Aunt Hannah's kindness either.

I needed to remember why I was here, keep my head down, and stop getting sucked into Fulton Academy bullshit. And that meant avoiding Donna.

CHAPTER 14

Donna

CLINKING GLASSWARE AND POLITE LAUGHTER punctuated the soft Christmas music playing in the background.

I resisted the urge to tug at the tight waist of my A-line red dress. I wanted to be wearing something dark, short, and plunging, and the only thing I wanted cutting into my waist was a strong arm. I took a sip of my soft drink, wishing it were vodka, or at least champagne.

"Can we bail yet?" Harlow yawned next to me. She was in a gold dress with red details, the two of us matching each other in all but attitudes—at least outwardly.

The cream of Devilbend society, and quite a few prominent San Franciscans, were mingling around our house, drinking mom's best champagne and eating delicate hors d'oeuvres. Our annual Christmas Eve *Eve* party was very different from the last party held in this house—the one that celebrated Mena's birthday, where we made a mess and people got wasted and I started falling for . . .

"Give it another half hour, Harls." I leaned down, keeping my voice low. "Make an effort to talk to someone. It'll make Mom and Dad happy. Then you can grab Mena and Amaya and slip out. I'll cover for you."

"Fine." She rolled her eyes. "Thanks, D."

She wandered off and struck up a conversation with an up-and-coming TV starlet who had recently hired Mom's company to remodel her entire penthouse apartment.

Mena was standing with her parents and Joseph and Vicky Frydenberg—Will's dad and his much younger latest wife, who looked bored out of her mind. Thankfully, Will hadn't been able to make it.

Amaya was nowhere to be seen, but her mom had the attention of several men as she told a story over by the roaring fireplace, her infectious personality and the ample cleavage on display keeping everyone enthralled. Like mother, like daughter.

I smoothed the nonexistent wrinkles from my dress and got back to mingling. Several family members and close friends had come out, but there were also Mom's and Dad's important clients, business partners, and colleagues. Our family Christmas would be a much more relaxed, fun celebration over dinner tomorrow night, then presents on Christmas morning. This party was more a way for my parents to nurture professional relationships.

Networking made the world go round, and I wasn't going to waste a single opportunity.

The dean of Fulton Academy was there, and I'd briefly considered raising the issue of my internship with her—along with Mr. Kirke's less than satisfactory handling of the situation—but I just made small talk instead. You had to pick your battles, and I knew that one was lost.

I chatted with my aunt and uncle for a bit as Harlow pulled Mena away and they slipped out to find Amaya. Then I gave Amaya's mom air-kisses and complimented her on her dress.

No one noticed my friends leave the party. I wished I could ditch too—ignore everyone, take this fucking dress off, put on my thigh-high boots and go to Davey's, or even just steal a bottle of champagne when the caterers weren't looking and hang out with the girls.

But I had goals, ambitions, responsibilities. So I shoved those juvenile urges down and headed through the crowd to greet the newest guest, my smile genuine for the first time that evening. Jasmin looked a little uncertain, but I couldn't blame her. She knew no one here, and the people in attendance could keep the legal center going for another thirty years with change from their couches. Which is exactly why I'd made sure Dad put her on the guest list.

"I'm so glad you came." I gave her a hug.

"Thank you for inviting me. You look beautiful, Donna!"

"Thanks! Come meet my parents." I led her over to

my mom and dad and did the introductions. Once they were chatting easily, I moved away.

I caught up with Uncle Heath and his wife, Serena. They'd been friends with my parents since college and Uncle Heath had inherited his father's chain of successful stores—GoodGrocer. When all the horrible bullying Mena had been dealing with came to light, he immediately offered to fire the parents of some of the kids involved, his face going red at the dinner table. I'd threatened the assholes with exactly that, but thankfully, the bullies had been dealt with by the police instead.

"How's school going?" he asked.

"Great." I smiled. "All As and breezing through my AP classes."

"That's my smart girl. Come, let me introduce you to Suzanne Brandy. She's a partner at Paulsen and Price." He gently took my elbow and led me to a small group of people by the eight-foot Christmas tree near the bay window.

I knew Suzanne would be there, of course. I'd spent time looking over the guest list and googling anyone I didn't know. She was married to Andrew, a recent business associate of Daddy's. I'd been planning to speak to her at some point regardless.

"Suzanne, such a pleasure to see you again." Heath barged into their conversation, and a couple of people excused themselves, leaving only the lawyer and another woman I wasn't sure I knew. "This is Donna— the Meads' oldest and California's next great legal mind."

I laughed and dropped my gaze. He was right, of course, but this old-money crowd still subscribed to the idea that it was unbecoming of a young lady to be too confident or proud. "You're too kind, and you have to say that. Hello, lovely to meet you."

She shook my outstretched hand. "The pleasure is mine. I'm always happy to meet young people interested in the legal field. Your home is beautiful."

"Thank you. My mother designed every inch and managed the painstaking remodel."

"She's very talented."

"She is." I beamed.

"Heath, you know Raine." Suzanne gestured to the other woman standing with us. "Donna, this is Raine Clayton."

"The founder and CEO of BestLyf." I turned my winning smile on her and stuck my hand out. "Pleased to meet you, ma'am."

"Likewise." She took my hand in a firm, confident grip. We were about the same height, but I was in heels and she was in flats. Her chestnut hair hung loose around her shoulders, and she wore very natural makeup and understated jewelry. She could have been anywhere between forty and sixty years old—either she just had one of those faces or the plastic surgery she'd had was excellent.

We made small talk for a little while, but the longer I stood there, the more I kept seeing the astronomical number I'd spied on that rental statement a couple months ago.

"You know, Raine"—I gave her a polite smile, which she returned before taking a sip of her champagne—"I actually volunteer right near the BestLyf offices."

"Oh?"

"Yes. It's a stunning building. The lobby always looks so inviting yet professional. I have no doubt my mother would give it the interior design tick of approval."

"Thank you. That's so kind." Her eyes crinkled at the edges as her smile widened. "Where do you volunteer? I think it's so important for young people to give back to the community." The last was delivered to the small group of people beginning to gather around us, who all murmured their agreement.

"I volunteer with Devilbend Community Legal Center every two weeks," I told her. "It's right on the corner near your building. Actually, I believe you own the building that the nonprofit rents."

"Do I?" She chuckled, and everyone else did too, not that she'd made an actual joke. "I own so many I can't keep track of them all, dear. I have a team of people managing all my assets."

"Of course." I smiled sweetly. "It's so wonderful that you allow a nonprofit to rent the space. I believe it's just as important for corporations to give back to the community as it is for young people." I threw her words back at her. "If you'd allow me to be so forward, I do wonder if you'd consider looking into this particular property personally? The rent is reasonable for such a prime location downtown, I'm sure, but every penny saved could go toward helping disadvantaged members of the community. It is the season for giving, after all."

Out of the corner of my eye, I saw Uncle Heath bring his scotch up to his mouth, trying to hide an amused smile. But my focus stayed trained on Raine Clayton.

She cocked her head to the side and studied me as if she were seeing me for the first time. Just as the silence was about to extend to an uncomfortable length, a slow smile graced her face. "You're a C3, bordering on C2, *and* easily an A2 also. Remarkable for someone so young."

"Oh, I was thinking the same." Suzanne nodded enthusiastically, looking between us.

"Uh, thank you?" I laughed lightly, trying not to show how much this nutcase was confusing me. "I don't think I'm familiar with those terms."

"Oh, I'm sorry. I live and breathe BestLyf principles. I sometimes forget not everyone knows our lingo. It basically means you're confident and assertive. Not many teenagers are. The combination can come off as arrogant at times."

I frowned. Did she just call me arrogant? But she barreled on before I could respond.

"You have rare leadership talents—the kind one is born with. The kind people undertaking leadership seminars would kill to have."

"Thank you. That's very kind of you to say." She'd given me several compliments, but I itched to probe her about the arrogance comment. I wasn't arrogant. Was I? There was something imposing about her presence, despite her understated look. Or maybe because of it. But the way she spoke, so articulately and with such certainty, was a little mesmerizing.

"Raine is amazing, Donna. Her program got me from a graduate position with an unknown legal firm to being considered for partner at Paulsen and Price within five years. I've learned so much! You should look into their Young Minds program."

"Yes, I think you'd be an ideal candidate." Raine smiled at me warmly, as if she were already proud of the achievements I had yet to accomplish. "And I promise to look into this little rent issue." She waved her hand dismissively and took another sip of champagne.

"Thank you. I'll certainly look into your program." If it could fast-track my plans for the future, I'd be an idiot not to. Maybe I could escape this crushing pressure sooner and start enjoying my life before my forties. *Wow*! What a depressingly middle-aged thought to have. Where the hell had that come from?

"Donna excels at all she does." Uncle Heath gently squeezed my shoulder, the pride in his face so obvious you'd think I was *his* daughter. But Raine was now engaged in conversation with some of the other people gathered around her and was no longer paying attention to either of us.

A tall man in a dark suit walked past in my periphery, and for a moment, I could've sworn Hendrix had just waltzed uninvited through my parents'

Christmas party. A quick glance told me it was someone whose name I didn't know, possibly my mom's PA, but that didn't stop the bone-aching urge to turn in his direction from coursing through my body.

The tight waist on the dress felt like a rope around my middle, holding me back from chasing him down. My breathing got shallow, and the conversation I was supposed to be a part of faded into the background.

Every time I thought about how he'd acted the night of the party—how he'd seemed to know what I was feeling and what I needed before I even said it—I got this weird panicky feeling in my chest. My mind couldn't seem to articulate what was racing through it, and my body got fidgety and restless.

I didn't like it.

It was inconvenient and unwanted. The only way to deal with it was to remove the trigger. So I'd started avoiding him. I had the girls help me keep tabs on him under the guise of keeping an eye on a troublemaker, but really, I used the information to avoid bumping into him at school.

The frustrating thing was, the more I avoided him, the worse my reaction was any time I spotted him—or thought I did.

I took another sip, trying to bring myself back to the present. I was being rude, but I'd lost all interest in this conversation, these people, and this party.

Jasmin pushed through the crowd, the worried expression on her face snagging my attention and giving me a good excuse to bail.

"Could you all please excuse me? There's something I need to attend to." I smiled politely and left, catching up to Jasmin just as she reached the makeshift bar area in the foyer.

"Can I get a scotch on the rocks, please? Actually, make it a double." She leaned on the bar heavily as the bartender moved off to pour her drink.

I nudged her shoulder. "Talking to my dad has driven you to drinking?"

"Donna." She straightened, looking at me warily.

I frowned. "Shit. It actually did? What did he say?"

"No, it's not like that. He was lovely. I . . ." She took a deep breath and gave me her customer service smile. "It's Christmas. We don't need to talk about this. Are you having a drink?"

The bartender placed a glass of amber liquid in front of her, and she took a big sip and winced slightly.

"I'm eighteen," I reminded her. "And you run a legal center."

"Ha! Yeah, right. Sorry."

"Jasmin, come on. What's going on? I'm not going to be able to stop worrying. You may as well just tell me."

She watched me warily for a moment, then took another sip of her scotch and nodded. "OK, let's sit somewhere."

Shit. A sit-down conversation. What the hell was this serious? As trepidation clawed at the base of my rib cage, I led her to a chaise lounge in the foyer, away from the party going on in the main living area of the house.

Jasmin was a direct woman—she had to be in her field of work—and she cut right to the chase. "I'm so sorry, Donna, but I have to terminate your volunteer position at the center, effective immediately."

I reeled back as if she'd slapped me. Of all the things I thought she might say, that wasn't even on the list. "What? Why? What did I do?"

"You didn't do anything. You're perfect. But through talking to your father and one of his financial advisors, I realized you or your family are behind a very generous donation we received recently."

"Oh god." I gritted my teeth and resisted the urge to cause a scene. "That was supposed to be anonymous. They shouldn't even be talking about it at a party, for god's sake."

"It was anonymous." She covered my hand with hers, her other tightening around her drink. "And they didn't mention the donation or break any kind of confidentiality. But the mention of certain umbrella companies and trusts . . . it was just business talk for them, but the names were enough for me to put two and two together. I had to make sure, so I pulled your father aside, and he confirmed my suspicion. It was a very generous, kind thing for you to do. Which is why it's so hard for me to have to let you go."

"You didn't have to ask Dad about it. It was anonymous. You could've let it stay anonymous."

"You know I couldn't do that." She gave me a look full of regret. I did know that. She was a stickler for the truth, a tough woman with a strong sense of right and wrong. It was why she was so good at her job.

"I know. I'm sorry. I'm just frustrated. But I still don't see why this means I have to stop volunteering. It's not illegal to donate both money and time, is it?"

"No, it's not. But we have our own company bylaws. We take several students as volunteers every year—most of them use it on their college applications, and along with the connections they're able to make with the attorneys who come to volunteer their services . . . the situation is rife for exploitation. We can't accept money from volunteers or their families. I'm so sorry, Donna, but your donation was very generous. There's no way in hell the board will let me return it to keep you on board for another couple of months."

The fact that she'd even considered returning the money told you all you needed to know about this woman's character.

"I'm so sorry." I wasn't even sure if that was the right thing to say.

"I'm sorry too. But listen, you don't even need us anymore. You've volunteered for over a year. I'm going to write you the best letter of recommendation that ever was, and I just know you'll get that internship with Horowitz, Ross, and Shore."

She didn't know it had already been awarded to someone else. I hadn't even told my parents. I needed this on my college application more than anyone knew. What the hell was I going to do now?

"Right. Of course." I smiled and got to my feet, my hand sliding out from under hers the same way the floor felt as if it were sliding out from under me.

The dress was squeezing all the air out of my lungs; my vision was starting to blur at the edges. I needed to get out of there immediately.

"See that man in the pale blue suit? He's had three champagnes, and I know for a fact this is his sweet spot for opening his wallet. Go schmooze him into a donation for the center."

"Donna, I'm not worried about that right now. Are you OK?"

"I'm totally fine." I squeezed her shoulder; my breaths were coming in shorter and shallower. "I'd introduce you myself, but I really need to go to the bathroom. Sorry."

I turned on my heel and rushed away before she could stop me.

Avoiding everyone's eyes, I took purposeful steps across the foyer. Joseph Frydenberg and Raine Clayton were standing in the corridor leading to the powder room, locked in an intense-looking conversation, but I hurried past, too weighed down by my own shit to worry about Will's dad having another affair.

I managed to control my steps and my breathing until I was in the kitchen with only the catering staff to witness my face falling, my shoulders slumping, my breaths turning to desperate pants for oxygen. But they were all too busy to notice me at all. I stumbled to the back door, steadying myself on the frame while clawing at the front of my dress.

I couldn't breathe. *Why couldn't I breathe?*

Rushing into the dark night, my vision flickering in and out, I walked past the patio and reached behind me with frantic fingers to yank down my dress's zipper. The pressure that had been cutting into my waist all night finally eased, and I gulped down cold air, my feet still carrying me away from the light and noise spilling out of the main house.

My heel caught in a groove between pavers, so I kicked off my shoes and continued down the path barefoot, relishing the sting of the cold night air as my dress slipped down my shoulders.

I walked to the pool and dropped the dress at my feet. My toes touched the curved edge of the pavers in the same spot Hendrix's boots had been that night.

At the thought of him, a sob tore from my throat.

More uncertainty, more confusion.

I wanted him here, but I hardly knew him. He'd probably make me feel worse, but I just wanted him to hold me the way he had at the Halloween party.

I *hated* that I wanted that, that I craved comfort from some guy. I was supposed to be strong, independent, smart. How the hell was my life falling apart this badly?

I didn't know what to do with myself. Going back to the party was not an option. Finding my friends in this state was not an option. There was only one thing to do—keep moving forward.

I stepped off the edge and into the frigid black water.

It enveloped me, wrapped its smooth coolness

around every inch of my body, muted the faraway noises of the party. It wasn't *his* embrace, but it was an embrace of sorts. A muted oblivion I craved more the longer I held my breath and stayed under.

The burning in my lungs made me feel alive. I opened my mouth, squeezed my eyes shut, and screamed. Air bubbles burst from my mouth, floating up, up, up as I released all the pent-up ugliness inside me into the water.

Once I had no air left, my body reacted on instinct. My feet and arms pushed me to the surface, and I gasped, spluttering and coughing, taking air into my lungs once more. But I felt cleansed. I'd let all that other, ugly air out, and I was taking this new, fresh air in.

My limbs felt drained when I reached the edge, and I leaned on the side of the pool to catch my breath.

I needed to clear my head properly, reset, have a break. I needed Davey's. It had been weeks since I'd gone, reluctant to return after what happened with Hendrix in the alleyway. For some reason, I couldn't imagine taking any other guy out there.

But enough was enough. I just needed to not think about anything for a little while so I could get back to thinking clearly. Going to Davey's was the only surefire way to do that. I'd have to wait a few days, just get through Christmas, then Harlow would go into a routine of staying up to a stupid hour and sleeping half the day, and Mom and Dad would go back to work until New Year's. It would be risky, but I could make it work. After all, the risk factor was half the appeal.

Mind made up, I felt better already. And I was shivering.

I waded to the stairs at the end of the pool and dragged myself out, dripping disappointment and failure all over the travertine.

I pulled my dress on over my soaked underwear and tights, slipped into the house through a side door, and locked myself in my bedroom.

CHAPTER 15

Hendrix

"HUH?" I GLANCED AT SHADY WHEN HE BUMPED my shoulder, but almost instantly, my eyes were drawn back to the good girl gone bad.

For all the effort she put into playing a party girl—the messy hair, the heavy makeup, the slutty clothes—she still looked as if she owned this dump and the whole damn town. Even that motherfucking leopard-print minidress somehow looked sophisticated on her. Some women just had that inexplicable class you couldn't hide. It was why anyone with a dick was watching her as intently as I was as she danced along to some grungy shit. Two games of pool had completely ground to a halt, the bikers at the tables drooling over their own beards as they leaned on their pool cues.

"Dude!" Shady whacked me on the shoulder this time.

I didn't hesitate to shove his skinny ass back.

"What?" I scowled, and he threw his hands up, his mouth twitching into a smile.

"Are you listening at all?" He righted himself on his barstool and took another sip of his bourbon and dry.

I took a long sip of my own drink—mineral water with lemon—and tried to remember what he was talking about. I had no fucking clue. I'd tuned him out completely so I could watch her.

My eyes started to drift to the dance floor again, but I ground my teeth and stopped myself.

"Yeah, yeah. I heard you," I mumbled to Shady, hoping it was vague enough to fool him. No way in hell was I about to admit I was distracted by a quality piece of ass.

"Sweet." He sat up a little straighter. "So, you're in?"

Fuck. That couldn't be good. With Shady, he could be asking for anything from a lift home to a kidney.

"That's not what I said." I gave him a reproachful look. "I'll think about it."

He eyed me for a second, eyes narrowing in suspicion, then nodded. "All right."

Hopefully I hadn't just agreed to consider selling a pound of pills to the spoiled rich kids at my school for him. The guy had a big heart, but his sense of morality was beyond skewed.

Shady downed the rest of his drink and waved the bar chick over. I could no longer stop my eyes from looking for Donna in the crowd.

She was definitely a complication, but I couldn't

seem to get her off my mind, her smell out of my nose, the feel of her ridiculously soft skin from under my palms. She was *everywhere*, and I wanted her to be *nowhere* so I could get through the next few months and get the fuck out of this town, maybe even this country.

I wanted her gone so badly, but when I scanned the crowd and couldn't see her light hair or ridiculous dress, I frowned. Where was she? I'd only looked away for a few minutes to get Shady off my back.

Did she take another guy out to the dumpsters? My teeth clenched so hard I was close to cracking one. I was half off my barstool before I knew what I was doing, but then Shady's hand appeared on my chest.

"Seriously?" he said. "What the fuck is up with you tonight, bro? I don't think you've heard half of what I've said."

The urge to pick his lanky ass up and throw him over the bar was overwhelming, but this was why I didn't drink anymore. Just as quickly as the murderous rage came over me, I leashed it, shoved it back into its cage, and slammed the door shut. I'd die before I threw another fist.

I rolled my head and took a deep breath . . . and that's when I spotted her.

She came out of the ladies' room, quickly wiping away the look of disgust that marred her perfect features. I laughed under my breath and lowered myself back onto the stool. She liked to play the bad girl, but she was grossed out by the nasty bathroom in the dodgy bar. You can take the girl out of the private school, but you can't take the privilege out of the girl.

My eyes tracked her as she made her way toward the bar, but I looked away before she got too close. I couldn't have her catching me staring like a dweeb. I wouldn't want her to get the wrong idea. As I turned away, my eyes landed on Shady's amused expression.

He looked over my shoulder, then back to me and grinned. Shit.

"Now it all makes sense." He chuckled.

"I don't know what you're talking about," I mumbled, taking another sip of my soda water.

"Her name is Donna." As if I didn't already know her name. As if I didn't know what she looked like when she came on my fingers. "But don't get your hopes up. She just comes here for a bit of fun."

"Isn't that why we all come here?" I raised a brow.

He laughed. "Yeah, but Donna . . ." He shook his head and blew out a big breath. "She's amazing in the sack, but she's fucking crazy, man. Just be careful."

Of course she'd fucked Shady. Had she opened her legs to every douchebag in this dump? For the second time that night, I resisted the urge to do violent damage to one of my only friends in this world.

"Noted," I informed him, my attention already drawn to the other end of the bar. She was leaning over it with her ass sticking out, the bar chick checking out her tits. Half the women here were into her too.

"Want me to intro? I'm not weirded out by sharing pussy if you aren't." Shady leaned forward and broke my line of sight. "Hell, she'd probably be into a threesome if you're game."

Three times—that was *three* times I'd wanted to drive my fist through his teeth in the space of half an hour. Because of *her*.

I opened my mouth to tell him to fuck off, but before I could, something behind me caught his eye.

"Shit. Never mind. I gotta go talk to a man about a dog." He downed the rest of his drink and disappeared into the crowd without even waiting for a response. I didn't even want to know what shit he was getting into now.

My view of Donna was unobstructed again. I tried really hard not to stare, but it was fucking impossible when I knew what her tits felt like in my hands. Now they were resting on the bar, and I wanted to pulverize the bar. This was ridiculous. I huffed, disgusted with myself, just as she looked up and our eyes met.

She glared at me and paid for her drink. Something inside me stirred at the anger in her gaze. The two times we'd hooked up, she was livid. It was as if my dick had learned that anger in her eyes meant action. I adjusted myself as she marched over, her shoulders back, tits and hair bouncing.

I gulped my drink, both dreading and craving whatever was about to come.

She leaned one hand on the bar and propped the other on her hip. "We hook up a couple of times, and you all of a sudden think you have the right to follow me around? Seriously?"

I turned my head but kept my body facing the bar, shielding my vital organs from her perfectly manicured claws. "I'm pretty sure I'm the least creepy guy in this dump, but whatever."

"Stop deflecting, Hendrix. Did you follow me here?"

I frowned, letting some of my frustration show. "You may be under the delusion that you own Devilbend, but in case you haven't noticed, Dorothy, this isn't Kansas. No, I didn't fucking follow you, and I have just as much right to be here as you. Which, technically, is none, since we're both underage."

She scoffed and crossed her arms. "OK, *mom*. Just stay out of my way."

"You're the one who came over here and started screeching at me. I'm literally just sitting here minding my own business. *You* stay out of *my* way."

Her lips pursed as her breathing quickened slightly, those perfect tits swelling with every inhale. It took more than a little effort to keep my eyes off them, but I did. I gave myself a mental high five and smiled. I knew I looked every bit the self-satisfied asshole she thought I was, but her obvious fury only made my smile wider.

This was kind of fun.

"What are you doing here anyway?" She chugged her drink and didn't even wince, making me wonder if she was pulling the same trick with the soda and lemon I was.

"Same thing you're doing here." *Lies.* But she didn't need to know that. To drive my point home, I looked over her shoulder, spotted a tall brunette with waves down to her jean-clad ass, and eyed her up and down the same way every other deadbeat had been ogling Donna all night.

She followed my gaze and scoffed. "You're such a pig. Just stay out of my way."

Without giving me a chance to reply, she moved back to the other end of the bar, but I watched her check out the brunette as she passed. She had that appraising look all women had when sizing up their competition—pursed lips, one raised eyebrow, the quick up-and-down glance.

I covered my mouth to hide the grin I couldn't hold back.

This was a dangerous game Donna Mead and I were playing, but it was the most fun I'd had in a long time.

Unfortunately, the brunette must've noticed me checking her out, because she suddenly appeared in front of me, blocking my view of Donna.

"Hi." She smiled and looked at me through long lashes. Her glossy lips wrapped around a straw, and she took a long pull of her drink.

She was pretty, and I probably would've gone for it had I not still been hard for the infuriating, entitled bitch who had just walked away.

I gave her a disinterested "hey."

Her boobs pressed against my arm as she leaned in to say something, but between the loud music and my every sense acutely keeping track of Donna, I didn't hear a word. She just wasn't going away though, and really, she didn't deserve to be led on.

I looked at her properly. "Listen, can I be honest?"

She nodded.

"I'm interested in someone else. When I checked you out, I was just trying to make her jealous."

She pouted but gave me a smile. "The cute blonde?"

"Yeah." My eyes sought her out in the crowd again. She was dancing with some thirty-year-old-looking motherfucker with a beard and hand tats, but she kept glancing in my direction. Was she trying to make *me* jealous?

"She's a lucky girl."

I scoffed. "I don't know about that."

"Is she still looking?"

I glanced over her shoulder. "Yeah."

The brunette gave me a cheeky smile and leaned in, trailing a hand up my arm and across my shoulders. Then she tilted her head and tucked it into my neck. I wrapped an arm around her waist and angled my body into her. It would've looked as though she was kissing my neck and I was into it. I mean . . . I wasn't *not* into it . . . but only because I knew it was probably making Donna furious.

"You smell amazing too," the brunette said. "Such a shame."

"Thanks for being cool about it." I gave her hip a squeeze.

She shrugged and smiled one last time before turning and making her way to the exit.

Do not look at Donna. Do not *look at Donna.* Do not look at Donna.

I downed the rest of my drink and mentally patted myself on the back for not looking at Donna as I got off the barstool and headed for the exit too. It was time to go home. If Donna happened to think I was leaving with the brunette, that was her problem.

But as I skirted the edge of the dance floor, I couldn't help taking a glance.

Right away, my eyes caught the flick of her light hair as she turned, the hand-tat guy leading her toward the bar. Another guy with a low ponytail and a bit of a beer gut leaned into her other side, and she laughed at whatever he said.

She glanced behind her, and I slunk into the shadows, leaning back against the wall. Something didn't sit right, and I wasn't willing to admit to myself that I hated seeing her with two lowlifes. So I stayed and watched like the creep she'd accused me of being.

They went to the bar and ordered drinks. Three glasses were delivered—two with amber liquid and one with clear. At least she was still smart enough to stay sober.

Hand tats told some kind of joke, getting her full attention as they all laughed. While she was facing him, ponytail reached into his pocket and dumped something into her drink.

I pushed off the wall, my hands tightening into fists. What the fuck? Did no one else see that?

Of course fucking not. Everyone here was too drunk or high, too wrapped up in their own shit. Before I could bulldoze my way through the crowd and stop her, they cheersed, and she gulped down most of her drink in one go. I had no idea what they'd given her, but I wasn't sure I could take them both. I just knew I couldn't let her out of my sight, couldn't let them take her from here.

This was none of my business—I'd been heading out the door anyway—and Donna was a bitch, but she didn't deserve this. *No one* deserved this.

So I hung around for a little while and watched.

She stumbled over her own feet while standing still, and hand tats steadied her before sharing a grin with ponytail. My vision went red, thoughts of tearing the fuckers to pieces assaulting my mind. But I had to keep my shit together.

Keeping Donna in my periphery, I scanned the crowd and spotted Shady at the end of the bar area. I beelined for him, bumping into drunks and bikers as I went. Donna was leaning heavily on the bar now with her head in her hands, while the two men hovered like the predators they were.

"Shady." I interrupted his conversation with a smack on the shoulder, barely sparing him a glance.

"Hendy, bro, I'm in the middle of some business here," he ground out.

I grabbed him by the collar of his tracksuit and leaned in close. "Some pieces of shit just drugged Donna. I can't take them alone. Come on, man."

I wasn't above begging, but I hoped the asshole's humanity would kick in before I had to.

Shady got to his feet and excused himself from the conversation he'd been having, ordering another round of expensive whiskey and stating he'd be right back after he took out the trash. Then he gestured to two of his buddies.

I kept my focus on Donna. Her feet started falling out from under her, and the two scum propped her up on either side and started helping her stumble toward the exit.

I rushed toward them, no longer caring if I had to take the two of them alone, no longer caring if I had to take *twenty*.

We cut them off barely ten feet from the door.

"Let her go," I growled, already reaching for her. Her eyes rolled into the back of her head, then focused, then rolled again.

"Back off, asshole." Ponytail scowled. He was even uglier up close.

"Hen . . . hel . . . h . . . ," Donna mumbled. Was she trying to say my name or "help"? It didn't matter. She was getting both.

Shady and his guys finally caught up. They didn't ask questions. They simply shoved the two shit stains out of the way as I stepped in and wrapped my arms around Donna. As I held her delicate frame against my chest, her legs gave out, her arms went completely limp, and her head rolled back.

Panic choked me; the shriveled thing in my chest passing for a heart constricted, then started hammering.

I scooped her up and pushed the door open with my shoulder. All I knew was that I had to get her out of there. Maybe to a hospital.

Shady caught up with me halfway to my car.

"How's she doin?'" He brushed some hair off her forehead. Lucky for him, both my hands were busy holding the unconscious waif of a girl.

"I don't know," I growled. "What the fuck did they give her?"

"Just a roofie."

This time I growled but no words came out. *Just* a roofie?

Shady gave me a sharp look as we stopped at my Tesla. "Chill, bro. She won't remember shit in the morning, but she'll be fine. They were trying to knock her out, not kill her. Rohypnol is a benzo—it's like she's taken a couple of xannies. It's not gonna kill her or anything."

In place of an answer, I gave him an instruction. "Get the door."

"You want me to take her, man? I'll take care of it. I've known this chick for a while." He opened the car door wide and stepped out of the way.

"No," I barked. I didn't trust anyone with an unconscious Donna, let alone a guy who went by Shady. But I forced my tone to lighten up as I lowered her gently into the passenger seat. "I got it. She goes to my school. We . . . I know her. I'll make sure she's safe."

Shady remained silent as I fastened the seat belt over Donna's limp body.

"You sure?" His eyes flicked between us as I straightened.

"I'm sure. Are you sure that's what they gave her?

Maybe I should take her to a hospital."

He cringed and rubbed the back of his neck. "I wouldn't, bro. It would look hella sus, you bringing in a chick you hardly know, roofied. Aren't you supposed to be staying out of trouble?"

I didn't give a shit what kind of trouble it landed me in. I wasn't about to risk someone's life—not again.

"Anyway"—he shrugged—"it's definitely Rohypnol. We beat it out of 'em pretty quick."

I sighed, said goodbye to Shady, and got into the driver's side. Even though I didn't care what kind of questions a hospital visit would raise, I knew Donna would. No one knew about her secret little walks on the wild side, but maybe it was time they did.

CHAPTER 16

Donna

I wasn't sure if the pounding in my head had woken me or if waking up had caused the pounding. All I knew was that I felt like shit.

I groaned, squeezing my eyes shut and mushing my face farther into the pillow. My stomach felt as if it were doing somersaults while twirling my intestines into a knot. I was so fucking hungover that—

My eyes flew open, immediately making me wince against the light, but I had bigger problems. There was no way I could be hungover, because I hadn't been drinking last night. I never drank or did drugs when I went to Davey's.

Panic clawed at my throat as I forced myself to look around. The sheets were gray, the desk under the window cluttered, a TV sat in the corner. *This wasn't my room.*

Where the hell was I?

How did I get here?

What happened to me?

Fighting the bile rising up my throat, I lifted myself into a sitting position and couldn't help groaning again. I'd never felt this crap before—not even when I had the flu last year. And that was so bad the doctors nearly put me on IV fluids.

The fact that I had no idea where I was or any memory of how I got there was beyond disturbing. I wasn't an idiot—I knew what happened to girls in shady bars sometimes. It was why I went there—the danger of the *maybe*. I just never thought I'd actually end up . . . *oh god*. I sucked in several deep breaths, fighting for air through the panic and the nausea and the hot tears pricking my eyes.

Was I raped?

I swallowed a sob and, with shaky hands, pushed the comforter and tangled sheets off myself completely. I was still in my leopard-print dress, my thong still in place. The only things missing were my shoes, but I spied them on the floor at the foot of the bed.

I shifted my legs. I didn't feel sore between them, but would I? If I was out and didn't fight it . . .

The room spun, bringing on another wave of nausea, and I lowered myself back to the pillow with a pathetic half sob, half whimper.

I had to get the fuck out of there, but I couldn't even get my body to stand.

Closing my eyes, I forced myself to take deep breaths through the churning in my stomach and the pounding in my head. I needed to get my shit together and get up.

My eyes flew open again at the sound of the door opening, but the only movement I could force my body into was rolling onto my back and turning my head to look.

"Hendrix?"

He was barefoot, in sweats and a T-shirt that was baggy even on his broad, muscular frame. One of his hands clutched a bright pink mug.

"Oh. Hey. You're up." I'd never seen the asshole look so uncertain. His eyes flicked about the room, not staying on me too long. "How . . . uh . . . you OK?"

"Am I . . ." My bruised brain was struggling to keep up, not processing information at its usual rate, but I got there in the end. "No, I'm not fucking OK. What did you do to me?"

I didn't shout—I *seethed*, spitting my accusation at him, as hot as the liquid in his steaming mug.

He threw his free hand up and stepped away until his back was to the door.

Was he trying to block my exit?

"I didn't do anything to you. All I did was bring you here, take your shoes off, and tuck you into bed." His voice was calm, low, deep.

More confusion. Why couldn't I remember anything? "Whose bed is this?"

"Mine."

My eyes narrowed. "You expect me to believe . . . that . . . I . . . you . . ."

I growled and punched the bed next to me, then threaded my fingers through my hair. I'd never been this incoherent, *ever*.

"I didn't hurt you." Hendrix's voice was still calm, but now it had a hard edge to it. "I'm not a rapist. I've done a lot of bad shit—and one awful, unforgiveable thing—but I didn't hurt you. No one hurt you. You're safe."

I lifted my head to look at him, breathing hard. An infuriating tear fell down my cheek, but there was no pity in Hendrix's gaze. He looked tired more than anything—bags under his eyes, hair a mess, eyelids drooping. As if to prove my point, he yawned and took a gulp of what I assumed must be coffee.

"You look worse than I feel," I said as I slowly sat up again. The nausea was easing somewhat.

"Thanks," he deadpanned.

"What happened to you?"

"Someone had to make sure you kept breathing all night." He looked away, took another sip.

All night? "What the fuck happened to me, Hendrix?"

"What's the last thing you remember?" He dragged his feet across the room and plonked down into the chair at his desk, backward, his arms resting on the back.

I looked down and forced myself to really think about it.

I remembered dancing at Davey's, feeling all my worries melt away into the sticky floor and the heavy bass of the music.

I remembered Hendrix, the immediate pang of irritation, how hard it was to ignore his presence.

I remembered us bickering at the bar, and then . . .

"I was dancing with these two guys." I swallowed, my gaze still on his gray comforter. "You left with the brunette. We went to the bar . . ." I trailed off and looked at him. He was resting his chin on his arms, watching me, waiting. I cleared my throat. "Bea, the bar chick—she knows never to pour me alcohol, regardless of whether I order it or someone else does. It doesn't make sense . . ."

"Bea didn't pour vodka into your soda. One vodka doesn't make you pass out cold within twenty minutes. The two lowlifes you were hanging out with roofied you."

I blinked once, slowly. When I woke up in a strange bed with no memory of how I got there, I'd suspected as much, but having him say it in plain English brought the fact home. I dropped my gaze and swallowed around the lump in my throat. I *really* didn't want to cry in front of Hendrix Hawthorn—again.

"Are you sure . . ." I wasn't even positive what I was asking. That it wasn't any other drug? That it actually happened?

"I watched them slip it into your drink. Shady and his boys beat the details out of them while I got you out of there. I was going to take you straight to a hospital, but I wasn't sure you'd want that, considering no one even knows about . . . your visits to Davey's. So I sat in the parking lot googling the shit out of Rohypnol, and when I was convinced you weren't about to die on me, I decided to just take you home. But then I started getting paranoid about what kind of home situation I'd be dropping you into. So then I fished your phone out of your purse to call one of your friends, but you have a damn passcode on it. I was gonna ring Turner so I could talk to Mena, but by that stage, I was questioning whether to bring your friends into it at all. In the end, I decided to bring you here. To my place. I figured I'd pick up and explain if someone called, but it didn't ring all night."

Of course it didn't ring. No one even knew I was out of my bed. He finished off his coffee, his gray eyes boring into mine over the mug's rim.

He hadn't left with the brunette. He'd seen someone trying to drug me and stepped in to prevent them doing worse. He took care of me, stayed up all night to make sure I was OK . . .

I frowned at him, trying to figure it out. We'd hardly spoken, had two admittedly hot but mostly rage-fueled hookups. He'd said on more than one occasion that he wanted nothing to do with me, and I couldn't count the number of times I'd wished he'd just disappear and stop complicating my life.

He returned my frown, leaning back against the desk. "Look, believe what you want, but that's the truth."

"I believe you," I rushed out. "I'm just . . . not feeling the best."

His cloudy expression lifted, and he got to his feet.

"No wonder. Nausea and fatigue are common aftereffects of being roofied. It's like an extremely bad hangover—you might be super tired for a few days and nauseated, and you might have diarrhea. I can take you to the hospital to get checked out if you want."

"No." I shook my head, immediately regretting it as pain shot through my skull. "That was a good call. No hospital. No records. No one can know about this. And please never talk to me about having the runs again. Just . . . drive me to my car. What time is it?" Eventually someone would come knocking on my bedroom door.

"Your secret's safe with me, princess. You can shower if you want." He pointed to a closed door next to his desk. "I'll get you some breakfast. I have better shit to do with my time than play *Driving Miss Daisy* today, but you've had a rough night, so I'll cut you some slack and drive you to your carriage."

Despite the horrid way I felt, the hint of a smile pulled at my lips. Snark was familiar territory for us, and it was making me feel better.

He collected his empty mug; gave me an exaggerated, mocking bow; and closed the door with a soft *click* on his way out.

I checked my phone and cringed. It was just after nine. Harlow would still be in bed, and Mom and Dad had mentioned brunch with the Frydenbergs. I'd been planning to be in bed when they left, but now I probably had two hours max before they got home. I hoped that was enough time to drive to Davey's and back.

But first—shower. I could've skipped it to save time,

but I felt gross, dirty. I dragged my ass out of Hendrix's bed, doing my best not to think about the fact that I was *in Hendrix's bed*, in his room, in his house. What would he be doing if I wasn't here?

In the bathroom, a wave of nausea hit me so fucking hard I literally collapsed onto the floor. Luckily, I was close enough to the toilet that I was able to get to it before I vomited, my stomach spasming violently.

Once I was positive I was done puking, I pulled myself to my feet and found a clean towel and some dark gray sweats folded neatly on the counter. I frowned, struggling to reconcile this thoughtful side of him with the antagonistic prick I'd gotten to know and . . . er . . . just know.

After a quick shower where I was forced to use his shampoo and bodywash, I dressed quickly, pulling the sweatshirt over my head. When I paused and brought the fabric up to my nose—closing my eyes and inhaling the fresh, clean scent with just a hint of cinnamon—I froze.

The mindless act had me wondering if I hadn't been given some other drug the previous night—one that altered your personality. I scowled at myself in the mirror, wrenched the sweatshirt back off, and threw it into the far corner.

Grudgingly, I pulled my leopard-print dress back on but wore it like a tank, tucked into the too-long borrowed sweats.

I stashed my bra and thong in my purse and headed for the door, but I paused just before my hand touched the doorknob. What if his parents didn't know I was here? I didn't want to get him in trouble. I also didn't want to deal with any more human interaction than absolutely necessary.

Before I could make a decision, the door flew open, nearly whacking me in the nose. "Fuck! Watch it!"

The surprised look on Hendrix's face melted into annoyance. "Who the fuck just stands in front of a door like that?"

"Who the fuck goes barging into a room so violently?"

"It's my room."

"I could've been naked." I crossed my arms, fully aware that it was pushing my tits up—and getting way more satisfaction than I should have when he glanced down at them.

"Were you?" His voice dropped, and he smirked.

I rolled my eyes. Even if I wanted to entertain the idea of hooking up with this infuriating asshole again, I still felt like death warmed up. The shower had helped, but it wasn't magic.

"Can we get going? I need to be home before anyone realizes I'm not."

"Do you want to eat something first?"

My stomach roiled at the mere mention of food, and I shook my head, breathing through my nose.

"OK." He rubbed my back for a moment but didn't linger. In a few seconds, he'd pulled on some socks and tennis shoes and jammed a baseball cap onto his head. I wished it was that easy for girls to get ready. I wished anything was that easy for me. But perfection took time and effort.

He led me through the silent, empty house and out the front door. I wanted to ask where his parents were, if he had siblings, but I kept my mouth shut. It was a nice place, not as big or ostentatious as mine, but respectable. I supposed it would have to be if they could afford to send him to Fulton Academy.

Once we got on the road, his Tesla gliding smoothly around corners, I realized he lived only a few streets away from me. I ducked lower in the seat and sighed. I'd have to drive forty minutes to get my damn car, only to come back to essentially the same place.

He was silent until we hit the freeway, then he reached over and turned on the stereo. Metallica blasted out of the speakers, and I cried out at the pounding in my head, clapping my hands over my ears. He turned it down. I glared at him and turned it *off*.

"No music. Just . . . no anything. God, I wish the sun would fuck off." I covered my eyes with my elbow and groaned. It was a chilly winter day, but the California sun was shining as brightly as ever. *Dick.*

Hendrix's cinnamon scent hitting the back of my nose made me crack an eye open. He'd leaned over to open the glove box and was pulling out a pair of Ray-Bans, which he handed to me. They were super dark, and I jammed them over my eyes immediately.

I looked over and studied him from behind the anonymity of the shades. Once again, he'd done something thoughtful without being asked.

Who the fuck are you, Hendrix Hawthorn?

I pushed the thought away as soon as I could. He'd already thrown me off-balance. I needed less Hendrix in my life, not more. What I needed more of was control.

As I studied his profile—the slight kink in his nose, the way his jaw tensed and relaxed as he chewed his gum, the corded muscle in his forearm as he gripped the steering wheel—I realized I still hadn't thanked him. I may have decided to keep him out of my life and my thoughts, but he had saved me from something I could hardly think about without feeling as if I might vomit.

I may have been a bitch, but I gave credit where it was due.

I cleared my throat and sat up a little straighter. "Hendrix?"

He hummed in response, keeping his eyes on the road.

"About last night . . ."

"Yeah?"

"Thank you."

He shifted in his seat, but before he could speak, I rushed on. "I know you don't like me, and I don't like you, so what you did for me last night—it means a lot. You could've just walked away. I wouldn't have blamed you. I got myself into that position. But you didn't. You could've been putting yourself in danger by doing that. Anyway, I'm rambling. Point is, I know it was no small thing, you stepping in and stopping them from . . ." I had to swallow and take a breath, but I made myself say it. ". . . from taking me. Maybe raping and killing me. You may very well have saved my life, and I'm grateful."

He was silent for a bit longer.

"You didn't," he finally said, and I frowned in confusion. "What you said about putting yourself in that position—don't blame yourself. I mean, going to Davey's is stupid and dangerous, but it is not your fault that those skid marks decided to drug you and hurt you. That's on them."

"I'm not victim blaming myself, you jerk. I know it wasn't my fault. I'm trying to thank you."

"Fine. Good. You're welcome." His hand tightened on the steering wheel, and he chewed his gum a little faster.

I stared out the window, wondering briefly if it was even safe for me to be driving yet. But I was feeling better after the shower.

It wasn't long before we were pulling into the empty parking lot of Davey's. Miraculously, my white BMW was still there and not stripped for parts, despite how out of place it looked among the cracked concrete and chain-link fencing.

"Donna." Hendrix's serious tone made me pause as I unfastened my seat belt.

"Yeah?"

"Are you going to stop going? After last night . . ."

I bristled and took Hendrix's sunglasses off so I could narrow my eyes at him properly. The thought had crossed my mind. Was the sense of freedom, the brief escape that Davey's provided, worth the risk? Shit had gotten pretty real the night before. But who the fuck did he think he was to assume he could ask me that?

"I don't know," I gritted out, reminding myself he'd done me a solid and I should cut him at least a little slack. "But that's not really any of your concern, is it?"

"Jesus." He rolled his eyes. "Why do you have to be so fucking defensive all the time? I'm just trying to look out for you."

"Why? Why do you give a shit? I'm nothing to you. We're nothing. I appreciate what you did last night, I really do, but that doesn't give you an automatic right to have an opinion regarding my life."

I got out of the car, my purse and heels clutched to my chest, not even caring that I was barefoot in a parking lot probably covered in needles.

"Thanks for the ride." I tried to say it in a neutral tone, but I was so riled up and raw from everything that it came out sounding sarcastic. Frustrated with myself, and the entire situation, I slammed the door shut.

His tires threw up dirt and gravel as he peeled out of the parking lot and disappeared.

Good. I didn't need anyone else trying to control my life. I had enough of that from society, from my parents, from my own damn self.

I hobbled to my car, scrambled into it quickly, and locked the doors. It felt as if someone was watching me. I knew it was just paranoia, but it still made my heart hammer in my chest and my hands shake a little as I reached for the ignition.

I'd wanted a thrill when I started coming to Davey's, an adrenaline rush. But I never wanted this.

CHAPTER 17

Hendrix

I DROVE STRAIGHT HOME, GRINDING MY TEETH and intentionally speeding—something I hadn't done since I'd left New York. I knew it was stupid, reckless, could send me right back there. But nothing else seemed to ease this infuriating pressure in my head, the incessant need to *do something* thrumming through my body.

I'd stuck exactly to the limit on the way there, unwilling to put Donna in any unnecessary danger—she did that plenty herself. But I'd be lying if I said it wasn't also to get more time with her.

She smelled like my shampoo, and her delicate, warm body was so close, drowning me in her scent mixed with mine. I wanted to pull over at least six times and just hold her, but I resisted. She would've kneed me in the balls and taken off with my car, and I wouldn't have blamed her. Not after what she'd just gone through.

That girl was spiraling. I didn't really know what her deal was, hadn't figured her out completely yet, but she'd been sloppy. Donna Mead was many things, but she was *not* sloppy. It had been desperation driving her, and she'd let her guard down.

Was it me? Maybe my presence had distracted her. No, fuck that! I wasn't about to blame myself for some despicable shit a couple of lowlifes pulled.

I just wanted her to stop going there before she got raped, murdered, or kidnapped into human trafficking. I'd carried her lifeless body out of there the night before. *Excuse me* for being concerned.

But no, all she saw was me sticking my nose into her business. God, she was fucking infuriating. Least of all because I wanted to *not* care. I wanted to call her a bitch, say I didn't give a shit what she did with her life, and actually mean it.

Lost in my rage-filled thoughts, I nearly shot past Aunt Hannah's house before slamming on the brakes and skidding to a stop.

Gripping the steering wheel so hard I felt as if it might snap in half, I forced a few deep breaths down my throat. When that didn't fucking work, I growled and got out of the car. Maybe blowing some shit up on a big screen would distract me.

I barreled into the house and slumped onto the couch, but instead of reaching for the remote, I found myself just clenching my fists repeatedly, thinking about how fucking helpless she'd looked passed out in my bed all night.

"Hey."

I shot to my feet at my aunt's casual greeting, every muscle in my body tense.

"Whoa." Her eyes widened in surprise, her OJ halfway to her mouth as she leaned against the wall. "Sorry to interrupt your intense scowling session there. You all right?"

"Shit." I ran my hands through my hair for about the millionth time in the past twenty-four hours. I was going to go bald at this rate. "Sorry. I . . . you just startled me. I'm fine." I forced a smile that felt fake to its core and lowered myself back to the couch. "I thought you were spending the day with Robbie."

"He got called into work, so I came home." She made her way over to sit down, took a sip of her juice, and looked at me expectantly.

"What?" I tried, and failed, to keep the irritation out of my tone.

"We had a deal, Hendrix. You come to me if you're in any kind of trouble. You're clearly not fine. Start talking, kid."

"I'm not a kid," I argued childishly.

"Then act like it and tell me what's going on."

Damn her and her logic. "Look, I'm not in any kind of trouble, OK? I promise. I'm sticking to our deal."

"Yeah, well, the deal included emotional and existential trouble, so . . ." She gestured for me to start talking.

I gave her a withering look. "I don't remember agreeing to that."

"Should've read the fine print." She took another sip of OJ. "Spill."

Her banter was a good distraction for about two minutes, but the restless, tight feeling in my body just wouldn't leave. Maybe talking about it would help. And my aunt was literally the only person I felt I could trust right now.

"I don't really know where to start."

"How about at the end?"

I laughed despite myself. "Usually people say start at the beginning."

"Yeah, but fuck them. Tell me where you just came from. Obviously it has something to do with this. Then we can work backward."

How the hell was I supposed to tell her I'd just come from dropping off a drugged girl at the seediest bar in the state? Hannah was cool, but even she wasn't *that* cool. Not to mention this wasn't technically even my problem.

"I . . . look . . . it's not really my story to tell. When I said I wasn't in trouble, I wasn't lying."

"But someone else is?"

"Not yet, but she will be if she keeps going like she is. But the fucked-up thing is that when you asked that, my first instinct was to say, 'Not if I have anything to do with it.'"

"Are you romantically involved with this girl?"

I snorted. "Trust me, there's been no romance."

There'd been heat, sexual release, a pull damn near impossible to resist, plenty of hurtful words, but no romance . . .

"OK, so then why do you care so much?"

"I don't know!" I pulled at my hair again. "That's a big part of the problem. I wanted to just come here, keep my head down, get good grades, and finish high school before figuring out how to make my life *mean something* after what I did. I didn't even want to make friends. I don't want anything to do with this. But every time I see her . . . doing some stupid shit, I just want to shake her. I see that desperate, caged-animal look in her eyes, and I know exactly how she feels, even if I don't really know her at all. Because I used to feel like that. I used to have that look in my eyes."

"You want to save her from making your mistakes."

I paused, thought about it. "Yes."

"You can't save people who don't want to be saved, Hendrix." She got a knowing, almost faraway look in her eyes, and I had a feeling she was talking about more than just my current situation.

"That's just it though. I think she does. She just won't admit it. And then she makes me feel like shit when I try to be there for her."

"Does she know? About . . ."

"No." I shook my head. "No one knows, and I'd like to keep it that way."

"Fair enough. But I think you should talk to her. In

a real way. Try to explain where you're coming from. Lay it all out, and then you have to be OK with what she does with that. You can't force someone to accept your help, but you can say your piece and move on knowing you did all you could."

"She won't talk to me." I slumped against the back of the couch.

"Make her." She shrugged. "You're a big strong man."

"I thought I was a kid."

"Clearly, I was mistaken."

"Did you just advise me to manhandle an innocent young girl?"

"I did no such thing. A man knows how to make someone hear him without resorting to violence or childish yelling." She gave me a pointed look.

I sighed and stared at the ceiling. She was right. I had to make her listen. This churning, unsettling feeling in my gut wouldn't go away until I did.

I got to my feet. "OK. I'll be back."

"Now?" Hannah bugged her eyes out.

"No time like the present. Life's too short. Carpe diem, et cetera, et cetera."

I grabbed my keys and waved over my shoulder as I headed right back to my car.

It took less than ten minutes to drive to her house. The big black metal gates were open wide, her ostentatious driveway curving up and around a bend. The top of the house was just visible in the distance.

I slowed down, nearly came to a stop ... then pushed down on the accelerator and drove off again, swearing under my breath. I'd driven over here determined to make her listen, but with no idea what I wanted to say.

After pulling over around the corner, I pinched the bridge of my nose. What exactly *did* I want to tell her? I definitely didn't want to detail my whole sordid past. I wasn't ready to talk to anyone about that, let alone the girl who'd managed to get under my skin more than anyone ever had.

Nearly half an hour went by as my mind wandered off on tangents, the same frustrations looping around and around, half-finished sentences floating past. None of it felt right.

I was getting nowhere.

"Fuck it." I started the car.

Driving around the block took almost as long as it had taken me to drive there in the first place, as the properties in the area were massive. I pulled into the driveway and made slow progress up the hill, then parked away from the imposing front doors, on the other side of the fountain.

No way was I going to slink up to that front door looking timid and unsure, so I squared my shoulders, ran a hand through my hair—*again*—and walked up the stairs steadily and confidently.

I rang the doorbell and resisted the urge to fidget as I waited.

Donna's mom pulled the door open—there was no

way the petite blonde in three-quarter yoga pants and a loose shirt was a servant. Plus, Donna and Harlow looked like her.

"Hello." She gave me a friendly smile, a hint of curiosity in her gaze. "How can I help you?"

This wasn't my first time introducing myself to rich, proper people or to the parents of a girl I wanted to speak to. I'd had more privileged pussy than I could count—way more practice at this than I cared to admit.

I pulled my Ray-Bans off and flashed her a grin. "Good afternoon, ma'am. I'm so sorry to bother you during the holidays. Please accept my apologies for showing up unannounced. If it wouldn't be too much trouble, I just need to speak with your daughter."

She watched me for a moment, amusement replacing the curiosity in her eyes. "Don't you kids all have cell phones for that?" She was teasing me. I liked her. Is this where Donna got her quick wit?

"Yes, we do, Mrs. Mead, but this is a conversation I'd prefer to have face to face."

"OK then." She looked me up and down one more time. "I'm guessing you're here to see Harlow?"

The younger sister appeared at her mother's side before I could respond, sliding over the highly polished marble in knee-high socks and an oversized hoodie. "Did I hear my name?" She hip-bumped her mother, then looked at me, and her eyes widened. "Ooh! Wow! This should be good. I'll get Donna."

She ran off as suddenly as she'd appeared.

Mrs. Mead raised her eyebrows and cocked her head. "Donna?"

"Yes, ma'am." I nodded, pressing my lips together.

"Come on in then." She stepped to the side and waved me in.

CHAPTER 18

Donna

I'D JUST DONE UP THE CLASP ON MY BRA WHEN Harlow barged into my room without knocking.

"You'll never guess who's here." She grinned, jumping up onto my bed like a deranged blonde gnome.

"What? Who?" I pulled on a pair of baggy sweats and dug around in my wardrobe for an old hoodie I hadn't worn in years.

She waited until the damn thing was half over my head before dropping the news. "Hendrix Hawthorn."

"*What*?" The word was barked out, but the thick fabric muffled my voice. I scrambled to pull the garment on the rest of the way and caught Harlow's ankle, sending her flopping down onto the bed. "What do you mean Hendrix is here? I'm not in the mood for pranks, Harls."

She shrugged, looking way too amused. "Don't know what to tell ya, sis. He's charming the yoga pants off Mom in the foyer as we speak. And he *specifically* asked for you."

"Fuck." I released my sister and raced for the door, not even caring about my unbrushed, wet hair.

As soon as I'd gotten back—just barely beating my parents home from their brunch—I'd taken another shower. The previous night had left me feeling dirty and off, not to mention I couldn't stop smelling Hendrix's fucking shampoo on myself. I'd had to drive home with my windows rolled down, the frigid air cooling my rage and washing the scent from my nose.

After I thoroughly shampooed—twice— conditioned, and scrubbed every inch of myself, I'd been looking forward to putting on some warm clothing and taking a nap. Oblivion seemed like a really good idea.

But no. Hendrix fucking Hawthorn had to ruin everything.

What the hell was he thinking coming to my house? Was he really going to snitch on me to my family? Maybe I shouldn't have been such a bitch to him when he dropped me off. I really didn't need this shit right now.

I rushed to the landing, then forced myself to slow down as I descended the stairs.

There he stood, chatting to my mom in the same outfit from earlier, his T-shirt stretching over his broad shoulders.

"Hello, Hendrix." I kept my voice even and detached as I reached the bottom.

"Hi, Donna." He gave me a tight smile.

"Hendrix tells me he goes to Fulton with you girls, but he seems to have expertly avoided mentioning what he's doing here." Mom chuckled, and Hendrix's smile became more genuine.

"Beats me." I shrugged. "But please excuse us while I find out."

I pulled Harlow's tennis shoes on—the only footwear by the door that Magda hadn't collected yet—and stepped outside.

"It was a pleasure to meet you, Mrs. Mead," Hendrix told my mother, and then I heard his footsteps follow me down the front stairs.

When I reached the bottom, I turned on him and crossed my arms. "What are you doing here?" I demanded, keeping my voice low and my expression neutral in case someone was watching from the window.

He stuffed his hands into his pockets. "I just came to talk."

"This couldn't wait?"

"Until school starts again? So you can keep avoiding me? Will there ever be a good time, Donna?"

Movement in the corner of my eye caught my attention, and I looked over to see my mom and Harlow standing in the bay window, not even remotely hiding the fact that they were watching us.

I rolled my eyes and took off. "Come on."

Hendrix grinned and waved at them before following me around the house all the way to the pool area.

"OK, so talk." I cocked a hip, squinting against the

sunlight glaring off the pool. It was already giving me a headache.

He huffed out a breath and ran a hand through his hair. Hints of auburn glinted under the direct sunlight, and I had the sudden urge to run my fingers through his dark hair too, see the colors shift at my touch.

"Look," he said, "I don't know why we keep ending up at each other's throats, and I'm sorry for driving off on you earlier. I just want to talk to you about Davey's."

I threw my head back and groaned. "Not this shit again."

"I don't want to argue. Just, please, hear me out."

I gave him a look, not even trying to mask my displeasure. "Will you leave if I do?"

He pressed his lips together and nodded, and I plonked down onto a lounger. Standing was starting to make me feel woozy again.

Hendrix sat down across from me and leaned his elbows on his knees. "Why do you go there?"

"Why do you care?"

"You said you'd hear me out."

"Yeah. I never agreed to answer questions."

"For fuck's sake, why do you have to be so difficult? I'm trying to help you."

"*Why do you care?*" I enunciated each word. I couldn't figure him out, and it was pissing me off. "Are you into me or something? You wanna be my boyfriend? Is that it?"

I was mocking him, but I also wasn't ready to hear his answer to that question.

I didn't think I could stand it if he said yes; everything would change.

I didn't think I could stand it if he said no; *nothing* would change.

Before he could answer, I barreled on. "Because this is never going to happen. And what's more, I'm not interested in being with someone who thinks they can control me, tell me where I can and can't go. My plan is to eventually settle down with William anyway."

"Will?" He looked somewhere between perplexed and disgusted. "That cardboard cutout of a guy? What could you possibly see in him? And what do you mean you plan to eventually settle down with him? This isn't 1876. You're either in love with the guy or you're not."

"I didn't ask for your opinion on my life choices, asshole! And I don't have to explain jack shit to you."

He ignored that and kept picking apart what I'd said. "And I'm not trying to control you. I'm trying to *understand* you, maybe help you avoid making the same mistakes I did."

"What the actual fuck are you talking about?" I dropped my head into my hands. Usually I at least partly enjoyed the challenge of verbal sparring, but today, I was just exhausted, beaten down. All I wanted to do was go to sleep. "You can't keep demanding to know deeply personal shit about me while not offering up any of your own, Hendrix."

He was silent for a long time. I just enjoyed the peace and quiet and watched a line of ants marching between the pavers near my feet.

"I moved here from New York, where I was born and grew up."

I lifted my head to look at him. He was in the same position across from me, but he was looking out at the view beyond the pool now, squinting against the sun just as I had.

"My parents are just as filthy rich and influential back home as yours are here," he continued. "I went to the best, most exclusive school on the East Coast—the only place harder to get into than Fulton. And I ruled that place. I'm not saying that to talk myself up. You know exactly what I mean, because it's the same position you're in at Fulton. People look up to you, follow your lead, want to be your friend. You can ruin their lives if you really want to. That's why I came to you at the very start—I knew if I wanted to be left alone, the quickest way to ensure it would be to piss you off."

He sighed and looked me dead in the eyes. "I know what it's like to have all those eyes on you, because I had them. I know what kind of immense pressure you're under, because I was. I may not know exactly what makes you crave the depravity and danger of Davey's, but I know that look in your eye. The desperate one that tells me you'll do anything to keep chasing that feeling you get. I had it too. Until I went too far. I did something . . . unforgiveable. Something that ruined *everything*. I just want to help you avoid it."

"What did you do?" I couldn't help myself. I had to know.

He winced and rubbed the back of his neck. "I can't

talk about it. I . . . I'm not sure if I can trust you with that. Yet."

"You know I could just find out, right? You've given me enough information to do some digging. It wouldn't take much."

"I know. But I also know you like a challenge." He smiled, but it didn't reach his eyes. And he was right, damn him. I wanted to hear it from his own lips.

"Donna, I know you're a strong, intelligent, independent woman." I bit the inside of my cheek to keep from smiling at the compliment. "I'm not trying to tell you what to do. But you know just as well as I do how dangerous Davey's is. After what happened last night, that should be painfully obvious. It's just not worth the risk anymore. Please stop going there."

He made good points, but it still felt as if he was telling me what to do, and I hated that beyond measure.

"No." I sat up and crossed my arms. "I've been going there for over a year. Last night was a first, and I won't let it happen again."

"For the love of . . . just. Let's try something else. Whenever you get the urge for some danger, just come to me. We'll go speeding on highways, or I can take you to an abandoned warehouse and we can break shit if you need to let off steam."

I was shaking my head. He didn't get it.

"Is it the random hookups? If it's sex you're after, I'm more than willing—"

"Don't." I pointed a warning finger in his face and got to my feet. "This conversation is over. You've said your piece. Now leave."

Motherfucker thought he was god's gift to women and his dick would solve all my problems. The arrogance. Although . . . if he fucked with his dick as well as he had with his fingers . . . No! I cut that train of thought right off.

He stood too, putting his Ray-Bans on. "If you continue to go to Davey's, I will find out, and I'll have to tell someone."

"Tell who? Who would even believe you?"

"Your friends? Your family?" He shrugged. "I'll just keep talking until someone takes it seriously. If you die and I did nothing when I knew you were going there . . . I can't have that on my conscience, Donna."

"Oh, so this is about you and your conscience? Fuck you!"

He started up the path back to the front of the house as I stared daggers at his back.

"I'll be watching you," he called over his shoulder.

I stuck both middle fingers up at him and gritted my teeth.

Once he was out of view, I took the other path up to the house and let myself in through a back door. Hoping Harlow and Mom were still glued to the front window, watching Hendrix leave, I rushed up the back stairs and into my room. I'd just lock myself in there and refuse to speak to them until they dropped it.

Mom was nowhere in sight, but Harlow and Amaya were perched cross-legged on my bed, looking at me with expectant expressions. As if it were fucking story time at the library and they were a couple of five-year-olds.

I heaved a defeated sigh and shut the door, leaning back against it. "Hey, Amaya. What are you doing here?"

"Harls texted me that you had an interesting visitor. I came right over." She grinned.

"And you didn't think to invite Mena?" I gave my sister an exaggerated look of disappointment.

She shrugged. "I did. She had to work. But demands a full blow-by-blow when she gets off."

"Blow-by-blow?" Amaya repeated, barely containing laughter.

Mirth bubbled up inside me too, and my shoulders began to shake. "When she gets off?"

All three of us burst into laughter. For the first time that morning, I felt a little better. They were being nosy and annoying, but at the end of the day, I knew they cared. They wanted the best for me, just as I wanted the best for them.

"OK, that's enough with the stalling." Amaya wiped the tears from under her eyes and fixed me with a look. "Spill."

I dragged my feet across the room and flopped onto the bed, face-first. "I don't wanna," I mumbled into the soft comforter.

Harlow kicked my hip. "Start talking or I'll tell Mom and Dad what really happened that time I had to get stitches at the back of my head."

I turned my head to glare at her. "You wouldn't."

"D, come on." Amaya started running her fingers

through my damp hair. It felt like heaven.

"It's not that big a deal, really. He's just being annoying." What the hell was I supposed to tell them? It all revolved around my trips to Davey's, and I couldn't tell them that. They'd make me stop going, or worse— try to go with me. I couldn't put them in that kind of danger.

"There had to be a damn good reason he came to our house," Harlow argued. "This is more than just your usual mutual disdain for each other."

"Just admit you hooked up with him. We won't judge you," Amaya said matter-of-factly.

I sat up. "What makes you think we hooked up?" Was it that obvious? Did other people know? God, I was completely losing my grip on reality.

They both looked at me as if I were an idiot.

"He came to your house." Amaya started listing things off while Harlow helpfully ticked them off on her fingers. "He braved meeting your parents. You were spotted talking in the kitchen at Mena's birthday." I knew that moment of weakness would come back to bite me. "You were spotted talking at the Halloween party. You thought he was hot that day we saw him at the gym. He riles you up like literally no other person on the planet. Your sexual chemistry is ridiculous, like some fanfic level of heat."

"Are you guys running an investigation or something? I feel attacked."

"Why won't you tell us?" For the first time, Harlow actually sounded a little hurt.

I had to tell them something, and it could definitely *not* be about Davey's or how spectacularly I was failing at everything lately—not until I fixed it. And we *had* hooked up; it wouldn't even be a lie.

"OK, fine, yes, Hendrix and I—" I didn't even get to finish the sentence; their excited squeals and proclamations of "I knew it" cut me off as they completely lost their shit, started bouncing on the bed, then pounced on me.

We ended up in a tangle, our heads at the foot of the bed.

"When?" Harlow demanded.

"Where?" Amaya added.

In the back of a dirty alleyway at a seedy bar just after I nearly fucked some guy whose name I don't even remember. "Um, a couple times. Once at school."

"At school?" they both yelled in unison.

"Yeah. I gave him a blow job in Mr. Kirke's office while everyone was in a staff meeting." I covered my face with my hands and laughed.

"Respect." Amaya nodded.

Harlow remained silent, a look of slight disgust on her face. "I don't need all the gory details."

"Well, I do. Is he hung? I bet it's huge. I can tell by how he walks."

"Oh my god, you're ridiculous." I laughed.

"Eew!" Harlow reached over me to smack Amaya. "Why didn't you tell us?"

"I don't know." I sighed. "It's not like it's going anywhere. It's not serious. It can't be. And I have

Will to consider."

"Fuck Will." Amaya frowned. "Actually, don't. He's never been able to even make you come. I don't know why you keep stringing that wet blanket along."

"I'm just trying to think about my future."

"Is that why Hendrix was here?" Harlow asked. "He wants more—in the future?"

"Yeah. Kind of." At the end, I was still a little confused about it all. Did he have feelings for me? Or was he just on some weird crusade to stop teenagers from doing reckless shit? Thinking about it was making me exhausted.

"Can we please stop talking about it?" I pleaded. "I'm not really sure where we stand, and I don't want to deal with it right now. I have a headache, and I just wanna take a nap."

"OK, fine." Amaya sighed and got off the bed. "Movie tonight."

"That sounds great." I meant it.

"I'll text Mena." Harlow was already bent over her phone as she headed for the door.

I breathed a sigh of relief that they hadn't pushed for more info. I had to be careful, and I had to make sure Hendrix didn't pull a stunt like that ever again.

CHAPTER 19

Donna

I FORCED MYSELF TO TAKE THE STAIRS ONE AT A time instead of bounding up them in twos. The auditorium was bursting, almost every Fulton student and staff member packed into the state-of-the-art facility for an assembly.

Ms. Perry, the headmistress, stood on the stage in a pale blue pantsuit, talking about Fulton Academy's charitable endeavors over the Christmas break. Half the students had already tuned out or were surreptitiously playing on their phones.

I was looking for one particular student.

I'd seen him file in with the others just moments before my phone had vibrated in my pocket, and I'd waved the girls in ahead of me as I checked the notification. It was an email from Stanford.

I'd read it, and immediately the walls started closing in.

I had this inexplicable urge to just . . . *move*. Leave. Get in my car and drive away. But I didn't think my shaky hands could steer effectively. And for some reason, my stupid brain couldn't stop thinking about Hendrix and the way he'd argued, *pleaded* with me to let him help.

I didn't want his help. I didn't need it . . . and yet I found myself slipping into the auditorium through a side door and scanning the blank, indifferent faces. They were so calm—bored even. Didn't they know my heart was about to burst out of my rib cage?

As I climbed, I checked each row for those broad shoulders, that messy hair, those sometimes cruel eyes that seemed to see me better than anyone else ever had.

"Miss Mead," Mr. Monroe hissed, a reproachful look in his bespectacled eyes. He was easily the hottest teacher at Fulton, but he was also the meanest. He had his hands clasped in front of him, one of several teachers standing throughout the auditorium to keep an eye on the students. "Take a seat. The headmistress is speaking."

"Sorry, sir. I'm looking for another student. I've just come from the office with an urgent message for him." The lie rolled off my tongue so easily even I was impressed, especially considering the tempest raging inside me.

He eyed me suspiciously for a moment, but I didn't falter. I was student body president, a top student, liked and respected by students and staff. I never got in trouble. Finally, he nodded. "Make it quick."

We'd drawn the attention of several students nearby, their curious gazes looking for any distraction from the boring speeches below.

My eyes finally locked with Hendrix's. He was sitting a few rows from the top, three empty seats and two juniors between him and the stairs. I kept eye contact, unable to break it if I wanted to, letting the desperation enter my gaze. He frowned and shifted forward in his seat.

I climbed farther up, watching him, begging him with my eyes.

When he got to his feet and shuffled past the other students, my heart kicked up a notch, even as some of the pressure around it eased.

I met him at the end of his row, gestured with a tip of my head for him to follow me, and kept climbing. His feet brushed against the carpet close behind mine, and the back of my neck tingled from his scrutinizing gaze.

Dear Miss Donna Mead,

Thank you for your application . . .

My steps faltered, and Hendrix's hand shot out to grip my upper arm, holding tightly. He released me as soon as I was steady, and I picked up my pace.

At the top of the stairs, he followed me inside the projector room and shut the door behind us.

I stood facing the dark room, finally allowing my chest to heave, my face to fall. This room had a professional digital projector for screenings of films the visual arts students made, as well as several bulky lights and a control panel for school plays and performances.

An assembly didn't require any of those bells and whistles though, so the space was empty and silent. A few people definitely would have seen us slip in, but I was sure none of the teachers had—one of them would've come through that door by now to demand what we were doing.

"Donna." His voice was low, cautious, but curious. "What are we doing in here?"

We receive a large volume of applications each year, and as such are unable to offer a spot to most applicants . . .

I squeezed my eyes shut, taking a steadying breath that didn't steady me at all, then turned to place my hands on his chest.

"I'm taking you up on your offer," I whispered, hoping he mistook my heavy breathing for arousal and not the clawing panic inside me.

The smooth muscle under my palms stiffened as he narrowed his eyes. Just touching him, being close enough to smell that heady male scent with a hint of cinnamon, was already making me feel more grounded. But why wasn't he touching me back? I needed him to touch me.

"What offer?" His voice had gone low too.

"The one you made by the pool that day, when you demanded I stop going to Davey's and asked if I went because I wanted to get laid." I slid my hands up and over his shoulders, pressing my breasts against his front.

"If I remember correctly, that was around the time

you told me to get lost." He was still refusing to touch me, but his breathing was getting heavier.

I shrugged and dragged my nose up the side of his neck. "I changed my mind. I want to fuck."

His hands finally gripped my hips, his fingers digging in. "Yeah, well"—he licked his lips and swallowed—"I don't."

"Liar." I growled, then bit his earlobe.

He hissed but didn't back away.

This game we played, this back and forth, was making me wet already. The anticipation was building, the adrenaline of an unlocked door and the entire school sitting on the other side only driving it higher. It was the perfect distraction from what I'd just learned.

One arm banded around the middle of my back, making me arch against him. His other hand threaded into my hair, and then he was kissing me. Intensely. Forcefully. His tongue immediately demanding my mouth. It was exactly what I needed. Unlike when we argued, I didn't have even a sliver of an urge to fight him. I wanted to give myself over completely and let him consume me until nothing else mattered.

Too soon, he broke the kiss and lifted his head out of my reach. I opened my eyes, panting, and frowned. "What the fuck? Don't stop."

He grabbed a fistful of my hair and pulled lightly until my head was tipped back, at his mercy. "What happened?"

"I don't know what you're talking about. Stop being a pussy and fuck me."

He smirked, then dipped his head, took my bottom lip between his own, and sucked. Just as my eyes started to close in satisfaction, he bit—not enough to draw blood but enough to send a jolt of pleasure shooting through me. But before I could tell him to do it again, he was back to staring down at me, denying me.

"Stop deflecting. I saw that look in your eyes, Donna. You looked like you'd seen a ghost—of a person you just murdered. Tell me what's going on."

I rolled my eyes and returned my hands to his front. "It's nothing. Seriously. Can we please just fuck before the assembly ends and someone comes in here?"

Did I seriously just plead with a guy to fuck me? *Ugh*! Who the hell even was I anymore? I pushed the indignation down and loosened his tie, but I got only three buttons of his shirt undone—barely a peek at the strong, muscular chest underneath—before he put a stop to that.

He wrenched my wrists away from his shirt, then pinned them both behind my back in one big hand. With my arms restrained behind me, my chest jutted forward. He stared at my tits and licked his lips. He wanted this. Why was he being so difficult?

The hand not holding me captive wrapped loosely around my throat, and I had to stop myself from moaning. But he didn't linger there. He dragged it down over my collarbones and to my left breast, then squeezed gently. His thumb brushed over my aching nipple, caressing it over the fabric.

"You want this?" he asked, his voice husky, his dark

eyes looking down on me.

"Yes," I hissed impatiently. Wasn't that exactly what I'd been saying this whole time?

"Then start talking, princess. Nothing in this world is free. You and I know that better than anyone."

His hand was still working my breast, making me pant, the pressure between my legs building.

And then suddenly he went perfectly still.

I frowned at him.

"Talk," he demanded.

"Fine," I gritted out, and his hand immediately resumed its ministrations. "Uh . . . I had a fight with my sister. She . . . ruined my favorite sweater."

"Bullshit." He dragged his hand down my rib cage, over my belly, between my legs, but stopped with his fingers flat against my pelvis, just shy of where I wanted them most. "Try again."

"Fuck, OK." He started to rub me over the fabric of my pleated skirt. "Uh . . . um . . ." It was getting hard to think. "I got a C on my last math test. My parents are going to be so mad."

He chuckled, the sound reverberating through me. "There's no way in hell you've ever made anything below a B plus. Come on, Donna. I'm losing my patience."

I was just about ready to wrench out of his hold, done with these stupid games. But then his hand slipped up under my skirt, and his fingers skimmed the edge of my panties. He moved the fabric aside and teased me with the lightest of touches.

"Oh god. Uh . . ."

His finger circled my entrance, gliding easily through my arousal. "Jesus, you're soaked," he whispered. "Come on, Donna, put us both out of our misery so I can drive my cock"—as he said that word, he slid a finger inside effortlessly, making me gasp—"into this warm, wet heaven between your thighs. Tell. Me."

"It's nothing. For fuck's sake. I . . . it's . . . I'm just moody because I'm on my period, OK?" I blurted.

He froze, his finger still inside me, and I realized what I'd just said. He looked down, then back up at me with a raised brow. I grimaced.

With an amused smirk, he pulled the finger out and held it up between us. His middle finger was slick with my arousal and nothing else. I wasn't due for another week at least. He held it there for a moment, giving me the finger with my own wetness all over it, then put it into his mouth. His cheeks hollowed out as he sucked on it, and he tipped his head to the side.

"Fucking delicious. But no tangy, metallic aftertaste. Try again."

"God damnit." I gritted my teeth so hard a jolt of pain shot through my jaw as I wrenched out of his hold.

"Tell me something real." The teasing lilt was gone from his voice. "I'm here, I'm not going anywhere. I'll make you feel good. Just fucking tell me something *real*, Donna."

We are pleased to inform you that we are offering you early acceptance to . . .

I cracked. There were so many things going through my mind, so many feelings coursing through my body, something had to give. I buckled and got into his face.

"Fine. You want to know what happened? I got into Stanford. Early acceptance."

"Is that not what you wanted?" he asked, but there was no confusion in his face, no judgment. He was simply asking.

I paused for a second, some of the tension draining from my shoulders. The next words came easier than I thought they would. "It's what I've wanted since before high school. But when I read that email ... I felt nothing. Empty. No, that's not right. It wasn't nothing. It just wasn't what it was *supposed* to be. There was no excitement, no joy, no pride at my accomplishment, no urge to jump up and down and tell my friends and family." I licked my lips, staring at his teal tie, and forged on. As if I could stop at this point anyway. "I read that email, the culmination of everything I'd worked for all these years, and it felt like the ceiling collapsed. Everyone else just strolled on by, heading into the auditorium, oblivious to the fact that I was holding the entire goddamn building up over our heads, with my knees ready to buckle."

I looked into his eyes, no longer trying to hide the emotion I was feeling yet could hardly label.

He took hold of my upper arms and stepped closer, his eyes searching mine. "Thank you for telling me. That couldn't have been easy."

Tears pricked at the backs of my eyes, and I had no idea why.

"I don't want to cry, Hendrix," I told him. "I just

want to forget for a little while. Just make me forget. Make me feel good."

He stared at me for another beat, the air between us getting charged. In the auditorium, a round of unenthusiastic applause went up as students carrying wind instruments filed on stage, ready to play a version of our school song.

He leaned down and whispered, "I can do that. I got you, baby." Then he kissed me—a bruising, distracting, dizzying kiss.

I moaned, but before I could wrap my arms around him, his lips were gone, and he was pushing me roughly around until his front was flush with my back.

Hot cinnamon breath washed over my ear, sending shivers of anticipation through my body. "Everyone thinks you're little miss perfect, all your ducks in a row, such a good girl. But I know you, Donna. I know the depravity you crave, the need humming under your skin."

He squeezed my shoulders, and I leaned back into him, but in the next instant, his warmth at my back disappeared.

"Take your panties off," he ordered.

I swallowed, the logical, in-charge Donna bristling at the tone. But she was already fading—along with her stresses and anxieties. Dark Donna was taking over, even if I wasn't wearing come-fuck-me boots and a low-cut top.

I reached under my skirt and pushed my underwear down my legs, purposely arching my back and sticking my ass out as I stepped out of them.

"Give them to me." His hand appeared at my side, and I placed the small piece of gray fabric in his palm.

As soon as my panties were tucked into his pocket, he reclaimed the space between us, his hands on my hips, his steel-hard erection pressing into my ass. I ground back against him, and he released a shaky breath.

"Undo the buttons of your shirt." He kissed and licked the side of my neck, and I tipped my head to give him better access as my fingers fumbled with the buttons. Another round of applause went up in the auditorium just as I managed to get them all undone, the entire school applauding my efforts.

This was so fucked, so dangerous, doing this here, behind a door that didn't lock, with Mr. Monroe literally feet away.

And I was loving every damn second of it.

Hendrix dragged his hands down the sides of my legs until he reached the hem of the skirt, then clasped the fabric and dragged them back up. My bottom half was completely exposed as I stood there in knee-high uniform socks and sensible black shoes, trembling with the anticipation of feeling him inside me.

As his hands continued up my ribs, the skirt fluttered back down, but then he was exposing me in another way. He seized the two sides of my unbuttoned shirt and yanked them apart, making me gasp. Almost instantly his hands were on my breasts, grabbing, kneading in rhythm with the grinding of his hips.

A soft moan escaped me, and I reached back for something to hold on to. My hands clawed at his pants—closed around the fabric at the sides of his thighs.

He dropped his right hand, reached under the skirt, and grabbed me between the legs as his left hand pushed into the cup of my bra. His fingers dug into my flesh, and he started to walk us forward.

"You're not a good girl at all, are you?" He was panting now, his words strained. "Sneaking out to bars, keeping secrets from your friends and family, fucking tattooed men with criminal records. You like the danger, crave it, get off on the prospect of getting caught."

I whimpered. His hands weren't doing anything, weren't rubbing or caressing or stroking me. I was desperate with need, my pussy clenching and relaxing, seeking some kind of relief. And his words only drove me higher.

Usually I hated it when he said things about me that were true, when he had me figured out. But in that moment, I *loved* every syllable. I was his, and I couldn't wait to see what he'd do with me.

He stopped us just in front of the dead control panel and long narrow window, the entire auditorium of three hundred people visible below. Any one of them could turn around at any moment. Would they be able to see us up here in the darkness?

The prospect made arousal flood through me, wetness gathering between my legs and soaking Hendrix's fingers.

"Oh, fuck," he breathed, rubbing me up and down a

few times, spreading the wetness all over my thighs. "You're so fucking wet. You love this, don't you? As much as you love the danger of Davey's. Anyone could walk in at any moment and catch us. Anyone could look up and see my hand down your bra. You're not little Miss Mead at all—you're not a good girl. You're a bad, *bad* girl, Donna. And you want me to fuck you in front of the entire school, don't you?"

"Fuck. Yes."

He rubbed my clit roughly, and my eyes rolled into the back of my head.

"Holy shit." I panted, bucking my hips to meet the movements of his hand. "I'm gonna, I'm . . ." Already, the intense feeling was building, that inevitable pressure in my lower half.

I threw my head back against his shoulder and moaned. The sound was too loud. I knew it as soon as it escaped my mouth. Had someone heard? *Shit*!

The thought of it pushed me over the edge, pleasure coursing through my system.

Hendrix gripped my jaw with his free hand and turned my head, capturing my mouth with his. He kissed me passionately—tongues swiping, teeth bumping—and swallowed every sound I made as I came apart on his hand.

"Shh!" he whispered against my lips as I panted, my vision returning. But Hendrix didn't give a fuck that my knees were going weak—he wasn't going to give me a break.

"You need to keep your mouth shut or this stops

right now. I can't get expelled for fucking you at a school assembly."

"Fuck you." It sounded weak and half-assed. "I can't exactly control it."

He licked my lips, then pushed me forward over the control panel. I threw my hands out, but the only area not covered in buttons and knobs was at the top, which meant I had to stretch my hands almost completely out. That left me pretty much lying on top of the thing, all those knobs and buttons pressing into my front.

Hendrix leaned over me and rubbed his erection against my ass. "I thought you were in control of everything at all times," he taunted, his voice gravelly.

I had no witty response. I didn't give a shit anymore. I just wanted him inside me.

With one hand, I reached back and fumbled at the waistband of his pants, but he slapped my fingers away and did the job himself. The rustle of fabric was followed by the distinct sound of a foil packet opening, and a few seconds later, my skirt was flipped up over my lower back.

His hands kneaded my ass, and then his hard length was at my entrance. The head of his cock entered me, stretching me, and I groaned.

He pulled out. "For fuck's sake, Donna. I'm not messing around. You need to be quiet."

I shifted and lifted myself slightly, looking over my shoulder. He was so impossibly gorgeous, his face flushed, his lips slick from kissing me, his swollen cock standing proud. I focused on his intense stare. "I'm sorry, OK? I'm not doing it on purpose. I'll try to be quiet, but you have my permission to do whatever the fuck you need to shut me up."

His eyes darkened at that, and I turned to face the front again.

Ms. Perry was back on the stage, talking about prom or a new mentorship program or . . . something. It was impossible to focus on anything other than the insanely hot man about to be inside me.

Hendrix's hand appeared next to mine as he once again leaned in close and positioned himself at my entrance. His free hand ran through my hair, and he caressed the back of my neck with his knuckles, sending shivers down my spine. The touches were gentle, sweet.

Which made the contrast of what he did next so much more intoxicating. As he pushed into me, his hand clamped over my mouth, muffling any sounds I made.

He took two slow, deliberate strokes, his body learning mine, then started to fuck me in earnest. His hips slammed against my ass mercilessly as his fingers dug into my cheek, keeping me silent.

I watched the assembly begin to wrap up as Hendrix pounded me from behind. I could see everything below, but I wasn't seeing any of it. Every fiber of my being was focused on him. His hand on my face, the taut muscles of the arm next to me, the hard, warm, wet, stretching, punishing freedom . . .

Another orgasm washed over me, heat spreading from my core all the way to the tips of my toes and fingers. Hendrix buried himself deep inside me and rolled his hips, his body collapsing over mine as he panted through his own release.

Even through the fog of my own orgasm, I was impressed at his control, his ability to remain silent.

His hand over my mouth eased, and he brushed some hair off my cheek before pressing his forehead against my temple. For a few seconds, we just breathed the same air. We just existed together in this moment, and I felt as if I were floating on a cloud of possibility.

CHAPTER 20

Hendrix

WITH ONE LAST KISS TO HER TEMPLE, I PULLED out and . . . realized I'd fucked up. Big time. Hooking up with Donna at Davey's and in that office was one thing—we hardly knew each other, we had this angry sexual tension going, it was hot, and that was that. But what we'd just done—it was so much more than sex. She'd told me something real, shown me a part of her soul. I'd known what she craved and given it to her.

And now, as I tied off the condom and buried it under a muffin wrapper in the trash, a tightness settled around my chest. I actually gave a shit what happened to her. I was *emotionally invested.*

Fuck.

My princess was feeling trapped in her ivory tower, and I knew exactly how she felt, what that could lead to.

Her arousal was still slick on the base of my dick, and I was already missing her warmth, her tight body writing under mine, her labored breathing against my hand. I wanted to make her forget her life again, help her find oblivion in ecstasy over and over and over until nothing else mattered. But this wasn't some fantasy where we could just run away and spend the rest of our lives fucking in a cabin in the woods.

Donna cleared her throat as she finished buttoning up her shirt. "Can I have my underwear back, please?"

I did my pants back up, tucked my shirt in, straightened my tie, took my sweet-ass time to respond. "No," I told her with a slight twitch of my lips.

Her eyes narrowed. "Hendrix, don't be ridiculous. I need my underwear. I can't go back to class like this. What if I trip or something and my skirt goes flying up?"

"Then don't go to class." I ran my hands through my hair and brushed the creases from my uniform. The assembly had finished, and a cacophony of sound drifted in through the narrow window—students all talking over one another, feet shuffling toward the exits. We backed farther into the darkness, closer to the door.

Donna finished straightening herself up as well, her appearance as pristine as possible without a mirror or a brush. Then she gave me a firm look.

"I don't have time for this. We need to slip into the crowd as everyone's leaving so we don't get caught. Give me my panties." She reached for my pocket, but I brushed her hands away and backed up against the wall.

I could see that look in her eyes returning—the one that hardened her against the world. She was retreating, probably freaking out about all she'd told me, seconds away from running from me yet again and avoiding even acknowledging what just happened between us. But I was done letting Donna Mead walk away from me. I was done letting her walk away from her problems. I was done letting her control everything. She'd been doing it for years, and it clearly wasn't working for her.

"You can have them. In ten minutes."

"What?" She frowned and glanced at the door. Our window was closing.

"Meet me at the east entrance in ten minutes, and you can have them back. Bring your coat."

"Hendrix, I'm not going to skip class to . . ."

I didn't hang around to listen to her enraged demands. I just opened the door, made sure no one was looking, and rushed down the stairs until I was close enough behind a group of freshman girls to look as if I was exiting with the rest of the students.

I resisted the urge to look over my shoulder and check if Donna was doing the same. She was a big girl— she'd figure it out.

As I passed through the auditorium's double doors, I accidentally caught the eye of Mr. Monroe—my English teacher. The guy was the youngest staff member at Fulton but easily the most hard-ass. He had the best opportunity to connect with his students because of his youth, but I'd never even seen the dude smile, let alone crack a joke.

He frowned at me before pushing his glasses back up his nose. I had no idea what that was about, but I smiled back politely and breezed on past. The only surefire way to get caught doing something dodgy was to act as though you had something to hide.

Between going to my locker to get my stuff and walking out to my car, I questioned my decision to cut class about a thousand times.

I was breaking my vow to keep my head down, stay out of trouble, and get past my senior year without any hiccups. I was also breaking my aunt's trust.

I got into my car and sighed, drumming my fingers on the steering wheel. Maybe I should just go back inside. If I hurried, I wouldn't even be late for gym. But then Donna would be left standing on the sidewalk alone, and she'd be pissed. And hurt, even if she didn't show it. I couldn't let her down—especially after I'd manipulated her into coming.

Sighing, I pulled my phone out and shot a quick message to my aunt.

> I'm skipping school for the rest of the day. I promise it's important and necessary. Can you please cover for me if the school calls?

I started the car, but her reply was instant.

> Thank you for telling me. I'll give you an alibi.
> But I expect a full and detailed report tonight.

I pulled up to the curb at the east entrance just as Donna slipped out the door. This was where the younger students were picked up and dropped off by their parents, nannies, and drivers. The area was packed with Escalades, Audis, and BMWs in the morning and the afternoon, but it was deserted as Donna rushed down the stairs.

I expected her to lean through the window, demand her underwear, maybe sic the football team on me. But she surprised me by jumping into the passenger seat immediately and throwing her designer backpack into the back seat.

"Drive," she demanded as she put her belt on. "Your tree-hugging car's windows are not tinted. The last thing I fucking need is to be caught skipping class with the likes of you."

"Yes, ma'am." I let the dig slide and took off.

The drive was surprisingly uneventful. Resigned to her fate, Donna jammed her black sunglasses on and remained silent as I tried to figure out where to take us.

When all else fails—comfort food.

I took us to a fast food drive-through, and after a half-hearted argument about how she couldn't eat that crap, Donna rolled her eyes and got the same thing I did. Cheeseburgers and milkshakes in tow, I pulled back onto the road.

"Should've got some chickie nuggies as well," Donna mumbled, her head buried in the paper bag.

"Chickie nuggies?" I grinned. She was fucking adorable, with her delicate, manicured fingers stuffing several fries into her mouth at the same time.

"Shut up." She laughed around a mouthful and shoved some fries into my mouth too. I gave her finger a nibble before she could pull her hand out of reach, and she smacked me on the shoulder. "That's what my sister calls them. She's got us all saying it now."

"It's cute. More fries," I demanded and opened my mouth wide, angling my head in her direction but keeping my eyes on the road.

"Fuck you. I'm not cute," she protested but deposited the salty, potatoey goodness into my mouth anyway. "Where are we going?"

"Ah, good question. Very deep. So many answers." I nodded and opened my mouth again.

She rolled her eyes and shoved more fries in my face. "I meant physically, like, right now, in this car, where are we going? Not existentially, smart-ass."

"Hmm. How about ..." We were well out of downtown Devilbend, the buildings thinning out, the speed limits rising. A sign for a turnoff caught my eye. "Oak Hill Park?"

The turn came up before she could answer, and I took it, but Donna remained silent beside me. We followed signs for the parking lot, intermittent sunlight shining down through the thick canopy of trees.

Unsurprisingly for a Thursday afternoon, the lot was mostly empty, no tourists or hikers in sight.

Donna turned to me as I cut the engine, her hands digging into the top of the paper bag. "I'm not getting out of this car or handing over your greasy burger until you give me back my underwear."

I pursed my lips to stop myself from smiling. We both knew I could overpower her if I really wanted to.

Reaching into my pocket, I fished out the small piece of cotton and handed it over. She deposited the takeout bag in my lap and pulled her panties up, shimmying into them under her skirt, then promptly got out of the car.

I followed her up the grassy hill to a nearby picnic table. The sun was coming and going behind grayish clouds—the kind that threatened rain but were just as likely to float away before a single drop reached the ground. It was fresh out here, the air chilly whenever the sun disappeared, and I was glad I'd made her bring her coat.

We settled onto the top of the table, our feet propped up on the seat. As we started to unwrap the burgers, Donna hesitated and looked around.

"Something messed up happened to Mena and Turner here," she said before taking a bite.

I paused with my burger halfway to my mouth and looked at her. "Do you want to leave?"

"Nah, it's fine." She shook her head. "I just realized where we are, that's all. Being reminded of what went down a few months ago just makes me angry every time."

"What happened?"

"Uh . . ." She picked at her burger. "It's not really my story to tell."

She was loyal and fearless—a fucking lioness personified. I took a few bites of my burger to avoid staring at her. "Does it have anything to do with how Turner reconnected with his little sister?"

I'd been training with Turner a few times a week since I joined the gym, and we'd hung out plenty. He'd told me most of how his mom and sister disappeared a few years back and how he and his dad had been searching for them, only to find his sister here in Devilbend and his mom murdered. He had a bit of a conspiracy-theorist streak, convinced that BestLyf—some corporate life-coaching company—was behind it all, but he was a really cool guy otherwise.

Donna's eyebrows rose slightly. "He told you that?"

"Yeah. That's what being friends with someone entails. You tell them things about yourself. Sometimes the things aren't very pretty."

She ignored that, and we ate in silence, listening to the birds chirping in the tall trees, the occasional gust of wind rustling the branches.

When there was nothing left to occupy our mouths, I turned to face her, lifting one knee onto the table.

She closed her eyes and sighed. "Don't."

"Don't what?"

"Please, Hendrix, don't start with trying to figure out my deep dark secrets again. We had amazing sex during a school assembly and got away with it. We're actually getting along. Can't we just leave it at that?"

"If what happened between us had been just sex, yeah."

"Oh, please. Don't tell me you're catching feelings now. I have enough shit to deal with."

She was going back to her defensive default, because that's what she always did when shit got hard or confronting. Did I have feelings for her? Fuck me, but yeah, I was probably getting there. But this wasn't about that.

"I'm not trying to put a ring on it, you psycho." If combative snark was the only language she could understand, then that's what I'd speak. "I'm talking about the desperate way you looked at me in the auditorium, the shit you told me about your early acceptance and how it made you feel like the roof was caving in, the fact that you go to Davey's and fuck dangerous men as a way to release the insane amount of pressure you feel every single day."

She blinked at me once, twice, not saying anything as her brows knitted. She was a smart girl, smarter than me, probably smarter than half the teachers at our school—surely she wasn't surprised that I'd figured her out.

"I don't know why I told you that earlier." She pursed her lips.

"Because on some level, you know that I get it. I may not understand feeling deflated after achieving a massive thing, but I definitely get feeling like the entire world is collapsing on top of you. I've been there."

"Will you tell me about it?" she asked, her eyes going a little wide. Was she scared? Deflecting?

"We're talking about you right now." OK, maybe I was deflecting too.

"Isn't that what being friends with someone means? Telling them things about yourself that aren't very pretty?" She threw my own words back at me.

"Is that what we are now? Friends?"

She sighed and ran her hands through her hair, pulling at it a little. "I don't know what we are."

I shrugged. "Doesn't matter right now whether or not we're friends. But you do have some actual, bona fide, ride-or-die kind of friends in those chicks—the ones you keep posting pics of with hashtag DevilbendDynasty." I'd witnessed firsthand how close they were, how they defended one another, took care of one another. Their friendship was real, not shallow and on the verge of backstabbing like so many rich, popular girls at my old school. "Why haven't you told them about any of it?"

"They . . . I . . . the thing is, we really are ride-or-die, as idiotic as that phrase sometimes sounds." She rolled her eyes. "But they'd try to talk me out of it, and when that failed, they'd go with me. Even Mena, who's had more than her fair share of violence, would risk getting hurt. I can't do that to them. This is *my* shit. *My* damage to deal with." *Alone.* She didn't say it, but the implication was there. This was something she felt she had to handle alone.

I dropped that topic before we started arguing again. "OK, then will you tell them about your early acceptance?"

"Yeah." She leaned back on her hands, turning her face up to the sun. It was likely to disappear behind a cloud again at any moment. "They'll be happy for me, proud of me."

"No doubt. It's an amazing achievement. But that's

not what I meant. Are you going to tell them you don't want it?"

She sat up straight and narrowed her eyes on me. "What makes you think I don't want it? I busted my fucking ass for that."

I didn't say anything. I just watched her steadily. That was a knee-jerk reaction—the response she'd conditioned herself to have. But we both knew what she'd said to me in that dark little room, and I'd seen that panicked look in her eyes in the auditorium.

After a few moments, she got to her feet. Her eyes darted from left to right, distant and unseeing, as she chewed on her bottom lip.

"Your friends and family love you and support you," I said. It was more than I could say about my own, but I pushed that stabbing pain away for the moment. "They'll understand. Just tell them you don't want to be a lawyer anymore."

Her gaze shot up. "Who the fuck do you think you are to tell me what I do and don't want? You have no idea what you're talking about. I can't just change my mind."

"Why?" I leaned my elbows on my knees, fixing her with a challenging look. The sun disappeared behind a fat cloud. "You're eighteen, your whole future in front of you. You have every privilege, every opportunity imaginable. You can literally do whatever the fuck you want, and you're going to force yourself to follow a path that's clearly suffocating you?" Did I resent all this? Maybe a little. But I'd also put myself in this situation where my own future was tenuous, so I didn't really have a right to be upset. I deserved much worse.

"Fuck you, Hendrix. It's not that simple. I have plans. People expect certain things from me. I've put in so much work for this. I ... it's ... you ... *ugh!*" She turned away in a huff, breathing hard.

"It's not worth it, Donna. Trust me. Life's too damn short." My hands clenched into fists, and I forced myself to release them. This conversation was making me frustrated and angry too.

She spun to face me once more, her hair flipping. "What would you know about it? God, why do you care? Just leave me alone."

I didn't exactly make the decision to tell her my deepest darkest secret, but the conversation had descended into another fight, and I was getting nowhere. She'd shared something pretty big with me in that dark little room—a truth she'd probably never even spoken aloud. Baring my soul to her, even in desperation and anger, almost came naturally.

I pushed off the bench, the nervous energy making it impossible to sit still, and spread my arms wide.

"I fucking killed someone!" I yelled, my horrific truth bouncing off the ancient trees in the park.

CHAPTER 21

Donna

I STARED AT HIM AS HIS WORDS SETTLED INTO the cold earth at my feet.

The logical part of my brain was questioning if I should be afraid. He'd been popping up wherever I went, had been demanding to know things about me, had driven me out to a deserted park alone, and then said . . . he told me . . .

I fucking killed someone.

. . . killed someone.

. . . killed . . .

Even as I wondered if I was safe with Hendrix, I struggled to accept the truth of those words. Maybe I hadn't heard him right.

"I'm sorry, what?" I tried to swallow, but my throat was so dry, so tight.

And yet I wasn't running from him; my body wasn't poised to defend itself. Yes, my logical mind had raised all the obvious alarms, but in my gut I *knew*. Hendrix would never hurt me. Not like that. He wasn't a threat to my physical safety—just my sanity.

He rubbed his eyes with the heels of his hands, then released a massive sigh as he collapsed onto the bench, his body sagging as if he hadn't slept in a month. "I'm sorry for just dropping that on you like that. I didn't mean to . . . I never wanted anyone to know, but I need you to understand the whole, abhorrent truth about me—what I am."

"You're scaring me." I wrapped my arms around my middle, but I couldn't tear my gaze away. I didn't mean I was worried he'd try to kill me—the very conversation was frightening. I was scared of what he was about to tell me, what it would change. For him, for me. For this thing between us.

But of course, he took my words wrong. He hadn't looked at me since he'd blurted out his confession, and he still didn't look at me as he reached into his pocket and pulled out his car keys.

"I won't hurt you. I'd rather die than ever hurt another person, especially you. Take the keys. Leave if you need to. I get it." He tossed them onto the corner of the picnic table closest to where I was standing.

I hardly even glanced at them. "Hendrix, tell me what happened." I didn't want to know, but I *had* to know.

He swallowed and released another big breath, his lips trembling. "Back in New York, I told you the kind of school I went to, the kind of people I hung out with. We got away with so much because our parents were so influential. The teachers were too afraid to discipline us. We all thought we were untouchable, invincible. But we all had this ... " He shook his head. "... this *restlessness*. Me most of all. Something inside me was constantly screaming and thrashing, and the only time it would quiet down was when I was driving my fist through something. Or someone. Those guys and I, we started getting into fights. At first it was against each other, betting obscene amounts of money on the outcome. Eventually we started hanging out with people who were intimately acquainted with the darker side of the city—people who were more than willing to take our money and hook us up with other sad fuckers looking to beat the shit out of anyone."

He stared at the ground beneath his feet and opened his mouth a few times, but he couldn't seem to get the next words out.

That restlessness he described, the screaming on the inside—I felt that in my *bones*. I moved forward to stand directly in front of him, and that seemed to snap him out of his inability to speak.

"There was this guy at my school." He leaned back against the picnic table, his hands hanging between his knees. "He wasn't like us. He wasn't rich, didn't walk around like the world owed him something. The school was bigger than Fulton, more students. I didn't know everyone, hardly cared enough to know my so-called friends. Anyway, there were several scholarship students and ..." He choked, his lip trembling again.

"Austin was one of them. We used to get into it sometimes. He had his own group of friends—we didn't move in the same circles—but he wasn't scared of me like almost everyone else. He always had a comeback to any bullshit taunt we threw his way, and he never seemed bothered by it. Like he knew he was smarter than all of us combined, and we wouldn't matter in a couple more months. He was probably going to cure cancer or some shit. It had never gotten physical between us. The guys and I, we kept the fights discreet, off school property. We may not have cared about punishments from teachers, but we sure as fuck cared about pissing off our parents.

"The thing is, I'd been getting less and less capable of holding back that restless fury—that thing that writhed inside me all the time and was only silent when I was hurting, or hurting someone else. The most fucked-up thing is that I don't even remember what led up to it. It was after school, the guys and I had just walked around the corner, Austin was there, and one of my friends said something to him. Austin shot a comment back. I have no idea what it was, but it enraged me. I let it bring that monster out. I didn't care that we were in public, in our school uniforms, with teachers just around the corner. I just lost my shit."

He paused and looked up to the sky. Tears slid down the sides of his face, but he didn't try to wipe them away.

For the first time since he'd started talking, he looked at me. Each word that followed was a struggle, forcing its way up his throat. "I threw a punch that landed on his jaw. He wasn't expecting it and lost his balance, fell backward, hit his head on the pavement. He never got up again."

"Holy shit," I breathed, wrapping a hand around my throat. My own eyes were stinging.

His gaze was intense, as if now that he was finally looking at me, he refused to let me go until I saw all his twisted insides. "I killed him, Donna. Me. I did that."

"I . . . wha . . . how long ago was this?" Why hadn't I seen anything about it in the news? This felt like a big deal. But then I remembered that people died all the time, and usually the rest of the world couldn't care less.

"Just under a year ago. I was supposed to graduate last year, but I stopped going to school. My parents spent an obscene amount of money and called in many favors to keep me out of prison. They even managed to have me tried as a minor so this wouldn't be on my permanent record and tarnish my future." He said those last words with a sneer.

"They were worried about my job prospects and their reputation when Austin didn't even have . . ." A sob tore free from his chest, and my own tears finally overflowed. "He was an only child, his mom a single parent. They were all each other had. I . . ."

He dropped his head into his hands.

I stepped into his space, between his legs, and gripped his shoulders. My throat was so tight I had to cough before I could speak. "It was an accident,

Hendrix. An awful, tragic—"

"No." He leaned out of my reach. "It was stupidity, it was pride, it was ego, it was not thinking through the consequences of my actions. I was a walking, talking cliché. It could've been avoided."

"No arguments here." He was right on all fronts. I knew guys like him—like the guy he used to be. "But you didn't mean to kill him."

I stepped closer and pulled him in again; he let me, but his hands remained in his lap.

"No, I didn't. I didn't think about him at all. I never thought about anyone else and how my actions could impact them. That's who I was. That's the guy who killed someone. I don't want to be that person anymore."

"You're not." I said it definitively, and I meant it. My arms wrapped around his torso, the urge to give him comfort impossible to resist. He leaned in to return my hug and rest his head on my chest.

For a few moments we were still. Just me holding a broken boy when I was barely keeping my own damn self from falling apart into a million incompatible pieces.

"After the trial and everything was over"—his words were warm on my chest, his tears soaking my shirt— "Austin's mom reached out to me. My parents and their lawyers and their fucking publicist all advised me against seeing her, but I went. I didn't give a shit what they thought. I was a mess, but she'd lost her son—I'd taken her son—so I was going to do anything that woman asked of me. I was ready to walk off a cliff if she demanded it. Told her as much when I walked into her living room and dropped to my knees before her, blubbering like a child. And you know what she said to me? Austin wouldn't want that."

Another round of sobs shook his shoulders, and his arms tightened around me—as if I was the only thing keeping him from collapsing completely. I didn't know what to say or do. I just held him, crying right along with him.

"Austin wouldn't want that," he repeated in a hoarse voice. "That's the kind of person I took out of this world. We talked for a long time, and in the end, she told me she forgave me. She said she couldn't go through the rest of her life carrying hatred in her heart. Then she made me promise to do all the things Austin couldn't anymore—live my life, make something of myself, leave the world a better place than I found it."

We fell into silence after that, the birds continuing to chirp and the clouds continuing to pass above.

After a while, Hendrix leaned out of my embrace, dragging both hands down his face. "I've never told anyone that. Not since it happened. Not the whole, full thing."

"Why did you tell me?" I didn't feel worthy of his deepest truths, not after the way I'd treated him.

"To make you understand why I'm being so weirdly intense about you going to Davey's, about you telling your friends and family how you feel about your college acceptance. We're so similar, you and me. And I'm terrified you'll—"

"What?" I took a step back, my anger rising again. It was too much. It was all just *too much*. "You think I'd kill someone because I'm not sure I want to study law? I would never do that."

"No." He closed his eyes wearily. "I know our situations are different. I'm worried you'll get *yourself* killed."

My phone started buzzing in my pocket. Desperate for an out from a conversation I still wasn't ready to have, I wrenched it out. It was Drew—school had finished ten minutes ago.

"Hello?" I answered, giving Hendrix my shoulder.

He got to his feet. "Seriously?"

"Hey, Big D! Where you at, girl?" He sounded as though he was in the car. He lived right near Oak Hill Park.

"I told you not to call me that." My response came out harsh—not at all like our usual light banter.

"Are you OK?" he asked.

I glanced at Hendrix, now standing in front of me with his arms crossed. "I need a lift. Can you pick me up from Oak Hill?"

"On my way."

I hung up, and Hendrix got in my face again. "You can run from this all you want, but it's going to catch up with you at some point."

"Yeah, well, that'll be my problem and not yours."

"All the shit I just told you makes no difference whatsoever?"

"That's your life. Not mine. I'm fine!" I yelled. A

flock of birds took flight from a nearby tree.

"Really? You're just going to keep pretending your way into a life you never wanted? How long until you're married to fucking Will Frydenberg, in a job you despise, and the only thing keeping you going is a daily dose of Xanax?"

"Fuck you. I'm not pretending shit. You're the one driving around in an electric car, trying to fix *my* problems like doing good deeds will make you into a different person. You can pretend all you like, but at the end of the day, you're just a thug." I managed to stop myself from saying *murderer* somehow, but I still felt like shit as soon as the sentence left my mouth.

He bared his teeth, the fury in his face nearly masking the hurt my words had inflicted. "Yeah, well, you can't get off unless it's with a thug, so whatever. I may be a thug, but what does that make you?"

The sound of Drew's matte black Audi coming up the drive was like the splash of a life preserver after I'd been in the water long enough to start swallowing some. I glanced over my shoulder just in time to see him pull up, then turned back to Hendrix, already walking backward. "You're the one who told me I need to stop fucking losers. So just stay away from me."

He turned around and smacked the remnants of our lunch off the table.

Breathing hard, I turned and jogged down the hill. When I pulled the handle of the back door on Hendrix's Tesla, I thanked my lucky stars it was unlocked, grabbed my bag, and rushed over to Drew's car.

"Drive. Go. *Now*," I demanded. Not that Hendrix was calling after me or trying to catch up. I ignored the pang of disappointment that brought and reminded myself I'd just ensured he wouldn't. I usually loved it when people called me a bitch—more often than not it was just their way of saying I was being too assertive as a woman, speaking my mind too loudly, refusing to take their shit.

But in this moment, I knew I'd been a bitch to him, in all the worst ways.

Drew glanced in my direction. "You all right?"

"I'm fine. Can you drive me back to school? I left my car there."

"Sure." He pulled onto the main road. "What's going on with you two?"

"Nothing." Not anymore. Not ever. I'd made sure of it.

"Didn't look like nothing. You need me to get the guys together and take care of it? Just say the word."

I sighed and forced a smile. "You're sweet to offer to inflict violence on my behalf, but it's not necessary. I promise. I've hurt him way worse than he could ever hurt me."

I hadn't meant to say that last part, but it was true. Drew kept silent, but I could feel more questions on the tip of his tongue.

"Drew, can you please not tell anyone about this? I've handled the situation, and no one needs to know. I promise."

"If you're sure." He sighed.

"I'm positive. Hey, what were you calling me about?"

Drew and I texted, but we rarely called each other. He must've wanted to talk about something important.

"It can wait. Looks like you've had a hard enough day." He squeezed my knee and returned his hand to the gearshift.

I sighed and looked out the window at Devilbend flying by. Was Hendrix right? Would I end up in a life that felt as if it were flying past as I watched from the other side of the window?

CHAPTER 22

Hendrix

MY FEET POUNDED AGAINST THE TREADMILL AS sweat poured down my face. My lungs were screaming, my heart thundering so hard it felt as though it might give out.

I gritted my teeth and kept pushing.

After Donna got into Drew's car and left, I'd driven straight to the gym, every inch of my body itching to just do *something*. It was better than punching a tree in the park, better than driving to Davey's and getting absolutely wasted, better than finding some unsuspecting dude in a back alleyway and beating the shit out of him. I couldn't punish anyone else to get this feeling out, so I'd punish my own body.

The person I really wanted to punish was *her*.

That wasn't true, not really. Yes, I was angry, furious, but I was hurt more than anything. I'd spilled my guts to her, told her the deepest, darkest moment of my life, and she . . . she just . . .

I grunted and swung my heavy arms a little harder, pumping my legs.

I'd told her about Austin because I wanted her to understand how fast and how horribly bad shit could turn when you were searching for an escape. No, she wasn't getting into fights with randoms as I had been, but she was spiraling in her own way—*exactly* as I had been. The only difference really was that she preferred to fuck dangerous guys and not fight them. Why couldn't she see that?

But maybe that was my mistake—I'd told her because I wanted her to change her behavior. I'd told her as a way to get her to do what I wanted her to do.

No, that wasn't entirely true either. I didn't think I'd be capable of saying all the things I'd said to Donna if I didn't want her to know them. Not because it would be a wake-up call for her, but because I wanted her to know me—every deep, dark, horrific part of my soul. I wanted her to *know me*. And still want me.

But she didn't. She'd run from me like the monster I was.

Maybe I was going about this whole thing the wrong way. Maybe she needed to hit her rock bottom, just as I had, in order to recognize that something needed to change. But how was I supposed to just sit back and watch her get hurt, possibly killed? Especially now that I'd gone and grown fucking feelings for her, like a moron.

"Hey, bro!" Turner appeared in front of the

treadmill, his smile more a grimace. I frowned, wishing he'd go away, wishing everyone would just go the fuck away, but he reached over and hit the Stop button.

"Dude!" I panted, bracing myself on the guard rails. "I was . . . still . . . going."

"Yeah, well, I can't let you get hurt, so . . . how about you take a break and we talk about what's bothering you?" He crossed his arms, and the biceps bulged out. He was a fit guy when we met, but he'd gained definition over the weeks we'd worked out together.

"I'm not gonna . . . get hurt . . . I just need . . . to keep running," I ground out, beyond frustrated with how hard I was breathing. My legs were starting to shake a little now that I'd been forced to stop. Useless meat stumps . . .

"I can't let you keep going, man." Turner frowned, looking more worried by the second.

"Why?"

He sighed. "It's my job to make sure people don't hurt themselves. You're sweating so much it's dripping on the treadmill, which is fucking disgusting"—he made a face—"but also a slip hazard. Not to mention you're so out of breath you can hardly talk, and the only reason you're still upright is because of that death grip on the handrail."

I glared at him, still working to catch my breath.

When I said nothing, Turner raised his eyebrows and pointed to the changing rooms. "Go shower. I'll wipe this down for you and get you a Gatorade so you don't pass out."

I kept glaring at him as I hobbled off the machine. There was no point arguing; he wasn't going to let me move on to weights.

After I stood under the shower for a long time with my hands propped against the tiles, my lungs and heart returned to normal function. I put my school uniform back on and walked out of the shower cubicle.

Turner was sitting on a bench with his back against the lockers, tapping away at his phone. He looked up when I came out and held out a bottle of blue liquid.

I flopped down next to him and had a long drink.

"What's going on with you?" he asked. "You looked like you wanted to murder someone out there."

My spine immediately stiffened, and I stared at him with wide eyes.

He leaned away from me, confused. "What?"

I shook my head and relaxed my posture, dragging a hand down my face. For a second there, I thought maybe Donna had told all her friends, that she was warning everyone to stay away from me again. Except this time, she had a very real reason for it. But that didn't make sense. Turner wasn't acting scared and suspicious—he was concerned for a friend. Me. I didn't deserve him.

"I can't talk about it. It's ..." I pressed my lips together so hard it almost hurt.

Turner rested his hands on his knees. "When I found out about my mom, that she was dead, that my little sister had seen the whole thing happen ... all I wanted to do was pretend it wasn't real. I'd spent years dreaming about the day I'd get to hug my mom again, and then suddenly I found out I never would. You know, I don't even remember the last time I hugged her. It must've felt so insignificant, like there was so much certainty there'd be another one, that I didn't think to commit every detail to memory." He turned to look me in the eyes. "Anyway, point is, my little sister needed me, Mena needed me, so I couldn't just curl up into a ball and pretend it wasn't real. I had to face it. And the only way I could do that was to talk about it. To my therapist, to the police, to my dad, to my girlfriend. Every time I shared a bit of how I felt, it was a little easier to carry all the pain and the heartache."

He was telling me I needed to talk about my feelings. That cocky asshole part of me I'd worked so hard to eradicate wanted to roll his eyes and call him a pussy with a punch to his arm. But he was also, in a roundabout way, telling me that he had trusted me with his darkness, his pain, and maybe I could trust him with mine.

But there was one key difference between our situations. "What happened to your family, you were in no way to blame for that." I held his gaze, my jaw tight. "I appreciate you being so honest about all this heavy shit in your life. But my story is the complete opposite. I'm not the victim here. I'm the bad guy."

"There's nothing you can tell me that will make me think less of you."

I sighed and looked up to the ceiling. He was so wrong. I really didn't want to lose Turner as a friend, but

I couldn't keep lying to him either. That wasn't friendship. Not to mention, now that Donna knew all the gory details and was more pissed at me than I'd ever seen her, it was only a matter of time before everyone knew. It would be better if he heard it from me anyway.

For the second time in a day, I told someone the full story of the worst thing I'd ever done. I didn't go into as much detail as I had at the park, and I didn't break down crying, but I didn't try to sugarcoat it either. I also told him that I'd told Donna and we'd ended up in another fight, but I didn't tell him why I'd told her—I was still keeping her secrets.

"I took Austin from his mom, just like Boyd Burrows took your mom from you," I finished. "All that pain you feel, I'm the cause of that for someone else."

Turner sat back against the locker, mirroring my pose, and released a big breath. "Did you set out to kill him? Deliberately end his life?"

"No. But—"

"Do you feel bad about what you did?"

"It's the single worst mistake of my life. I'll never stop feeling like shit about it."

"Did you learn from it? Are you trying to be a better person?"

"Every single fucking day. But nothing I do can take back the fact that I *killed someone*."

"No, what's done is done, and you have to live with that. As far as I see it, it was an awful, horrible mistake that ended in a horrific accident. All you can do is keep living your life in a way that honors Austin's and make sure you don't willingly put any more hurt out into the world."

He stood up and faced me. "As for Donna, I don't know what's going on between you two, but she's not a bad person. Everyone calls her a bitch, but that's only because she's so unapologetic about standing up for what she believes in. She's a good person deep down. Just like you. You'll figure it out."

I stared up at him, struggling to process the casual way he was still accepting me as a friend despite it all. Tears stung the backs of my eyes as he pulled me to my feet and into a hug. We patted each other's backs, holding on for a second longer than our usual hellos.

"Thank you, Turner." All the things I wanted to say to him but couldn't find the words for, I injected into that thank-you.

He shrugged and smiled. "I gotta get back to work. Go home. Do *not* get back on that treadmill." He gave me a pointed look and walked out.

I took a few moments to get my shit together before grabbing my stuff and leaving, waving to him on my way out the door.

The sun was starting to set as I walked around the corner to where I'd parked, my head bent, my mind on what a batshit day it had been.

Apparently, it wasn't over.

I looked up to find Shady leaning against the side of my car, smoking a cigarette. He was in jeans and high-tops, a tracksuit top zipped up under his open coat. With a grin, he pushed off the car and held his arm out wide.

"Hendrix, my man!"

"Shady." I gave him a fist bump and a half smile. He was a good distraction and cool most of the time, but it was a little odd he was out here, waiting for me. It put me on alert. "What's up?"

"Listen." He stepped in closer, took another drag of his smoke, and lowered his voice. "I'd love to shoot the shit, but it's freezing out here, and I got another matter to attend to."

"OK." I unlocked my car and threw my gym bag into the back before turning back to face him.

"I just need to know if you've given any more thought to what we talked about." He dropped the butt of his cigarette onto the ground and put it out with his toe.

"What we talked about?" I frowned, trying to remember the last time I'd seen him. It was the night Donna was roofied. We'd sat at the bar, talking shit, sports, movies, nothing serious. Then I'd spotted Donna, and I couldn't remember a single word Shady had said after.

"Yeah, man. There's a fight night this weekend, and the people in charge need an answer." He bounced on his toes, looking at me expectantly.

Every muscle in my body stiffened; it was a battle to relax my jaw enough not to speak through gritted teeth. "Shady, I don't remember us talking about any fight night, and I don't know what this is about, but I want nothing to do with it."

He licked his lips and flicked a glance over his

shoulder, a flash of worry entering his gaze before he covered it up with a sly grin. "I know you used to be into it back in NYC. Don't you want an opportunity to put some of those arrogant pricks on their asses? Guys like the dickheads you go to school with? They'd stand no chance against you, man."

He thought he was paying me a compliment, but my blood was boiling. His cousin had been the only one who stood by me in New York after all my so-called friends turned their backs, and Shady had been good to me since I got here, but surely even he must know what he was asking of me.

"Shady, turn around, walk away, and never raise this with me again."

The sly grin fell from his lips, and his eyes darted from side to side. Then he sighed and gave me the first genuine look I'd ever seen on his face. "Hey, man, I'm sorry. You said you'd think about it when I mentioned it last. I didn't know you weren't paying attention. The organizers just wanted me to put a little sweetener on top, extra money, bitches, that kind of thing. They really want you, man. They think your history would add an extra . . . *element* to the entertainment."

They thought the fact I'd killed someone would make the fight more interesting—in case I did it again. Scum-sucking pond dwellers.

I looked over his shoulder and spotted a dark SUV parked a few cars down, the two hard-looking middle-aged motherfuckers inside not even hiding the fact they were watching us.

"What the fuck are you mixed up in, Shady?"

"It's not my scene, man." He leaned in even more, lowered his voice further. "You know how I said Davey's is kind of a neutral ground? Well, I'm not the only one who hangs out there, if you get my drift? Not the only one who does business there. These guys who run the fights . . ." He sighed and shook his head. "I try to steer clear of them, but they noticed we hung out and . . . persuaded me to persuade you, if you know what I mean." He shrugged and stuffed his hands into his pockets. "Don't worry about it, man. I'll tell them you're not interested. I'll take care of it."

I'd never seen Shady scared of anything. I knew he was into some dodgy-as-fuck stuff, that a lot of people were afraid of *him*, so the fact that he was doing someone else's bidding . . . a cold dread settled in my stomach. For Shady and what kind of danger he was in. For Donna and what she was walking into every time she went there.

"Would it help if I made it clear I wasn't interested?" I flicked my eyes over his shoulder so he knew I'd spotted our audience.

He watched me for a second, then gave a tiny nod.

I grabbed him by the collar of his jacket and shoved him back. "Never ask me that again! We're done, you lowlife son of a bitch," I bellowed.

He held his hands up and grinned at me, walking backward, then dropped a serious look onto his face before turning around.

I let the rage show on my face as I got into my car,

slammed the door, and sped off as angrily as I could manage in an electric car that was whisper quiet.

The little bit of hope my conversation with Turner had given me—that not everyone would see me as a violent monster—was smashed to pieces, its jagged remnants left on the curb where I'd spoken with Shady.

As I parked the car and trudged into the house—my body sore from my punishing workout, my shoulders sagging from the crushing despair—I didn't know what to think anymore. Which side of the fence would Donna land on once she calmed down? She had said nice things when I'd poured my heart out to her at the park, but did she mean them?

On top of that, the run-in with Shady had shaken me. I kept running over the entire day's events, my mind twisting every single look, every single word, until I had no idea what was real anymore.

My aunt was on me before I even finished taking my shoes off.

"Hey." She leaned against the archway leading to the kitchen, a steaming bowl in her hands. "Want some ramen while you tell me every single detail of your day?" She grinned, then slurped some noodles into her mouth.

I dropped my school bag and my gym bag to the floor and sagged against the wall, not even trying to hide the despair on my face.

Hannah's eyes widened, and she abandoned the bowl on the kitchen island before rushing to my side. "Hendrix? What happened?"

So many things . . . but there was only one my mind

couldn't seem to stop obsessing over.

"I told someone what I did. All of it. I didn't hold back."

"And?"

"And she threw it back in my face." It was so much more complicated than that, so much else had happened, but I was just so *tired*. I didn't have the energy to explain it all.

"Oh, Hendrix." She took my hand, cocking her head to the side and looking at me with pity. "I'm so sorry."

I didn't want her pity, nor did I deserve it.

"Today feels like it's been three years long. I'm so tired. Can we please talk about it tomorrow?" I begged.

She nodded and gave me a watery smile. "Come eat something."

I squeezed her hand and followed her into the kitchen. I didn't deserve her kindness either, or her ramen, but I was broken, and I'd take it anyway.

After an almost sleepless night, I made my way to school the next morning still with no idea what to do next—about Donna, about Shady, about how ridiculously complicated my life had become. This was exactly why I'd wanted to keep to myself in Devilbend. But I'd failed even at that.

I was tired and deep in my own dark thoughts, so it wasn't until walking up the main stairs to the entrance that I noticed how everyone was acting.

People were steering clear of me, but that wasn't anything new. What was new were the looks they were throwing me, the hushed whispers. Students were glancing in my direction, wide-eyed, but looking away just as fast. Some of the younger students even turned around and rushed away when they spotted me.

A heavy weight settled in the pit of my stomach. I rushed up the rest of the stairs and into the school, ready to deal with whatever fresh hell was coming my way next.

Inside the doors, I came to a complete stop, the blood in my veins turning to ice. My eyes made a slow sweep of the hall as I let it all sink in, including the looks on everyone's faces, and then I took off again.

There was only one person who could've done this.

Practically snarling at anyone who got in my way, I stalked through the school with a single-minded purpose—find Donna Mead.

I was going to wrap my hands around her delicate little neck, and not in the way her freaky ass liked. I wanted to feel her throat under my palms as I squeezed the air out of her. I wanted to feel those fragile bones snap under my hands. It was the only way to make her pay for this—the only way to make sure that bitch never hurt someone with her petty, privileged attitude again.

CHAPTER 23

Donna

I TORE THE PAPER DOWN AND CRUMPLED IT, already rushing to the next one. My hands were full of large torn-down photocopied pages, and as the newest one fell to the ground, I cursed and jogged to the nearest trash can. I was only halfway up the corridor, frantically darting from one side of the lockers to the other to get them all down before more people showed up, before Hendrix saw it.

Logically, I knew it was pointless. They were all over the school, every wall of every corridor covered in identical posters that read, "Hendrix Hawthorn is a killer." The words were in red, stark against several newspaper clippings all photocopied over one another like some macabre collage.

Had someone overheard us talking in the park? I was pretty sure Hendrix hadn't told anyone else in Devilbend about it. Who could've done this? Who would go to this much effort? I racked my brain the entire time I attacked the red-and-black paper, ignoring papercut after papercut in my futile effort to stop this from happening to him.

The only other person I was certain knew was Harlow. After Drew dropped me off at my car the day before, I'd driven straight home. Magda was in the kitchen, stirring a giant pot of something that smelled delicious. She wanted me to taste it, and usually I would have been more than happy to, but I told her I had to go to the bathroom and went straight upstairs.

I was a little numb, my mind not quite able to focus on any particular thought or problem. It had all gone so wrong.

Harlow popped her head out of the bedroom as I got to the top of the stairs. "I've been calling you for half an hour." She frowned. "You OK?"

I glanced at my bedroom door, then bypassed it and went to hers instead, wrapping my sister into a hug and breathing in her smell. Her arms held me tightly.

"Donna, you're scaring me," she whispered into my shoulder.

I pulled back and cleared my throat. "Sorry. I'm fine. Do you have a minute? I need your help with something."

"Yeah. What's up?" She was still watching me warily.

I looked in the direction of the stairs. The faint sounds of Magda moving about the kitchen, the radio on in the background.

Shuffling Harlow into her room, I softly closed the door behind us. "I need you to look into something for me."

The last time I'd said those words to her, we were digging up dirt on the assholes who bullied Mena at her old school. There wasn't anything really illegal about what I was asking. I just wasn't sure I'd be able to find the information myself. And that's what I needed in that moment. Hendrix had told me quite a story, but I needed facts, evidence. I needed something solid to hold on to so I could begin to put my racing thoughts in order.

Or maybe I just needed to not deal with it alone. For once, I wanted someone with me as I dealt with something heavy.

Harlow flopped into her computer chair, and I shoved a pile of clothes off the spare chair in the corner before pulling it over to sit next to her.

She keyed in her password, and her three screens came to life. "What are we looking for?"

"I need to know why Hendrix moved here."

"Uh . . . OK. Do we have something to go on? I need a starting point. Maybe his old school."

I sighed. "I know why he came here. I mean, he told me what happened. I just want to check that—"

"You don't believe him? What did he tell you?"

"No, it's not that I don't believe him exactly. I just . . . fuck." I dropped my head into my hands. How could I articulate to my sister that I just needed to give my brain something to focus on?

"I just need more information," I finally said and

lifted my head to look at her. When she simply raised an eyebrow, I kept talking. "We ditched school this afternoon, and he told me what happened last year, why he transferred here. He, uh . . ."

The words lodged in my throat. He hadn't actually told me not to tell anyone, but it still felt wrong, as if I was betraying his trust when he'd kept all my secrets. *So many secrets.*

But Harlow wouldn't tell anyone, and I needed some clarity. I swallowed and just said it. "He told me he killed someone. It was unintentional, a horrible accident, and he feels like shit for it. I just need to know more."

Harlow stared at me. "Jesus, fuck." She breathed out, then turned to the screens.

In the end, she didn't do much of anything I couldn't have done myself; it just took a fraction of the time. A search of his name and New York brought up countless results—his family was prominent in society there. That led us to the name of his school, which led us to Austin's full name and allowed for more detailed searches. There was an obituary, a few articles.

I got more details, put names to faces, but really, I didn't understand it any better. I didn't understand why he got under my skin so badly. Why I'd lost it at him even after he told me about the person he killed.

"This is some heavy shit, D." Harlow leaned back in her chair. "Did he . . . what's going on between you guys? Are you OK?"

I looked into my sister's eyes, so full of concern, and

the urge to spill it all was almost palpable. But I couldn't do that. My heart quickened at the very thought of it. I was the responsible one, the one who took care of her, the one who did what she was supposed to so that Harlow could do whatever she wanted. I needed a new plan, a way out before I could say anything to anyone. I just wasn't sure what it was I needed a way out of . . .

"I don't know what's going on between us," I told her honestly. "It's more complicated than I can even explain to myself. But please, don't worry. I've never felt unsafe with Hendrix. Not even when he told me about . . . that." I pointed at the screen.

"OK. You wanna talk about it?"

I got to my feet as it dawned on me. *I'd never felt unsafe with Hendrix.* How often had I wished someone would be for me what I was for so many other people—protector, defender, confidant, safe place to land? He'd been exactly that and more from the first time I saw him at Davey's. I'd just been too busy fighting against it to realize it.

I was a fucking idiot.

"No," I whispered, my thoughts far away. I leaned down and kissed my sister on the cheek. "I just need to think for a while. Thank you."

The next morning I texted the girls, asking them to make their own way to school, and headed in early. I'd planned to wait for Hendrix in the parking lot so I could talk to him, swallow my pride and apologize, but I needed to pee, so I ducked into the school—and that was when I saw the posters. *Everywhere.*

I'd started attacking them immediately and had still barely made a dent. I'd only managed to do one hallway and the stairs leading to the back entrance.

"Donna!"

At the sound of Amaya's voice, I looked up from stuffing paper into the trash can.

Amaya, Harlow, and Mena jogged up to me. Other students were milling about too, and I glanced up at the clock. It was only another twenty minutes until the first class.

"Did you tell anyone?" I demanded, my focus on Harlow.

"No." She shook her head. "I would never . . . oh my god."

"Help me get them down," I demanded.

"Have you told a teacher?" Mena asked as the others started tearing down posters.

"No." I shook my head. I'd been so panicked I hadn't even thought of it. "I just started tearing them down as soon as I realized."

"I'll go find someone." Mena rushed off toward the office.

She'd hardly disappeared around the corner when Hendrix came storming down the hallway. The girls stopped ripping down posters as the few other students in the hall darted out of his way. He was furious, shoulders tight, eyes narrowed, scowling—and he was heading right for me.

I knew what this looked like. I rolled my shoulders back and steeled myself, facing him.

He stopped right in front of me and smacked the pile of papers out of my hand, his fist crunching around one as the rest fell to the floor.

"It's a little late for that, isn't it?" He cocked his head and leaned in. Anger was rolling off him in waves, but his voice remained low, seething. "Why bother taking them down when you went to so much effort to plaster the entire fucking school?"

I forced my own voice to come out steady. "Hendrix, I didn't do this."

He chuckled, the sound devoid of any humor. "Oh, of course. The princess doesn't get her hands dirty. You had the help do it for you."

"Hendrix, I didn't do this," I repeated, my fists clenching at my sides.

"You're fucking unbelievable." He was so close now, I could smell the cinnamon on his breath, feel the heat of his rage. "I know I got on your nerves, but all I ever did was try to help you. What I told you yesterday was . . ."

He squeezed his eyes shut for a second, beating back the pain that flashed for just a moment across the stormy pools of gray.

"You keep saying you want me to leave you alone—*fine*. We're done. You're on your own, Donna. If you end up dead in a ditch, I no longer give a shit. I'm done with you, you spiteful bitch."

He took a few steps backward, balled the piece of paper in his hands, and threw it before turning around and storming out. The ball of paper hit me in the chest and bounced to the ground harmlessly, but I flinched so hard. My whole body stiffened with the impact—of his words, his rage, his hurt, all directed at me. And I knew I deserved it. I wasn't responsible for the posters, but that pain in his face—that was my fault.

Tears stung the backs of my eyes, but I forced them back. There was no way in hell I was going to let myself fall apart in front of all these people.

More and more students were arriving every minute, most of them now throwing me confused, curious looks. Mena rushed back from the office, but several teachers had appeared already, tearing the rest of the posters down while trying in vain to keep the students calm.

The girls surrounded me, all looking worried.

"Donna, what's going on?" Amaya kept her voice low, her arms crossed.

I looked around at the chaos once more. I couldn't stand there and talk to them. I needed to do something.

Drew was standing a few feet away. One hand rested on his hip while the other rubbed the back of his neck as he took it all in. But unlike everyone else, there was something more in his eyes—fear.

I narrowed my gaze on him.

"Donna?" Harlow asked, placing a hand on my shoulder.

But I shrugged her off and marched right up to Drew.

He startled when he spotted the murderous look on my face. "Hey, D."

"Cut the bullshit, Drew." I got in his face. "Start talking."

"I . . . I'm . . ." He backed away, his eyes flying about the hall, unable to meet mine.

I shoved him, and even though he was practically twice my size and mostly muscle, he let himself stagger back a step. "Who did it?"

He sighed and leaned in. "It was Will. He—"

I didn't wait for him to finish. I had a name. I turned around and stormed toward the front entrance.

"Donna, wait! I have to tell you . . ." Drew called after me, but I ignored him and just kept going.

The girls fell into step beside me, but I didn't want to drag them into this. I didn't want them to find things out about me I wasn't ready for them to know.

"Amaya, I need to know who else knew about this and why I didn't." I glanced at her. She looked determined, ready to stand by me regardless of the fact she had no idea what this was about. They all had that same look.

She nodded and turned back around.

"Can you two find out how the faculty didn't notice this before students started arriving? And any other info you can get."

Harlow looked hesitant, but Mena pulled her away, heading back to the office.

I jogged down the ornate front stairs and rushed toward the back of the parking lot. Will parked in the back because he was always too late to get a better spot, and because it made it easier to do the other things that made him consistently late to class.

I pulled the door to his Bentley open, not even remotely surprised to see his pants down and Nicola leaning over the center console, giving him a blow job.

They both startled at my sudden appearance. Nicola flinched back against the opposite door, while Will was slower to react, tucking his dick back into his pants as he sighed. "Donna, what the fuck?"

"We need to talk," I snarled. I didn't want to talk. I wanted to hit him, punch him, kick him while I screamed all my frustration out. But that wasn't how my parents had raised me. That wasn't who I was.

Nicola scrambled out of the car and straightened her clothes, eyeing me with fear. "I'm sorry, Donna. I know you and Will ... but you're not technically together, and I ... just please—"

"Shut up." God, she was irritating. I opened the back door and threw her school bag onto the path in front of the car. "I don't give a flying fuck whose dick you wrap those Botox-filled lips around. Get lost."

Her eyes narrowed in anger, and she scooped her bag up and stalked away, muttering "bitch" as she went.

Will got out and fixed his tie. "Was that really necessary?"

"What the fuck is wrong with you?" I asked.

He looked at me as if I were an idiot.

"I know you're responsible for Fulton Academy's new décor." I let the sarcasm drip from my lips. "And I want to know why."

He eyed me for a second, the disinterested

expression melting away into something more calculating. "You really are spreading your legs for that thug," he said, and my stomach plummeted. "I didn't quite believe it when Drew mentioned what he'd seen, but, shit, I don't think I've ever seen you this worked up."

Unbelievable. That arrogant, spoiled, useless piece of . . .

I slapped him. The feelings welling up inside me—ugly, awful, frightening feelings—couldn't be contained any longer, and the next thing I knew, Will's head was turned to the side, and my hand was stinging from the impact.

I curled it into a fist and dug my nails into my palm, using the pain to keep me grounded.

Will fixed me with a blank look, not even reaching up to hold his cheek. "You think you can hurt me?" He chuckled. "You're just a little girl, playing princesses and castles while there's a whole big, dangerous world all around you. Nothing you do can hurt me, Donna."

"You're jealous I fucked another guy, so you're going to ruin his life? How petty, William, especially considering your mediocre cock is still slick with Nicola's saliva."

"I don't have time for this." He swung his bag over his shoulder and slammed the car door shut.

"Don't you fucking walk away from me." I got in his path.

He looked at me as if I was boring him, absolutely no emotion on his face. Will was not at all what I always thought him to be. He was cruel and cold and empty. I couldn't believe I'd considered a future with him.

"Do yourself a favor and stay out of this, D. Now, unless you want to finish what Nicola started, get out of my way."

He didn't wait for a response—just shoved past me and sauntered off toward school.

What an absolute piece of shit of a human being. And he'd set his sights on Hendrix because of *me*.

A sob clawed its way up my throat, but I swallowed it, forced my eyes to remain wide open until they felt raw—until I was certain I wouldn't cry. Not yet.

The bell rang, and it was almost a relief to have something functioning the way it was supposed to. My world was crumbling around me, and I held the sledgehammer in my hands, but the bell tolled anyway.

I had no idea what to do next, how to fix it. So I pulled a calm, detached expression over my face, smoothed my uniform, and walked steadily back to school.

I sat through classes, said the bare minimum to my friends, listened to the announcement from the principal assuring us we were all safe and the culprits of this "prank" would be caught. But I didn't really pay attention to any of it. I spent the entire time going over everything in my head. Every interaction between Hendrix and me, every word, every touch, every loaded look.

I made myself recount all the horrible, vicious things I'd said and done to him. And in the end, it wasn't me who had broken him. In the end, I'd wanted to do the very opposite, but his downfall was my fault anyway.

I was failing in every single area of my life, barely holding it together on a good day, but this . . . this was the worst thing I'd ever done.

I wanted it all to just . . . stop.

CHAPTER 24

Hendrix

THE GLOW OF THE TV WAS THE ONLY LIGHT IN the room as I slumped on the couch, controller between my hands. I was half-heartedly playing with randoms on the internet when someone knocked on the door.

I didn't even glance up. It was probably Robbie, although he usually just let himself in. Aunt Hannah had gone to bed not even half an hour ago.

I'd called her right after my run-in with Donna, completely lost, and she'd left work and come right down to the school. She marched me up to the office and flipped her shit, demanding to know how this had happened, why none of the staff had noticed before the students arrived, what the fuck they were paying their security staff for.

The headmistress calmly answered all her questions while I sat in a chair, scowling at the edge of her desk. Apparently, most of the teachers and admin staff entered the school through a side door that led directly to their offices. The security guard who opened the student entrance in the mornings hadn't bothered to peek inside before walking to his post by the front gates. One of the janitors hadn't shown up to work that morning, and they were still investigating.

She'd probably paid him off, and in a way that he wouldn't even know who he was dealing with. I had to give her that—she was damn smart.

The knock came again, more insistent this time, and then indiscernible voices, hisses—someone arguing.

I rolled my eyes and focused back on the screen. I didn't want to deal with people, didn't even want to *think* right now. It was probably some kids from my school, here to play some prank, or maybe even their incensed parents come to threaten my aunt. The calls from worried, outraged parents had started pouring in as soon as we left campus. People didn't want their kids anywhere near me.

When we got home, I told my aunt everything that had happened between me and Donna over the last few days, leaving out the graphic sexual details. I blamed myself—I'd gotten myself into this mess by not leaving her alone, and I deserved those posters, really. I deserved their fear and contempt and disgust. I deserved their rejection for what I'd done. But I couldn't fight the disappointment, the hurt. I guess I was still human after all.

My aunt listened to it all and, in the end, said she was proud of me. *Proud of me.* For doing what I thought was right. She assured me Fulton wouldn't be able to kick me out, despite how loudly the other parents complained. I was getting good grades, and I'd completely stayed out of trouble. I was a victim in this situation.

That didn't sit well with me. I didn't feel like a victim—I felt like the monster they all now knew I was. But I appreciated her unflinching support anyway.

The knock came again, even louder. I gritted my teeth and glanced toward the stairs. They'd wake my aunt up if they hadn't already. The thought that it could be someone here to harass her was the only reason I tossed the controller down and stormed to the door.

"Get off my property or I'm calling the police." I put a little grunt into my voice, making it firm, threatening, but not too loud—I didn't want to disturb my aunt.

There was a second of perfect stillness and then: "Hendrix, we need to talk to you." The voice was feminine, but it wasn't Donna, and she didn't sound angry. I frowned, wishing the side panel by the door wasn't frosted.

When I didn't respond, another female voice, this one much more demanding, said with a single thump against the wood, "Open the damn door." Amaya. It was definitely her, and that first, uncertain one had been Harlow.

I shook my head and turned to leave. Maybe I *would* call the police.

There was more arguing behind the door, hushed words. Was Donna with them? Standing there with a smirk while they manipulated me into . . . into . . . *shit*, I didn't even know what else she could possibly do to me.

"We don't have time for this." Mena cut across the others, surprising me with the seriousness in her voice. "Hendrix, please open the door."

I sighed, already regretting the decision, but because it was Mena—the only one of them with some goodness in her soul—I turned back around and wrenched the door open.

It was just the three of them.

"What the hell do you want? Here to do your overlord's bidding?" I set my feet wide apart, blocking the door.

"We've been trying to call you. Why didn't you answer?" Amaya frowned. Always on the attack.

I hadn't looked at my phone since I got home. It was probably still on my bed, where I'd dumped everything before changing into sweats. "Why would I want to talk to you? And how the hell do you know where I live?"

"It's in the school records." Harlow waved that away as if it were no big deal they had access to the school records. "We can't find Donna, and we're starting to get worried. We wanted to check with everyone she could be with before telling our parents or the police. Have you seen her?"

I ignored the pang of worry that made the back of my head tingle. She didn't deserve it. Not anymore. "I haven't seen that bitch since this morning, and I don't give a flying fu—"

"She didn't do it." Mena stepped forward and

gripped my arm, looking up at me with those doe eyes. I could see why Turner was so protective of her—she looked like the perfect meal for a wolf. "Donna didn't put those posters up. She didn't know anything about it. It was William Frydenberg."

"What?" I frowned. They had to be lying. But why? What game were they playing now?

"It's true. She confronted him about it, and they got into a fight. She slapped him. And Drew confirmed it when Amaya asked him. It was Will. Donna didn't know anything about it, I swear. We would know if she'd planned something like this. I would've talked her out of it."

"She's been acting weird all day," Amaya cut in before I could argue, slam the door in their faces. "She was really detached, hardly talked to anyone, just kind of went through the motions."

Harlow was on the verge of tears. "When we got home after school, she just shut herself in her room. She didn't even come down for dinner. When Mom went to check on her, she said she was sick, but when I went to her room after everyone was in bed, she was gone. Her car is gone, and she's not picking up the phone. *Please*, Hendrix, do you know where she might be?"

"Why do you think I'd know anything?" I was still a little wary, but the implications were slowly sinking in, making my shoulders tense. Mena wasn't one to lie, and I couldn't deny the fear in Harlow's eyes. Even Amaya— who I'd never seen bothered by anything—looked worried.

It could be a trick, another game, but I didn't think it was. Maybe I was just desperate for it to be true. I so badly didn't want it to have been her who'd ruined me.

"We know you two have been hooking up," Amaya answered. "We know there's more to the story, but that's not important right now."

I watched them for a few moments longer, trying to hold on to my anger, my hurt. But in my gut, I knew this was the truth. Donna hadn't done it. It was Will and . . . they had a history, maybe even a future from what she'd told me . . . they'd argued . . . she'd be blaming herself. On top of everything else.

"Fuck." I dragged a hand down my face. "I know where she might be."

I pulled on my shoes and grabbed my keys off the side table. "I'll drive, but you three need to be prepared. This . . . is not going to be pretty."

***

I white-knuckled the steering wheel, wishing for the first time I'd spent dear Dad's money on some obnoxious sports car instead of the Tesla. Not because the Tesla wasn't fast—it was. It glided through the night, practically flying toward our destination. No, it was the absolute silence of the high-tech machine that made me wish for something with an engine that grunted. I wanted a beast under me, one that growled with all the rage I wished I could let loose.

Amaya sat next to me in the passenger seat, Mena

and Harlow in the back. For the first twenty minutes of the drive, I'd told them everything—how Donna and I first met at Davey's, how she'd been going there for months, the early acceptance and her constant self-destructive behavior. Every single one of their questions I'd answered without hesitation.

She'd kept my secret—it was Will who'd exposed me, I was sure of it now—and I was betraying all of hers. I wasn't sorry. I had half a mind to call her parents and put them on speaker as I let it all spill out. It was the only thing I could do until we found her. The only thing keeping my fear at bay until we could figure out if she was . . . I couldn't let myself think the worst.

I'd texted Shady before we took off, asking him to keep an eye out for her, but he hadn't replied.

The girls had all fallen into silence. Amaya was staring out the front window, watching the headlight beams illuminate the road as it whipped past. Her eyes were a little wide, her chest rising and falling with labored breaths.

I wanted to look into the back seat, but I was pretty sure the other two would be wearing matching expressions, and I had to focus on the road.

We were nearly there, and I needed to keep my shit together. I needed to figure out how to get the three girls to stay in my car while I went inside and looked for her. All three of them would certainly fight me on it, demand to help me look, but I couldn't risk them getting hurt— Donna would never forgive me.

I should've been thinking of a way to convince

them, should've already started making my case as I pulled onto the dim, run-down street, but I couldn't get my mind off what we'd find.

The worst-case scenario—the one where she was dead in a ditch, as I'd practically told her that morning I hoped she would be—was too hard to even consider. But there were so many other scenarios. What if someone spiked her drink again and took her? What if she pissed off the wrong person? What if she'd gotten in an accident on the way here? What if she'd already found some biker dude with a cocky attitude and big biceps? What if they were already out in the back alley where I'd . . . where we'd . . .

What if she wasn't even there and we'd wasted precious time?

I was so lost in the worry, the rage, the abject fear of what we'd find—or wouldn't—that I nearly missed the turn. I slammed on the brakes and yanked the steering wheel toward the parking lot entrance. The sudden force sent us all flying to the side, and I reflexively threw a hand out to catch Amaya across her abdomen. But the car was the epitome of precision and safety, and it corrected my sudden moves, not even sliding out as we pulled into the lot.

Amaya covered my arm with hers, breathing even harder now.

"Sorry," I muttered. She just shoved my hand away without saying anything.

I slowed considerably as we neared the entrance. The bouncer was there, looking mean as ever as he nodded to a group of rough guys heading through the front door. The one at the rear of the group wasn't even trying to hide the gun tucked into the back of his pants. Beside them, a woman leaned over and vomited right on the footpath.

Mena made a sound of disgust as Harlow finally found her voice. "This is where Donna has been coming secretly? Jesus."

Amaya just stared, jaw tight.

I steered past rows of cars toward the dark corner of the lot where I knew she liked to park. As we approached the area, I wasn't sure if I was hoping to see the flawless pearlescent finish of her BMW in among this filth—or if I was hoping to find nothing at all.

CHAPTER 25

Donna

I TOOK THE TURN INTO THE RATTY STREET A little too fast. Then I overcorrected and weaved from side to side until I managed to force my car into a straight line again. The adrenaline sent a hit of pleasure shooting through my veins, even as some addled part of my brain screamed that I was an idiot who'd get myself killed before I even got to Davey's.

I knew I shouldn't have been driving after drinking—I'd *never* done it before—but I was beyond caring.

After school, I'd shut myself in my room, unable to face anyone, unable to really process everything—not just that day but the last several months.

I'd failed. How spectacularly I'd failed at *everything*. I had no idea where to go from here. *Me*. Donna Mead. I prided myself on how organized and prepared and determined I was in all things. But suddenly I found myself sitting on my bed, staring out the window as the light disappeared, with absolutely no fucking idea what I was supposed to do now.

Every time Hendrix's face popped into my mind, I fought back tears. I'd failed him the most. And I knew—*I knew*—if I let those tears fall, if I gave in to the emotion, I'd fall apart, and no one would know where to even start putting me back together.

All the king's horses and all the king's men . . . the wall I'd fallen from was so, *so* tall.

When I'd realized I was sitting in pitch blackness, I reached over and turned on the lamp by my bed.

My reflection stared back at me from the dark glass of my window. I didn't like what I saw, so I looked away.

I wanted to go away. Make it stop. I just wanted to be able to breathe. To be someone else for a while.

Dark Donna . . .

I didn't even wait to make sure everyone was asleep before leaving the house; I just waited until it sounded quiet. No one even noticed me walk—not sneak—down the stairs, get into my car, and leave. No one even cared.

After leaving my house, I decided that maybe getting blind drunk was a better option than going to Davey's. I wanted oblivion, but I didn't really want to hook up with anyone who wasn't . . . I didn't want anyone but *him* touching me.

Don't think his name.

So I drove to a liquor store and used my excellent fake ID to buy an obscenely expensive bottle of scotch.

It wasn't until I was back in my car and the smooth scent of the liquor hit the back of my nose that I realized why I'd picked that particular alcohol. I never drank scotch, but I'd craved something smoky, spicy—because it was the closest I could get to the cinnamon that clung to Hendrix. That stupid gum he chewed ... the scent always lingered, it was always on his tongue, in his kisses, on his breath as he told me he hated me.

I ground my teeth against the threatening tears and took a big swig, the alcohol so smooth it hardly even burned my throat. It just warmed my chest and belly, already numbing the pain, already giving me something else to focus on.

With every drink, I forced myself to think of other things that weren't him. Campfires, cigars, the smoked cheese Harlow and I had gorged ourselves on during our last family trip to Paris.

I didn't know how long I'd sat in my car, drinking and trying not to think about Hendrix, but nearly half the bottle was gone when I decided I did indeed need to go to Davey's. I couldn't go home, and I didn't want to sit in the car alone, crying and drinking. It was the one place that never failed to let me get lost, let me forget everything.

As I pulled into the parking lot, I made myself breathe, focus. I couldn't go smashing into parked cars. Not when I'd finally made it. Even though I was a fucking mess, that little part of my logical brain had managed to remind me to take the back streets instead of the freeway, to drive slowly. I was irrationally annoyed at how long it had taken to get here. Self-preservation was so weird . . .

I parked the car in the back of the lot where there was more room, where I was able to park across two spots at a weird angle and hit the divider without anyone noticing. Then I grabbed the bottle from the passenger seat, swung the door wide open, and hauled myself out. My vision blurred, and I took a moment to steady myself before walking toward the front entrance, leaving my car open, my purse just sitting there, the keys still in the ignition. Nothing mattered anymore.

I took another swig as my heels crunched in the gravel, my footing uneven. I'd changed into a low-cut gray top and applied dark eyeliner before I decided it actually didn't matter what I wore. My school skirt and socks had stayed on, and I'd added a pair of heeled Mary Janes to complete the weird ensemble. I was pretty sure I looked like some slutty porn version of a school girl with my cleavage hanging out and the heels on, but I didn't care.

I had no idea who I was anymore, which version of myself I was *pretending* to be. The clothes were a representation of all the lies I'd told to everyone, to myself. Of this ugly downward spiral I was on and didn't care to prevent.

The good girl gone bad . . . *rotten to the core.*

"Donna." My name. His voice, so rough, so demanding, no—*pleading.*

I gritted my teeth and took another swig from the bottle. I'd pushed the image of his tortured face from my mind so hard that now I was hearing him in my head.

"Donna!" Louder, more insistent. The sound of crunching gravel wasn't just from my own unsteady steps.

I stopped. He was here. My heart soared.

He was here. My heart plummeted into the dirty gravel at my feet.

I turned, resigned. But I didn't see Hendrix. No, the first thing my addled, fucked-up mind latched on to was Harlow.

My sister stopped, her eyes wide, taking me in. There were a few feet between us—an entire ocean, the Grand Canyon. Mena stood next to her, tears trailing down her cheeks unabashedly as she watched the train wreck I'd become, had been for so long already. Amaya was on Harlow's other side, hands on hips, breathing hard. The other two were shocked, worried, upset, and Amaya probably was too, but she was the most like me. In the moment, she was ready to take charge, ready to get answers, ready to fix the situation.

Well, I wasn't a *situation*, and this couldn't be fixed. I frowned, fighting the dizziness from the alcohol. "What . . . how did you know . . ."

That's when I spotted Hendrix. He was standing behind my friends, his face cast in shadow from one of the few lights still operational in the parking lot.

He was here. He'd come after me despite everything. *He was here . . .*

He'd brought my friends here . . .

What had he told them? Who else knew?

I narrowed my eyes, homing in on the one person who could make me feel more angry—*more alive*—than any other. I focused on Hendrix as my world fell apart.

"What the fuck have you done?" I sneered, my breathing getting faster and faster.

He blinked but didn't look surprised I was turning my rage on him.

"You've ruined everything." I seethed, taking a few wobbling steps forward.

As one, my friends moved toward me, ready to steady me, to break my fall. But maybe I needed to crash into the filthy gravel, let it scrape away all the ugly parts of me until nothing but clean, raw blood showed. I couldn't look at them.

I threw the bottle between us, stopping them in their tracks. The bottle didn't even break—just thumped to the ground and started spilling amber liquid.

Gravel dug into my soles as I tugged off my shoes and kept moving toward Hendrix on unsteady feet.

"I told you to keep your mouth shut. I told you not to tell anyone. I told you to leave me *alone*." I threw my shoes to the ground, like a toddler throwing toys.

I was directly in front of him now, wishing I'd kept the shoes on so I wouldn't have to look up to meet his resigned stare.

"I told you!" I screamed into his face.

He pressed his lips together but didn't respond, hardly moved other than the rise and fall of his labored breathing. He was barely keeping it together too.

But I didn't give a shit. This was *my* mental breakdown. He could wait his turn.

The realization that that was what was happening to me—that I was acting like a completely unhinged, crazed lunatic—was the last straw. Because that's what I was.

Unhinged.

Driving drunk.

Throwing things.

Screaming at people.

Crazy.

Lunatic.

The tears I'd been holding at bay all day burst out of me—a dam breaking. But even as I started crying, *sobbing*, I railed against what was happening to me. What I'd allowed myself to become.

"Why?" I cried as I shoved Hendrix. He hardly even leaned back at the force of my hands on his chest. "Why did you tell them? They know. They can see. I'm . . . I begged you . . ."

I pounded his chest with my fists, pulled at his sweatshirt. "You told them my secret but I kept yours!"

When the reality of the situation washed over me, I made myself look up into his eyes again. His jaw was tight, a muscle jumping in his cheek as if he was grinding his teeth, his eyes blazing with emotions I was not equipped to decipher in my current state.

But he was still there, still standing as solid as a stone pillar.

How many times had he saved me—*from myself?*

I sobbed, the energy draining out of me as I dropped my gaze.

"I kept your secret." The anger that had edged my voice just moments before drained away, and I gripped his sweatshirt. "It wasn't me, Hendrix. I didn't ... I would never ... I'm sorry."

His hands landed on my back just as my knees wobbled. He was finally touching me, finally holding me.

"Please believe me. Please, please, please ..." I had no idea what I was pleading for. My voice was barely above a whisper as I sagged against him.

I fully expected him to push me off, dump me on the ground and walk away. It was all my fault. *It was all my fault.*

"No, it's not." His low voice reverberated through his chest. My whole body shook with emotion, and my knees buckled.

But Hendrix was there, his arms tightening around me, keeping me from falling.

I was heavy in his arms, a dead weight, a burden. But he'd never let me down, never wavered, even as I'd pushed him away at every step. And he didn't waver now, didn't let me fall.

His strong arms banded around my back as I clung to him, one hand going to the back of my head.

"It's OK, baby," he whispered against my hair. "It's going to be OK."

A small glimmer of peace flickered in my chest at his words, a tiny bit of sanity returning, reminding me he was here, that I was not alone, that my friends had come too.

Harlow. Mena. Amaya.

They were all here, all watching me unravel, watching Hendrix hold me together.

My addled thoughts were interrupted by my heaving stomach.

"Shit." I lifted my head from Hendrix's chest, gave him one wide-eyed look, then leaned to the side and vomited.

CHAPTER 26

Donna

IT DIDN'T TAKE ME LONG TO REALIZE THE BED wasn't my own. The light on my face was coming from a different direction from where my window should be, and the pillow was softer than mine. It also smelled like Amaya—that feminine, light perfume my friend wore.

My head ached. It felt as if someone were squeezing it between big, strong hands, every thought coming through a fog.

I remembered most of the previous night—I was never the type to lose memory when drunk, even when I polished off half a bottle of scotch. Thinking about the amber liquid made my stomach spasm, and my mouth filled with saliva.

I forced a deep breath down my nose and blew it out, then another and another, until the urge to puke subsided. There was nothing left in my stomach to vomit out anyway—I'd just be retching and feeling even more miserable.

Squeezing my eyes shut against the light, I rolled into an even tighter ball and snuggled farther into the bedding. For the first time since I'd learned to tell time, I didn't give a crap how late it was. Nothing mattered other than how utterly broken my body felt. My mind and my heart weren't much better.

After I'd started puking all over the gravel, Hendrix had stepped behind me, out of the firing line, so he could hold me. With one arm wrapped around the front of my shoulders and the other low on my hips, he held up my full weight as I vomited the entire contents of my stomach. The sudden sickness must've roused my friends from their shocked stupor. Soft feminine hands appeared at my forehead to pull my short hair back, and someone else produced a bottle of water and a wad of tissues.

After that, Hendrix carried me to my car, and my friends buckled me in and drove me away. I hardly heard what they said to each other, hardly registered Mena giving Amaya directions out of the seedy neighborhood as Harlow ran her fingers through my hair, my head in her lap.

I managed to walk myself up to Amaya's room—thankful I didn't have to suffer the indignity of having my girls carry me up—and passed out as soon as I collapsed on her bed, totally spent in every way imaginable. Judging by the T-shirt and underwear I'd woken up in, they'd taken the time to change me and tuck me under the covers.

I sighed in frustration and threw the covers back, keeping my eyes closed. More than anything, I just wanted to go back to sleep, embrace unconsciousness, and pretend for a little longer that none of this was happening. But now that I was awake, I couldn't stop thinking, remembering, worrying. Plus, the awful pressure in my head and clammy, gross feeling in my entire body made it impossible to relax.

I cracked my eyes open and hissed at the light, then forced myself to lift up onto my elbows.

"Morning, sunshine." Amaya's bright voice was like talons against my brain. I glared at her, but it turned into a wince as another sharp pain shot through my head. My friend was sitting on the bed next to me, propped up against the headboard, her phone clutched in her elegant fingers.

"Were you watching me sleep? Fucking creep." My voice was hoarse, scratchy. Probably from all the crying and screaming at Hendrix. Also the vomiting. God, was I a mess.

"Don't flatter yourself. I was scrolling the gram while you snored. I was actually trying to decide whether to post this lovely pic of you." She showed me her screen, a sweet smile on her face. It was a picture of me sleeping, my mouth open, my face smooshed into the pillow. The one visible eye was dark with smudged mascara.

I lunged for her. "Don't you fucking dare!"

She laughed maniacally and leaned back, slapping me away.

"You started the 'beat her ass' portion of the intervention without us?" My sister's voice alerted me to her arrival, but I was too busy trying to pin Amaya under me to look. She was skinny, but she was fast.

"It stinks in here." Mena went to the window and threw it wide open; a gust of fresh, chilly air sent a shiver down my spine. My tousle with Amaya came to a natural end, both of us panting.

Amaya made a face. "Your breath is hideous."

"Come on." Harlow yanked the sheet off the bed, detangling it from my legs. "Go have a shower and brush your teeth."

"Then breakfast." Mena smiled from the window.

"Then interrogation." Amaya nodded.

"Intervention," Harlow and Mena said at the same time, making me think they'd already argued about how to approach this ... situation. I didn't want to be a situation.

I crawled off the bed and shuffled into Amaya's adjoining bathroom without looking at any of them. Her bedroom was luxurious, with soft furnishings, velvet cushions, and everything in rich jewel tones. The bathroom was just as dark and moody, black marble and muted gold fixtures everywhere.

Avoiding my reflection in the mirror, I hopped into the shower and scrubbed my face before using Amaya's toothbrush. I also did my best to avoid thinking about how much Hendrix had told them, what they thought of me now, what they'd said to each other while I slept.

Someone had left fresh underwear and sweats for

me on the bathroom counter. I changed quickly and stepped out to find my friends all scattered about the bedroom, sipping from steaming mugs. A tray with a fourth mug and a plate had been laid out on the bed—for me.

Shame burned the back of my neck as I sat down in front of it, the feeling as tangible as the droplets of water coming off my wet hair.

They'd made me plain toast and a cup of chamomile tea.

I nibbled on the toast, focusing on the food, on pushing through the queasy feeling in my stomach. No one said anything. The only noises were the occasional sips of coffee and the wind and birds through the open window. So weird for my usually loud, animated, opinionated friends.

I finished the first piece of toast and pushed the plate away, unable to stomach the second. Bringing the mug to my lips, I blew gently on the hot liquid.

I needed to get this conversation going, air out this odd tension between us just as the room was getting aired out by the fresh wind.

My first sip was pleasantly warm as it made its way down my throat. I sighed and opened my mouth to speak, but . . . I wasn't sure where to start, so I closed it again and frowned into my tea. I was kind of sick of always being the one to start the conversations, to take the lead. I felt like shit. If they wanted to talk, they could talk. I was just going to nurse my hangover.

"How are you feeling?" Mena sat down on the bed

next to me, her kindness immediately making me feel guilty for what I'd just been thinking.

I swallowed and took a deep breath. "Like shit."

I looked up into my cousin's face. There was no judgment, no pity, just a readiness to listen, maybe a little worry.

"Good." Amaya took a sip from her mug. She was sitting in a magenta armchair in the corner. "Serves you right for what you put us through."

"You really had us scared, D." Harlow sounded unsure whether she wanted to scold me or plead with me. She was perched on the bench under the window, one leg propped up as she leaned on her knee.

"I'm sorry I worried you guys." I sighed. If Harlow—if any one of them—disappeared like that and I found them in the state I'd been in ... "Last night was ... yesterday ..." I couldn't find the words. Because it wasn't really about yesterday. It was about months, years, *all of it*.

Harlow moved my tray to the floor and sat cross-legged in front of me. "What's going on with you? Why won't you talk to us? Let us help?"

I shrugged. "I don't know. I just ... you all have your own things going on, your own problems. And it's not like there was some catastrophic thing that happened. It was just one thing after another piling up, and I didn't want to burden you. I thought I could handle it myself—that I *should* handle it myself. But shit just kept building and building ..."

Amaya snorted, and a bit of frustration shot

through me. I stared her down as she slammed her now empty mug on her desk and came to stand by the bed. This was just her—how she reacted to hurt—but I didn't want to deal with it.

She spoke before I could say anything I'd regret. "That's a load of shit, Donna. You didn't want to burden us? So, it's OK for you to help Harlow with her homework and get her out of trouble with teachers, it's OK for you to listen to me bitch about my mom, it's OK for you to rain down hell when Mena was getting bullied, but we can't be there for you? You're not a goddamn robot. You can't do everything yourself, and it's bullshit that you didn't trust us to help you."

"What? I trust you girls with my life." I reached out and took her hand. She let me, but didn't break that hard stare. "Devilbend Dynasty is not just a silly hashtag to me. This has nothing to do with me not trusting you and everything to do with my fucked-up head."

I needed them to understand that this was all because of my need to handle my own shit—maybe because I was the oldest, maybe because of how driven everyone in our family was, maybe because I'd fallen into a pattern of showing everyone a tough, unshakeable face. Who knew why I was the way I was? It was something to figure out later, but I needed them to know it had nothing to do with how I felt about them.

"What did Hendrix tell you?" I asked.

Amaya just stared.

"A lot," Mena finally answered.

"He pretty much didn't shut up the entire ride

over." Harlow rolled her eyes.

"About Davey's? Why I go there? What I do there?" They nodded.

"About college? The early acceptance?"

More nods.

"About . . . us?"

"He was scant on details about that," Harlow said.

It was time for more honesty. I swallowed and looked at each of them. "I'm sorry I lied to you, kept things from you. I'm sorry I didn't come to you for help and support. But please, don't leave me. I need you girls."

"No one's leaving you, you idiot." Amaya finally flopped down onto the bed and squeezed my hand back. "Just talk to us."

Surrounded by my friends, I told them everything—the internship I didn't get, the volunteer position I'd idiotically lost, the early acceptance that made me realize I didn't want to go to law school, the way going to Davey's made me feel free of it all for a little while, how the danger of hooking up with hard men made me feel alive.

They listened to it all, held me, supported me, asked questions, reassured me we'd find solutions. They were exactly the kind of friends I hadn't given them a chance to be. I promised myself I'd never shut them out again. Then I promised them, out loud.

After talking it through properly, in detail, with three sounding boards—it didn't feel so insurmountable. It no longer felt as if I was single-handedly holding up an entire building. I'd speak to my parents, hard as it would be. I'd figure out what I wanted to do after high school. I'd lean on my friends more for support and guidance. In fact, now that they knew it all, I felt a little silly for how much the pressure had gotten to me, how spectacularly I'd fallen apart the night before. But they made me feel better about that too.

We sat on that bed for hours.

I even told them about Hendrix, the full story this time—how he'd caught me at the bar, how we'd been hooking up, how he'd been trying to keep me safe, trying to help me.

"Well, shit." Amaya rubbed the back of her neck. "Now I wish I'd let him come home with us."

"Huh?" I looked between them.

Harlow chuckled. "Yeah, he wanted to help us take care of you, but Amaya barked at him to back off and just drove away."

"All we had to go off was his word." Mena crossed her arms. "For all we knew, he was the reason you were so messed up in the first place."

"What's going on with you guys now?" Amaya asked. I'd told them everything that had happened, but even I had no idea where we stood. The things we'd said to each other, the way I'd repeatedly pushed him away . . . He'd come for me last night, helped my friends save me before I got seriously hurt, but that didn't mean all was forgiven. That didn't mean he'd want anything to do with me after all I'd put him through.

"I don't . . ." I bit my lip. That wasn't entirely true

anymore. I knew what I wanted. "I don't know where I stand with him. If he can forgive me. But . . . shit. I really like him. More than like him. I think he might be the real deal."

"He believed us, last night." Mena rubbed my shoulder. "When we told him it was Will and not you who was responsible for the posters. He helped us find you. He still cares."

"Yeah, but Will . . . it's still my fault. I don't know if I can even ask him to forgive me for how awful I've been."

Before anyone could say another word, Amaya cursed and frowned at her phone. It had been vibrating with notifications the entire time we'd been talking, but that wasn't anything new. She had a pretty big following on Instagram. "Is Drew blowing up anyone else's phone?"

Mena and Harlow pulled theirs from their pockets. I had no idea where mine was.

"I have twelve missed calls." Mena frowned.

"Same. And no messages." Harlow looked around at us.

Amaya's phone buzzed again. She rolled her eyes and picked up. "Why are you blowing up our phones? We're kinda in the middle of—"

We could hear Drew's voice on the other end but couldn't make out what he was saying.

Amaya sat up straighter, the annoyance draining from her face to be replaced with something more serious. "We're at my place. Just come here."

Another moment of silence, then she hung up and looked at us all. "He's freaking out. Something about Will and . . . Hendrix."

I shot to my feet. "What happened?"

"I don't know." Amaya's voice remained calm. "But he was already in the car. He should be here any minute."

I rushed to the window overlooking her curved driveway, and sure enough, a few minutes later, Drew's Audi came tearing toward the house. As soon as the car slammed to a halt, Drew jumped out and rushed to the door. His footsteps pounded on the stairs, and then he was standing just outside Amaya's room, breathing hard.

"Shit." He ran both hands through his hair. "I shouldn't be dragging you into this. Never mind."

He turned to leave, but we all lunged for him at the same time, shouting over one another. Between the four of us pulling at his clothes and scolding him, we managed to drag him back into the room. He took a seat at the foot of the bed, and the four of us lined up in front of him, blocking the door.

"Drew, what is going on?" I demanded. It felt good to have that steel back in my voice, the strength returning to my spine. "Are you OK? Is Hendrix?"

"Yeah, Hendrix is fine." He waved that away, then fixed me with a look. "It's you I'm worried about."

"Me?" I raised my eyebrows, not giving anything away. Had he found out about my meltdown somehow?

"Will . . ." Drew swallowed. "Will's lost the plot, and

I don't know what to do. I don't want to drag you girls into it, but I'm worried about you, D—what he might do. And I . . . I don't know how to make them stop."

He ran his hands through his hair again, and I shared worried glances with the girls. Mena sat down next to him and rubbed his shoulder, just as she'd been rubbing mine earlier.

"You're not making any sense," Amaya said. "What don't you want to drag us into?"

He released a big breath and leaned his elbows on his knees. "Last year, just before the school year ended, some of the guys and I . . . we got into some shit."

"Stop being vague," I demanded.

"Fights. We started going to these illegal fights Will somehow found out about. At first it was just to watch, make bets. But after a while, some of the guys started fighting too. It was fun at first, a rush, all that money passing hands. But the people running it . . . the opponents they were pitting the guys against got tougher and meaner, and we started walking away with more bruises and less money. And then they wouldn't let us walk away at all."

"Luke and the guys. The car accident." I clenched my fists, forcing my breathing to remain even. Over the summer, four of the guys on the football team had been in a horrible accident, and none of them could play anymore. "They were hurt in a fight and not an accident."

Will shook his head. "No. It was a car accident. It just wasn't exactly *accidental.* The people running the fights got in touch after, made it clear. That's what would happen to anyone else wanting to leave."

The words coming out of Amaya's mouth were filthy even for her. Harlow wrapped her arms around herself.

"You're all a bunch of fucking idiots," I said calmly. "You couldn't just hire some hookers and trash your daddy's yacht like regular rich assholes? You had to go and get involved in some dodgy fight club? That is the most toxic-masculinity, stupid-ass bullshit I've ever heard."

"I know!" Drew pleaded, hands splayed out. "We all lost interest pretty quickly, but they wouldn't let us leave, and now . . . I don't know what to do."

"What does this have to do with Hendrix? With me?"

"Apparently, they tried to get Hendrix to fight before, invited him, but he said no." Because he'd vowed never to lift a hand against another human being again. Despicable trash-bag assholes . . . "So, the posters exposing him—they're trying to bait him, make him angry. Someone's decided he'd make them a lot of money, that he's worth the trouble of . . . coercing. And Will seems to be in with this shit way deeper than I thought. I should've known." He gritted his teeth. "It was always Will with the information on the next fight, always Will making the first bet. I don't know what the hell he's doing, but that's why he put the posters up. It had nothing to do with jealousy over you. But now that he knows how much you care . . ."

The blood drained from my face. Even as a weight lifted—relief that it wasn't because of me Hendrix had been exposed—another heavier one settled in the pit of my stomach.

Drew nodded, as if he could see the horror washing over me. "After you laid into him yesterday, he realized that you and Hendrix—that there's something more there. And I'm worried he'll try to use it. Use you to get Hendrix to do what he wants."

Drew heaved a massive sigh, a punctuation to the clusterfuck he'd just dumped on us.

"Why haven't you gone to the police?" Amaya asked.

"Honestly? I'm scared." He rubbed his thighs, as if his fear was something to be ashamed of. "All the others are too. We don't want to get charged with anything, and we don't know if we'll get dragged down with the rest of them. Plus, I'm worried if Will finds out it was me . . . he'll tell the others and . . ." He was scared for his life. He actually thought these people might kill him. Considering the state Luke and the guys had been in, I didn't blame him. "Plus, it's not that simple. We never know when or where the fight will happen until the day of, sometimes just hours before."

Harlow stepped forward with a pen and a piece of paper. "Can you write the addresses down for me?"

Drew nodded and started to write things down as I mulled over what he'd told us. When he was done, he handed the paper to my sister, who had already situated herself at the desk and was filling Amaya's computer screen with weird windows of text.

"Thanks for the warning, Drew," I said and meant it. "But I'm not sure what we can do about it either. Maybe it's time we told our parents? There's got to be a way to get the police involved and keep you safe."

Drew nodded, but he looked solemn, drained. "I was thinking that too, but I can't really go to my dad." Drew's father had never laid a hand on his son, but he was a cold, unfeeling man who was always happy to point out failures, never successes. "I was thinking, maybe, with all your connections in the legal field . . . I don't know."

He was hoping I'd know what to do, who to speak to, how to handle this best. Because I always had answers, always had a plan, was always willing to do whatever it took for my friends.

I was tired, hungover, and sick of everyone thinking I was unbreakable. But Drew was a friend, and I had my girls with me all the way.

My hand closed over his. "We'll figure it out."

I didn't know how, but we would. Together.

"Shit." Harlow's wide eyes were scanning the screen as if to double-check—*triple-check*—what she was seeing. Then she turned to us, her hands gripping the edge of the desk. "Those addresses aren't random. I figured out what they have in common. Or rather *who*. We have a big problem, you guys."

CHAPTER 27

Hendrix

THE SHEETS WERE POOLED AROUND MY HIPS, my wide-open eyes staring at the dark ceiling. I'd tried to go to bed after watching a movie with my aunt, but I'd just ended up lying awake, wrapped in the gloomy silence.

It had been a full twenty-four hours, and I still hadn't heard from Donna or her friends. I'd wanted so badly to follow them home, barge into the house and help them take care of her, but I knew they'd just had a bomb dropped on them. She didn't make it easy on any of us. So I gave them space, didn't call or text. But as I stared into the blackness, running everything over in my mind for the millionth time, I wondered if that was a mistake.

Maybe she was waiting for me to reach out, show her I cared. I frowned at the thought. Hadn't my actions over the past few months shown that already? Yeah, I'd told her friends shit she didn't want them to know, but I had no other choice.

It was kind of bullshit that, after everything, she hadn't even texted to tell me she was OK. But then, it wasn't as if we were together—she didn't owe me anything. And I didn't owe her jack shit either. So I'd deleted every message I'd half written throughout the day.

The uncertainty was killing me, but I was done chasing Donna Mead.

With a frustrated sigh, I sat up, rested my elbows on my knees, and rubbed my sore eyes. I'd hardly slept after coming home the night before. I was exhausted, and yet I was still completely incapable of sleeping.

Resigned to putting on another movie to drown out my thoughts, I was just getting out of bed when a sound from the window made me pause. I turned toward it and frowned. It sounded like a tap, maybe a branch knocking against the glass. Except there wasn't any wind—or any trees near my window.

The sound came again—a low *ping*, something solid but small hitting the glass. I edged toward the window and pulled back the curtain.

Donna stood in my yard, her hand raised as if she was about to throw something, but she lowered her arm when she saw me. That crazy bitch was throwing pebbles at my window even though we both had perfectly functioning phones.

I shook my head, torn between amusement and annoyance. What the hell?

She held my gaze for a moment, then folded her arms and cocked her head, silently gesturing for me to come outside.

I pinched the bridge of my nose and sighed, but when I looked at her again, I knew I'd go. I'd go wherever she wanted me, whenever she needed me. Because I had it bad for the petite blonde bundled in a gray coat, standing in my yard in the middle of the night.

After giving her one nod, I turned from the window to pull on sweatpants and a hoodie, then picked up my shoes and padded softly down the hall. I wasn't trying to do anything behind my aunt's back, but I didn't want to disturb her either.

The night air was crisp and cold, and I zipped the hoodie all the way up as I stepped out the back door. Donna turned and walked to the back of the yard as soon as I appeared, edging past the shrubs at the bottom of the property. I stuffed my hands into my pockets and followed.

Donna waited for me on the walking path that ran down the backs of the yards, along a nature reserve on the other side. She waved her phone at me, then silently held her hand out and gave me an expectant look.

This behavior was weird even for her.

"You wa—"

She slapped her hand over my mouth, cutting off my words. I was so stunned I didn't even know what to do. With her phone still in hand, she pressed one finger to her lips in a silent order to be quiet.

I frowned at her.

She ran her hand over the pockets of my hoodie, making my abs tighten at her touch, then moved to the ones on my pants. Several dirty jokes ran through my mind, making me smirk, but I remained silent. Even so, she still gave me a withering look as she located my phone and removed it.

My smile remained in place as she hid both phones under a bush and gave me another "let's go" gesture. She was acting really weird, but I still followed without hesitation.

We walked the silent path shoulder to shoulder, the half moon and occasional back porch light the only illumination.

Once the path veered away from the houses and into the woods, Donna finally spoke.

"Sorry about that. Harlow insisted on no phones."

"Uh . . . what?" I chuckled. "That doesn't actually explain anything."

"I know. Just . . . come on." She picked up the pace, and after another few minutes of walking, we emerged into a clearing surrounded by trees.

Harlow and Amaya were bundled into coats, shoulders up near their ears against the cold. Next to them, Turner had his arms around Mena, pressed in close behind her. But it was the presence of Drew—the quarterback of the football team and Will's friend—that made me pause.

Every muscle in my body tensed, ready for . . . I wasn't even sure what. I had no idea what this bizarre situation was about.

"Dark woods. Middle of the night." I made a show of looking around. "Are we planning to sacrifice a virgin or something?"

Drew and Amaya both snorted while Harlow grinned. "There's no virgins here, trust me."

"Hey, man." Turner nodded to me from across the clearing. "There's something you need to know."

I rolled my shoulders and stepped forward to join their weird little circle. Turner was my friend. I could trust him. "OK. And this something I need to know couldn't have been put into a text or a phone call?"

"No phones." Harlow's tone brooked no arguments.

"Relax." Donna rolled her eyes. "We ditched the phones, as instructed."

Baby Mead nodded but gave me an apologetic look. "Sorry. I know it's weird. But when you're dealing with corporations, you don't take chances. People worry about governments spying on us, but most government departments are running Windows XP on hardware that belongs in a museum. Meanwhile, Google knows more about you than your own mother, and *we let them.* It's willful ignorance. And it's because corporations have the money and the latest tech. So . . ."

"Riiight." I squinted at her. She had the hood of her purple coat up, her blonde hair tangling with the white fur trim. No tin foil hat in sight, and yet . . .

"Hey, before we go any further." Drew stepped forward and held a hand out. "I'm Drew. I know we haven't met properly, but I just want you to know that if

D trusts you, so do I. Also, I had nothing to do with the posters yesterday. That was all Will."

I looked at his outstretched hand, then frowned at him, keeping mine firmly in my pockets. After an awkward silence, he cleared his throat and looked away. "Fair enough, I guess."

I turned to Donna. "What the hell?"

"I just wanted to warn you about . . . you have a right to know why . . . uh . . . right, I should probably explain about Will first . . ." Her eyes darted around uncertainly. I'd never seen Donna unsure about what to say.

"Oh, for fuck's sake." Amaya threw her hands up and let them flop back to her sides. "This idiot and his friends"—she pointed to Drew—"managed to get themselves involved in some seedy fight club. Now the dangerous bad men won't let them leave. Apparently, these same men have tried to lure *you* into the seedy fight club, but you have more than half a brain and said no."

I raised my eyebrows. I was pretty sure that was a compliment.

"But they really want you," Amaya continued, "because of your super violent past, and they don't like being told no, so the posters were their way of intimidating you. Will seems to be more involved than any of those half-brained idiots realized, so he was the one behind that little stunt. Drew's had enough and is worried about them dragging Donna into it, so he came to us to spill his guts. Harlow did some digging, and it turns out Will's dad owns all the properties where the fights have been taking place. He's a businessman with ties to several big corporations, but he seems to be giving a lot of money to BestLyf. Which is why Harlow insisted on no phones."

She rolled her eyes as if she thought it was preposterous that anyone would try to spy on a bunch of teenagers, and I was inclined to agree, but whatever. The phones didn't really matter right now.

"Harlow found other documents with names and dates that match previous fight nights, along with figures we suspect are the profits. Drew seems to think they're not going to stop trying to recruit you, and they may try to use Donna to do it because you clearly have the hots for her. She also has the hots for you, because all she could think about all afternoon was making sure you were warned and safe. Also, sorry if I was a bitch to you last night. I was just worried about my friend and didn't know you were a decent guy."

With a dismissive wave of her hand, she looped her arm through Harlow's and stomped her feet against the cold, apparently done talking.

Most of us gaped at her. Donna had her hand over her eyes, her short hair obscuring half her face.

Harlow was grinning at Amaya. "Holy shit, you actually said sorry for being a bitch?"

"And she called him a decent guy!" Mena bounced on her toes.

"Out of all that, that's what you choose to focus on?" Donna shook her head, incredulous.

Everything Amaya had blurted out—some of it shit I already knew, some of it making other things click into place—finally registered properly.

Without even thinking about it, I took a step forward and blocked Donna with my body, holding my arm out for good measure. "What do you mean they're trying to use Donna? Is someone threatening her?" I tried hard not to speak through my teeth, but my words still came out on a growl.

Donna slapped my arm away and stepped in closer to my side. "And out of all that, that's what *you* choose to focus on? You're the one they've already come after."

I huffed. "I can take care of myself."

"What? And I can't?" She crossed her arms.

I groaned. "That's not what I'm saying. You're a fierce independent woman and all that shit, but these are dangerous people who—"

"Is this some kind of foreplay for you two?" Drew cut in.

Everyone burst out laughing while Donna and I sealed our lips shut and avoided looking at each other.

"Can we focus please?" Turner sounded serious. "We need to figure out our next move. If BestLyf really is involved in this . . ." He shook his head. My friend was already convinced that company was evil—this would only be more proof for him.

"We don't exactly have evidence they are," Harlow hedged. "I just thought it was worth noting that Mr. Frydenberg was giving them substantial amounts of money each week."

"How do you know what kind of money Frydenberg is giving anyone?" I asked.

"It's better not to ask." Mena bugged her eyes out at me.

Harlow gave a nonchalant shrug. "I'm not a pro. It's not like I could hack into all his accounts or anything like that, so I definitely don't have the full picture. I just got access to a few folders on his computer."

"This is ridiculous." I rubbed my temples. "Why are we freezing our balls off in the woods discussing this and not going to the police?"

They ran me through the obstacles, the lack of evidence, why Drew and the others were scared to come forward.

"I'll talk to the police, man." Drew looked at me earnestly. "I just want to make sure that when I do, it counts—that my friends will be safe, that Will and his dad can't weasel their way out of it."

"We need evidence." Amaya tucked her chin into her scarf.

Everyone fell into silence, the only sounds those of animals scurrying and the flapping wings of some night bird.

I wanted so badly to just turn around, walk back home and get under the covers, pretend I didn't know any of this. I didn't want to get involved in this shit. But I already was, whether I wanted to be or not. And there was no way in hell I was going to sit around and risk Donna getting hurt.

An idea was forming in my mind, but the potential for trouble—exactly the kind of trouble I'd promised Aunt Hannah and myself I'd avoid—was pretty damn high.

"Are we being stupid not telling our parents about this?" Mena's voice was low, hesitant.

"Maybe." Donna ran her hands through her hair. "But telling Drew's dad or Amaya's mom?" They both cringed. "Probably do more harm than good. Telling your parents or Turner's dad? They'd just go to the police. Telling my parents? Dad is friends with Joseph Frydenberg and would almost certainly confront him, maybe warn him unintentionally. I don't think it's worth the risk."

"So, what? We do nothing?" Drew sounded frustrated. Of course he was. He'd been dealing with this exact conundrum, stuck in this impossible situation, for a year. Grudgingly, I felt for the guy. He may have gotten himself into this position, but at least he was trying to get himself out.

"Donna, is what Harlow has on Frydenberg enough to connect him to the fights, charge him?" Even if she didn't want to be a lawyer anymore, my girl still had more legal knowledge than anyone I knew.

"On its own? No. We would need to show proof that the fights happened on his properties. Then the fact that he owns them, coupled with the documents Harlow found and Drew's statement, would be grounds enough to dig into his affairs further, search his properties and businesses."

"Drew, are you sure Will is involved in organizing this shit?"

"Yeah." He huffed. "It's all on his phone. I've been watching him for a while, and I've noticed a few texts, other things that would prove it. They make everyone surrender their phones at the doors for the fights, but Will somehow always has his."

"If Will was at the fight when the police showed up, would that be enough reason for them to check his phone?"

"Yeah." Donna nodded. "Anyone caught participating in illegal activity would be searched and questioned."

I blew out a big breath. "Then we make sure Will is there when the police bust up the fight."

"How?" Drew asked, but Donna was already shaking her head, giving me a reproachful look.

"We give them what they want."

"Dammit, Hendrix, no." Donna shoved me, but her hands stayed on my chest. "I'm telling you all this to keep you safe, not so you can get yourself into a dangerous-as-fuck situation."

I smirked at her, but it didn't reach my eyes. "How's it feel, princess?"

"It's not the same." She seethed. "After what you told me . . . you shouldn't have to do this."

Donna knew how abhorrent the idea of violence was to me now, and here I was, about to throw myself into an actual fighting pit. She was trying to look out for me, just as I'd been trying to look out for her all this time. Only difference was, she'd been doing stupid, dangerous shit as an escape. I was about to do some stupid, dangerous shit for a good cause. For her. To protect her.

I rubbed her upper arms and spoke in a low voice, ignoring the others. "Better me than anyone else. My soul is already black."

She shook her head, her gaze pleading.

"You two done whispering sweet nothings over there?" Amaya barked.

I stepped away from Donna and fixed her sister with a look. "Get everything you have on Frydenberg ready to send to the police."

She nodded, and I turned to Drew.

"Keep us updated on any changes, but don't go to the next fight if you can avoid it. Just be ready to talk to the cops when it goes down."

Another firm nod.

"The rest of you, we all need to pretend like nothing's changed. Especially around Will. We should definitely not be seen together."

"Also, don't text or call each other about this," Harlow rushed to add.

"I'll get word to Donna when I have a date and location for the fight," I said. "If I don't check in twenty minutes after going in, that's your confirmation Will's there. That's when you do all you can to get the cops there."

"We'll make it happen." Turner looked determined.

"All right." There was nothing left to say, so I turned

to walk back to my house. The others moved in the opposite direction—to where the path led to another street.

"I'll be home later," Donna called, then caught up with me, pulling on my elbow. "Wait. Can we talk?"

I just kept walking. "There's no other way, Donna. It's late, and I haven't slept in two days. I'm exhausted."

"It's not about that." She kept pace, looping her arm through mine.

I slowed down and peered at her. Her expression looked uncertain—almost nervous. I wanted to pull her against me so badly, kiss her little nose, which was almost definitely frozen in this weather. But I had no idea where we stood. Not wanting me to get killed was a long way from actually wanting . . . whatever. I hadn't even allowed myself to fully consider what *I* wanted from *her*.

But that look on her face . . . she didn't look as though she wanted to lay into me or use me as a distraction. It looked like something else. Something more.

"OK," I said, relenting. "But let's get out of the cold."

She nodded. Her hand slid down until it joined my hand in my pocket, and we threaded our fingers together.

CHAPTER 28

Hendrix

DONNA AND I WERE SILENT AS WE COLLECTED our phones, crossed the yard, and made our way up to my bedroom. I didn't drop her hand until I was closing my bedroom door with a subdued *click*.

She was draping her coat over my desk chair when I turned around; I had to stop myself from rushing over to tidy up the mess of books and papers and pens littering the surface. The sweatshirt she was wearing underneath had a neon-pink pair of puckered lips on the front. It was so clearly not hers it made me smile faintly.

I took a few soft steps toward the lamp, then decided against it. Our eyes were already adjusted to the dark, and the curtains I'd left open earlier were letting in enough light. The moonlight made her hair look silver, ethereal, the soft angles of her face cast in gentle shadow as she looked around. Her eyes wandered to the desk, the bed, the window, everything but me.

I came to stand directly in front of her, not even sure what I wanted her to say. But she was here, and I couldn't find it in me to be anything but pleased.

She looked up at me and swallowed, reached out, then dropped her hands and balled them into fists at her sides. She was clearly anxious, but her brave eyes never left mine as she licked her lips and took a big breath.

"I'm sorry," she whispered and clenched her jaw—as if the words didn't taste right on her tongue. Or as if she was bracing for my response.

I frowned. "What for?"

"All of it," she breathed. "For being a bitch to you when you first got here, for making your life hell, for not seeing you were just trying to help me, for not seeing what I was doing to you and to myself. The willful ignorance . . ." She shook her head, that silver-blonde hair falling partly over one eye. "For blaming you for my friends seeing me in that state last night. For the posters and Will and Drew and this whole mess. I'm sorry for all of it."

She squared her shoulders and gave me one firm nod, ready to accept whatever I threw at her, however I reacted. So strong even in her humility.

I moved closer and allowed myself a single touch—a brush of my fingers against her temple as I tucked that lock of hair behind her ear—before I forced my hands down to my sides. Just because she was here, just because she was apologizing, didn't mean she wanted more from me.

"I gave as good as I got." My voice was as low as hers

but just as decisive. "I goaded you, Donna, and a part of me wanted my life to be hell. I didn't feel like I deserved happiness, friends, light after what I'd done. As for the other shit, I chose to follow you and push you, and I was probably crossing lines and sticking my nose where it didn't belong, and for that I'm sorry too." She shook her head and opened her mouth to object, but I rushed on before she could. "As for Will and Drew and that whole mess—I promise you none of that is your fault. I was getting dragged into that shit before Will realized there was anything between us. That's not on you."

She searched my gaze for a long time, then gave a tiny nod and a barely audible "OK."

"OK." I resisted the urge to pull her against me, hold her, protect her, devour her. There was barely a sliver of moonlight between us, our bodies drifting closer and closer.

"Hendrix?" Those round, perfectly imperfect, mismatched eyes still held me prisoner in my own room.

"Yeah?"

"Thank you. For sticking your nose where it didn't belong. For pushing me. For seeing what was happening when no one else did—when even I didn't let myself see the extent of it."

"I'd do it all again in a heartbeat, take every mean thing you said and did, to make sure you were safe."

"I know." She reached up and finally touched me, gripping my shoulders. "I know . . . I . . ."

My heart beat so fucking hard in my chest I was sure the thudding would wake the neighbors. I dared not speak as she tried to get whatever she was trying to say out. But with a slight shake of her head, she gave up on words altogether.

Instead, she lifted onto her toes and tilted her face up to mine, her eyes already half-closed as I reacted to her—naturally, instinctually. My hands went to her back as I met her halfway in a kiss. Her nose was still cold from being outside so long, but her lips . . . her lips were warm and soft and perfect.

She kissed me with such tenderness—such purposeful, gentle tenderness—that it felt as if this kiss were our first. Despite all the other times we'd kissed, all the other depraved things we'd done to each other.

This moment felt more raw and honest than any of it. The softness of that chaste kiss filled me with such contentment that I would've been happy to simply stand there and hold her—just like that—for the rest of the night.

It was Donna who teased my lips with a hint of her tongue, asking for more. I gave it to her, opening my mouth to hers, kissing her deeper, holding her tighter, my fingers digging into her back.

It was Donna who unzipped my hoodie, who whipped her own off before mashing her lips right back to mine. I helped her get all our clothes off until we were skin-to-skin. She was so hot against me, her body so soft and perfect, my cock in agony where it was pressed between us.

It was Donna who nudged me toward the bed until I was sitting down and she was climbing over me, straddling me. We moaned against each other's lips as our breaths turned to pants, as we caressed and kissed and licked and gripped, moving seamlessly together. So seamlessly I almost forgot to grab a condom before she slid down my length.

All the other times had been rushed, frenzied, as much fighting as it was fucking. But this time, in the quiet darkness of my warm bedroom—this time it was slow, deliberate, *intentional*.

Before, the sex had been about release—hers and mine. About Donna getting that rush of adrenaline. About her easing the insane pressure of constantly being in control by giving up control of her body to me.

Now, as she took her time lowering herself onto me, this was not about control or danger or release. This was Donna showing me with her body what she couldn't seem to say with her words.

She pulled back to look at me as her hips met mine, her knees splayed wide, my hands in her hair, on her ass. I groaned deep in my throat at the sensation of being so completely inside her, so carnally connected.

For a few moments she just sat there, not moving against me as my granite-hard cock twitched inside her warmth.

Breathing hard, she pressed her forehead to mine and finally found her words. "I want this, you, all of you. I want you, Hendrix—in my body, in my life, in my heart. I want . . . more."

I kissed her forehead, her eyes, her cheeks, her nose, which was finally as warm as the rest of her. "I want more too. Everything. Even if I don't deserve it. Even if it makes me selfish."

She took my face in her hands and trailed her thumbs down my cheeks. "You do deserve it. You deserve happiness and light and . . . love. I love you."

An indescribable feeling washed over me—something warm and intense and overwhelming and terrifying all at once. No one had ever said those words to me with such conviction.

"I love you," I told her with just as much certainty.

Only then did she start to move against me. Her core ground against my pelvis, not even bouncing up and down—as if she couldn't stand to not have me inside her for even the fraction of a second it would take to thrust back in.

We stared into each other's eyes as we worshipped at the altar of this crazy, cosmic thing between us. And I watched as the orgasm washed over her face, her legs twitching at my sides, her whole body going tense and then so, so loose. I drank in every second of the ecstasy she was finding with me.

And then I flipped us over and lowered her gently onto the bed, claiming her lips in a kiss. My tongue moved in rhythm with my hips as I pumped in and out and in and out, but it didn't take long. I came inside her, so deep, and moaned into her mouth. She held me close through it, clawing gently at my back, my ass.

After our breathing evened out and we cleaned up in my bathroom, we curled up on my bed with the blanket drawn up to our chins. Outside the window, the light was starting to turn that grayish indigo that signaled a new day.

"It's dawn," she whispered against my arm and placed a little kiss there. Her bare ass was against my crotch, her hot little body pressed to mine. Even our legs were tangled.

"I guess that means you have to go soon." I squeezed a little tighter, not ready for her to run away as she always did.

"Nah." She reached for her phone. "I think I'll stay. The girls can cover for me."

I smiled against the soft hair at the back of her head and was asleep before she even finished writing the text.

***

For the next few days, we all went back to our lives and pretended that nothing had changed. Everyone acted as though I didn't exist, and I went about my business with my usual disinterested look on my face. It was so fucking hard not to smile though, after what Donna and I had shared, after how we'd managed to come out the other end after all we'd been through. I wanted to grin like a fool. She was as frustrated by it as I was. More than once, she pulled me into an empty classroom for a secret kiss, and on Tuesday night, I got home from the gym to find her in the kitchen with Aunt Hannah, chatting and cooking dinner.

I wanted to forget everything else and just . . . be happy. But I kept it all locked down tight. Seeing Will's smug face at school was enough of a reminder why I needed to bide my time just a little longer.

The school hadn't been able to prove who'd put all the posters up, the cameras having conveniently failed that day, so no one was being punished. But I knew it was him, and he knew I knew. I could see it in his smirk, the way he looked down his nose at me, the taunting glint in his eyes. When I was looking at William Frydenberg was the only time I let my true feelings show—my disgust, my disdain, my rage at who he was and all he represented. I let him see how badly I wanted to beat his ass every time I passed him in the halls. I figured it would only serve to prove I was serious about changing my mind and wanting to get into the ring with him.

I'd texted Shady the day after our little meeting in the woods, telling him I wanted in but only if I could fight Will. Said I had a score to settle. He'd replied with a thumbs-up and nothing more. I resisted the urge to push him, ask for more info, show my impatience.

For now, we had to just sit and wait.

I used the gym to thrash out my frustration. On Wednesday afternoon, I finished a brutal leg session with Turner and hobbled out the back door to find Donna leaning on the wall.

I didn't even say hi. I just checked that no one was around before dropping my gym bag and diving in for a kiss. She laughed against my mouth as I pressed her into the concrete at her back. It was just about dusk, the street lights starting to come on, and I wondered if we could get away with a quickie, if the parking lot was too exposed. My girl would totally be up for it too—she was freaky like that.

"Daaaamn." The sound of Shady's voice was like a bucket of cold water being dumped over our heads. He strutted up to us from the corner of the building and leaned against the wall, grinning. "I might be jealous at this new development if I wasn't sporting a semi. But please, don't let me interrupt—I like to watch anyway."

He bit his lip and scanned Donna's body without a lick of shame.

"Shady." Donna gave him a tight smile. "You know I don't do jealousy."

"Yeah, but you never wore that uniform for me, baby girl. What makes *him* so special?"

We looked at each other and couldn't hold back the genuine smiles. She was special—more precious to me than anything.

"What's up, Shady?" I said, keeping my eyes on Donna. Her arms were wrapped around my neck, her tight little body still flush with mine. I hadn't missed the little flash of excitement in her eyes at Shady's suggestion to watch us. I was pretty open-minded, but I knew they'd slept together on more than one occasion, and I wasn't sure I could control my own jealousy. Not yet. I wanted her all to myself for a while.

"Shit." Some of the teasing tone left Shady's voice as he looked between us. "This is the real deal then? You two are a thing? Didn't see that one coming." Then he grinned. "Nah, I'm fuckin' with ya. Saw this coming a mile away!" He threw his head back and laughed.

Donna finally dropped her arms. I put some distance between us but kept one arm propped on the wall next to her head.

"Stop messing around." Now Donna had gone serious. "What are you doing here?"

"I gotta talk to your man about a dog," he said.

"You can talk in front of Donna. She—"

"No, it's OK." She looked over my shoulder; people were coming out of the gym. "I should go anyway. Call me later."

She gave me a quick peck on the lips and pushed off the wall.

Shady leaned forward and puckered his lips, raising his eyebrows expectantly, but she just flipped him off and sauntered away. I smirked as we both watched her disappear around the corner.

Once she was gone and the people from the gym were in their cars, Shady turned a dead serious expression on me. "What the fuck you doin', man? We both know you have no interest in those fights."

"I told you. I have a score to settle. I'll only come if your people can guarantee Will Frydenberg will be in the ring with me."

"Not my people." He crossed his arms and tipped his head back, watching me for a few moments.

I stared him down, not faltering.

"OK." He gave a disappointed shake of his head, as if he wanted to say more, and turned to leave.

"Shady." He stopped. "Do you go to the fights?"

"Sometimes."

I glanced around the darkening parking lot one more time. He'd looked out for me in his own way, and he'd made it clear he wasn't on board with this fight club bullshit. "If you happen to have other plans for this particular fight . . . that might not be a bad thing."

I raised my eyebrows, hoping he got my gist.

But guys like Shady operated in gray areas, were fluent in ambiguity. He cocked his head to the side, then slowly nodded. "All right."

Without another word, he walked away.

The next day, around lunchtime, I got a text message from an unknown number. It contained an address, the word *tonight*, and nothing more.

CHAPTER 29

Hendrix

THE ADDRESS WAS FOR AN ABANDONED factory in an industrial district about an hour out of town. It was massive, and the adjoining properties were far enough away that no one would hear any noise coming from the squat but sprawling building I'd just pulled up to.

I'd asked Donna to check if Drew had gotten the same message, not daring to piss off the younger Mead sister by contacting him myself. Donna and I had been texting each other freely—it fit with what the Frydenbergs suspected of our relationship anyway—but we dared not discuss the fight or our plan. Donna's text to Drew had been masked as her asking him for the address because I was being stubborn and wouldn't tell her. He was home sick that day, but Donna confirmed he'd received the text too.

As soon as I got word to the others, Harlow sent all

the evidence from Joseph's computer in anonymously—directly to a cop Donna knew from the legal center where she used to volunteer, knew wasn't dirty. Harlow had been corresponding with him, though she'd refused to come in and make a statement, and had told him to be ready near the factory that evening.

I got out of the car and walked slowly toward the building. Half the windows were smashed, and weeds grew between the cracks in the concrete. Not a single light was on, either outside or shining from within, but even without light, it was clear there were no other cars parked near me and no other people hanging around. Maybe everyone was already inside. Maybe they were instructed to park at the back.

Still, as I neared the building and looked for a way in, my steps slowed. It was too quiet. Was it possible the fight was set up in some underground area, away from prying eyes and ears? I wasn't sure, but something didn't feel right.

"Right on time, my man!" Shady emerged from the shadows near a side door set deep into the wall. He was in one of his tracksuits, the cocky grin firmly in place.

"Hey, dude." I slapped his hand and thumped his back, looking around. No one—not a single other person—was in sight. "I thought you had other plans."

He shrugged. "They fell through. Couldn't miss your debut in the ring!" He laughed, then turned for the door and gestured for me to follow him. "Everyone parks in the back or down the street. I figured you wouldn't know where to go since it's your first time."

The heavy metal door creaked as he pulled it open, but when we stepped inside the warehouse, I grabbed his shoulder. "Thanks, man, I appreciate it." Then I lowered my voice. "You can go now."

He dropped the bravado to give me a rare serious look. "Nah, I think I'll stay."

Stupid petty criminal. I sighed, but he was already walking away before I could say more. I was trying to save him from getting arrested, and he was sticking by my side out of some misguided sense of loyalty? Fine, his problem. I had to stay focused.

I texted Donna, knowing my phone would probably be taken at any moment.

Heading in now.

Shady led me past rows of dilapidated, rusting machinery and sagging conveyor belts. The rest of the space was bare, covered in dust and grime. Broken windows high above our heads let in beams of weak light as rats scurried in the shadows.

We rounded a corner, and several floodlights set on high stands flared to life. I pulled up short and squinted, my eyes adjusting to the sudden brightness.

Two figures stood in the middle of the starkly lit area. Two men, and no one else.

My whole body tensed, hands curling into fists at my sides. Something had gone very wrong.

The space did indeed look as though it was set up for a fight. A rough circle had been painted on the dirty concrete floor, plenty of space around it, and there was a balcony overhead on one side with what looked like empty offices behind the railing. But clearly, I was the only one who'd come here expecting to see an illegal fight ring.

"Hendrix Hawthorn." The man standing next to Will had the same brown hair, the same build, the same sneering mouth. They even stood in the same pose. Will's dad had his hands in the pockets of his long coat, worn over a suit and tie, while Will's were in the pockets of his Fulton Academy varsity jacket. "I've been told you want to settle a score with my son." A pause, a cold grin. "Have at it."

Will rolled his neck, his full focus on me.

I gritted my teeth and threw a murderous look at Shady.

He just flashed me that stupid grin. "You're a cool dude, but business is business."

That spineless son of a bitch. He retreated to lean against the staircase leading up to the balcony, whipping his phone out as if he was already bored.

"You see, the thing about dealing with criminals is you have to remember they're self-serving at their core," Mr. Frydenberg explained to me as if he were giving a lecture. "They're always going to do what's in their best interest. And Shady here is going to prosper greatly from our new mutually beneficial arrangement."

Shady just gave him a thumbs-up, hardly even raising his eyes from his screen.

"Criminals and businessmen both," I said, rolling my shoulders.

He laughed low. Will took off the varsity jacket and

draped it over the railing next to Shady, loosening up too.

I was going to beat his ass into this disgusting concrete until his every breath was a gurgle. His dad looked as if he'd hardly stepped foot on a treadmill in a decade, his gut poking out of his coat—it wouldn't take much to get him on his ass either. Shady would be running by then; that's what rats do. But I'd catch him. I'd chase him down and . . .

And . . .

Austin's face flashed in my mind, his eyes wide but unseeing, blood slowly pooling around his head. For a split second, I was back on that street in New York, once again realizing what I'd done. How irrevocable it was.

I had so much adrenaline pumping through my system, so much rage and outrage, my body practically screamed at me to start throwing punches. But I also felt sick to my stomach. All three of the men standing before me were the lowest kind of trash, but I refused to take another life. I couldn't have that on my conscience. Not again. Not *ever* again.

I forced myself to take a deep breath, flex my fingers and not curl them back into fists. I knew I'd walk away from this broken in more ways than I could count—if I even walked away at all—but my decision was made.

"I'm not going to fight you, Will," I said, proud of how steady and clear my voice sounded. "I was never going to fight you."

"Oh, you're going to fight me." Will sneered, slowly pacing back and forth, closing in like a hyena.

"No, I'm not." I shook my head. "I'm done with that shit. No amount of threats and intimidation were ever going to get me to throw another punch. Sorry you wasted your time putting all those posters up. Hope you didn't get too many paper cuts."

"Stop being a pussy and hit him!" Joseph's voice echoed in the cavernous space. Like a good little boy, Will immediately moved to obey his father.

He sprang forward, throwing a wide right hook. But he wasn't quick enough. I ducked out of the way and backed up, hands raised in front of me. I wasn't going to fight him—but I was going to defend myself as long as I could.

Will growled and came for me again. Football had made him fast, strong—he was relentless. I batted his swings out of the way, dodging and weaving, but eventually I started to get winded.

He pulled back, dancing on his toes, waiting, but his face had lost some of its confidence. If this was for real, if I'd actually stepped into the ring with him, I would've already won—and he knew it.

"Do I have to do everything myself?" Joseph barked and shrugged out of his coat, letting it flop to the filthy ground, before loosening his tie. They both advanced on me. I considered running, but what was the point? They'd catch up—eventually. Even if it wasn't before I reached my car and got away, they'd find me and do what they planned to do. Might as well get it over with.

I tried to get away from them, duck out of their reach, but it was two against one. After some grappling and shoving, Joseph managed to grab my arms and held me by the elbows as I thrashed.

Pain exploded in my skull with Will's first punch, and my eye felt as if it had burst in its socket.

Is this what Austin felt, right before he stopped feeling anything at all? Or was there no pain whatsoever for him?

I saw the next hit coming and tensed, but it still hurt like a motherfucker when Will's fist collided with my core. My insides clenched, and my stomach roiled. I half hoped I'd puke all over him.

Like a little bitch, Will backhanded me, but he was wearing a ring, and it split my bottom lip open. The hit rattled my brain even more after that initial punch. It threw my head to the side, and for a moment, I caught a glimpse of Shady. He was still leaning on the railing, still casually scrolling through his phone. *Unbelievable . . .*

He glanced up and winced, but my full focus was taken up by Will's fist smashing into my ribs. I coughed and wheezed, doubling over as much as possible with his father holding me tightly.

Finally, Will took a few steps back, breathing hard.

I spit blood onto the concrete and fixed him with as firm a look as I could manage through a rapidly swelling eye. "I was never going to fight you," I repeated. "The police are already on their way." I prayed that was true— or at least that they would believe it enough to leave. What if the police came past, saw it was as quiet as I thought when I arrived, and didn't bother to check inside?

Shady's chuckle echoed. Will grinned before stepping a little closer. "We both know the cops aren't coming. And even if they do, what are they gonna find?" He spread his arms wide and looked around. "All I see is a man and his son protecting their property from a known murderer."

"You think you can get one over on me, boy?" Frydenberg's mouth was close to my ear, but he was practically yelling anyway. "I've been in business for years. Been running circles around the police *and* everyone in this town. I have eyes and ears everywhere. You think I don't know about that little weasel Drew? My son has been keeping an eye on him for months. Weak piece of shit. Shady's already taking care of him. I'm going to personally watch the life drain out of your eyes, and then I'm going to feed you to the rats. And that little whore of yours? Well, I guess she's just going to have to forget you ever existed. Just like everyone else."

He talked about business as if what happened here was the same as his stocks and mergers and emails. He insinuated he was having Drew and me killed as if it was just part of a bad day at the office. But when he mentioned Donna, that's when cold, unadulterated rage coursed through me.

I growled, then threw my head back as hard and fast as I could. It hurt like a bitch, another blow to my already aching skull, but the crunch of his nose when I connected was beyond satisfying.

Will's eyes widened and he rushed forward, but it was too late. I'd startled Frydenberg enough to wrench out of his hold and shove him toward his son. They stumbled but quickly righted themselves, both of them watching me with surprise.

I bared my teeth at them like an animal, fists clenched, eyes narrowed. Warm blood was trickling from my split lip down my chin, but I didn't bother to wipe at it. I knew I looked feral. I *felt* feral—I wanted to tear them to pieces with my bare hands for even *mentioning* Donna. But I wasn't going to attack. I wasn't going to be that guy anymore.

"OK. That's enough of that." Shady strode forward casually, clicking his fingers and then slapping his hands, the sharp sound like a punctuation.

"Stay out of this," Frydenberg barked at him.

Shady just cocked his head. "No. And for the record, I don't like people taking credit for my work. You wouldn't know my buddy here was even planning to bring your operation down if it wasn't for me. Your idiot son was ready to fight him at the actual fight night tonight." So there was another location, an actual fight. "I'm the one who got Drew out of the way. Unthankful bitch."

Frydenberg was ready to beat both our asses now, but before he could say anything, I shook my head at Shady and scowled. "I thought you might be a decent guy somewhere underneath all those tracksuits."

He laughed as if I'd made a hilarious joke. "Well, I don't know about that." He moved closer until he was standing shoulder to shoulder with me, facing Will and his dad. "But I did also save your ass."

"What?" the Frydenbergs and I all asked at once, frowning. Senior stepped forward, pointing a finger at Shady as if he were telling off a toddler. "Listen here, you lunatic, I'm—"

Shady cut him off by placing his thumb and forefinger between his lips and letting off a piercing whistle.

"I'd get on your knees, bro," he muttered to me as he did exactly that, putting his hands behind his head while Will and his dad stared in confusion.

Before Shady's first knee hit the concrete, the empty factory exploded in a cacophony of sound. Several heavily armed men poured down those rickety stairs he'd been leaning against, guns pointed, shouting at us all to get down on the ground. More came in through a back door beyond the bright floodlights, and within moments, about a dozen police officers surrounded us.

I took Shady's advice and placed my hands behind my head, cringing against the pain in my torso as I slowly lowered myself to my knees.

Joseph raged, cursed Shady and me to hell, vowed bloody murder. Spit flew from his mouth as he screamed at the police that they had no idea who they were dealing with. Will was as silent as his father was frantic while they cuffed him. When the officers pulled the two of them past us, the look on his face was stoic, but I could've sworn I saw a bit of relief in his lowered gaze.

Once they were out of sight, the three remaining

police officers lowered their weapons and approached us, but instead of cuffing us as I thought they might, they helped us to our feet.

A guy with brown eyes and a salt-and-pepper five-o'clock shadow nodded at Shady. "You better hope your info is good. That's a prominent member of Devilbend society we just arrested."

"It's good. And here's junior's phone. I already forwarded the voice recording of senior's little villain rant before you all showed up. You should have enough to charge them both from that alone." He pulled an iPhone out of his pocket and handed it over to the cops, who sealed it in an evidence bag. I glanced at the varsity jacket Will had draped over the railing next to where Shady had been standing.

"You're lucky we got other anonymous tips on both these locations. They were enough to justify a bigger force than we initially planned. A lot of arrests tonight." He grinned, as if he ate arrests for dinner and tonight he was having a feast. Donna and the others were responsible for calling in this address; I wondered who Shady had gotten to report the actual fight.

"We good?" Shady raised his eyebrows.

The cop eyed him up and down. "For now." Then he turned to me. "We'll need to take your statement, but I think an EMT should check you out first. Can you walk, son?"

"Yeah." I gripped my ribs but hobbled out of there on my own two damn feet.

"That was a dumbass thing to do," the cop said to

me as he hurried ahead, one hand resting on the butt of his rifle. "Next time you might not get so lucky."

I resisted the urge to give him the finger. All things considered, shit could've gone much, *much* worse. Instead I turned to Shady. "You're an asshole."

He chuckled. "Maybe."

"You couldn't've let me in on your plan?"

"You couldn't've let me in on yours?"

Fair point. "I told you to stay away so you wouldn't get caught up in this shit."

"Yeah, but you know how it is, man. I saw an opportunity, and I took it. Everything worked out." He winked at me.

As we emerged into the night through the same creaky door, I realized Shady was a fucking genius. And I needed to be more careful around him. He'd wanted to be rid of the people running the fights and making his life difficult, and maybe he'd wanted to help me out on some level too, but at the end of the day, he was always going to look out for his best interests first. He hadn't told me jack shit because if the police hadn't shown, he'd still be in with Frydenberg. I had no doubt he would've handed me over if shit hadn't gone to plan. It was a win-win for him.

The area outside the factory was lit up now. A few cop cars and a van had converged near where I'd parked, and several police officers were milling about, talking on their radios, searching the property—doing whatever the fuck it was they did after busting bad guys doing bad shit.

I just wanted to sit down, go to sleep, maybe have Donna run her hands through my hair while I nestled my face into her tits.

As if I'd summoned the little hellion, her pearl-white Beamer came screeching around the corner and pulled to a stop next to my Tesla. She burst out of the car, and several cops tensed.

"Hendrix!" she bellowed as they approached her.

My heart lodged itself in my throat at all those guns pointed at her, but before I could yell, run, do *something*, they realized the little blonde chick in jeans and an oversized hoodie—my hoodie—was not a threat. The cops lowered their guns and just held their arms out instead, trying to herd her back.

"Don't you touch me." She pointed in their faces. "I'll sue the department so fast and so hard none of you will be able to sit for a month."

Despite the fucked-up situation, I chuckled. She was glorious when she was livid, and now that it wasn't directed at me, it was hilarious. *And* she'd cracked an anal joke.

"What is she even doing here?" The plan had been for Harlow to send the address to the cop she'd been emailing as soon as the agreed-upon twenty minutes were up. In the meantime, the others were supposed to make anonymous calls from various public phones—which are not that easy to find anymore—while Drew headed down to the station to make his statement. Donna's role was to wait for my call and, if I was arrested, come down to save the day with the lawyers the Meads paid an exorbitant amount of money to keep on retainer.

"Apparently Drew didn't head to the station like he was supposed to and wasn't answering his phone. So weird!" Shady grinned. "Then she found out the fight had actually gone down at a completely different spot—man, these rich people gossip when their kids start getting arrested. When she didn't hear from you and couldn't get any information out of the cops, she blew up my phone demanding to know what I knew." He raised his arm to wave at her. "Over here, baby doll! It's OK, guys, that's just my girlfriend!"

Reluctantly, they let her pass, and she jogged over to us.

"You told her to come here?" I gritted my teeth. If she'd gotten here five minutes earlier . . .

"Psh! Naw, man. I got ninety-nine problems. I don't need rich bitch drama on a night like this. Not like she didn't have your last known whereabouts though. Must be true love." He placed both hands over his heart and fluttered his eyelashes at me.

"You fucking prick!" Donna put the momentum of her jog behind a shove to Shady's chest. He actually staggered back but laughed at the same time. Then she noticed me, and those gorgeous mismatched eyes went wide. "Oh, shit. Oh my god, what did they do to you?"

Her hands ghosted over my chest as she scanned my face. I must've looked even worse than I felt, because tears welled in her eyes, and her bottom lip quivered. Donna *never* cried in front of other people.

Keeping one hand braced against my aching ribs, I cupped her cheek with the other and pressed my forehead to hers. "It's OK. I'm OK. I'm still standing."

She just breathed, ragged, trying to get her emotions under control.

"How'd you get here so fast?" I tried to distract her.

"I was parked halfway between here and the nearest police station where I thought they'd take you." She still looked as if she was fighting those tears, as if she was losing.

I quirked up the side of my mouth that wasn't bleeding and tried for humor instead. "You should see the other guy."

"The other guy is just fine." Will's cocky voice made me look up, and Donna froze. A police officer was leading him past us toward the back seat of a cruiser, while his dad was already being assisted into another one next to it.

"Bro, you're in handcuffs." Shady gave him an incredulous look. "You lost."

Before he could reply, Donna turned toward him, putting her back to me. "You're a piece of shit, Will. I hope you and your dad both rot in jail. And Hendrix might be too noble to hit you, but I'm not." Lightning quick, she threw a punch. It was wobbly and off-center, but it still landed, making Will's head snap back a little.

"Ow." He lifted his hands to his face, prodding his nose, then balled them into fists at his chest. "What the fuck, Donna?"

I wrapped my free arm around her middle and

pulled her back, wincing through the pain, as another cop rushed over.

"Ma'am, you need to step back." The cop leading Will had let him pause, but now she was holding a hand out. "I'm going to have to place you under—"

Shady stepped forward and threw a punch of his own. His was much more powerful and accurate, and Will cried out in agony as blood started pouring down his face.

The cops rushed in, grabbing Shady and shuffling Will into the cruiser. Donna was forgotten as they roughly cuffed Shady's arms behind his back and arrested him for assault.

Donna and I both raised our eyebrows at him.

"What?" He shrugged and grinned. "I like hitting people. Also, that guy was a dick. And I got a reputation to uphold."

He winked at me as they dragged him away.

One of the cops eyed Donna disapprovingly, her hand hovering over the cuffs at her belt. But then she glanced at me—I made sure to look extra pathetic—and gave us both a warning look before walking off.

Donna turned to me as the two cruisers carrying Will and his dad peeled out of the lot. With a hiss, she held her hand out. "Holy fucking shit, that hurts so much."

I smiled at her, and more blood trickled out of my busted lip. "I hope the pain was worth defending my honor."

Her face was dead serious as she replied, "It was."

An ambulance pulled in, lights flashing but siren off. I slung my free arm around her shoulders and started shuffling toward it. "Let's get that checked out, Rambo."

"Me? You're the one who looks like you went into the ring with Ronda Rousey."

"You know who that is? I'm impressed."

"Don't fucking patronize me, Hendrix."

We bickered all the way to the ambulance. It was the perfect distraction from the pain of every step.

CHAPTER 30

Donna

THE WEATHER WAS WARM ENOUGH THAT WE could have the windows down as Hendrix drove us to school. With both our sunglasses firmly in place and Post Malone blasting from the speakers, we held hands over the center console. That car practically drove itself anyway.

The girls wanted to give Hendrix this boyfriend moment—driving his girl to school—so they were meeting us there.

I was looking forward to getting back to classes, routine, some semblance of normalcy, but I knew all eyes would be on us instantly, and I wasn't sure I was looking forward to that. We hadn't been to school for about a week with everything going on between our families and the police. Plus, Hendrix had needed time to heal from his injuries.

The EMT and the two separate doctors his aunt had

insisted he see all said he was very lucky. Nothing was broken or permanently damaged, but he did have some internal bruising, and his ribs were black and blue. It made me wince every time he took his shirt off. While the bruises did finally seem to be fading, the cut on his lip was going to leave a scar. I'd told him "chicks dig scars" and distracted him with a BJ, and he hadn't seemed too put out by it after that.

His parents hadn't even bothered to fly over to check on their son. I'd overheard a stilted phone conversation with his mom while he was waiting in the hospital to be x-rayed and tested, but he hadn't spoken to his dad once. His parents really were trash, and I was glad he had his aunt. Hannah had been frantic with worry and pissed Hendrix hadn't told her what was going on, but in the end, she admitted she was proud of him—for the way he handled himself and the way he stuck to his values throughout the whole terrible ordeal.

We pulled into the student parking lot at the busiest time. People were arriving, walking up to the entrance, some hanging out and talking—it was still a good twenty minutes until the bell.

The lot was filling fast, but my spot right near the front was empty. Hendrix rolled to a stop and looked at me over the top of his sunglasses, the sun glinting off the frame. A lock of hair fell over his forehead, and I resisted the urge to sweep it back, run my fingers over his scalp, pull him in for a kiss . . .

I rolled my eyes but smiled. "I'll allow it. But only

because I'm in the car with you."

He laughed low, the sound sending a shiver down my spine, and pulled into my spot.

Amaya's purple Jag was on one side, and Drew's matte black Audi was on the other. They were all milling around on the path in front of us, chatting, leaning against the hoods of their cars.

Shady's men had released Drew as soon as Will and his dad were taken into custody. Apparently, they'd picked him up on his way to school the morning of the fight and had been the ones replying to anyone who texted his phone. Drew had been nearly out of his mind with worry, but they wouldn't let him leave the suite at the Hilton they'd stashed him in. They'd actually treated him pretty well, hadn't gotten violent—much—and had explained the whole situation before letting him go.

He was so relieved that Will and his dad had been arrested—that his nightmare was over, that we were all OK—he hadn't even reported Shady or pressed charges. I tried not to think about what would've happened to him in the hotel room had things gone sideways and the police never showed up.

The Frydenbergs' arrests had shaken the Devilbend community to its core. No one had suspected Mr. Frydenberg of being involved in anything illegal, let alone the extent of what the police discovered.

His lawyers put up a good fight, but ultimately, the evidence was too damaging. They'd managed to get Will out on parole by arguing he was a victim of his father as much as anyone, but he was being strictly monitored until his trial date.

As we'd hoped, the info Harlow had dug up was enough for the police to launch a massive investigation. Joseph Frydenberg was practically running a crime empire while moving about in California's high circles and pretending to be an upstanding citizen. It appeared he had some legitimate businesses, but he'd also been at the helm of an operation responsible for multiple fight rings across the state, drug dealing, prostitution, all kinds of things.

He might have been able to get away with a slap on the wrist—he was, after all, filthy rich and not above buying his way out—but he'd embarrassed a lot of people in Devilbend who had invested in his business ventures. Not to mention the fact that he'd put so many people in danger, that his thugs had been responsible for the accident that nearly killed Luke and the other guys. The rich and famous of Devilbend were going to make sure he went away for a long time—they were going to ruin him, *bury* him. If he ever got out of jail, he'd never step foot in this town again, let alone do business.

Raine Clayton, the CEO of BestLyf, was denouncing him as vehemently as all the other people who had been at my parents' Christmas party. She'd brushed off questions about his regular sizeable donations, and her PR machine was working in overdrive to squash any suspicion in that area. They'd put out only one statement, making it clear they had no involvement with Joseph Frydenberg past his being a member of the organization, like so many other prominent Americans, and that they'd been unaware of the illegal activity. The press was so preoccupied with all the other constant bombshells surrounding the case, no one hardly looked in BestLyf's direction.

Turner was more pissed than any of us about that. "That is such a load of shit! Those people are evil incarnate and were so involved in this," he'd raged a few days after everything came out. Every time a statement even mentioning BestLyf appeared in the press, he'd lose his shit and go on a tirade about what had happened to his mom and what he and his dad had discovered. He'd only calm down once Mena dragged him out of the room.

It wasn't that I didn't believe Turner. I'd seen Raine and Joseph talking at our party that night, and she gave me weird vibes, but there was no way to prove BestLyf had done anything illegal. The sums Frydenberg had handed over were substantial, but there were no laws against making donations—and both sides claimed that was exactly what they were. The police were attempting to seize some of the money as proceeds of crime, but BestLyf's legal team was wrapping that up in so much litigation it would probably be years before the government got their hands on it—if ever.

"You ready?" Hendrix squeezed my hand as he pushed a button, and all the car windows soundlessly slid up.

I'd let him see my apprehension when he'd picked me up, but I'd had the ride over to steel myself, and I wasn't about to show vulnerability to any of these people.

With him by my side and my girls having my back, it didn't feel so much like a mask anymore. I wasn't hiding. I was just reserving the most private parts of myself—the real parts—for those closest to me.

"Ready." I gave him a genuine smile.

We got out of the car together. Heads turned, whispers sounded, but we ignored it all and just joined our friends.

I gave the girls and Drew a kiss on the cheek each, and Mena started showing us photos of an elaborate makeup look she'd done over the weekend. She was so talented.

Next to us, Drew sat up a little straighter on the hood of his car and nodded to Hendrix. "Welcome back, man."

Hendrix watched him for a beat, and I waited with bated breath. With everything going on, we hadn't really had a chance to talk about Drew, but I knew that whatever my boyfriend decided, there would be no changing his mind.

The side of his mouth quirked, and he held out a fist. "Thanks, man. Good to be back."

They fist-bumped, then did that sideways high five, and I breathed a sigh of relief.

Amaya snorted. "Men."

"I know, right?" I shook my head. It was that easy. No conversations necessary; they were just friends now. Drew asked how Hendrix was healing, Hendrix made out as if he was practically back to normal (lies), and just like that, they launched into a conversation about baseball.

Mena frowned at my sister, who kept glancing over my shoulder. "Why do you keep looking at the front gates?"

Harlow shrugged. "I'm waiting for Mom to pull up. I can hardly believe she let Donna out this morning."

I laughed, but it ended on a groan. "She nearly didn't. She made Hendrix come inside and promise to drive carefully and to text her if we needed anything. I'm so glad Dad had to go on his work trip. I think if they were both home, they would've insisted I take another week off."

Mom and Dad had been . . . hovering. For the first time since I could remember, they were more worried about me than Harlow. Mom was worse than Dad, even coming in to check on me in the middle of the night as if I were a toddler. She'd startled me awake several times.

But they'd both been pissed, *livid*, when they first found out what we'd done—that we hadn't told them the second we found out Will and Drew were involved in something illegal, that we got *ourselves* involved. I knew most of it came from a place of worry for us, so I did my best to remain calm, take the verbal lashing, and act appropriately contrite.

Once they'd calmed down, I did the mature thing and told them everything. I went through every detail of what we found out—glossing over Harlow's potentially illegal methods of getting the information—why we chose not to tell anyone, how the night had played out. They were grudgingly happy Hendrix was willing to go to great lengths to protect me like that but still didn't condone his reckless actions.

I left out my regular visits to Davey's—figured my parents didn't need to know how many guys I'd fucked—but I told them about how I'd been feeling suffocated, pressured, and overwhelmed and that I didn't want to go to law school anymore.

With everything else that had happened, they were hardly even bothered.

"You do whatever you want, go to whatever school you choose, study arts for all I care." Dad waved a dismissive hand, his hair a mess, an empty glass sitting on his desk. "We just want you to be happy and safe."

"You're not mad about all the work I've put in over the years going to waste? All the connections I've made and . . . and . . ."

"Honey." Mom scooted closer to me on the couch, and Dad pushed off his desk and came to sit on my other side. "We're not mad at all. We want you to be successful, but what that looks like is entirely up to you. Above all, we want you to be happy. And safe."

I nodded, a lump forming in my throat. "I just want

you to be proud of me, and I feel like I'm failing."

"Donna." Dad took my hand and made me look at him. "We are proud of you. So proud of you. No matter what."

My tears spilled over.

"We love you so much, honey." Mom wrapped me up in a hug.

That was pretty much the end of the conversation. The following week had been focused more on Hendrix's recovery, police statements, and my parents constantly reassuring themselves I was safe and well. They'd been hovering over Harlow and me both, but I was definitely copping more of it after opening up about how I'd been struggling.

I shook my head and pushed the memory away, taking a deep breath of the fresh, sun-soaked spring air. I still got a bit misty thinking about what an emotional roller coaster the past week had been.

Nicola walked past with Luke, and they both smiled at me and waved. I smiled and waved back. A lot of the guys from the football team had been at the fight when the police busted in, and were arrested. Every single one of them had walked away without being charged— thanks to expert lawyers, their parents' influence, and their enthusiasm to testify against the Frydenbergs. Nicola and I had talked, bitched about Will, and we were cool now.

"Let's head in." Amaya picked up her bag, linked arms with Mena, and took the lead. Drew slung an arm over Harlow's shoulders, and they were cracking jokes and messing around before we even reached the front stairs.

Hendrix threaded his fingers through mine and kissed the top of my head as we followed our friends into the school.

People stared and whispered, none of them daring to come up to us and actually ask about what happened, but by now the whole school knew everything that was public knowledge. The stares and whispers were just as much about the fact that I was walking into school hand in hand with the guy they'd all thought I despised just a week ago. I smiled to myself.

At the start of the hallway where all the seniors' lockers were, we pulled up short so we wouldn't collide with Mr. Monroe. He was barreling past—students parting in his wake, some even turning to walk in the opposite direction to avoid him—but he stopped when he spotted us.

"Welcome back, both of you." His lips twitched slightly in what I thought might constitute a smile. He was in a charcoal sweater, the shirt underneath buttoned all the way to his throat.

We mumbled our thanks.

"It's been brought to my attention that you've withdrawn your applications for some of the colleges you applied to," he said, looking right at me.

"Uh . . . yea . . . yes, sir." He was an English teacher and not even *my* English teacher. He must've seen the confusion in my eyes.

"Mrs. Fielding is on leave, and I've been asked to

step in and assist for a short time." His lips pressed together slightly—clearly he wasn't thrilled to be helping with careers counseling. "Please come see me if you'd like to discuss options. You too, Mr. Hawthorn."

With another tiny smile, he stalked off again, clutching a pile of papers at his side.

Hendrix and I looked at each other with raised eyebrows, then burst into laughter. It was so good to be back—hanging out with my friends, dealing with Mr. Monroe's moods, getting ready for classes. As much as I'd felt suffocated by some of those same things in the past few months, the familiarity of it all was weirdly bringing me comfort.

The others had already dispersed, so we hurried off to our own lockers. I quickly grabbed my books and rushed over to Hendrix's side just as he closed his.

Pulling his shoulder down, I leaned in to whisper in his ear. "I'm not wearing any underwear."

His eyes squeezed shut, and he groaned low, gripping my hip and moving in close. "Why would you tell me that? I really don't want to spend all day with a semi, Donna."

There was an edge of annoyance in his voice, but his gaze was pure lust.

"Who said anything about all day?" I whispered against his lips. Then, without kissing him, I started to back away. "Meet me at our spot at lunch."

He frowned. With a grin, I turned and rushed off to class, fully aware he had to go in the opposite direction or risk being late.

"What spot?" he called after me. "Donna! What spot?"

I rounded the corner and picked up my pace. He'd figure it out once the lust cleared a little and he could think straight. Now I just had to make sure I made it to the little room at the back of the auditorium before he did.

NOTE FROM THE AUTHOR

Thank you so much for reading Like You Hurt! I really hope you enjoyed it and you'll consider leaving a review. As an indie author, reviews make a massive difference when it comes to my book reaching other readers. Even a sentence or two helps!

ACKNOWLEDGEMENTS

A lot goes into putting a book out. The process is long and sometimes painful and there's no way in hell I could ever do it all on my own. I'd like to thank, from the bottom of my heart, the following people for always having my back, constantly supporting me, and doing all that you do to make my work better at every step along the way: my family and friends, my beta readers, my ARC team, Sam Dove, Christine Estevez from Wildfire, my editor Kirstin Andrews, and all the members of my reader group – The Snow Lodge. To all these people, and to every single reader, thank you! I'm able to live my dream because of you.

I always make sure to thank my husband in the acknowledgements, but this time around I'd like to shower him with a little extra praise. Because, to be honest, if it wasn't for John, I'm not sure how I would've gotten through the past few months at all – let alone finished writing this book and put it out. Between what a frightening and unsettling place the world has been lately, and some of my own personal struggles, it's been a really rough couple of months. I paused at this very spot for a long time while writing this because I struggle to put into words all that he means to me – all that he is to me. John has been everything I needed and more at every step, every high and every low – and there have been some serious lows lately. I honestly don't know what I'd do without him.

ABOUT THE AUTHOR

Kaydence Snow has lived all over the world but ended up settled in Melbourne, Australia. She lives near the beach with her husband and a beagle that has about as much attitude as her human.

She draws inspiration from her own overthinking, sometimes frightening imagination, and everything that makes life interesting – complicated relationships, unexpected twists, new experiences and good food and coffee. Life is not worth living without good food and coffee!

She believes sarcasm is the highest form of wit and has the vocabulary of a highly educated, well-read sailor. When she's not writing, thinking about writing, planning when she can write next, or reading other people's writing, she loves to travel and learn new things.

To keep up to date with Kaydence's latest news and releases sign up to her newsletter here: kaydencesnow.com

Join her reader group here:
facebook.com/groups/KaydenceSnowLodge

Or follow her on:
Facebook: facebook.com/KaydenceSnowAuthor
Instagram: instagram.com/kaydencesnowauthor/
Twitter: twitter.com/Kaydence_Snow

Goodreads:
goodreads.com/author/show/18388923.Kaydence_Snow
Amazon: amazon.com/author/kaydencesnow
BookBub: bookbub.com/profile/kaydence-snow

ALSO BY KAYDENCE SNOW

THE EVELYN MAYNARD TRILOGY
Variant Lost
Vital Found
Vivid Avowed

DEVILBEND DYNASTY
Like You Care
Like You Hurt
Like You Should (coming soon)
Like You Know (coming soon)

STANDALONES
Just Be Her
It Started With A Sleigh